THE ULTIMATE PAYOFF...

After ten minutes' ride deeper into the woods, I suddenly seemed surrounded by people. First another cyclist, his head well down, sped past me. Approaching me, I saw three other men on huge horses, the one in the middle seemingly hedged in by his two companions, who appeared to be protecting him.

The cyclist coasted rapidly downhill. He's going to crash, I thought, there surely wasn't enough room to pass the riders. But he slid to a halt twenty yards or so away from them, and I saw him lift one of the water bottles from a rack on his handlebars, as if to drink from it. But then, in a flash, he threw the thing expertly, like a grenade, the canister soaring up over the horsemen before landing in the middle of them.

It exploded on impact in a fan of light. The quiet had been shattered. And I knew, somehow, that it would never be quiet again. . . .

"THE WORK OF A MASTER OF THE FORM, THIS BOOK HAS THE TIMELINESS OF A PAGE ONE STORY."
—*Times-News* (Erie, PA)

THE
OXFORD
GAMBIT

Joseph Hone

FAWCETT CREST • NEW YORK

THE OXFORD GAMBIT

Published by Fawcett Crest Books, a unit of CBS Publications, the Consumer Publishing Division of CBS Inc., by arrangement with Random House, Inc.

ISBN: 0-449-24436-9

Grateful acknowledgment is made to the following for permission to reprint previously published material:
The Viking Press: "Prologue to a Saga" is reprinted from *The Portable Dorothy Parker,* Copyright 1931 by Dorothy Parker, Copyright © renewed 1959 by Dorothy Parker. Reprinted by permission of Viking Penguin, Inc.

Printed in the United States of America

First Fawcett Crest Printing: August 1981

10 9 8 7 6 5 4 3 2 1

For Julia and Dick

Every man has a creed, but in his soul
he knows that that creed has another side.

—JOHN BUCHAN
A Lucid Interval (1910)

PROLOGUE

"Lindsay!"

She called from the drawing-room window, half open on the warm spring afternoon, looking over the dry moat and the croquet court toward the Oak Walk, a line of old trees that led away from the house into the forests that circled it. He kept his bees there, in hives between each tree, where they faced a long slope of rough meadow that fell away to the loch and backed onto the vegetable and pleasure gardens that lay behind the house.

"Lindsay?" She called again, more loudly. "Teatime."

She could see the bee smoker on top of the first hive by the nearest oak tree a hundred yards away, a wisp of gray trailing up into the still air. And she had seen her husband there too, ten minutes before, using the bellows at an open hive, shrouded in a black veil and a battered straw hat, tending his bees for the first time that year after the winter.

She went back to the little rosewood desk by the piano and tidied away her papers, glancing quickly through the letter she had almost finished to her daughter in London.

Sunday, March 21, 1976

*Glenalyth House,
Bridge of Alyth,
Perthshire,
Scotland*

Dearest Rachel,

It was such fun having you up last weekend and we were both so pleased about the concert.

L. has started on his bees this afternoon, it's so fine and warm, like summer, tho' the daffodils aren't completely out yet and the trees hardly in bud at all—but everything curiously still and balmy so that you can hear voices sometimes (it must be the forestry men who are here again) way across the loch on Kintyre hill. He didn't think he'd get down to his bees before he went back to London. And now he's been so happy getting them organized that he'll hate to leave—and I'll hate to see him go. I wish these bees would keep him here. Still, they will—soon. And thank goodness he doesn't see it as "retiring"— but as a start, a new start. His bees have always mattered to him as much as us, I think, though he would never admit it. And I don't mind that at all. We have to have other things besides people in our lives. And I think perhaps L. has found this more with his bees than with his real work in London. So it's nice to think that the honey this autumn, for the first time, will be the real thing for him, a business and not just a retired old gentleman's hobby. I'll be down, of course, for the Flower Show and your birthday concert and will see you then....

She looked out at the croquet court again through the tall windows, but there was still no sign of her husband. She turned and glanced at the tea tray—oatcakes which Rosie from the village had made that morning, and a brown earthenware kitchen teapot that had been brewing on the mahogany drum table for nearly ten minutes. She picked up her pen and finished the letter.

Must stop now. Tea's getting cold and I'll have to call him again—he's so tied up out there puffing away with his old bellows he can't have heard me the first time.

All love, Madeleine

She sealed the envelope and moved to the windows once more. Still he had not come, so she went out into the big hall, where she, was surprised to see the front doors shut and to hear their terrier, Ratty, scratching furiously outside.

She opened the large door and the dog looked up at her with curiosity. "He's not in the house, silly. He's somewhere with his bees. Come, we'll go and find him." But the dog seemed unwilling to follow her. "Come on, Ratty!"

She walked out onto the columned porch and round to the side of the big square house and stood on the croquet court.

"Lindsay—teatime!"

She sang the words out, shading her eyes against the afternoon sun that sloped down on her from above the rim of fir trees on a long hill away to the west of the house. The dog stood expectantly by her feet, its nose quivering slightly, smelling the air, head pointed doubtfully toward the woods.

"Where are you?" Madeleine called, moving on across the lawn in the direction of the line of oak trees.

A small wind sighed, running down from the wooded hills, through the oak buds, rustling the evergreens and the dead winter grass in the meadow. A bee swung past her head, droning away toward the forest. The bellows smoked on top of the first hive and the breeze caught the smoke and spiraled it gently round her face—a long-remembered smell of burning corrugated paper.

"Lindsay?"

She moved down the row of trees and came to a hive with its roof off. She touched the felt covers and lifted one corner gently. In the new honey frames beneath she saw the bees for an instant, a furry mass, busily crushed together, starting to replenish their stores with a loud murmur. Two pigeons flapped violently out of the branches above her; a pheasant squawked somewhere in the woods nearby, and the little dog whimpered at the end of the walk. It had not followed her and it fidgeted now, chasing its tail, wary of the bees and lost without its master.

She called once more. But nothing answered; no voice but hers in the loud spring.

BOOK ONE

THE PUZZLE

1

I tried to work again this afternoon, going upstairs to the attic in the cottage which I have made into a study. But from my window I could see the sky, quite blue, almost balmy, for the first time this year, after months of damp and gray—light fluffy clouds sailing over the small hills of this part of Oxfordshire where I have come to live.

But I was impatient again, for something I couldn't touch, something that was surely happening, somewhere out there in the world at that very moment, as I sat at my desk thumbing the typescript of the book on the British in Egypt I'd been working on for the past few years. I had started to read again my chapter on the Suez debacle and its aftermath, a period I'd lived through in Cairo twenty years before. But the writing seemed cold and irrelevant on the page, so far removed from the blazing heat and anger—and yet, for me, the love—of those years: the smell of lime dust and urine and burnt newspapers sweeping up from the back streets of the city; the rumor of sour bread and burnt kebabs that they cooked on a barrow at the corner of my street by the Nile, rising up in the baking air past our open bedroom window, where I lay with Bridget through the hot afternoons, doing the one thing we did so willingly and well then...

I was impatient for that, perhaps—something like that again—some dangerous reality and not this studied history in a calm world: the Cotswolds, where it seemed I'd been asleep for many years. I had felt like Mole in *The Wind in the Willows* all that day: Mole waking on the riverbank that first real day of spring, coming out into the light on the water after the bad dreams of winter, getting his house in order before setting out on his long adventure.

I was not yet tired of country life last Christmas. But now that spring had come and some nameless cure was taking place in me, boredom had begun, nibbling away at my days, making each of them several hours too long.

The mornings were all right when I worked—and most afternoons when I journeyed over the small hills. But the evenings were difficult. There was no pub in my village, while the one three miles away was empty on weekdays and full of television playwrights and producers at weekends. Sometimes I watched their work on the box at home in the evenings, and that was worse.

The village, quite lost in the folds of high sheep pasture ten miles or so beyond Woodstock, was more than attractive; that quality alone would have ruined it years before. It was inviolate: a manorial hamlet, almost all of it still owned by an eccentric army officer, the last of his line and rich beyond the dreams of avarice, so that he had no need of weekenders or modern bungalows in his village—and what's more, before I came, had once taken a shotgun to some intrepid London house hunters he had found admiring a ruined cottage on the edge of his estate.

Nearly all the tied cottages on the single small street had their doors and gable ends painted the same shade of very somber blue—except for mine, a neo-Gothic, red-brick cottage behind the church: not part of the major's empire, but which had belonged to the local sexton and I had bought from the church commissioners.

There was a unique fourteenth-century tithe barn by the manor farm with arrow-slit windows, and the small church, with its dumpy Anglo-Norman tower and ocher-colored stone, was a wonder in slanting sunlight, and considered perfect of its kind.

But I am no rural chronicler—and the Bartons, a colonial

13

family who came to live in the old rectory shortly after me, I fell out with one evening over sanctions in Rhodesia and have barely seen since. The major and I have never met at all. But I am not alone in that. He is not a social man. The vicar, a persistent and oversocial Welshman, now from another village, bearded me several times early on, believing me to be a television dramatist, and suggested I compose a Christmas masque based on the career of a local seventeenth-century divine whose voluminous and uncollected papers, he told me, were available somewhere deep within the Bodleian Library.

I disappointed him, I'm afraid. Though I still sometimes go to church. The place has a very simple whitewashed nave, with the original brick showing through on the window corners, and old pine-box pews that smell of candle wax.

I chose this village nearly four years ago specially for its isolation—when they "retired" me, after the fracas with the KGB in Cheltenham. McCoy had seen it differently, though, and had offered to recommend me for an M.B.E. on the Foreign Office List, since for him, needless to say, the whole business had ended in vast success. Instead I took the £15,000 gratuity they had offered and told McCoy I hoped never to see or hear from him again.

"Don't be like that, Marlow," he'd said, in his ugly Belfast voice, words and tones no real Foreign Office man would have used, for of course we had both worked for a far less intelligible government department: the—and I find it hard even to write the words—the Service: D.I.6 as they call it now. British Intelligence: the Middle East Section in that terrible glass tower in Holborn.

It was accepted by the small farming community that I was an academic of some sort, a suggestion I planted soon after I first came, when I told the postmistress, Mrs. Bentley, I was researching the story of one of the English Crusades, a sort of medieval regimental history, as I put it, of their campaigns in the Near East. Subsequently, neither she nor the other villagers inquired further about my work, doing no more than to wish me well at it from time to time.

I was not, I should say, entirely a recluse. Once a girlfriend I'd known in Paris years before came and stayed with me, arriving with her husband—an overeducated young man who held a position in the Banque de France—in a large silver Citröen which blocked half the village street for a weekend.

They spoke to me at length and in French of their recent journey among the Danakil tribe in the lowlands of Ethiopia. After I'd seen them off in Oxford I happened to spot a secondhand abridgment of Churchill's *History of the English-Speaking Peoples* and read it for a week.

Better friends came too, at fairly long intervals and yet repetitively, for I have never been part of any wide circles. It was the walking I enjoyed most after my leg wound healed. The physiotherapist had recommended it, but I soon found it pure pleasure and took to the hills like an alcoholic, strolling the old Roman roads and empty lanes in every weather.

Yet, as they say of childbirth, one comes to forget even the worst kind of pain and one day a few weeks ago I realized I might be coming to an end of my rural needs. I had started, not talking to myself, but worse—holding imaginary parties in the small dining room of the cottage: scintillating affairs with old friends, many of them dead, which spilled happily over into the other rooms of the place as I wandered through them, sherry glass in hand, imagining it zibib from Egypt or some other sharp foreign drink from long ago.

On that particular evening, I had begun to re-create the annual reception for the Queen's Birthday at the old British Residency on the Nile, where I had worked in the mid-fifties. By sunset I had summoned up a bevy of dark Nubian waiters, each slashed at the waist with a royal-blue cummerbund, carrying silver trays of iced martinis high over their heads, pushing through the guests under the flame trees on the long lawn which, in those days before the corniche road was built, went all the way down to the river.

At the end of the evening, the furniture all askew and the sherry bottle empty, I felt a terribly sharp bite of social disappointment that my friends had left. I felt, in my small cottage, the weight of huge empty spaces around me, echoing reception rooms and verandas; I smelled the mud of the low water riding on the breeze over the Nile and heard the evening cry of the muezzin, harshly amplified from the mosque tower by Kasr-el-Nil bridge...

I realized when I woke with a headache next morning that I had finally cured myself—but that if I stayed much longer in the country I should get ill again.

That was last month: I tried to forget about it and returned to my book. But this morning the fire has come back and I have drunk nothing. Tomorrow, I know, I shall go to London.

15

THERE was a reason, had I needed one: my solicitor, who also handled my finances, such as they were, had written sometime before, suggesting a visit to discuss the possibility of some "judicious reinvestment," as he put it—an unnecessary thought to my mind, since what little money I had, in the hands of a well-known Irish brewery, appeared judiciously placed already.

Barker, an Englishman of a lost kind who had only one eye, tended to the legal problems and finances of many retired people from the Service. He had once been vaguely attached to it himself, in 1942, as a captain in charge of a commando company; he had been invalided out, with partial vision, after a sten gun had blown up in his face while he was on secret maneuvers in Scotland before the Dieppe raid. His had been a short, inglorious war. He had subsequently tried to recompense for this by maintaining contact with a world of derring-do—in the shape of elderly brigadiers with tax problems and younger men in the SIS whose marriages had gone astray.

He had moved offices since I had last seen him, and now sat, back to the window, on the top floor of an old Georgian building in Jockey's Fields, up from High Holborn: a judicious man indeed, surrounded with his comfortable club furniture, but still with the remnants of unsatisfied activity in his face. He fidgeted while he talked, charging and releasing the silver cap of a ball point like a rifle bolt.

"I rather think Metal Box might be worthwhile," he said, gazing to one side of his desk where a stack of old tin deed boxes ran halfway up the wall.

I followed his gaze, misunderstanding him. "Metal box? I don't have any—"

"Oh, no. I meant the company who make them: containers, foil, wrappings of all sorts."

"I see. What's wrong with the brewery?"

"Nothing. But I hear—confidentially—there's to be a new rights issue with MB: two for one. If you bought in now...It might keep you going for another year."

"At most?"

"At most, if that." Barker was like a doctor staving off bad news: one suspected he had something worse up his sleeve. "Inflation. Your money is not what it was and really a year is too long. It may run out sooner. Had you thought of any kind of—work?" he added, very diffidently. "You used to, didn't you? The Service..."

I shook my head. "I'll have to think of something," I said, "but not that."

"Of course your cottage must have increased in value—a great deal. You could sell—"

"No, not that either. That's the last thing I want. London again, a flat, a job."

"Well..." Barker paused, letting the future hang in the air like a bankruptcy. "We'll have to think of something."

I've forgotten what else we spoke about that morning, except that we agreed to move some money on to Metal Box in a last bid for solvency, since what struck me after some minutes in Barker's new office, and absorbed me more and more while I was there, was the view from his window. Towering up over the old slate roofs of Gray's Inn, not more than a few hundred yards away, was the monstrous glass block I'd worked in for ten years: naval recruitment at the front with sundry other government offices upstairs, including my own in the Mideast section of Intelligence.

Indeed, from where I sat I could actually see the window of my old office in Information & Library, the eighth floor, fourth along, where I had thumbed through *Al Ahram* on damp Monday mornings, waiting for Nellie with the coffee trolley, or gazed out all afternoon at the concrete mess they were making round St. Paul's throughout the sixties, before checking my watch against opening time.

More and more often, during Barker's meticulous financial suggestions and provisos, my eye would wander back to the glass façade over his shoulder. And I found, having first recognized it with distaste, that I had begun to think about it with fascination, as a man experiences an extraordinary sense of déjà vu that haunts him for the rest of the day. I was drawn by incidental memory deep inside the building, through the security checks with Quinlan, the old Irish Service Corps sergeant in the hall, up the murmuring lifts and along the windowless corridors, permanently invested with the lavender-smelling disinfectant they flushed the latrines with, hearing the *thwack-thwack* of busy typewriters running up top copies "For Your Eyes Only" with a single flimsy for registry that more often than not in those days would find its way to Dzershinsky Street by the end of the week.

It was an eerie feeling, sitting safe in Barker's big red

leather chair, huddled among his reassuring nineteenth-century deed boxes, their white lettering naming old families in Herefordshire and great houses in the southwest, while looking out at this glass castle gleaming in the sunlight, an architectural chaos, where all the bad fairies lived and I had worked passage for a rotten decade that had ended nearly ten years before.

Henry, in his old tortoise-shell specs, had gone from that eighth floor in 1967, sent packing by Williams on his last long journey down the Nile—and so had I, sold out by the same man, from that meager office with its scratched walnut furniture, half carpet, and the hatstand I never used, finding solace by comparison in the hospital wing of Durham Jail, where—framed by this same Mideast Intelligence section—I'd been sentenced to almost a lifetime's incarceration less than ten years before. Even the duds who had left this building in one piece had few reasons to be grateful to anyone in it, while the best usually found death or exile in the small print of their contract halfway through their time there.

And yet, as I say, I was drawn to it. Even the worst memorials serve to remind us that we have lived once, and seen happiness with friends in certain streets when it was evening, had lunch with them on good days or weekend picnics in a Bloomsbury square: that there was some pleasure, despite the horror of the times.

Drinks with Henry, for instance, in that wine bar down the Strand: the champagne he always ordered, back from some mission, running his finger down the frosted side like a child playing on a clouded windowpane, celebrating a safe return from some folly in the East; the married commuters from Sevenoaks and their secretaries sipping sherry and whispering sweet mischief over candlelit barrels while we spoke of more distant intimacies—Ahmed's cloudy news from behind the bar at the Cairo Semiramis and what had passed that week by the pool at the Gezira Club.

These days one can find the past preserved in squalid modern brick and glass as much as in old deed boxes—and so it lay now, across the roofs from me, like a temptation one knew was wrong and thus could not resist.

THE wine bar was empty at eleven-thirty, after I'd left Barker's and walked down to the Strand in the hot summer sunshine. The candles on the barrels were unlit and the manager, an accommodating and sleekly brilliantined Jeeves whom I had known well in the past, must long since have died or moved. But otherwise the place seemed exactly the same as it had been ten years before, almost to the day, when I had last sat here with Henry, swapping gentle taunts about the fatuous vacuity of our lives.

Even the salted crackers were the same—too dry and crumbly for pleasure, tasting of old paper.

And one never forgets a smell—which brought it all back quicker than anything: a musty sourness embedded in the wood and in the furnishings, of wine spilled over many years, that had remained like a coward in the room long after all the happy tribe had left.

I took a glass of Beaune with me and sat down in the far corner. I thought of my finances and of Barker's polite warnings. I prayed I wouldn't have to leave my cottage, which already, after only a few hours in London, beckoned me like a woman. "A job?" as Barker had hinted. I was unemployable.

I gazed at the snack menu to take my mind off the idea. "*Pâté de foie à la Maison:* 95p"—a nerveless mix of liver and old bottle ends still doing time after more than ten years at three times the price. The place began to sicken me with its bland constancy, a stage set always for the same production, with the same props and the same cast waiting for curtain up at lunchtime: the silly bowler-hatted City men strayed adventurously beyond Throgmorton Street, lunching with fast women, account executives probably—long-nosed and forty who laughed too much; gossip writers from the staider papers; a lone bishop, his purple bib showing like a sore thumb; and country gentlemen in tweeds, up in town for the day without a table in Simpson's, who took the set lunch upstairs in the small restaurant after two rash glasses of South African amontillado below.

They were beginning to come in all round me now and I was just about to leave, thinking of a more piquant lunch in Soho and some easy film in Leicester Square afterwards.

I saw him almost from the moment he pushed open the glass doors, coming in out of the sunshine like a harassed refugee. The thin figure sloped up to the bar in his dark and slightly grubby pin-stripe suit and the old navy-blue pullover, same as ever, tight around his neck, so that just the knot of some regimental tie peeped out like an apology, which nonetheless could be fully displayed in an emergency and astound everyone with the truth. For Basil Fielding actually had all the right credentials. He hadn't changed, either, in ten years. I couldn't see his face clearly as he moved behind some people to make his order at the bar. But I could remember it well enough, now that the man himself had given me the outlines: the always badly shaved cheeks and chin, stubbled like fine white sandpaper, the slightly blue, spittle-encrusted lips, the ears that dropped thinly down either side of the large face rather like an elephant's, the air of apologetic dejection. Fielding looked so shifty you couldn't believe it of him. The devious expression was like a bad caricature, for his eyes always hovered on the edge of such real laughter it made him seem incapable of dishonesty or malice. Or so I had thought in those former years.

Basil had been the wandering minstrel of our Mideast section in the old days, almost a licensed jester, a sad man who yet rejoiced. His job had been ill-defined, most particularly by himself. But it had been in Protocol, even he knew that. It was his function to control liaison and run such formal paper work as existed between our own and other Allied intelligence services, particularly with the CIA. Though I remember once he had lunched at the Soviet Embassy, on some diplomatic pretext or other—for he was officially on the Foreign Office list—and had returned that afternoon with a more than useful piece of information about the rocket base in Baikonur, extracted by Basil from a surprised military attaché, like a poacher tickling a trout.

There wasn't really much doubt about it: behind the inefficient footling exterior, Fielding possessed some nameless gift. He was a man who could lull people with his inanities while all the time calculating just how much he could rob them of without their noticing. While he hemmed and hawed and groaned with platitudes, I remember—as though hurtling through some cosmic black hole—that was when he was at his most dangerous, when he had noticed some great potential out of the corner of his eye—some bureaucratic advantage—and was beginning his stalk toward it.

He hasn't seen me yet, I thought. Don't talk to him, I said to myself. Don't start anything. He hasn't seen you. And I turned my head away from him and blew my nose.

Perhaps this sound alerted him, was some sharp aural file index of his identifying me from afar. For the next thing I knew, he was beside me, standing diffidently over me, holding two glasses of wine in his age-marked hands—one at such an angle that some drops fell onto my table. I thought he might be drunk for a moment, or hung over.

"Marlow!—the last person...How are you? Haunting the old places?"

How apt Basil could be, like a fortuneteller who, ten years before, had divined my return here to the very hour and had come now to confirm his prediction.

"Saw you as I came in," he went on. "Hiding over there in the shadows. You're not meeting anyone, are you?" He gestured to the seat beside me.

"No—of course not. Let me get a drink." I stood up.

"I've brought you one."

"You knew I was coming here?"

"No!" he said, drawing the word out in mock horror, as though my thought was quite outlandish. "No, my goodness. Just a restorative. In for a whizzer," he said brightly, as if trying to jolly himself along with the phrase. And again I had the impression of some unnatural elation in Basil, some disorder in his day that had brought forth such fluent slang. "Darley's here," he went on. "And Jameson." He looked back toward the bar. "You remember?"

I did, vaguely. They had been tyros in my day: new field men making a mess of an old circle in Damascus.

"We're all going to church round the corner. The RAF place—St. Clement Danes," Basil went on, licking his dry lips and looking mischievously at me over the rim of his glass before taking a long quaff from it.

"Church?" I looked at my watch, I remember, the thought so surprised me—as though Basil, an unbeliever of all sorts in the old days, had taken now to some new faith that worshiped on an hourly basis.

"Memorial service. Alkerton. Sir George. Deputy head of SOE during the war, of course. Old fellow died a month ago. You didn't see it?" he asked, as though I might have been an essential witness in a street accident.

"No. I don't have much interest in that sort of thing now."

"No," Basil agreed, and drank deeply again. If not drunk to begin with, as I had thought, he now seemed intent on reaching that state as quickly as possible.

"Yes," he went on. "We're all going. Everyone's coming." His tone was that of a child anticipating a treat. "Drink up and have one at the bar with us. They'd love to see you again.

Darley and Jameson, I mean. You're still quite a hero in the department, you know—though what is it, ten years?"

"I'd rather not, Basil, really—"

"Come on, old man. They've *seen* you. It won't do any harm."

The silly phrase rang out with nothing but innocent temptation then: a day in town, some fine weather, a drink with old colleagues—what could have been more natural? And hadn't I been thinking of just such things all morning—the lure of the odd good parts of the past? And here it was, come timely, in the shape of Basil and Jameson and Darley—if not Henry. All the same, though not close friends, these three had never harmed me. They were innocent cogs in another part of a stupid machine, and their names, like those on some old colonial war memorial, suggested only simple comradeship that morning as the corks began to pop and the bishop took another half of Veuve de Vernay, the perfume of many freshly opened bottles beginning to invade the room and warm the stupid chatter all around me.

After a mild argument with Basil, I got up and went with him to the bar.

"Ah," Darley said carefully, holding out his hand, inspecting me like a masterpiece that yet might just possibly prove to be a fake. "'Home is the hero...'"

"'And the hunter home from the hill,'"...Jameson added in a deep sotto voce, before turning away and belching a fraction. They were drinking champagne, the bottle between them already badly depleted.

"Coming back into the ranks?" Darley asked.

"No," I told him. "I—I was just up in town. I'm not staying."

I felt like one of the tweedy men around me, awkward and guileless in this knowing, cosmopolitan atmosphere, anxious for Paddington at 5:10 and a first-class corner seat to Kemble junction. I didn't have the right words with me; I didn't fit.

"My goodness," Darley said vigorously, the drink beginning to talk in him, "but you'll have to come to the service. Everyone's coming. Church is just round the corner."

A week before I would have refused: the idea would have seemed preposterous. But a week before I hadn't started to dream of the old Residency on the Nile over an empty sherry bottle.

I didn't reply one way or the other. But I could feel the

drink seeping into me, too, laying a firm foundation of acquiescence.

"And lunch," Basil said in his humble way, eyes downcast, looking at me through his eyelashes like a virgin. "There's a fork lunch at the Special Forces Club in Mayfair afterward."

"Ah, yes," Jameson said comfortably, ordering the other half of champagne. "What a day. What—a—day!" He smiled beatifically, dragging the phrase out, then raising his glass and savoring the frosty bubbles. He was like Mole too, I thought, released from the underground into the sunshine that first day of spring. "We've taken the day off, you see," he went on. "All of us."

I suddenly saw the telegrams from Cairo and Beirut—the "extras" and the "ordinaries"—piling up all over our building and blowing unheeded along the corridors in that lavender wind, with only Quinlan, in his smart uniform and campaign ribbons, left to chase hopelessly after them. The whole of the Middle East—Arafat and Sadat and Gaddafi—who would do nothing untoward that day, who would go into purdah for twenty-four hours or lie prostrate tending their souls, and all because Sir George (the Dragon, as he'd been known) had passed on and was to be handsomely commemorated with a few hymns, a quantity of drink, and international truce among the Intelligence community.

A clock chimed twelve from some church nearby. We left the bar and fell out into the sun, dizzy with good will, like children released for the day on a king's funeral.

SIR George—as we knew now, at last, in a spate of memoirs and histories released by the thirty-year official-papers ruling—had been a hero during the war, channeling Allied support through Special Operations Executive to any number of Resistance groups on the Continent—though much of his effort, it had since been confirmed by the war historians, had unfortunately taken the form of saturation bombing: one agent placed on the Continent at the expense of ten caught and executed.

Certainly I didn't see many women or civilians in the church when we got there—widows or children from that war, bereft by Sir George's elaborate ploys. No doubt they preferred to keep their own private counsels today, sharing informal griefs, far from that loud and self-congratulatory church.

The congregation was official and extensive, filling every pew right to the back where we sat, spilling over to the very doors of the church.

We had heard the babble of many tongues as we came in, from hard-faced, white-haired old men—French, Dutch, Belgian, Scandinavian, Slav. They'd come in chartered planes, Basil told me, from all over Europe. And here they were, triumphant, as all survivors are, but now with more triumph still, because, in an old Wren church, rebuilt over the wildflowers and dead masonry of the blitz, they had come to celebrate a final victory. They had outlived their patron and master: the Dragon had been put away. They had at last succeeded him, and though it was too late to rule, for this one day they would be kings; memories could be deeply stirred, all sorts of heroism evoked—now, in the rich history of the church, where even the dirtiest wars became part of the Good Fight, and later, more informally, over a fork lunch in Mayfair.

Yet I didn't blame them—the old men in their severe suits, some tailored for one arm, the crimson of many decorations and orders peeping over breast pockets and around lapels. Theirs had been a better fight than ours had ever been in the glass tower half a mile away. That was obvious, and I felt an interloper, a spy in a glittering council chamber, suddenly seeing for the first time the whole map of the Grand Design.

I don't suppose that more than a quarter of the congregation knew the words or the music of the first hymn, "To Be a Pilgrim." But the voice of the whole church, like the rising frenzy of a victory parade, hit the vaulted roof by the start of the second verse, when people had found their stride, miming the words where they didn't know them.

Then the choir sang an anthem—"Per Ardua ad Astra"—accompanied by trumpeters from the Central RAF Band—the sweet-harsh sounds piercing the silence in a long voluntary when the voices had died.

An air marshal read the first lesson: "'I have lifted up mine eyes unto the Lord and seen my salvation...'"

The second hymn had not such a sprightly tune and there was a more ragged response to it. The words, too, were less easy and many among the foreign congregation dipped into their hymn sheets in confusion. Perhaps because of their failure to do the hymn justice even at the end, a restlessness fell over the church just after the start of the address, given by an old comrade-in-arms of Sir George's.

"Nobody can be all things to all men. And there are people—some of you here, indeed—who will have had your disagreements with the Dragon. He was never a man to beat about the bush. But that you *are* here, however many bones you picked with him in the past, is a measure of his—and your—constancy and success."

Now the restlessness seemed to have congealed and isolated itself some three or four pews ahead of me—there was a strange movement of heads and flurry of broad backs. Then I saw what it was: a middle-aged man in a white Burberry had slumped across the pew in front of him, and friends or colleagues on either side were trying to revive him, pulling his head back and opening his collar. I couldn't see the man's face, but his thin hair was tossed about and his head lolled on a shoulder next him, falling sideways, right down on the pew behind, like a confident lover in the back row of a cinema.

They got him out, sliding him along the bench and onto the side aisle, just ahead of me to my left. His two friends held him, linking hands round his back, the man's arms dangling about their shoulders. Then they came past me, holding him up like a hooker going into a tight scrum, except that his legs trailed along over the flagstones like a marionette's. I have never seen anyone so dead.

But few people in the congregation had noticed. The address went on unabated. "...Sir George had many enemies. But at the end only one was undefeated: the Last Enemy..."

Life was imitating death, I thought, as I glanced at Basil beside me. There was a query in my expression, for he had been watching this little drama intently, as if he knew the man.

"What?—who?" I whispered.

But Basil dodged the question by moving out of his seat as quickly as a cat and following the grisly trio down the aisle. I heard one of the small side doors open and the man's feet scraping over a grating—and when I turned I saw Basil for an instant, framed in the doorway in his dark suit, standing like an expectant undertaker outside in the sun.

2

I remember thinking it was too soon for corpses—that Basil, for all his devious skills, could hardly have laid this on for me. Yet even so, that was surely the moment to have bailed out—away from that victorious church, celebrating death all too effectively—and found myself a back table at L'Escargot.

Instead I hung around after the service. I suppose I was curious: that dull passion of our trade which, though buried for years in Oxfordshire, could not have quite died in me and had now come again, warmed by drink and memory and by the vision of a Burberry with a body inside being humped out of a Wren church.

Basil was shifting about uneasily on the pavement like a bookie's runner when we came out. An ambulance had picked up the man some moments before, the siren trailing away down toward the Strand.

"Who was it?" Jameson asked. The Beaune had crusted on Basil's lips in the heat, and he licked them now, curling his tongue about like a flycatcher, as though trying to reactivate the taste.

"Jock. Jock McKnight. He was in Nine with me—just after the war."

"Nine?" Darley asked innocently.

"Slavs and Soviets."

"Heart?" Jameson inquired anxiously, straightening his tie, sobering up. This untimely death had cast a gloom over the whole proceedings.

"I should think so," Basil said. "He must have been getting on."

Basil peered round him, gazing inquisitively at the congregation as they left the church. Despite his medical verdict, he might have been looking for a murderer, I thought.

"Yes," he went on, continuing his inspection over Darley's shoulder. "We both worked on an interdepartmental committee years ago. It was set up to deal with Tito after he broke with Moscow. Jock was very good on the Slavs and Soviets. Pity. Ticker must have packed in."

Basil moved toward the main doorway of the church to speak to someone and we vaguely followed. There was a tub of laurel just inside the railings by the side entrance, and I put my foot up on the rim of the barrel to tie one of my laces while I waited.

Just as I put my shoe up a drop of blood fell on the toecap. Blood? Yes, it was certainly blood. The bright sunlight showed its color clearly now—dripping down over the shiny green leaves from somewhere deep inside the bush. Then I saw where it must have come from: there was a hymn sheet pressed into the middle of the leaves, about halfway up. I could just see the deeply embossed print on the cover: "In Memoriam: George Alkert—" But when I went to pull it out half the thick cartridge paper came away in my hand. The back of the sheet was sodden with fresh blood, and my thumb and index finger were soaked with it now, as if I'd just pressed my hand deep into a still-bleeding wound.

And there was another moment to run. And yet by then, one wanted to know: had Basil lied about the man's death or was he genuinely ignorant? And what of the man's two friends who had helped him out—were they indeed friends or enemies? And what of the man himself, who had obviously put the hymn sheet away into an inside pocket after the memorial address had started. Had he been shot with a silencer? And if so, by whom and why?

Cowardice, I sometimes think, is not so common as we like to imagine. We are more often rash to the point of bravery. And if not that, pride will usually prevent a retreat—even in some unimportant matter like doing the dishes before we allow ourselves to sit down for coffee. We set up borders and checkpoints for ourselves every day, small trials of strength, confirmations of nerve or integrity in a hundred small measures taken. So too, in larger issues, we will set ignorance, curiosity, or even superstition up against our better judgment—determined to prove that what is purely willful in our nature has more value than our sanity. The Greeks defied the fates in myth, but we sometimes do it in fact—sudden spendthrifts, goaded beyond endurance by the prosaic in our lives. And that was true of me, no doubt, as I followed the others down along the Strand, unwilling yet impatient, pushing through the lunchtime crowds.

The sun lay directly overhead now like a hot plate. Girls in thin dresses floated in the light, shrieking with sudden inane enthusiasms, turning quickly, stopping, getting in our way, exchanging brash and knowing looks with louts in cowboy boots, their faces happily cleaned out of thought or care. They had the nature of plant life unique to the city: miraculous fruit erupting overnight, blooming on tarmac and oil fumes—diaphanous-skinned girls, ready to drop at a touch into some lap on a bench down by the river.

I had forgotten the vigorous arrogance of London summer lunchtimes, the mocking youth of secretaries and long-haired clerks. What would I do walking off into those crowds alone? There was no girl to pick up there who wouldn't think me a middle-aged refugee from the mackintosh brigade; no bar to be easily propped up off Leicester Square with talk to strangers about prospects for the Derby; and to eat alone at L'Escargot would be to sit there wondering about the blood on my fingers. Then, too, there had been the shapes of death all morning in the summer air. An elephant will move away and die apart from its tribe, but humans are less considerate and tend to herd together in the face of mortality; when Basil hailed a cab near the Savoy and called me to hurry up, I quickened my step. It was too late to turn back then—even if I'd wanted to.

THE Special Services Club enjoyed a small leasehold at the back of a large Victorian town house at the end of a narrow cul-de-sac just off Park Lane. The front and grander part of this red-brick pile was now a smart but not exclusive gambling club, with a candy-striped awning reaching out over the front door. But that day it was the old tradesmen's entrance, twenty yards away, which commanded attention, as cars clogged up the narrow approach and old, stiff-shouldered, white-haired men embraced each other on the pavements, not yet sure of their direction, so that the lane was filled with guttural, Continental queries.

"C'est par là!"

"Non—c'est tout droit. Et prenez garde!"

"I'm not a member," I said to Basil, as he pushed his way ahead through the crowd.

"Be my guest," he said, glancing over his shoulder and looking at me, mischief flooding his eyes. Basil was considerably smaller than I, almost an overgrown schoolboy. And I saw him then as a sophisticated sixth-former abroad with a group of younger boys, pressing us forward toward the first forbidden delights of a brothel.

The heat and the crush inside the club was so great that my first thought was to try and rise above into some cooler airs. Another bar was open on the first floor, we were told, and we all made our way up to it, threading between old men already exhausted, sitting on the stairs underneath photographs of their former glory, great moments from Europe's clandestine past: Jean Moulin with a machine pistol among Resistance comrades on some scrubby hill; Randolph Churchill in a huge sheepskin coat playing chess over a bottle of rakia somewhere in Yugoslavia.

At the top of the stairs we came into a long, gilded dining room where a white-laid table, groaning with food and drink, ran along all one side, and three big bow windows, wide open, looked over a small courtyard at the back; a chestnut tree sprang up from the middle of it, some of its mint-green spring leaves almost touching the windows. It was less crowded here; there was a drift of a breeze coming in, mixing with the sharp, tart smell of lemon and gin and the sound of cracking ice as it drowned in tonic. Basil rubbed his hands judiciously and licked his lips once more. Then, after an interval in which he seemed to calculate the quantity of alcohol available and equate it satisfactorily with his future capacity, he moved off to do battle at the long white table.

And yet he must have drunk no more than tonic water most of that afternoon. Certainly an hour later, when he introduced me to the man in the billiard room, he was totally sober—a different Basil, no longer the inane schoolboy, no longer deferential: Basil in command.

I'd been talking to a middle-aged Frenchwoman about her experiences in the Resistance: how in 1943 she had been put on top of the notorious lime quarry outside Meudon and faced by a German Wehrmacht major with a Luger, anxious for information about her comrades.

"I didn't tell him, though," she said.

"Why didn't he shoot you then?"

"I didn't know—at that moment. I was taken back to Paris—then sent to an ordinary prison camp, and released eventually. The major 'lost' my file—on purpose."

"Why?"

"He fell in love with me—there, on top of that quarry. He'd been interrogating me for days before."

I was astonished and not prepared to believe the story—and I said so.

"No, it's true," she said. "There are some stories from that war which ended well."

"How do you know—did you meet him again?"

Basil had come up next to me meanwhile, and was pressing me for a word, but I persisted with the woman.

"Yes," she said, smiling. "I did. He survived the war. He traced me in Paris afterwards. I married him," she added simply. Then she turned and looked round the room, searching someone out. "There. He's over there," she said.

I followed her glance and as I looked a man pushed through the crowd, coming toward us, glass in hand: quite an old man, upright, smiling, with the remnants of fair hair.

She introduced us. "My husband," she said.

We shook hands. Then Basil forced me away. I was glad I didn't stay longer. I didn't want to know anything more about it, yet I walked on air with Basil into the billiard room, thinking how wrong I'd been about life, life only as defeat.

"This is the Prime Minister," Basil said, as we pushed our way into a gloomy, paneled room with long clerestory windows high above the covered billiard table: a room where the sun had never been, and where sad old men had played with sticks and balls for a hundred years. In the far corner a group of Continentals—a French army officer in a kepi and a one-armed man I hadn't noticed before in a wheelchair—surrounded a figure brandishing a pipe.

"Oh, yes?" I said. "Was he in the Resistance? I didn't know."

The wine I'd had, without much food, had begun to play in me sometime before, and I felt I could see the afternoon out nicely now, with one or two more drinks and a few jokes before dinner, and then early bed in a club I belonged to not far down the road.

Basil paused at one corner of the billiard table, trying to negotiate a passage between two excitable old partisans who were playing a war game with matches on the green baize cover.

Basil said, "He wants to meet you."

I thought he meant one of the men in front of us and I half held out my hand before Basil pulled me on toward the corner of the room.

And then I was face to face with the Prime Minister, his sage, plump head nodding rhythmically in answer to some elaborate explanation from the French officer about De Gaulle's dissatisfactions in 1940—a matter the Prime Minister clearly felt uninterested in. Our arrival provided him with a thankful exit, and he turned to both of us, smiling at me hugely, shaking my hand with surprised bonhomie, as if I were a long-lost relative come to praise him on "This Is Your Life."

"Mr. Marlow," he said, again with the hint of deeply considered joy in his voice—here at last was the only person in this gathering that he really wanted to meet—"how good of you to come." He turned to his companions. "Would you excuse me for a moment?"

The Prime Minister put an arm round my shoulder and led Basil and me some little distance along the wall of the room, to where there was a small raked stand of old cinema tip-up seats where members could watch the billiard games. We sat down in line abreast—the seats going *clank-clank-clank* as they took our weight—like louts settling into the back row of a local Odeon, noisily and abruptly. And I thought that no more conspicuous meeting with a Prime Minister, about something presumably confidential, could have been contrived. Yet perhaps I was wrong: here in this room crowded with the clandestine, in a building packed to the doors with old secrets now come to a fine and alcoholic bloom, who would have suspected the start of any new conspiracy?

"I won't waste your time," the Prime Minister said, in a

way which suggested he was rather more anxious not to waste his. "You're one of our best men, I understand"—and again, before I could contest this, he seemed about to put his hand on my arm, as though he too was uncertain of the truth in this statement and was anxious to persuade me of it by touch. But at the last moment he withdrew his hand and started to light up his pipe instead.

"I'm sorry, sir. But I'm not—" I looked across at Basil in the far seat. He was leaning out toward me, the PM between us, his face a mask of official rectitude.

"I'm afraid I'm not one of your men at all, Prime Minister. There's been some misunderstanding—"

"No, of course you're not one of our men—not officially. But it was you, wasn't it, whom we have to thank for that business in Cheltenham five or six years ago? The names of those Soviet diplomats you got for us—a hundred of them or more, not a bad bag—half the KGB men they had over here. We owe you a great deal for that."

"I was involved in that—yes. Regretfully—"

"We all have regrets, Mr. Marlow. We wouldn't be human otherwise. I have many myself. The point is—" He cleared his throat and picked a piece of burning ash from the bowl of his pipe. Then he relit it again, with another consequent delay, before he found his stride and began to puff vigorously. "Point is, something rather serious has come up which I think you can help us on."

"I don't work for Intelligence any more—"

"No, of course you don't. And that's just why we need you. Let me explain briefly. Then Fielding here can fill in all the details afterward. Primarily—at the moment—this is a political problem..." Again he stopped to tend his pipe.

"I'm not a politician—"

"You mustn't keep saying 'No,' Mr. Marlow. I'm not just a politician either. I'm also head of the security and intelligence services in this country. And that's why I've asked to meet you—unofficially, of course." He glanced round the room, smiling broadly, a happy old King Cole taking appropriate obeisance from his courtiers, while apparently chatting to me about nothing more important than next week's cricket with the West Indians.

"I wanted to meet you," he went on, turning to me without dimming his smile a fraction, "because I know you've had your doubts about working for us in the past—" I was about to assent to this, but before I could, he really did put his hand on my arm. "Now I *understand* those doubts, Mr. Marlow. Doubts are part of every considered response. I've had them myself. But in this instance I wanted to see you myself—personally—to reassure you that this directive comes right from the top and isn't some harebrained scheme dreamed up by a lot of backroom Intelligence crackpots." He stopped once more and sucked hard at the dying bowl. Then he looked for his lighter. "This job has my personal authority—right down the line. And Mr. Fielding here is answerable to me over it, as well as to his own department. It's a matter of *possibly* the utmost importance. I say 'possibly' because as yet we simply don't know how real the threat is. However, after this morning's incident with McKnight at the church there's no question—we're in deep."

"So he was killed, wasn't he?" I looked across at Basil.

"It seems so," Basil replied diffidently, as though options lay even beyond the grave.

"And there's the point," the Prime Minister said, his smile gone and a deep seriousness flooding his face; he was obviously winding up toward his peroration. "McKnight is the third to go in as many months. Dearden, Phillips, and now McKnight."

"What links them?" I asked.

The Prime Minister took his pipe out and looked at me carefully, essaying a shade of deep drama. "That's my out cue, Mr. Marlow. I have to get back to the House. Fielding will give you the rest of the details. I'm here just to give you my *word*: this is 'official'—no tricks involved. We need you."

He stood up and his seat whipped back with a loud bang. Basil and I stood up—and there were two more loud bangs. People glanced at us. The Prime Minister took my hand, leaning toward me. "*I* need you," he said finally, in the soft, steely tones of a false lover. And then he was gone, an aide touching his arm and leading him forward to the top of the billiard table where toasts were about to be proposed. The Prime Minister made the first, raising a tulip-shaped glass of champagne: "To Sir George—his memory. To you—his colleagues in adversity. And to all those who fell secretly in the cause of a better world."

There was silence in the long, dark room as everyone raised his glass. A dead, smoky heat rose up to the clerestory windows. I was stunned and suddenly very tired and the drink had quite deserted me.

"Come on." Basil nudged me, whispering. "Drink up. Your country needs you."

"YOU are a cheat, Basil. My God—I should have seen it the moment you stumbled up to me this morning, spilling the wine. You were playing the Trojan horse."

We'd left the club and taken the underpass over into Hyde Park, and had paused now at the beginning of the sandy ride down Rotten Row, looking along the sloping avenue of heavy chestnut trees. Basil had taken one of his shoes off and was shaking some grit out of it.

"Let's walk on the grass," he said.

There had hardly been any rain since the start of May. Spring had come and gone in a weekend and the sky was cloudless now—a tired, dusty blue as though it had been summer for a long time. I felt as if I'd been with Basil for a week, too, and not a few hours—and I was tired of him, as a host who had betrayed me, yet with whom I still had to tie things up before exchanging formal good-byes.

"A cheat?" Basil said carefully, as we struck off toward the Serpentine. He looked hot in his old pin-stripe and the long lobes of his ears were red with excitement. "Nonsense, Peter. You heard the Prime Minister—"

"I suppose you followed me this morning—the whole thing was arranged. Barker must have told you about my coming up. Well, let me tell you—" I said aggressively.

"Wait a minute—"

"*You* wait a minute. The short answer is 'No.' I'm not doing any more jobs for you—or the Prime Minister."

Basil said nothing. He looked up at me and smiled gingerly, like someone admiring the bravery of a fool.

"I've been caught twice before with you people," I went on. "The first time gave me four years in Durham Jail—and the second a bullet in the leg. I've had all that," I stormed.

"You also had fifteen thousand pounds," Basil said vaguely, looking aside at a half-naked couple throwing a Frisbee over a prancing dog. "Don't blame Barker, by the way. He only confirmed what we knew already. You're broke, Peter. Stony broke."

"I can sell my cottage. I can get a job," I lied.

"What?—with four or five thousand on the mortgage still

to pay? That won't leave you with much. And a job?—at forty, with your experience: a few years teaching at some wog prep school, ten years thumbing through *Al Ahram* with us, and a criminal record? You could get a job—washing dishes, Peter, and you know that. So let's stop talking cock, my old man. You need money—and we'll give it to you. More than the fifteen thousand you had last time. And something substantial to open the account." Basil loosened his tie and blinked in the hard light. "God, if this is only June, what's it going to be like later on? Never mind, we'll have some tea in a minute. I want to take you to an hotel near here. Because it's not just the money. There's something else that will interest you about this job—partly why we've asked you to do it."

"What?"

"Come—I'll show you." He looked at his watch. "Teatime. Should have started by now. We're going to have some tea: some iced lemon tea and some expensive cream cakes, Peter. You can make up your mind after that—and I'll tell you about the job then too."

How confident he was, I thought. And yet I had to admit that I shared some of his confidence: with this money I wouldn't have to lose the cottage—that was my first thought. The wine bill could be paid, all that San Patricio sherry— and the new radials that my car needed all round. We turned off before the Serpentine and walked south toward Knightsbridge.

"Tea and cakes, Basil," I said. "It's just blackmail. You think I can be bought for that?"

Basil shrugged his shoulders. "You were always such a moral fellow, Peter. Well, you simply can't afford them any more. That's the long and short of it. Besides, this isn't immoral: you can see it's straight. Why else the PM?"

"You people could con even him," I said.

I should have walked away and left Basil then, sweating on the pavement, waiting for a break in the traffic before we crossed over to Wilton Place. But I thought then that my life had been too full of what I ought to have done. Besides, Basil had set the whole thing up so skillfully that I couldn't resist moving on to this next carrot: what could he possibly have in store for me over a glass of iced tea and a plateful of cream cakes? It was as simple as that—and Basil knew it, looking

35

at me confidently, when we finally managed to cross over and made our way toward the Grand Hotel.

THE lobby was quiet and nearly empty, for this was a small Grand Hotel. But once through the beveled glass doors and into the gilded tearoom, we sank into a pool of gentle privilege, the tact of money, a crowded well-being. We took a table right at the back, while the rich chatted softly over Royal Worcester tea services, nurtured by attentive waiters sailing round their tables, hands held high with plates of hot scones and Viennese chocolate cake.

A samovar of tea, a huge silver-plated edifice, bubbled in the center of the room—and beyond it, standing by the window like a dark exclamation mark against the white net curtains that filtered the afternoon sun and gave the room the feel of a watery, lemon-gray aquarium, was a woman—raven-haired and deeply bronzed, playing the flute.

They say you never forget a face. But I did then, and it was clear that Basil, looking at me carefully and then up at the dais, wanted me to recognize something, to remember someone.

"Well?" I said, looking at the £5-a-head tea menu. "You normally do your business here? Never miss a trick to ham it up, do you? I'll have the Welsh rarebit—and a beaker of cold tea."

Basil smiled ominously. "It's ten or fifteen years, isn't it? Or have you seen her since?"

"Who?"

Basil glanced up again at the woman in the pale smock dress, her copper-colored arms floating up and down as she nursed the instrument, which obscured her lips and chin. Perhaps that was why I hadn't recognized her sooner—as I did then, a second before he mentioned her name.

"Rachel Phillips."

It was her short parting, just an inch or so long, right above her brow, and the bouncy, untutored hair that ran away from it down either side, enclosing her head in a windy circle of dark curls, that jogged my memory and made my stomach turn suddenly: hair that I'd run my hand through with such pleasure years ago. And, before I'd fully appreciated her identity and presence here, I remembered a time on the lake in Scotland, below her house in Perthshire—the first

36

time I'd ever looked at her properly, with love, out in a rowing boat, nearly twenty-five years before.

And my first thought was: Did Basil know about this, too? Had he been hiding on that wooded shore with binoculars? And I thought, Yes, Basil must know practically everything, even that far back perhaps. And I wasn't angry to begin with, as one isn't when an outsider, a relative or a friend, admires someone one loves, when one has first introduced them into the family circle. Instead, for a moment, I was grateful to Basil, as though he were a long-lost uncle come to commend my choice of wife almost a generation after the engagement. And indeed, having run the gamut of childish infatuation and advanced on love, Rachel and I had once thought to marry and had met with little encouragement either from ourselves or our circles.

Subsequently, in our twenties and until she had married ten or so years before, we had shared each other intermittently, but without any permanency, for when she had wished that, I hadn't—and by the time I changed my mind she had moved on to other dreams. We had grown together, home from boarding schools through years of holidays, in thoughtless leaps and bounds but with as many angry retreats. And when we had loved afterward it had been with the same extremes of pain and excitement. Our exaggerated feelings for each other always retained the flavor of nursery antagonisms: petty squabbles over toys or idyllic trysts behind the laurels, trysts that in turn had become the bitter quarrels and loves of adulthood without any change in their childish nature; antipathies and desires which never benefited from growth or reason.

That Basil should bring me to her again, in the tearoom of a London hotel, her cool music flooding the spaces all around us—well, as I say, I was charmed at first. But a moment afterward I was afraid. Basil rarely did anything without the long view in mind. I remembered a seemingly innocuous quarrel he had once inaugurated with a young visa clerk in our travel section which had ended in the man's being sent down for fourteen years at the Old Bailey. Basil had spotted a flaw in the fellow long before anyone else. And now Rachel, for some reason, had swum into his sights—in a matter which, for some other reason, I was to be linked with her. If I feared for her, I feared as much for us as well.

Basil intended some meeting between us—I sensed that clearly, it was part of his plan. But had he any idea of what such a renewal would mean to me? Had he really spied out that personal terrain? Gazing across the water at us from a lakeside perch, children touching each other in a boat, or seen us through the window of that shabby blitzed flat we had once shared at the back of Notting Hill Gate? Did he know only the softness and easy humor we had found together in those early days in London: lying on that broken sofa, as I had done, listening to her practice behind a closed door in the bathroom, the only privacy she needed then? Or had he waited until the weekend, and been another customer in the small corner store in Ladbroke Grove, and seen the whirlwind row over what to buy and how much to spend on provisions for the following week?

Was my past that far back, long before I'd spied or married myself or come to such ruin in Durham Jail—all the life that had come before me now as precisely as in an old scrapbook—was that untouched part of me to be opened to the casual view, released by Basil from an airtight box and become, with all the other failed emotion, heir to real corruption?

"I want you to meet her—again," Basil said.

"I thought as much."

I breathed hard, restraining my anger in the polite room full of delicate music. A meeting, Basil would have thought, hardly different from one of his own held in those airless basement rooms in Holborn: hardly different indeed—in that it would have been just as devious. Rachel had always been proud of what she saw as her innocent carelessness in human affairs. She herself was a gift, she thought—like her music—which would inevitably be appreciated. In fact she knew well how wrong this view was, how frightened she was of herself— and so, like a spy, she constantly hid her tracks and changed identity the better to avoid the unacceptable reality of her person. Thus it was that a casual involvement with her took the course of a prolonged adolescence, while a commitment was a return to the heart-stopping trials of childhood. She had surprised me then, to depths unknown. I'd come to accept that music was her only passion—the one thing, besides her father, that she really cared about.

"You've been doing your homework, haven't you?" I turned on Basil with some bitterness. "How did you dig her out of my life? No one in the department could have known."

The waiter arrived before Basil could reply and he spoke to him with heavy humor. "Yes, don't forget, a double ration of pancakes..." For a thin man Basil had an inordinate greed in everything: a fat man was desperately trying to get inside him. He leaned forward now and tinkered with the carnations in a small silver vase between us.

"It's years since I last saw her—properly," I went on when the waiter had left. "It was before I joined the section in Holborn, before I went to Egypt."

"Your file, Peter—the forms you had to complete when you came to us. You gave her father as a reference. And why not? He was an old friend of yours and your family, and a distinguished man. But she was always more than a friend, wasn't she?"

That was true, I thought—unfortunately. How much better simply to have been a friend of Rachel's. And how she would have laughed at the idea—that crystal, mocking, serious laughter—laughter like a wild bell. Friendship required balance, foresight, discretion—and Rachel had few gifts there. She viewed friendship as a kind of failure, something second best, a slur on the real potential of human association which she saw in primary colors, in terms only of extravagant love or hate.

"But I left Holborn nearly ten years ago," I said. "My file must be pretty dead by now. How did you pick me out of the bag?"

"The files never die with us, Peter. You know that." Basil crushed a carnation bud and put his fingers to his nose. "In fact, with computers, they've taken on a whole new life. When this Phillips business came up six weeks ago we ran his tape through. Part of it included all official contacts made by or to him while he was in the Service: the names of people he'd dealt with overseas and at home here—a complete business directory, in fact. We have them on everyone now. Well, there was your name, among some hundreds of others. And I said to myself, Well, that's funny. What's friend Marlow got to do with Lindsay Phillips? They weren't in the same section, years between them. A look at your own file and the matter became clear: an old family friend; then the daughter—a few discreet inquiries. Forgive me."

"You could raise the dead, couldn't you, with your bloody files? But what 'Phillips business'? He was just a diplomat in the Foreign Office, surely."

"He wasn't. He's been with us for over forty years. And he's disappeared. That's the business."

I laughed. "This is where I came in, Basil. It's just like old Henry going down the Nile. You want me to find Phillips?"

Basil nodded. The waiter glided up to us with a feast of goodies, placing them carefully all over the small table, while Basil relished them in advance, seducing the éclairs and undressing the sandwiches with his eyes.

He nodded now again, sagely, licking his lips. "Yes," he said. "You're good at finding people if they're to be found." He took a buttery pancake and maneuvered a bowl of strawberry jam through the other dishes toward it.

"How does she fit in?" I asked, looking over at Rachel. "What's she doing here?"

"She plays here. Three afternoons a week—in the season."

"She used to be better known. I'm surprised."

"Why? They pay well."

I laughed. "She never needed money. That used to be our problem: she had too much of it."

Basil took no notice, biting into his jam-laden pancake. "Yes, they pay well," he said at last. "She needs the practice. But really—she likes an audience, doesn't she?"

That was true, I thought. Rachel had never really sought private admiration—she feared the ensuing commitment. In that sphere she preferred to give: to dominate in particular, or else to weep. It was only from a public, I remembered well from her early concerts, that she properly "received"—taking from the eyes of many an approval she refused in her personal affairs. So often "unworthy"—of me, or of life—in the light of a crowd her skin began to glow.

Basil paused before his next pancake and listened to the music. "Gluck's 'Dance of the Blessèd Spirits,'" he said. "Delicious. She does it beautifully, doesn't she?"

"I don't follow you, Basil."

"And beautiful herself, too. Wonder she hasn't married again."

"I hear the last one sank with all hands. That's probably why."

Rachel had once tried to be her age—in marriage. But she had failed, not from any lack of fidelity, I'm sure, but because the only fidelity she cared about was impossible. She wished at all costs to be true to herself, while yet ensuring that her soul should surprise her every hour. She walked into a new country each morning and threw away the map at bedtime. I had found it difficult to share these abrupt journeys she made about herself: the young German conductor I'd heard she'd married had obviously found it impossible. In exchange for certainties she offered a complete lack of restraint. But there never had been any real certainty, apart from her father. She and I had separated; the German had moved on, finding her, I suppose, the one score he couldn't interpret, and she had been left holding mysterious gifts—ones to which only her music could give a satisfactory form.

Basil continued to look across at her, his eyes becalmed for a moment trying to focus on some more sensual greed. "That nose—straight down from her brow like a ruler and eyes like black ink bottles. Greek-god department. No? And that skin..."

"She used to say anyone really in love with her was queer. Do you fancy her, Basil? Or are you pimping for her?"

He sighed, turning back to the table, before considering the merits of the creamy éclairs or the soft almond icing on the Battenberg cake. "We've been trying to help her, that's all. I told you—her father disappeared. Two months ago, up in their house in Scotland."

"You work for the missing persons bureau, do you?"

"You don't understand. Latterly Phillips was head of Nine: the Soviets, as well as Tito and all the rest of that Balkan crew down there. That's been his stamping ground since he rejoined after the war. And now—thin air. At least there were the bodies left over from the other two, Dearden and McKnight."

"They were in Nine as well?"

Basil nodded. "Dearden headed a circle out of Zagreb—he was a businessman there—covering Croatia, Slovenia, the Hungarian border areas. McKnight was his case officer, ran him from London—and Phillips, well, he was control—directly responsible for the whole operation."

"Head of Section personally responsible? I'm surprised."

"Not in this case you wouldn't be. This was grade-A stuff all the way: the Soviet threat to invade Yugoslavia, grabbing a good-looking Med port, Split or Rijeka; a takeover after Tito's death—all that. I'll give you the details later."

"I've had quite a lot already. And I've not agreed to anything."

Basil had bitten into an éclair, and the cream inside had

41

squashed out all over his chin. He dabbed at his face with a napkin.

"Nothing you couldn't get from the papers, Peter—if you read any down there on the wolds. And as far as Western Intelligence is concerned, you don't suppose we're looking the other way over all this, do you? Any fool must know that. Balance of power in the scales here: sovereignty of nonaligned nations, Little Red Ridinghood and the big bad Soviet wolf. Used to be brave little Belgium—and that set off quite a rocket, as I recall. Well, now it's brave little Yugoslavia we're having to go out and bat for."

"And that's where I come in—third wicket down? With the first three dead. Thanks. But I think this bowling is too fast for me, Basil."

Basil munched away before looking up at Rachel again and clearing his throat. "You come in—with her. Where you left off, maybe, all those years ago. With her—and her mother, too."

"Madeleine?"

"Yes. She's down in London at the moment. We want you to meet them both."

I smiled. "Officially?"

"Just the opposite. Officially we've got nowhere—which is why we need you. The Scots police, Interpol, his own section, half the special branch down here—we've turned the man inside out these past two months and found nothing. Just nothing."

"Maybe there is nothing. A lot of people these days walk out the door one morning and never come back. It's inflation."

Basil pursed his lips and sipped his tea for the first time. "You don't disappear one morning if you're Lindsay Phillips. A happy man: well married, nice family, lot of money, work he liked and six months away from retirement in a beautiful country house. You don't walk out on all that."

"Maybe he lost his memory then. Amnesia. That happens, too."

"Unlikely—when you consider Dearden and McKnight. Very unlikely."

"Kidnapped, murdered?"

Basil nodded. "Perhaps."

"Or perhaps he defected?" I said lightly.

"Hardly. Do you remember him?"

I had to agree. Lindsay Phillips had been like an early

idealized map of the world: everywhere you looked were the legends of honor and duty, the trade winds of patriotism and hard work. Major Lindsay Phillips was to me, at least when I was young and had stayed in his house during the war, the epitome of the good soldier—a man who, home from leave and reading the lesson in the little church on the edge of his moorland estate, seemed hardly different from his eminent forebears, commemorated there in bad stained glass above the pews: Victorian officers killed in the Ashanti wars or governor-generals buried in Westminster, emblemized now as St. George or the Good Shepherd. They were sunny, colored pictures—Camelot knights in armor or strong men with sheep on a green hill. "Brigadier General Sir William Phillips, Queen's Own IIth Hussars: Died at Glenalyth, November 1936: Faithful unto Death." That was the father.

"It doesn't make much sense, Basil—my succeeding where you've all failed. How am I supposed to find out any more than you did?"

Basil humphed. "A friend always knows more than an outsider: a close friend, an old friend." Basil tolled the bell of friendship as if he really believed in it—the one true faith which he had lost and I still in some way possessed.

"I'm to use my friendship with these people to spy on them, is that it?"

"Not at all. Not for a moment. Can't you see it from their point of view? Stop thinking about spying: *they* want to find out what's happened to him, more than we do. Don't you see? You'll be helping *them*."

"But without telling them I'm working for you—why that?"

"Because you tell things to a friend you wouldn't to a policeman. That's one obvious reason," Basil said impatiently.

"That's a real cheat. You assume the family has something to hide?"

"They may have," Basil said judiciously. "But that's not the point—as you know perfectly well. It's a matter of familiarity, longstanding association. In such circumstances people say things...one is in a position to learn." Basil left this idea of inquisitive friendship hanging in the air.

"Exactly. It's called placing an agent, Basil. A deep-cover illegal. The target here is the Phillips family and I'm to be dropped over the landing zone at the next full moon. Well, that's nonsense. I can't do it."

Basil stopped eating for a moment, starving himself to give weight to his next pronouncement. "Listen, the end justifies the means in this case. If you *can* help them, would you refuse to? And if you do manage to find out what's happened to him—well, they'll tell us in any case. So you need deal only with them if you like. And I'll make another offer: we'll leave it up to them—see if they make the first move. Madeleine Phillips is down here for the Chelsea Flower Show. You remember the family business they have up on their estate in Perthshire? Bee suppliers and that honey of theirs 'Glenalyth Heather'? Well, they've got a stand, and they'll both be at the show tomorrow. I want you simply to go round and introduce yourself, show your face—and we'll take it from there. I can't do fairer than that."

"What do you mean?"

Basil eyed the final éclair like an executioner—moved his hand toward it, but then, at the last moment, reprieved it. "I think they'll *ask* you to help them, Peter, without your doing anything."

"That's a long shot."

Basil looked up at the chandelier. "God help us." Then he shifted in his chair, taking a firm grip on himself. "I don't think you realize the situation, Peter—how desperate these two women are. A husband and a father just disappearing one afternoon. Someone you loved—not knowing. Not knowing *anything,* you see. And there's not even a body. People have an enormous need to tidy things up that way, you know. It preys on their minds: the corpus delicti. And they need it, dead or alive, the flesh or the bones. It becomes a kind of passion—to find out."

Basil killed the last éclair now, biting deeply into the chocolate icing. "Yes I think they may well ask you to help them. They're rather lost just now," he added, trying to master the cream filling.

"They must have fifty close friends, Basil—here and in Scotland. That won't wash—that I'm the only friend they'd think might help them."

"You're the only friend with a foot in both camps, though, the personal and the professional. You're the family friend and the Intelligence expert. And Phillips kept those two worlds quite separate. Anyway, we better get out of here before she stops playing." He gave a last longing look up at Rachel on the dais, then took out a crisp £10 note and left it on the table for the waiter.

"It's up to you," he said before he saw me looking at the money. "Yes, and that too. I told you: this is important—all the way along. And though I know you'd never do anything simply for money—you're far too serious for that—don't forget, you need it. Sherry is going up all the time and the beer is falling, even those Liffey water dividends."

"You're everywhere, Basil, aren't you? The bloody Light of the World. Who did you have looking through my window in the village?"

Basil leaned across to me, confidingly, so that I thought I was about to hear some trusting revelation about Mrs. Bentley the postmistress, or the nosy vicar.

"More things in heaven and earth, Peter. You can't expect to know everything. But that's why I fancied you for this: you *want* to know, don't you? You have a great need to find out, get to the heart of the matter. Well, here's your chance—with Lindsay Phillips. Go to the Flower Show, see what happens, and I'll come round to your club tomorrow evening."

"Can't I call you?"

"No. That's another problem—there's a leak somewhere in our section at the moment. Anything you and I do will be person to person for the time being. Six o'clock, shall we say, at the club?"

I nodded. Basil touched my arm. "Don't be so serious. You can always say no."

I glanced at Rachel away on the far side of the room, coming to the end of a piece, her eyes far away somewhere. She had dropped out of life, as if down a hole underground, into the heart of her music. I envied her that ability. I envied, too, this recurrent artistry which kept her young and gave her a secret world where she could happily spend a lifetime growing up. I have always been impatient for some kind of maturity.

Basil was right—though about the wrong person. I needed to know again about Rachel, not her father. Though I hadn't seen her for more than ten years, I suddenly felt the thought clearly in the sweet, cake-scented air—that as in the old days she and I could happily tease each other once again. We need to tease each other more than we know, and love may come to depend on it.

3

The big man in the crumpled candy-striped summer suit and loafers strolled along the southern rim of Hampstead Heath, toward where they were flying the new dual-stringed stunting kites, which swooped and fell about in the warm afternoon breeze, high up in the air above Jack Straw's Castle.

He turned to his companion, who was older and more formally dressed, speaking quietly in Russian. "I've not seen these kites—they're extraordinary. Could you send some home for me?"

Feydor Kudashkin gazed wistfully up into the sky. "The children would love them," he added.

"Yes. We've sent some back already," the London Resident said. "I'll get some for you. How many children do you have?"

Kudashkin didn't answer, his eyes fixed on the sky—sharp, clever blue eyes, with laughter in them; he had a thinly bridged, straight nose with an equally forceful, dimpled chin; nose and chin jutted out now like pincers, savoring the air, while the bright eyes were downcast for a moment, a hint of sentimentality creeping in over the edges, the eyes of an exile dreaming of home for the first time.

"Yes," he said. "They're about old enough." Then he turned

46

to the Resident and now he was precise, intent, his dream quite gone. "Are they difficult to use? I can't quite see how they work."

"They come with full instructions," the Resident said patiently. "I'll send some home for you."

The two men had moved on now, moving between the old beech trees, down the hill from the heath, toward Frognal.

"How is your accommodation? Do you need anything?" the Resident asked. "Since I'm your only contact here, and we are not likely to be meeting again, you'd better let me know now."

"No. I have everything."

"Everything we know I've given you."

"Yes, you've been most helpful. Apart from McKnight this morning. That may hamper my operations."

No change of tone or hint of criticism emerged in these last sentences. But the Resident knew that in voicing such a comment at all Kudashkin must equal or outrank him in the KGB hierarchy. Yet since he did not know—indeed, he thought, specifically had not been told—of this man's exact place on the ladder, the Resident, by way of professional revenge, did not attempt to placate Kudashkin or exonerate himself.

"They were my instructions. From Center," he replied simply.

"Not the intent. I speak of the method—and the place: messy, risky." Kudashkin used his words judiciously, without rancor, just as the Resident had been equally restrained and unruffled. They might have been two bored agricultural inspectors in some backward province, far from their Moscow homes, discussing an outbreak of fowl pest that had got out of control.

"Since we put Dearden down in Zagreb, McKnight was under twenty-four-hour close surveillance," the Resident went on. "Sleeping at his office and never out of his own house at weekends. But we knew he was going to the church this morning. He was an old friend of Alkerton's. It was quite straightforward."

But Kudashkin didn't appear to be listening; he was lost once more, looking up at the sky again, at a last vision of the kites dancing in the early evening light.

"You won't forget, will you? To send some home for me?"

They took a path down the hill now, and were soon in the

narrow streets above old Hampstead village, deserted at the fag end of the hot afternoon.

"But what about Phillips?" Kudashkin suddenly broke the silence again. "He's the one we want—yet he went to ground before either of them. I don't follow that—unless they're hiding him somewhere." His tone was intimate, almost possessed, the Resident thought, as if this search for Phillips had already absorbed half his career.

"His family certainly think he's disappeared. So do his colleagues. We know that. It seems genuine."

"It 'seems.' But that's not enough. We have to know exactly where he is—dead or alive. Unless we can account for Phillips his whole Yugoslav operation must be considered still active, which limits our operations over there severely. We have to *know*."

They went on down the hill, stopping just before Admiral's Walk, where Kudashkin, posing as a visiting American academic on sabbatical, had rented a basement apartment in a handsome Georgian house. "I'll leave you here, then," he said. "Use the ordinary post if anything fresh turns up on your side."

"Good luck."

They didn't shake hands, just drifted apart, immediately becoming strangers in the leafy street. The Resident watched Kudashkin go—the academic in old spectacles, hands in pockets, the casual stride, a big-boned easy figure with an air of *savoir-vivre*, his thin fair hair and deep-cut features giving him the look of an old fashioned Anglo-Saxon: a man in a crumpled linen suit, from Australia or South Africa perhaps, like thousands of other similar colonial visitors in London that hot summer.

His cover was fine, the Resident thought. But he was curious once more, seeing him disappear among the chestnut trees along the Walk, as to why Center had sent over such an obviously senior officer, as simply a hit man it seemed, or at least to do a job which, given time, he could easily have handled himself. Finding out what had happened to Lindsay Phillips was simply a matter of time and routine, the Resident thought, and he resented this critical interference from on high.

THE flowers bloomed heavily in the long tents, their perfume exhausted in the moist air, saturated now with a smell of trampled grass and bleached canvas. People shoved their way in from the stark glare outside, already sweating at ten o'clock, before struggling around the exhibits with vehement mania.

I had come inside to pass the time, since neither of the two women had been at the "Glenalyth Honey" stand on the central thoroughfare half an hour before. But now that I wanted to get out again I could hardly move.

A woman trod on my foot. *"Excuse* me!" she said, outraged. A Japanese couple, the little man focusing a Nikon carefully on a *Begonia grandiflora,* were quietly toppled over the ropes into the Belgian house-plant stand.

Someone started to jab my shoulder vigorously. I'd had enough. *"Excuse* me!" I said, turning.

It was Rachel, her mother pressed in behind her, almost lost in the crowd.

"Hello! It *is* you, I was sure—" she shouted, before the surge of people took her away from me like a tide. "What on earth are you doing here?" she asked when she was pushed back again. "Are you with someone? Come on out—it's impossible here."

Rachel's face was caught before me, close to me, held still in the vise of the crowd for a moment, set like a dark cameo against the splash of scarlet color in a bank of flowers behind her. Pinpricks of moisture glittered on her skin. A faint rose lipstick exactly filled her bow-shaped lips. Nothing moved. The sounds in the tent were turned off. Then the film started again. She was pushed away from me and I moved toward the exit behind her. But that instant was enough to set the intimate shapes of her face against my memory of her and re-create the whole person afresh: the marks in her skin, the deep-set eyes on either side of the too-straight nose, the flurry of thin curls round her brow. I saw these for less than a moment, against the crowded confusion of flowers and people all about her, yet they had the same effect on me as if I'd gazed on her, sitting still in front of me in a deserted room, for an hour. A second can give one a deeper insight into someone than an hour's steady gaze—for there, in the unexpected cast, the surprised moment, the half-open lips, the real person speaks. With language and time we can all pretend otherwise.

I greeted Madeleine outside, before we found ourselves caught in a queue for the toilets and moved away once more.

"Peter!"

There was surprise and enthusiasm in her voice and yet a sharpness in it too that I'd not remembered, and her smile was a thing produced, set up on fragile supports, a play that would not run long. Her eyes had not the natural depth of Rachel's, yet with the strain—and the tears, I suppose—of her loss, and the disguise of mascara, they looked deeper now.

Where Rachel tended to run amok in her life, Madeleine, I remembered, favored restraints. Yet, lacking Rachel's profligate outlets, she had a greater hoard of emotion than her daughter. Like her husband's bees she stored up rich feelings, a familial honey which she offered to those closest to her in small samples. Sometimes in the past I thought she craved a wider market for these gifts. Yet, if she was frustrated, this never appeared in her manner, where, most of all, she proved how much she was herself. Madeleine was in command of herself—not professionally, though she helped with the business management of their honey farm, but in the matter of her real temperament, the course of her life, the fate of her soul. And in these things one felt she had rarely denied either her will or her spirit. There had been, I remembered, something of a bright crusader in Madeleine—a crusader in some visionary cause which she wished to recruit you to, her face suddenly turned young and gold and sharp as frost under her ash-colored hair.

But now, always so young to me as a child (and she was, after all, a second wife to Lindsay, a dozen or more years junior to him), her face had aged in sadness, and given her an equality with her husband as I'd remembered him. She had become, in losing him, his contemporary.

We walked away from the crowded tents toward a display of garden furniture, the three of us chatting brokenly, exchanging odd notes of greeting.

"I'm sorry about Lindsay," I said at last.

Madeleine spotted a luxuriously upholstered garden swing seat and now she sat down on it suddenly, testing the cushions, pushing the bench to and fro delicately with her long legs. She didn't reply and I thought I had been wrong to remind her of her loss. But then she looked up at me from beneath the wide brim of her crisp linen hat, patting the place beside her, and I sat down next her while Rachel stood in front of us playing with the tassels on the awning.

"Peter, it's so nice to see you! Such a surprise. We don't

know—we simply don't know what's happened. But thank you. And let's not think about now. Let's hear about you—what are you up to here? It's years since we heard anything of you." She narrowed her eyes, looking at me with concern.

"Yes," I said. "I rather dropped out of life. I was in jail, you know..."

"Yes. We learned that." She paused and Rachel took up the running, crouching down now on her haunches, confronting us both.

"We thought you still *were*—in jail," she said brightly, without the care of her mother's voice, but with the fascinated curiosity that a child displays in hearing of some disaster. She looked at me closely, a smile waiting its cue all around her eyes. "A jailbird running the library, I suppose?"

She'd lost no time in starting to tease—taking my seriousness up again and seeming to stamp it, this time, with the final punishment of prison. Yet I didn't mind. Rachel's great quality was her almost complete lack of indifference. She cared more with her rudeness than others do with sweet words, and the only thing I'd ever come to fear in her was an expected response.

"They let me out—four years ago," I said. "I was—" I hesitated. "I was framed."

The word was so far removed from my previous life with both of them that it seemed meaningless to me now, a hieroglyph in the language of some vicious world that I had been part of for many years but from which, like some time traveler, I had escaped, returning successfully to an earlier, almost idyllic civilization that surrounded me just then in the shape of two women: one pushing lightly on a garden swing, the other gazing at me; the first in a cool dress and fragile hat, softening the marks of pain, whom one wanted to help from her retreat at any cost; the other, cheeky and surprised, bent over on the ground, swaying on her haunches as if about to spring, haphazardly, on a world all round her full of tempting choices.

I was surprised at Rachel's air of happy fancy that morning. For it was her world, surely—as much as her mother's—which had been brutally circumscribed by their loss. Rachel had loved her father unwisely and too well—and so had never been able to see me as more than a permanent lover, a temptation on the outskirts of her life, which had been my problem: legitimacy with her, I had thought then, would have been an easy substitute for maturity. Yet she may that morning, I suppose, since her relationship with her father was unrealistic, have decided to miss him in an equally inappropriate manner—with a touch of madness rather than conventional tears.

"Come, let's have some coffee," Madeleine said. She turned to me. "Peter? We've got a big thermos. You're free?"

I nodded. I was certainly free then, with no thought of Basil Fielding, not even a ghost now from that ugly world I had escaped from.

Billy, the manager of the honey farm, together with an assistant, dealt with inquiries in the front of the small exhibition stand, while we three sipped coffee on stools among a mass of beekeeping equipment at the back of the stall. I set my cup on a galvanized honey extractor, price £58, plus VAT, and brought the two women up to date on some of my life: Durham Jail, the disasters of New York, the end of things with the KGB in Cheltenham four years previously and the subsequent sherry dreams of Egypt lost in the Cotswolds. It was not an encouraging story. And I realized then how, for Madeleine at least, it might have been a story something like her husband's. Intelligence work, based as it is on the possible truth only through certain deceit, can never be really encouraging. And though Lindsay, of course, had always been "doing something in the Foreign Office," now I knew better, and I wondered if Madeleine would confirm this for me. She did.

"Did you know that was Lindsay's work—the sort of thing you've been doing?" she asked.

And there was the first opportunity for lying. "I used to wonder," I said, still trying to keep a foothold on the truth with them.

"Yes," she went on. "Which of course makes us think his—his disappearance was to do with that."

She took to the word "disappearance" hesitantly, with a kind of feigned surprise, as though he were a conjurer at a children's party who had vanished in the midst of an astonishing trick, but was there all the same, behind a curtain or mirror, and would show himself again any moment. Lindsay was for her, I could see—even in absence—an ever-present air that encapsulated her, a warm caul from which she never wished to be expelled. The almost childishly eager white-haired man with the half smile I'd remembered was there

52

next to Madeleine then, at that very moment—fully fledged in spirit, hovering on the brink of our discussion, an apt comment on the tip of his tongue—there, as a comfort to her, in everything except flesh and blood.

"How did he disappear?" I asked. "On Intelligence business?"

"Oh, I don't know." Madeleine dismissed the idea as if it had never happened. "I was never really part of his life in that way. A lot of people came up and talked to me—looked everywhere—but I couldn't help them. He kept that side of his life mostly separate from me, except that I knew he was doing it."

"Naturally, I suppose," I said.

"But it *wasn't* natural," Rachel interrupted scornfully. "That was the problem: living two lives like that. No wonder something happened one day..." Her voice trailed off.

Rachel looked at me, her blackberry eyes surprised and angry. Then her focus changed and she stared right through me, into a void. For her Lindsay had truly gone, and was not lurking behind the beehives at the edge of the stall.

"Anyway, Mummy, you knew more than that about his work. Don't be so cagey about it. You *knew*—"

"Not exactly what he did in London. I didn't." Madeleine changed tack now, became roused, the flash of the crusader that I remembered coming into her eyes again. I could see the two women had argued things in this way recently—and could equally see that nothing had been resolved. How could it? The deceits implicit in Lindsay's game are often immeasurable, even to experts. What could a familial love—even as strong as theirs—bring to deciphering them? Yet the two women wouldn't know this. Indeed just the opposite: they would have tried to use their love as a key, for they were part of a biblical tradition, a world of old-fashioned virtues; in Rachel's case a large house in Perthshire, a small moorland church, where she and her ancestors before her had learned over many generations that it was exactly this quality of disinterested love, and not any aptitude for clinical investigation, which would answer the most awkward questions. Love alone unbolts the dark, however impenetrable, they would both have thought. But probably not this dark, I felt just then: not Lindsay's dark.

"What do *you* think?" Rachel suddenly confronted me, her coffee forgotten. Madeleine looked carefully at me as well, a huge query in her face, and I could see Basil's plan taking vague shape in both their expressions.

"I don't know," I said, trying to deter them. "What do your friends think?"

"Like us—what can they think? You knew our friends—the Thompsons, the McAulays. What could they know about Intelligence—about agents and spies?" Madeleine bit these last words out with a touch of sad derision, like a nanny reproving an older child for still playing with tin soldiers.

I remembered these country neighbors at Glenalyth: the Thompsons—he was a solicitor in Perth—and the new-rich McAulays, who had to do with whisky and lived in the grand Hall near Glenalyth, where I'd gone to children's dances with Rachel: dreamy, tippling, sad Mrs. McAulay, who had passed quite away in a daze from strong malt one evening. As Basil had hinted, such good people would know nothing of these clandestine matters—and what's more, would have scorned the whole business if they had.

How far Lindsay had removed himself, I fully realized now, from the consensus of his background, his family, and his Scottish neighbors—for whom, as he had to me, he must always have appeared as the best and the brightest of the good soldiers: Marlborough and Merton colleges, the Foreign Office in the thirties—Rome, Paris, Vienna—a captain in the Argyll and Sutherland's, leading part of their advance up through Italy from Monte Casino into Austria at the end of the war, and finally Whitehall again—something suitable, in the long run, with suitably tactful honors every ten years: home-based with the Diplomatic Service, no doubt dealing with the Russkies, it was said by his intimates. But never too loudly: Lindsay Phillips, faithful servant, jaws of death and valley of the shadow, who had generously served his country long years but had come back at the last to Scotland and his honey, where his heart was...

How could such a man have his heart in any darkness? they would have said—and as Madeleine and Rachel far more vehemently believed, and with better reason. I could remember, over the years that I'd spent with them, so many incidents that showed evidence of his love for them; moments which were never exhibitions of affection but minute and continual evidence of it. He was a sure emblem of ease and kindness to his wife and daughter—and to Patrick, his dead son, too, whom I had been brought to live with as company during the

54

war; nine years old and gone with typhoid fever one Christmas in my time there. He was, for all of us, a comforting shadow, lingering in the damp, woody smell of his old country coats and hats and mackintoshes in the hall at the back of the house, a spirit that laid hands on you at odd moments throughout those long Scottish country days, who yet might suddenly materialize on the telephone, calling from London, or come driving up the stony avenue with Henty, his father's old chauffeur, beside him in the big green Wolseley.

In these many ways, I remembered, Lindsay was never absent. Yet now, together with his inexplicable departure, and Basil's information, the messages that came along the wire were incoherent notes of horror and distress—and Henty, I felt, would never again bring Lindsay from another overnight train at Perth.

"What exactly happened?" I asked.

The two women seemed to withdraw from the event, in the need once more to confront the actuality of their loss. But Madeleine took up the burden gracefully—one which Rachel couldn't face again, I think, for she moved away.

"I was in the small drawing room. Lindsay was outside dealing with his bees—I'd seen him a few minutes before. I called him in for tea but he didn't reply, so I went out and looked for him. He wasn't anywhere near the hives on the Oak Walk. So I looked around the garden—and then I got Billy and the others and we looked everywhere else all afternoon—the loch, the forest—and before then, of course, all the rooms, the attics, the yard, the stables. He hadn't taken the car or any of the bicycles; no one had seen him in the village, or on any of the roads. He'd just been out there on the Oak Walk one minute and then he was gone, totally—and we've not heard or seen anything of him since." She stopped abruptly, turning from me.

Her face had become so wan in the telling of this story that I couldn't bear it, and I didn't wait for any more of Basil's predictions to take effect.

"Could I help?" I asked. "Help you to find out . . . ?"

She smiled in assent.

"You might know more about it than the Thompsons. Or the McAulays," she added weakly.

I might indeed, I thought.

55

4

I noticed the man at the bar of my club before lunch: chalk-striped suit, a pearl tiepin, Jewish—an overneat, small, silver-haired fellow, with something of the air of a homosexual jeweler; meticulous in his responses, nodding his head repeatedly, obviously marking time over gin and tonics with an elderly companion, a stooped figure who had all the lineaments of a club bore.

He picked fastidiously at the bowls of olives and onions in front of him, saying "Um" and "Ah!" and "Yes" many times to some endless tale he was being told. I was at the counter, studying a large sherry, back from the Flower Show with an invitation to Wigmore Hall that evening and dinner afterward with the Phillips and some of their London friends. Rachel was giving a concert. It was her birthday too: she was thirty-eight.

I noticed the man because I had known him once—not well, but I had seen him about sometimes in Holborn years before. And then his name came to me: it was David Marcus, the Scots lawyer who had originally come to our Mideast section as a ferret, expert on double agents and potential defectors—common as rabbits with us then. They said he was

56

the man who never let go, and indeed, it was he who had finally unearthed Williams, his chief in the department, as a deep-cover KGB agent, an event which indirectly had led to my release from Durham Jail five years previously. Marcus had subsequently been promoted to Head of Section. But that had been years ago, and he could certainly only have gone upward since then. He had the vigorous tenacity and ambition of his race—he'd aimed for the mountaintop in my days at Holborn, and sure to be up there now, on the pinnacle, chipping away at the tablets. I'd never seen him in the club before—he struck me as a Garrick man, if anything—and I fancied, with the well-worn premonition that becomes second nature in this business, that he had turned up at the bar that morning to see me.

Sure enough, when the old ormolu clock behind the bar struck one and the members had partly straggled off to lunch, he made his move. There was now an open space on the counter between us. He turned, saw me, and made a passable imitation of surprise.

"Ah, Marlow—how are you?" He pushed a bowl of pickled onions toward me. I was several yards away and didn't move, merely smiled and nodded, a fish that wouldn't be tempted.

"Have another sherry," he went on, thoughtfully producing a tastier bait. He moved toward me, flourishing a five-pound note—a gesture that at once alerted Reddy, the normally somnolent Irish barman. Reddy looked up at us, his long arms now placed aggressively on the counter, as if about to vault it should I decline the drink. It was Reddy who made the meeting inevitable. I accepted a sherry. "A large one," I added.

"Nice to see you," Marcus said. The elderly bore stooped down, trying to muscle in, but Marcus would have none of him for the moment, impatience creeping into his gestures.

"Is it?" I smiled.

"Who is—?" asked the bore, lending a conspicuous ear.

Marcus looked at his watch. It was clearly going to be touch and go whether he could get his business done with me while maintaining his cover in the other man's company—something I could see he was equally intent on doing.

"What are you up to these days?" he asked brightly.

"Oh, a book on Egypt. What about you?"

Marcus put his hand into his jacket pocket and I thought for a second that he was going to produce a gun and shoot

57

me, either for my impertinence or for some devious professional reason, his legal restraints quite lost to him. Instead he took out a latchkey with a label on it, and continued talking. "I get around," he said.

"I don't doubt it."

"Why?" the bore said.

"Still the old things," Marcus added.

"And some new ones too, I shouldn't be surprised." I made little attempt to avoid the sarcasm.

"New *what?*" the bore interjected.

"New *horses.*" Marcus turned to him finally. He had the key in the palm of his hand now. "Our friend here—he and I have stakes in a horse together." Whatever he was up to these days hadn't dulled his imaginative response, I was glad to see. That had always been his gift, of course: to imagine answers to a problem—often, it seemed, sheer fantasies about a Soviet move or a possible double agent—before putting on his lawyer's wig and laboriously following them up and almost invariably finding the nightmare true.

"Oh," said the bore, "I had a dream once, night before the Derby, about a horse called Stardust. Put my shirt on it—"

"No," Marcus cut him off. "We have a hurdler. Over the sticks, you know." At the same moment Marcus slipped me the key, leaning toward me, saying softly, "Be there this afternoon. Three o'clock."

The address on the label was W.2—somewhere off the Edgware Road. I laughed on my way upstairs to lunch, and ordered a half bottle of Latour to go with the beef. I had been sad all morning at the Flower Show, for that had been real. This, on the other hand, was clearly high farce. Yet I knew too—it came to me soon enough, and even the rich wine couldn't dispel the thought—that though Marcus might play the horses, what he really found funny was horseplay with death.

IT was the largest block of flats I'd ever seen: ten stories and as big as Twickenham Rugby ground, on Kendal Street half a mile up from Hyde Park. My appointment was in Windsor House, through an archway and into a huge forecourt. There must have been about a hundred bell pushes outside, but the main door was open. I dangled my key, and a hall porter in his shirt-sleeves saw me past without comment. I'd finished lunch with an Armagnac in the club, so was feeling sweaty myself, but fairly perky as I took the lift up. I wondered if I should have had a gun.

I opened the lock on the heavy door while gazing impudently into the spy hole. Marcus was sitting on a tea chest reading the *Times* when I got inside, like the fox on the tree stump in *Jemima Puddleduck,* his little feet dangling off the floor, while another considerably larger man, a bodyguard, was by the window, looking out over the roofs into the depths of the lead-blue spring sky.

Marcus stood up, folding the *Times* carefully—then gestured, as if to a seat. But there was no furniture at all in the apartment, just a half-dozen tea chests, some of them open, with kitchen and other household equipment peeping out, together with two rolled-up carpets and a stack of empty picture frames against one wall. The place was empty.

"Oh, there isn't—" Marcus said.

"Never mind." I looked around the sterile room. I knew where I was: one of the "safe" houses—a refinement, often called "one-time pads," that D.I.6 kept in various large apartment blocks across London, each having the appearance of imminent occupation, but never lived in and rarely maintained for any length of time. The tea chests and old carpets could be picked up at a moment's notice and transferred to another vacant apartment, often in the same block. They were used normally for appointments with only one individual—for debriefing a defector or sometimes just for a single meeting with an outsider, as in my case. Though the tea chests, I knew, would contain enough food and other necessities to keep a man incommunicado in the apartment for a month. This fact, together with the presence of the muscular factotum, led me to suppose that Marcus, apart from wanting something from me, might impose unpleasant sanctions in order to obtain it.

I sat on a tea chest opposite him, the Armagnac still living in me, quite prepared to do battle. But Marcus didn't say anything. It was hot in the room. A bluebottle stirred viciously against the window; a huge puffy white cloud slid into view over Paddington. Summer was a strong rumor everywhere now. Finally Marcus sighed, thinking some deep thought. But I wasn't going to let him intimidate me with any *longueurs*.

"Well?" I asked sharply.

Marcus woke. "Ah, yes. Well, thank you for coming. And for going along with me over that old bore."

"I was curious. That's all."

"Coffee?" Marcus was starting to play the old switch-theme game, softening up the opposition, disorientating him. "Arthur? Brew up a kettle, will you." Arthur took an electric kettle from one of the chests and disappeared into the kitchen. It seemed I was probably the first person to use this safe house. Marcus was either playing it big—or else it was big.

"Of course, curious," he went on. "That's why Fielding got on to you. I can see that. I wanted to talk about that." He fidgeted with his cuffs. He was hot, I could see, but afraid to lose dignity by taking off his coat. I took my own off to further discomfit him.

"Why?"

"Well, we don't want you to look for Phillips. That's why," Marcus said apologetically.

"We? Isn't Basil part of 'you'?"

"Well, not exactly—"

"So who are you these days?"

"Basil's with the Slavs and Soviets: Section Nine. I'm Chief."

"Of the section?"

"Of the Service."

"I see."

Marcus suddenly came alive now, as if, in getting things straight with these little introductory word games and having so circuitously established his bona fides, we could now properly embark on the real business, a matter, it would seem, of lesser moment than his own credentials. "Yes, Marlow. We'd really prefer it if you didn't go along with Basil."

I kept the offensive. "You're going to have to tell me why, aren't you?"

Arthur put his head round the kitchen door. "Milk and sugar?" he sang out in a surprisingly thin, harassed voice, like a fretful waitress.

"Please," Marcus said.

"No sugar." Then I turned to Marcus. "You don't happen to have any brandy in those chests, do you?"

Marcus resumed without a smile or a comment. "No—I'm not going to have to tell you. But I—"

"The Prime Minister authorized this, you know. You're above him, I suppose?"

Marcus sighed again. "The PM is not in possession of all the facts—"

"He rarely is with you people."

"Marlow, are you going to *listen?*" Marcus said abruptly.

"Are you going to tell me the truth—or even take a stab in that direction?"

"Yes, I am—if you'd wait a moment," he added petulantly.

"Are you keeping Phillips somewhere?"

"No. We're not. He *has* disappeared. We don't know where he is. But we don't particularly want him found either, both for his own good and for his reputation—at least among his family and friends."

"He's gone over to Moscow?"

"I doubt it," Marcus said wryly. "Rather the opposite camp. Phillips, I'm afraid, was another sort of traitor. The right wing. So far out, in fact, he fell overboard completely."

"National Front?"

"Good God, no!" Marcus was briefly appalled. "Retired Army wallahs down in Devon. Vigilantes with handles to their names, that sort. As well as people in the Service."

I shook my head in wonder.

"No, it's true. There's always been a vaguely right-wing element in the Secret Intelligence Service. And since the scandals of the fifties and early sixties—Philby and that lot— together with Labour coming in again then, it's hardened very considerably during the last ten years—and around Phillips, we found out about six months ago. He was the kingpin."

"How? How did you find out?"

"No need for details. But we discovered he's put taps on the PM's office in Downing Street—bugs in the wall, the lot. We traced it back to him, kept him under close surveillance. There were two or three others, as well. Then just when we were sure and were going to pick Phillips up he disappeared, went under. Someone must have got word to him."

"The usual," I said. "But you still need to nail him, don't you? All the more so, I should have thought."

"Well—yes. At first I thought exactly that. 'Do everything—find him,' I said. And so we turned him over for two months. But absolutely nothing. So then I thought, Well, leave him. He's gone, he's out—drowned himself up in that loch of his in Scotland most likely. Let dead dogs lie. Because, you see, Marlow, if we did find him then he'd have to stand trial and there'd be no end of a rumpus."

"Indeed." A rumpus, I knew, after all the other scandals in our Service, was like a fifth horse of the Apocalypse.

"So you see, if you help Lindsay's family—or Basil—you'll be doing them a disservice, Marlow. They'll end up with a traitor, instead of—as now—a hero, albeit missing or dead."

Arthur brought us two mugs of coffee—cheap stuff, too much chicory. But I drank it, thinking. It gave me time. Of course there was one flaw in Marcus's story—so obvious he must have left it intentionally.

"Why haven't you told the PM all this?"

Marcus obviously found the coffee as bitter as I had, for he put the mug down and didn't touch it again.

"Oh, we *did* tell him. He knows all about what Phillips was up to. It was the PM who lied to you, Marlow. He wants him found all right—but not for the reasons he gave you, obviously. He'd like him found—and removed, if it were still possible, along with the others. He's livid with us now—all set for a rumpus."

Marcus paused, seeming to consider the awful effects of such a thing coming to pass: first three decades of Reds under the bed, now fascists bugging the PM's study. I could see if this came to light Marcus and his cronies would be in for a roasting.

"Well, naturally, I'm just as anxious to stall him. It's our Service, after all. Prime Ministers come and go. We have to live with our mistakes."

"And Basil?" I asked. "Where does he fit in? Does he know what you told me about Phillips?"

"No. At least, I hope not. And I'd thank you not to tell him, either. He's just anxious for kudos. And don't forget—Phillips was running a genuine grade-A job in Yugoslavia, against Moscow. That's all perfectly aboveboard. But it was cover for his real activities."

"But the other two—Dearden and McKnight. That was Moscow, wasn't it? So maybe they got Phillips as well?"

"Maybe they did." Marcus was pleased with this idea. He was very bland now, believing he had made his case secure with me. "That's certainly my opinion. *They* dumped him in that loch, or something—so that Zagreb circle is well and truly dead anyway. But Phillips still matters to us. We don't want a right-wing purge, a month in the Old Bailey and enough classified fodder to keep the *Sunday Times* "Insight" boys happy for a year. And that remains a possibility—if you go sniffing about after him."

"Especially if I find him, you mean?"

"Alive, I mean. If you find him dead that won't matter at all, of course. But we'd prefer it if you didn't bother, in fact—if you kept off it."

Marcus had gone just a fraction too far. He was hiding something; there was another, entirely different reason he didn't want me to go looking for Phillips—I had no idea what. Everything on the surface added up—I could see that. Phillips, though never authoritarian in my memory of him, did have a certain kind of very conventional, upper-class army background that could have led him to a clandestine right-wing position within the Service.

Very well, then, I thought. Marcus's scenario on Phillips was quite probable—except for two things. First, his not wanting me to find him, which seemed unlikely anyway—for if I did find him, alive, it would surely be no great trouble for Marcus to keep his mild treason under wraps, as he'd done with the other conspirators. No one knew of the matter so far in any case—and unless the PM himself let the cats run, there was no reason why anyone should. Second, there was the matter of Phillips's other official concern: the Zagreb circle, apparently instrumental in preventing Moscow getting a foothold in Yugoslavia after Tito's death. This, indeed, was grade A—an operation sanctioned from the very top and most likely being run in tandem with the Americans, who were more anxious than we to maintain that country's independence. And it struck me that no chief of an intelligence service could so lightly dismiss the loss of a principal operative in such a scheme, as Marcus had done—and that Phillips's work in this respect was, in any case, more important than his being discovered playing toy soldiers with some old colonial darling down in the Shires.

Well, let him hide whatever he wants, I thought. The matter had come into a private realm that morning at the Flower Show—a world beyond any that Marcus lived in or could apparently comprehend.

I said, "I'm going to help them anyway, Marcus. I offered to this morning. Purely as a private matter—unless you have in mind to lock me up here for a month."

Marcus didn't smile. "I see," he said, like a housemaster

63

confronted with a boy bigger than he was and about to prove it.

"Yes. I don't know that you do see, but this has really nothing to do with you, anyhow. I'm not interested in all your political stories. The Phillipses are old friends of mine. That's the level it's on as far as I'm concerned. I left your Service years ago—and it's I who have the extreme prejudice about it. If I find Lindsay it'll be for his family. What you do about it then is your own affair. There is a world outside yours, you know, of people and families, that's not part of your mad power plays. And I don't care if Phillips was trying to score on the right wing, not a bit: I wouldn't fancy it myself, but I understand it very well—it's his background after all, and you people taught him to fight for it over the years. Anyway, it's all absolutely insignificant in comparison with how a family feels about a man's disappearance—his possible death. And that's what I'm concerned with. So let's just beg to differ, shall we?"

Marcus eased his collar and sniffed. My response couldn't have surprised him; he seemed now, in his mind, to be addressing himself to the next item on an already prepared agenda.

"Beg, Marlow—that's the word all right. For, of course, I shan't authorize Basil's payment to you."

"You've been close on his tail, haven't you?"

"And will remain so—and on yours, I'm afraid. Why don't you give it up, Marlow?"

"You'd pay me more, would you?"

"Yes," he said lightly. So he *was* hiding something. But I laughed, rather than give any hint of sensing this.

"A few days ago I had the bank manager on the phone, murmuring about foreclosures, bald tires all round, and a sherry bill that looked like I was washing in the stuff. Yet here I am being offered a small fortune either way. I can't lose, can I?"

"Yes, you can, Marlow," Marcus said quickly. "I assure you you can."

"Thirty pieces of silver, indeed." I looked at him with distaste. "You don't intimidate me. And you won't. Oh, you can lock me up here, I suppose, but that won't last. Why don't *you* give it up? I told you—this is a personal matter now. I won't screw your pitch, whatever dull game you're playing. I give you my word on that."

Marcus nodded several times, looking at me closely.

"Very well, then. We'll see. I'd only add, Marlow, that no one can ever really give his word in this business. Not me, and not even your friend Phillips, who gave so many."

Marcus left this curious thought hanging in the warm air before showing me out, and when I looked back I saw Arthur carefully stowing the electric kettle away, deep within a tea chest. This caravan was obviously moving on at once. Marcus was covering his tracks against me already. As far as he was concerned our meeting had never taken place.

BASIL met me in the club that evening at six, wandering brokenly round the lobby in his smudged blue suit, gazing at the cellar notices and club functions as I came down the oak staircase. The valet had pressed my suit while I'd had a bath. Basil saw this from a distance, sizing me up, his shifty eyes detailing my clothes. Ah, he seemed to say, the clubman hero—up from the country to a world of snooker parties and dinner nights and Margaux '59, while I risk myself about mean streets and sterile offices; a lone pad in Kensington after a half pint and a divorced wife down in Cornwall.

What a liar Basil was, I realized again just then. He looked like an embarrassed retainer, a tradesman wringing his hands and doffing his cap, come to secure a debt from a gentleman in his London club. Whereas I knew now that it was Basil who held the advantage, who had me on a string, who had only told me half the Phillips story. I had suspected something of this, of course, since I'd first met him in the wine bar in the Strand the day before—known then that dealing with him was like disabling an octopus. Basil always had an extra hand to stab you in the back.

He looked worse than usual, if that were possible, hangdog and pale-faced, with the blood drained right out of the thin lobes of his elephant ears—a water biscuit now, wafer thin, who might at any moment disintegrate, flake away right there, in the middle of the hall, leaving just a pile of old clothes: a liquor-spattered pullover, minor public-school tie and a pair of dirty desert boots from Marks & Spencers. And I thought I knew why he looked like death warmed up: Accounts, as he'd probably discovered that afternoon, had held up my first payment on some technicality. His plans for me had been spiked by Marcus.

The library was empty. The two long windows were open

at the bottom, muslin curtains drifting slightly in the warm air, while in the distance the evening traffic rushed around Grosvenor Square.

"You look done in," I said. "The bar is open." I thought what a treat it might be if Marcus were to turn up again and see us both there, for indeed I'd not come to look on their apparent service rivalries as anything but a rerun of an old farce, endemic to British Intelligence since the war.

"No. No, I think here—"

We sat in two big leather armchairs by the long-dead grate filled with a grimy paper fan, stuffed dusty clubmen in dark suits, up to some weary mischief.

"Cheer up," I said. "I saw them this morning. I'm going to help them."

Basil's face didn't flower at all.

"Oh, good," he said at last.

And then I was surprised. He drew a long envelope from his pocket and passed it across to me. There was an inch-thick wad of new twenty-pound notes inside it.

"Five thousand pounds, to start with. Don't pay it in all at once," Basil said. "Sign the chit—not your own name. We've put you down as Wardell. Alan Wardell."

I looked at the flimsy Treasury receipt with its five carbons and wondered how on earth Basil had managed to outsmart Marcus. I supposed the money had come straight from some other secret fund directly administered by the PM. But I signed it anyway and put the money away. It bulged in my inner pocket, a Christmas present without end for a child.

"Cash?" I said.

"Well, one likes to be definite about money: keep one's word." Basil looked at me sharply, as though I'd tried to make a fuss about accepting it or was about to ask for more.

"No. I mean, it's usually by check. It was last time."

"Not in this instance. We don't want any trace between you and us—and you're not an employee of ours now, Peter."

Basil, just as Marcus had done, preened himself on his secret status and my public exclusion—the invisible membranes between us which we both saw, oppositely, as a division between the quick and the dead.

"So you saw them?"

I nodded. "It went like clockwork."

"What did I tell you."

"You told me. But now tell me more."

I didn't quite know what I wanted Basil to talk about, but I wanted to get him going on some kind of chat which might give me a lever into what was going on between his faction (and the PM's obviously) and Marcus's. It seemed that Basil was very much the PM's man, and though I wasn't going to tell him anything about my meeting with Marcus I wanted to see if this right-wing threat was the real reason for sending me after Phillips.

"Tell you about what?" Basil said, stonewalling.

"About our meeting, for example. You said there was a leak somewhere in your section—that I couldn't phone you. Is that how it's always going to be?"

"The leak? Oh, that's just a precaution. As you know yourself there have always been divisions in the Service. At the moment it's a slightly left-wing element causing trouble, one which Phillips was identified with. Well, quite a few of the traditionalists would be very happy if he never turned up again. So we're keeping you well clear of them, that's all: no open contact if possible, no phone calls. I'll use your club here for any messages. Put them up on the board in the back hall. You do the same for me. Either I or someone else will drop round here most days. All right?"

"Yes."

Basil picked up an old copy of *Country Life* from the table next to him and started to flick through the pages of fine houses. Our interview seemed at an end.

"Good," I said, while pondering Lindsay Phillips's remarkable transference from extreme right to left wings in the political spectrum, one that had happened in the space of a few hours, in the estimation of two of his colleagues. One of them was lying. Perhaps both were. I couldn't restrain a smile.

"Yes?" Basil looked at me sharply.

"Nothing."

We got up and walked toward the door. One thing at least was obvious: Basil and Marcus were on opposite sides of the fence in the matter of Phillips—Basil anxious to prosper the PM's cause by nailing these old men with microphones, while Marcus was equally anxious to forestall him. I was the patsy in the middle of what was no more than an unusually bitter internal squabble.

Basil wouldn't take any sort of a drink at the end of our meeting, sloping off into the evening without even wishing me well. That surprised me, too. Perhaps his merrymaking the previous day had filled him with remorse. But I doubted it; in the old days he'd been such a funny man—now the gift seemed suddenly to have died in him.

I watched him disappear into the rush hour, merging at once among the other preoccupied, anonymous figures. Basil had suddenly become like them, no longer a man of witty parts but someone who had turned in on himself, the better to hide some dangerous secret—a suburban murderer hurrying home to bury his wife's corpse.

I glanced at the piece of paper he'd given me before we left the library; he'd written down the name of the man in Scotland with whom I could safely connect in my investigations up there: Chief Superintendent Carse of the Perthshire CID, Court Buildings, Tayside, Perth. I knew the place well—a black Gothic pile, stained with years of mist and spume from the huge tumbling river right in front of it beyond the quayside—a river fed by all the streams of my childhood higher up, the burns and lakes that spread like fingers and hands between the hills, a whole lost world falling from the moors around Glenalyth.

5

A fat man in small gold-rimmed specs—an excessively large and jolly man like an apologetic bear—was marshaling our theater party in the long foyer of Wigmore Hall for Rachel's birthday concert that evening.

They used to say one never spots a rival in matters of the heart until it is too late. But I could see it then, almost the first minute I laid eyes on George Willoughby-Hughes, that he would always be someone's rival in this way, that he would pop up untimely, like an impertinent water diviner, searching out and tapping every intimacy, for he had that dangerous quality of adolescent energy allied to an equally childish vulnerability. He was the kind of man who would organize coarse Rugby parties on Wimbledon Common for his male friends on Saturday afternoons, only to have his bruises tended by most of their wives at odd hours for the rest of the following week.

He busied himself now, a man gloriously come into his own, bursting out of an old double-breasted thirties dress suit, surrounded by half a dozen of the Phillipses' friends, strangers to me but part, obviously, of a vast encircling intimacy to him. He held out his arms indiscriminately, turning about on his neat dancing pumps, facing one person while still addressing another, like a huge clockwork toy, a masterwork of greeting where the mechanism had lost synchronization with the slightly squeaky voice.

"June! Max! Come—come!" He looked beyond me imperiously, toward some new arrivals, then pushed forward to greet them. As he moved I saw Madeleine, who had been hidden by his great bulk.

I kissed her on the cheek. She wore a long, A-line skirt of midnight-blue velvet, topped by a close-fitting crepe blouse that formed a sort of ruff at her throat; the sleeves were of a thinner fabric that floated around her arms. The others, including her companion—an elderly man with a heavy beard—were all in evening dress.

"I'm sorry," I said, looking down at my lounge suit, a little tired now, two days out from home.

"It doesn't matter a bit. Come." She took my arm, looking over my shoulder. "Meet George."

And I knew at once who George was. I could hear him now, bounding about behind me like a frisky animal.

"George?" I asked quietly.

"George Willoughby-Hughes. You never met, did you? Rachel's agent, Rachel's manager, Rachel's"—she paused—"Rachel's lover," I thought she might finish with. But she smiled, saying simply, "Rachel's cross."

"Hello! Good man," George said, putting a hand on my arm and squeezing it. "Fine, fine. Wonderful. I've heard so much—"He looked beyond me again, already marking down another more urgent social call. "Just a minute, a moment—"He pushed past me. Then he turned back. "You're on the aisle: B-10. Behind Sir Brian." Then he was gone. Luckily Madeleine was still there.

"Sir Brian?" I asked her. I felt I almost needed a drink.

"Brian Allcock," Madeleine said. "The Professor—an old colleague of Lindsay's. Over there." She gestured with her eyes. It was the man with the heavy beard, a bird's nest of a beard and a long, studious, slightly eccentric face, like Edward Lear's in all but the nose, which was of ordinary size. He looked like a musicologist, rudely unearthed just a moment before from the pages of some fascinating but smudged manuscript: a myopic, romantic figure in a dress suit of Edwardian vintage—a man impossible to associate with any kind of secret derring-do. If a good cover were a prerequisite in his trade, then this man must, I thought, have been invisible in his work.

"And June—and Max," Madeleine said, turning me toward the most recent arrivals.

"Hi," said Max. June and Max were American.

"Friends of Rachel's—"

"And you! And of you—madam!" Max interrupted overcourteously, pushing forward, kissing Madeleine's hand.

Max was as short and thickset as his wife—or girlfriend—was tall. Max wore a frilly dress shirt and had barely any hair. His face had a youthful chubbiness, but the eyes seemed far older, and there was an unreal tan over the skin, not oily, but something assumed all the same with lotions or sun lamps, giving him a veneer of slight artistry and inevitable success. He wasn't old enough to look like a million dollars. Give that a year or two, he seemed to say: I still have a leasehold on youth—and the money will come soon enough, goddamnit...

In June's case, on the other hand, the cash had obviously been inherited already. A woman with a genuine tan and dark, Mediterranean hair, wearing a white silk sheath dress, she looked like someone born to lose her father's fortune gamely.

"Hi," said Max to me again, while June smiled at me from a height, beatifically. Her hand was so limp and damp I felt it would come away with mine if I held it too long, and drop like dough to the floor.

"Max writes musicals," Madeleine said. "With George. George does the music, Max the words. A lyricist," she added sweetly.

"Hi." Max addressed me thus a third time. He was no spendthrift with words. They must have been quite short musicals, I thought.

Then there was Marianne, George's wife. I could hear her loud, broken voice talking rapidly to someone over by the box office even before I met her, in the ever-more insistent tones of someone who can never get to the point of a story for fear of losing an audience.

Marianne was as verbose as Max was reticent. She was fiftyish and sad, a music copyist once, she soon informed me. She and George lived round the corner off Marylebone High Street, she added, among many other things. Marianne talked so much because her world was empty, and words could fill it for an hour or so, words to other people, huge verbal deposits (as I afterwards learned from her long silences with George) that she now banked among us with great clatter and alarming gusto.

"Well?" Madeleine asked later, looking me straight and too forcefully in the eyes, as if trying to hold on to something, to stop herself sinking in this pool of friendly emotion. Madeleine was sitting on the edge of a cliff. We had left the morning and the stark white tent filled with brilliant colors where she had hidden as a masked intruder. But here, where the drama was far more tense and subtle, the indistinct lines of emotion on her face suddenly reflected this and the pain became terribly clear once more. She seemed, as I watched her, before the concert started, to preempt the music—to hear it secretly herself and run through all its heartbreak before a note was sounded.

I thought she was about to break down and cry; I touched her arm. "What is it?"

"No. Nothing—of course. Nothing." She gripped herself mentally even as she spoke.

Her face changed then, brightened. Light spread into her eyes, seeped over the edges and crinkled all the valleys in her skin. Her face warmed as if by a lot of little fires, and the sad mold splintered off her cheeks right there in front of me.

Just as Basil an hour before had been a dark omen in his shabby suit, a Charon crossing Brook Street into the dull evening, so Madeleine was a harbinger now, marvelously bright, emerging from tragedy, a dove come to an ark where all of us had been lost many days far out on the waters. At that moment she cast out pain like a saint. Marshaled by George, with her glittering imprimatur, something—faith or art—would lock the doors in the hall and resolve everything for an hour or two.

The bell rang. The flock was finally gathered together.

"Well," Madeleine said, "shall we go?" She turned and led us into the evening.

I am no musician. I might tell some of this story more easily if I were. As it is, that evening and most of its characters must remain strange to me. Rachel is the one exception, since it was her particular problem which came to a head that night. She so craved an end to mystery, a less ambiguous connection with the world than that which art allows, that she forsook her music in this cause, and thus she entered my dull lists again—those she had escaped from years before: the ambush of verbal cause and effect, the dry rot of why and wherefore, the death rattle of explanation that lies across the border from what is simply felt.

But she gave up her music later, after that concert, and there is still that concert to describe. And here, too, since in the estimation of those who were there and knew about music, it was by far her best performance, I am faced with defeat in writing about it. Bad music, since it fails, easily falls into the realm of words. But if the harmony rises, finding perfection, each step it takes is one more giant stride away from language.

There is a crucial phrase in flute-playing, remembered from my days in Notting Hill with Rachel: "a good embouchure." This describes the essence of the whole business, in which the player's lips must be so formed and placed against the raised mouthpiece that the air stream strikes the edge of the hole in such a way as to produce a perfect tone. And tone, as I remember Rachel always said, is supreme; the rest is secondary. But, oh, the drudgery of it all—that comes back as well: of Rachel locked in the bathroom playing in front of the mirror for hours, developing that perfect sound. A proper stance, the right way of holding the instrument, ease in the complex fingering—unless one mastered these, tone could be lost. Playing the transverse flute well is almost a miracle, a juggling act with a half-dozen techniques, each to be kept up effortlessly. To reach perfection requires a mastery that is literally breathtaking, for here is an art where player, instrument, and music must come together as one perfect voice—a human voice, based on air, on breathing, and thus subject to an exactly limited capacity. But that evening one couldn't tell where Rachel drew breath: the music appeared seamless.

She played some pieces with piano accompaniment—Prokofiev's Sonata in D Major, Saint-Saëns's flute variations from the ballet *Ascanio*—and then Gluck's "Dance of the Blesséd Spirits," which she had played the previous day in the hotel. She ended the recital with a flute cadenza, the "Serenade" from Drigo's *Les Millions d'Arlequin,* which she made so light and haunting a thing that nobody moved or clapped for a long moment when she had finished.

73

What more to say than that it was perfect? Her music took her light years away from us that evening, on the small stage; she was a woman in a long green tartan skirt and white silk blouse, lost to us, and traveling deep into a world without words.

In one way her behavior after that evening was an attempt to be counted among ordinary mortals at last—and her release from the secrecies of music was, she felt, a necessary step in that direction. She told me later that she had come to live on too rarefied a plane, blind to the concerns of ordinary existence. Wrongly, as it turned out, she believed that her father had lived in just such an ordinary world and that to find him she must descend from her many pedestals and seek him in the undergrowth of a more mundane existence.

There were kisses and congratulations backstage afterward; I stood back from them, in the doorway of the small greenroom, crushed next to the end of a big grand piano in the corridor as people rattled to and fro, George trundling about like a sack of potatoes, flapping his arms and organizing flowers, beads of sweat pouring down his joyous face.

"Darling . . . dear . . . how wonderful . . ."

A lot of "dears" and "darlings" floated on the warm, over-scented air. I caught Rachel's eye for an instant, between the insistent pushing figures. I lifted my hand to her like an uncertain traffic policeman. And she, too, paused a second in her other greetings, to return an equally unfinished smile before her face disappeared again in the crush—a smile that to me, at least, spoke of tired failure and not success.

I turned and nearly walked straight into a huge beard: Sir Brian Allcock had been standing right behind me, equally on the edge of things.

"What a birthday present—for us!" he said. "What inspiration, elegance." His tiny, pale-blue eyes glittered above his heavy whiskers. He clapped now, involuntarily, banging his long fingers together several times as if overcome in retrospect. He perched behind me, owlishly, looking down on these exaggerated joys with incredulous wonder, as if at the mating antics of some obscure species. "A colleague of Lindsay's," Madeleine had told me. I was curious. Certainly he could have been no ordinary field agent, I thought. He was much older than Lindsay, too, in his seventies at least: a frail yet clamorous wraith on the outskirts of the feast.

"Yes," I said, smiling up at him with some sense of fellow feeling.

"The Drigo piece," he went on, gazing enthusiastically into the greenroom. "She played that incomparably. Better than he did himself. I heard him once—just before he left St. Petersburg."

"Indeed?" I answered.

I had no idea who this Drigo was. But St. Petersburg gave a date to the old man's reminiscence—a date and a place, too—pre-Revolutionary Russia. A *colleague* of Lindsay's—could he be that? I decided to risk a mild interrogation.

"You worked with Lindsay then, did you?" I asked easily.

"Uh!" the old man snorted, his beard bristling. "No, I never worked with him. I was his tutor—at the School of Slavonic Studies here."

"In the thirties?"

"Yes, about then. When he came down from Oxford, doing the Foreign Office exams." He stopped, seeming to run off into some old cubbyhole of his mind, searching for something. Finding it, but without wishing to explain it, he said vehemently, "Such a pity about him, such a stupid, dreadful thing." Then he seemed to dream again, casting his mind back to some dark pool in the past.

"Yes," I said. "Yes. I was hoping to help the family find him."

Sir Brian woke up and looked at me closely now. "You're one of his Intelligence people, are you?" He ran on in a great hurry before I could contradict him. "Well, what a damn silly business that was. I warned him about it—oh, yes, back at the time. Told him not to get mixed up with it; told him he'd be a prime choice, with his background, his gift for languages, his sympathies. It was all a very foolish thing, you see. And now look." The old man's eyes lit up and he raised his long, bony fingers like a prophet about to explain everything. But he didn't continue. His hands fell limply and he started to chew on his lips, as if he had said too much.

"Look—at what?"

"Well," he grunted—and then, sotto voce, "The Russians must have taken him back. He knew too much."

Sir Brian stalled again, looking down his nose at me triumphantly.

"Taken him *back?* He knew something—"

"Look here, young man," the old man interrupted me

quickly, in a sharply professorial tone. "I'm not here to teach you your business. You must know what he knew far better than I."

"Oh, I don't work for Intelligence," I said, realizing the lie suddenly.

"Goodness me." Sir Brian perked up in mock alarm. "I thought you said you did—and here am I giving away state secrets to every Tom, Dick, and Harry. Dear me, I must curb my tongue."

Again he appeared to do just this, biting his lips, chewing wisps of his beard. "Ah! Madeleine—Rachel." His beady blue eyes had found an out cue; he moved away from me abruptly, into the greenroom, to make his own little entrance and congratulations, a great bearded beanpole, seemingly an ineffective old eccentric, but possibly something else altogether: a man who found easy cover in these assumed peculiarities— a vain old man who perhaps knew something, and, if so, whose vanity might have betrayed him.

I stood with the others on the pavement outside, waiting for our transport, breathing the warm spring evening air— London air, after a long hot day, a faintly warm smell of tarmac and petrol fumes dying out now as Findlater's big gold clock down the street touched half past nine.

Taken Lindsay back? Because "He knew too much." A slip of the old man's slippery tongue, perhaps. But taken him *back*?

Rachel came out of the hall just then, and though I was standing some distance away from her, at the edge of the pavement, she called across to me, beckoning me with a smile to go with her and her mother and Sir Brian in their car. I had just time to note a look of frustrated disapproval cross George's features as he closed the door behind us, looking through the window into the dark interior, his big sad face like a moon about to disappear behind a cloud.

THEY still owned the big house in Hyde Park Square—on the north side, looking over the tall bleached plane trees in the narrow gardens, the only side of the estate not bombed out in the war and rebuilt: a row of formidable early Victorian town houses rising up, tier upon tier, like the decks of an old Atlantic liner. White-stuccoed, with tall porticoes and heavy doors, they stood imperiously among the clutter of modern "bijou" residences and apartment blocks that surrounded them on all sides. Encircled by this concrete mess, but protected by the stockade of the small park and its graceful trees, these houses had resisted everything and continued to insult their attackers, effortlessly, by their mere existence.

Such houses were cumbersome and awkward to run, even in the days when I had stayed there just after the war; now nearly all of them had been divided into flats—all except the Phillipses', which they had held on to through thick and thin and still possessed in an undivided state. It had been Madeleine's family home. Her great-grandfather, who had bought the house after the Crimean War, was, like Lindsay's, a military man; and her family, like his, had never given ground, nor lacked the money to maintain the grounds they held.

Nonetheless, what was an anachronism twenty years before today must have been practically unique. Lindsay's work, it was true, had allowed him to live in the house most of the year. Madeleine lived there for part of the time—every winter at least—while Rachel had organized a self-contained flat for herself on the top floor. Patrick too, I suppose, had he lived, might have made it his home—while after his death, and had I ever married Rachel, I suppose I could well have been living in part of it myself.

But even with all this real or potential habitation there were still half-a-dozen large rooms left over: a formal dining room, music room, library, study, spare bedrooms, and a billiard room. Most of these remained unused in my days there, and were heavily furnished in the original Victorian mode, with long, thick velvet drapes over the high sash windows—rooms ideally fitted for children's hide-and-seek on winter weekends or half-term holidays when I had come down with Rachel to London to see the circus or the Palladium pantomime; heavy rooms, smelling of polished mahogany, with mustachioed portraits of Imperial gallants floating down like trapeze artists on long wires from brass rails on either side of the ceiling.

Our car drove round the south side of the square to get to the house. I could see it now—the first few stories rising like a white cliff above the street lights, up into the darkness of Rachel's top flat, the few rooms which, even when we had lived together in Notting Hill, she had frequently returned to openly, by way of seeing her parents, but just as often surreptitiously, as I afterward found out. Already then, like a fifth columnist, in the midst of her life with me, she was starting to convert these rooms, planning her defection, organizing her separate return over the border to her real home.

This house, together with Glenalyth, was where her real life came from—and she a kite held to them on a string, let out to fly by her father. Of course, I had thought then to cut this string; instead, in her short time with me, I had only managed to bind her far more closely to this solid edifice and all the secure emotions it contained. What a fruitless quest I had made with her then, set on a shared life amidst the razed, postwar squalor of Ladbroke Grove. How could one set an Ascot gas heater and broken windows looking out on an already clamorous emigrant street against this heavy dreadnought of a house, a house that, together with its hardheaded crew, had forced its way successfully through a century of violent change, war and social riot, familial deaths and entrances, individual dissents and strengths, unsuitable passions and alliances—all of which were to be finally subservient to some stronger ghost, an intangible inheritance that still lived in this great pile of brick and mortar.

My association with Rachel seemed, in its shadow, to be nothing more than an illicit day trip, a foolish excursion round the bay, in which, luckily and quite without our deserving it, we had not been drowned. This house was my inanimate rival. If Rachel and her family had a real failing, it was that they hung on to their past, protected it, not with money, which to them was simply an adjunct, as natural as air, but with an uninquiring acceptance. To them their position in life was an ancient *fait accompli* with which, without knowing it, they insulated themselves against all outsiders and newcomers. They were like tightrope walkers in their estimation of themselves. Though they knew in some secret, quite unspoken place that their kind of life was a rare thing, a glittering performance above the multitude, they knew too, quite simply, that if they were to maintain this style in these drear times and among this new commonality, they must never look down.

But now the man who had lived in that house, who had governed its directions, maintained and nurtured and filled it so appropriately, had disappeared, suddenly lost his balance and fallen inexplicably from the high wire. He had, at last, broken all the rules.

* * *

GEORGE, who had somehow managed to reach the house before us, was at the open doorway, his face alight with secret anticipation. He kept us in the hall until the other guests arrived, then led us all upstairs to the first-floor drawing and music rooms. Here he fumbled with the handles of the double doors before finally managing to open them with a flourish.

As he did so a cataract of music swept upon us—a clash of timpani, followed by a sweet rush of violins and cellos, and winds—taking up and running vigorously along with the old Strauss melody. It was with some surprise that we gazed into the room, for at first we could see nothing but an empty floor and a long table laid out near the window for a buffet supper. But on entering the drawing room and looking round to the right through the open curtains that led to the music room behind, the matter became clear. Inside, on the heavy old dining room chairs arranged in several semicircles, was half a fair-sized orchestra, twenty or thirty people in evening dress rushing clamorously through the overture to *Die Fledermaus*.

George smiled, quite taken up for a moment, justifiably, with his *coup de théâtre*. Rachel embraced him.

"What on earth—?" she said, before disappearing into his bear hug.

"Your birthday present!" George shouted above the music, and the two of them stood there for a moment, arms linked, watching the performance. I thought of my own present for Rachel, something I'd seen in a Bond Street antique shop that afternoon, a Victorian silver brooch, something delicate and pretty but quite without the demon grace of this gesture, a gift that wouldn't endure beyond the evening, but was so bright and unexpected a thing that it was far more than a gift. It was Rachel's own life, a dazzling portrait, drawn from her, shown and confirmed to the world, and now returned to her keeping. George's affection for Rachel, I saw now, was no lugubrious thing, but a deep care which he could yet offer to her lightly, in the sweeping tones of half the London Philharmonia.

George, among his friends and good offices in the musical world, had managed to hire a section of the orchestra for this latter part of the evening. There were friends of Rachel's too, among the players, it was obvious, doing her honor and favor; some of them smiled at her, right in the middle of an elaborate *con brio* passage. They went on playing for half an hour—the easier, celebratory music of Lehár and Strauss, *Wiener Blut*

79

and suchlike, waltzes and polkas, but played them with an intense delicacy that gave the music a quite extraordinary, crystal-sharp effect, like flame cutting through steel.

Later we drank wine and some champagne and cut deeply into raised game pies and moist pâtés, the orchestra joining us. Of course it was a merry evening; it could hardly have been otherwise. And no doubt it had been intended as just such by George: a means of helping the two women to start again, to wipe out the pain of the past two months. In that, at least, he succeeded. Indeed, without his musical resuscitation that night it's doubtful if Rachel—and Madeleine particularly—would ever have had the heart to embark with me on the journeys they did. George's gift brought them back to life and made it possible for them to contemplate action once more, action that would fill the gap of absence. For once started on their search for Lindsay and for as long as they remained at it, they could believe in his existence somewhere, a life apart from theirs, which they would eventually discover, once more reuniting it with their own in one happy family. George it was, in his generosity and loving commitment to Rachel, who set the long fuse alight, and I the man who tended that flame so carefully. At the time who could have done otherwise?

6

"I don't know what he could have meant—it must have been a mistake," Madeleine said to me purposefully, over a late breakfast. I'd stayed the night in a spare bedroom, wearing a pair of Lindsay's pajamas. Rachel was still sleeping upstairs in her flat.

"Yes, it may have been. But that's what he said—that the Russians had taken him *back*."

Madeleine finished her coffee, carrying the cups and plates over to the sink, where she paused a moment, gazing out over the rooftops at the back of the house. The sky was again a leaden blue, and already, before ten o'clock, the day held a threat of heat in it that was beginning to leak out all over the city.

"He meant they may have kidnapped him," she said at last. "He must. But we went into all that in Scotland at the time, with the police and the people from Lindsay's office. We're only sixty miles from Aberdeen. Russian trawlers often call there—and there *was* one the day he disappeared. It stayed for more than a week afterward, though, for repairs, with the Special Branch people watching it all the time. But there was no sign of Lindsay and we've never had the slightest evidence that they may have taken him."

"All the same, why don't we speak to Allcock agaïn? I tried to last night, but he—"

"Oh, I *have* spoken to him, Peter," Madeleine interrupted. "And he said more or less what he said to you. He was very kind—he's one of Lindsay's oldest friends, after all—but a little scornful. 'The Russians have probably got him,' he told me in the end. Well, I thought that a little too melodramatic—and so did Lindsay's colleagues when I spoke to them about it. But maybe it's true?" She looked at me quizzically, one rubber glove half on, about to wash up.

"Well—maybe. I don't know. Just he seemed so certain about it. Who is Brian Allcock? What's his background?"

"Oh—eminent Slavic scholar. He taught for a while in Moscow, in the twenties, then at London University, wrote books on the culture and heritage of all the Slavs, was on endless committees—the British-Soviet Friendship Society in the old days and now the British-East European Society. All sorts of official things. And Lindsay consulted him a lot; traveled with him, too. They were friends."

"And his politics?"

Madeleine shrugged her shoulders. "He's not interested in politics as far as I know. He's an academic—sort of caricature of a professor, as you saw yourself. I've always thought him a rather fussy, self-important old party. But I get on with him—I suppose I rather tend to pull his leg."

"Was Lindsay close to him?"

"In a way. Well, no—not *close* really." Madeleine considered my question, frowning. "Lindsay admired him, maybe saw in him the brilliant teacher he might have become himself. And Brian in his turn took great pride in Lindsay—initially, at least—hoping he'd follow him in some academic line. Brian never married—and there was something of that, too, in the relationship to begin with, I think: the father-son business. Lindsay's own father wasn't easy, you know."

"He said he'd been in St. Petersburg?"

"Oh yes." Madeleine smiled shortly. "As a tutor with some of the decadent nobility there—before the Revolution. He's really a walking history of twentieth-century Russia. He even met Lenin: they had a glass of tea together in some station waiting room."

"I'd like to talk to him again."

Madeleine looked doubtful. "He's an awful old fusspot, you know. He'll probably just try and bite your head off again."

"All the same."

"Well, I'll phone him."

She moved to a kitchen extension, looking up his number on a big card above the telephone. She let the phone ring and ring but there was no reply.

"Funny," she said. "He's always there first thing in the morning. And there's an Irishwoman who cleans for him who comes in then as well." Madeleine looked fairly surprised.

"I'll go round and see him," I said.

Madeleine gave the number of a house beyond Russell Square, off Great Ormond Street on the southern edge of Bloomsbury. "The ground-floor flat," she said. "Only door on the right. You can't miss it: it smells of cat, rather."

I got a cab at once, luckily, on the corner of Edgware Road.

The house was in Rugby Street—the middle of a rather decayed, genteel, mid-Victorian terrace, opposite a pub a few yards away on the other corner. A woman opened the door very soon after I'd rung the bell—a doughty, red-faced Irishwoman with an old scarf turbaned round the back of her head, coming to a rough knot in the front, as if there was still a war on, St. Paul's was in flames up the road, and she had been halfway through listening to "Worker's Playtime" inside.

"Come on in," she said, the easy brogue still thick after probably thirty years in London. "The Professor's expecting you, said for you to go on in if you came. He's just down the road at the library. Be back any minute."

Before I had time to reply to any of this she had led me into a small drawing room on the ground floor looking over the street, very cluttered and rather dark and smelling of cat, as Madeleine had said it would; the sun streamed through the windows, hitting a recent explosion of dust motes like a searchlight.

"Just finished in here," the woman shouted happily, bending double in a corner and unplugging a Hoover. "Sit down. Sit down, do. He'll be back any minute." She seemed to want to reassure me and indeed I must have seemed surprised at my welcome.

So I sat down and she left me. The room was an Aladdin's cave filled with the treasure trove of many journeys to Russia and Eastern Europe: a grave, thin-faced icon of the Christ-

King with a silver halo stared at me from above an upright piano against one wall, a sheet of music by some unpronounceable Slav composer open on the stand; a rough, peasant-weave blanket in a deep scarlet covered an easy chair—and next to it, a Bosnian coffee stand with a fine circular brass top that had some strict advice from the Prophet beautifully engraved in classical Arabic around the edge.

On this lay a fat typescript—a doctoral thesis, it seemed, when I glanced at it, already open at the title page: "Part One: The Years of Hope: The Soviet Union 1917–1923." It was nearly seven hundred pages long, with footnotes as copious as the text. A heavy business, with a name and address on the bottom: "Arthur C. Pottinger, The Russian Institute, Columbia University, New York, N.Y."

The doorbell went and I jumped, involuntarily. The Irishwoman appeared from the kitchen and hurried through the room. "He must have forgotten his key," she shouted back at me from the front door. But when she opened it, it wasn't the Professor but another younger man who stood on the threshold: a big, easy-looking fellow in moccasins and a crumpled, candy-striped summer suit. He stood there for a moment, surprised, outlined sharply in the sunlight from the street. An American, I thought, and certainly the Professor's properly expected guest. A big-boned, strong-featured man in his mid-forties, with dark, deep eyes behind glasses and a lot of five-o'clock shadow rimming his jowls.

"Hi!" he said, suddenly breaking into action, his face creasing in a big smile, that smile of permanent good-fellowship which is the badge of most old fashioned Americans. The Irishwoman looked curiously at him, then at me.

"I'm sorry. There's been a misunderstanding," I said explaining my position.

"Well, that's perfectly all right," the other man said with extreme good humor, coming forward, offering me his hand. "I'm Art Pottinger. Just came by to see the Professor about my—" Then he saw his thesis open on the little table behind me. "Why, there it is. I asked him to take a look at it. We were just going to have a few words about it."

"Oh, I won't keep you," I said. "I only wanted a quick word with him myself. It'll keep; I'll come another time." I moved toward the door.

"Well, please, now—not on account of me." Pottinger held

his hands up deprecatingly. "Don't worry about me. My work can wait too. Who did you say you were?"

He had that nice American knack of asking a personal question and making it seem entirely appropriate and not at all impertinent.

"Just a friend of friends of his. Marlow. Peter Marlow. I was with the Professor last night, with these friends, at a concert. I just wanted to check something. It's not important."

"Well, wait a minute now. Why not, goddamnit?" Pottinger said expansively. "The Professor plays a lovely piano." He moved toward the upright in the corner. "Why not stay and ask him? Check it out with him and maybe he'd play us something. I guess he knows as much about music as he does about Russian history," Pottinger said like an admiring juvenile. "What concert did you get to? I've been trying to take some music in ever since I got over, just been too busy, I guess. Was it good—the Festival Hall?"

Again, he asked this question with such natural enthusiasm that I replied at once, just as naturally.

"No, Wigmore Hall—a girl called Rachel Phillips. She plays the flute."

"Oh. Rachel Phillips?" Pottinger said carefully, as if the name represented a piece of valuable china in his hands. "Phillips..." He narrowed his eyes, lending a visual confirmation to his mental exercise. "Yes, now maybe I have heard of her. She's good?"

"Yes, I think so."

At that moment a key grated in the door and the Professor walked in, carrying some books. He saw me at once and stopped dead, staring at me with considerable annoyance.

"Forgive me," I said.

The Professor, carrying his load under one arm, sidled across the room, quite fast, like a crab. Then he dumped the books down on the little Bosnian table so that the brass top jumped and clattered.

"I just dropped round," I said. "Madeleine called you earlier but you were out. We thought you might be able to help over something. But some other time—it's the wrong moment."

"Indeed it is—to say the least," the Professor said, spitting through his whiskers. He was breathing heavily, clearly put out, glaring at me with his little blue eyes like a fighting cock. He had seemed a wraithlike, ineffective figure the previous night, but now there was a ragged, dangerous edge to him, as if some nasty alarm had gone off in his soul during the night.

"I'll give you another call, if I may. Or Madeleine will," I said, moving toward the door.

"Yes, that would be more appropriate. Though I can't think how—" He was obviously going to finish this sentence with "—how I can help you." But he stopped halfway through, abandoning the thought ruthlessly, and it was just then I happened to look over at Pottinger, standing by the piano. His face was set, quite still, like an eavesdropper's—as though he, more than I, had been anxious to hear the end of the Professor's sentence. But at once he came back into vast good humor. "Well, now don't mind me! I can wait—I can come back." He was so anxious to help I was sorry to disappoint him.

"No, no—not at all. Nice to have met you and my apologies." I left the two men standing rather uneasily together, closing the door sharply. After I'd done so, I saw that the Professor had left his latchkey outside in the lock. So, without knocking, I opened the door again with the key, to give it back to him. Pottinger was standing much closer to the Professor now, talking to him, one hand partly raised. His easy charm had faded quickly and he seemed intent on something rather serious at that moment.

"He's gone for a holiday," the solid Irishwoman had told Madeleine on the phone next morning, with me listening on an extension. "Ah, an' sure, God love him, isn't that the way with him?, never knowing what he's doing from one minute to the next? He just upped and packed his traps after lunch and took off for Heathrow."

"Where to?" Madeleine had asked.

"Amsterdam," the Irishwoman said confidently, as if she knew that city intimately. "He said he was going to look at the flowers there. The tulips, he said."

"Did he say when he was coming back—or where he was staying?"

"At the end of the week he thought—but he'd be moving around a bit, he said."

I'd looked at Madeleine afterward. "Was he interested in flowers?"

"No. Not that I know of."

But that was the following morning, when the bird had flown. Before then several other matters had cropped up.

Immediately after I'd left the Professor's flat something worried me—I couldn't quite place it, but I was uneasy. So, having walked away from Rugby Street, I doubled back, first down to Theobald's Road, then up John Street, turning left halfway and along to where I knew I'd hit the Rising Sun, the pub opposite the Professor's house. I knew the area fairly well in any case—my old office in the glass house beyond Gray's Inn was only a few minutes' walk away. The pub was on a corner. The public bar entrance was hidden from the Professor's view but the lounge windows, round the other side of the corner room, gave directly out onto his street and I could see his doorway even standing back at the bar with a weak beer in my hand.

What was it about Pottinger? Or, rather, about his association with Allcock, an amalgam that had produced such an uneasy atmosphere. Was it simply my presence? I thought not. Singly, both men—the Professor the previous evening and Pottinger alone with me—had both rung true. But together they set off some alarm. They seemed to know each other rather better than they pretended, like adulterous lovers avoiding each other's gaze in the presence of a spouse: that was what worried me. And I remembered Pottinger's half-raised hand when I'd surprised them a second time—facing the Professor with a look close to the dictatorial, or at least not with the expected expression of a respectful student.

Before I'd taken a second mouthful of the warm beer it struck me that Pottinger might be with the CIA—or at least hovering somewhere in that line of country—and there was one way, possibly, to find out: to follow him, rather clumsily, when he left the Professor's house, and see how successfully, if at all, he tried to break the trail.

Well, the surprising thing was that when he did emerge, more than half an hour later, and I followed him rather clumsily up Great Ormond Street, across Russell Square, and toward the British Museum, he didn't try to break at all. I'm sure he saw me several times as he turned to look back at a Zebra crossing or caught my reflection in shop windows—he must have, yet he ambled along happily like a lot of other tourists that morning, just enjoying the sun.

And then suddenly he disappeared, at a point where it seemed impossible for him to do so; it was as if some huge hand had scooped him up while my back was turned for a second. He'd been looking into the window of the joke-and-games shop just opposite the British Museum gates, while I'd been on the other side of the street, my head turned up toward a poster on the BM railings for a few seconds. But when I looked across the road again the candy-striped suit had vanished. He wasn't in the joke shop, which was filled with half-a-dozen children making monkeys out of themselves with hideous papier-mâché masks; he wasn't in the Museum Tavern next door, fairly empty at that time; he certainly hadn't crossed the road toward the museum gates and he was nowhere down the street opposite. There was nothing I could do except admire his skill—or his luck perhaps, for I supposed at the time that he might have escaped me purely by chance, a thought I tended to dismiss next morning when I learned of the Professor's departure.

It seemed just possible then that Pottinger had come to warn Allcock of something, and that I had unsettled them both by my unexpected appearance at their rendezvous. But to warn him of what? And then I saw that it could well have been me: that the warning had only begun with my arrival there, and my speaking to Pottinger—for hadn't I told him that I'd come to ask the Professor something, to consult him over some point that had cropped up the previous night at a concert? A concert of Rachel Phillips's, as I'd also told him. And that point, which could well have emerged after I'd left the flat, was, What had the Professor meant by saying that Lindsay Phillips had gone *back* to Russia?

If I was right, then both Pottinger and the Professor had some previous interest in Lindsay—the Professor's knowledge sufficiently damaging to warrant his immediate exit from the country, thus avoiding any more awkward questions about Lindsay, either from me or, more awkwardly still, from the Special Branch.

In sum, the two men could indeed have a far more intimate connection than had originally been apparent, and their subsequent meeting had resulted in denying me some crucial knowledge of Lindsay.

I had no proof, of course. The Professor might have been no more than an old fantasist, whose theories about Lindsay's disappearance were mere dreams of exotic adventure, while Pottinger could well be exactly what he said he was: an American student of Russian history. And was there anything necessarily strange in the Professor's taking a spring holiday at short notice?

Nonetheless, I suddenly had doubts. For the first time, entirely through my own eyes and efforts, without recourse to the curious and conflicting evidence on Lindsay's past from Marcus and Fielding, I had stumbled on a much stranger glimpse of the man—a glimpse quite different from their mild political antitheses, and light years away from the loving and honorable vision Madeleine and Rachel cherished of him. Was Lindsay indeed a deep-cover KGB officer? Was he a mole buried at the heart of British Intelligence for far longer than Philby or any of the others had been? And had the Professor, given his longstanding Soviet connections, fallen naturally into the role of confidant and possible recruiter, while Pottinger, with equal ease, took on the part of Lindsay's KGB control?

I could have tried to check these ideas out there and then through Fielding and one of the counterespionage sections, but I didn't. I wanted to protect Madeleine and Rachel from their implications until I had found out for myself, quite certainly, that they were true. If they turned out to be false, I should have set up a cloud over Lindsay's reputation difficult ever to erase—since how, with absolute certainty, could one ever prove it? One could only prove them true should the Professor crop up in Moscow six months later, or Pottinger admit the truth at the hands of some brutal or skillful interrogator. So I let the matter lie.

At the same time these suspicions subtly altered the previous bias of my search for Lindsay. From that morning on everything I remembered or found out about his life I had to put not only against my firm image of him as a totally honorable man, but also against this seemingly impossible proposal that he was a traitor. I was looking for two men, I thought for a moment, before realizing that only one had disappeared. But which one?

7

Every individual life is a marvelous excess of lyric and tragic
information, while a family together creates an even more
profligate history, a huge unrecorded folklore of ancient intimacies, passions, truths, lies, hatreds—all of which have
sunk in time, buried layer upon layer in the years they have
lived through. Even an old and close friend has little hope
of properly gauging the real weight of their various previous
associations, of sharing their visions, or finding reasons for
their particular choices and antagonisms.

He may, with luck or patience, clearly isolate certain special moments in those lives—colorful occasions, times of distress, or even a precise incident from an afternoon long ago
which can be made to rise clear of time and live again like
a song. Or he may stumble upon a great flaw in the puzzle,
an appalling error in what seems at first to be a different
jigsaw altogether, the shards of another and quite barbarous
civilization. He may even attempt to fit these conflicting frag-
ments of life together. But who, without extreme intuition
or some quite visionary effort, will ever uncover either the
right picture or the whole picture?

Even a man's wife, I thought, looking across at Madeleine

in the drawning room, who has specially loved him, may be the most deceived—a woman who has shared more than anybody else with him who yet may be least privy to his secrets; for if we lie, and we will, it is those closest to us to whom we must lie most completely.

It was clear to me then, as I looked at that kind and vulnerable face, that my continued researches into Lindsay's life might bring renewed pain to Madeleine—and that unless through some lucky inspiration I could summon up the whole man, the unrelated, incidental details of his life which I might unearth could create a horror for her as deep as his loss.

I said, thinking of this, "How much did you really know about Lindsay's work?"

"Oh, enough. Quite a lot, in some ways," she replied at once. "I wasn't one of those golf widows in the Intelligence service, numbskulls who have to be made believe their husbands work in the Ministry of Transport. I knew from the very beginning what he was doing, and that it was important work."

"But the details?"

"Well, I didn't know all of them, obviously. But I did know the moment he became deputy chief of the old Soviet Section, Section Nine, after the Philby fracas in the mid-fifties—and that ten years later, when Stevenson retired, he took over from him as head of it."

"He told you all these things?"

"Of course. And other things, too: office politics mostly, personalities—who was trying to push who, that sort of thing. But naturally he didn't chatter about any of his actual Intelligence *plans*, if that's what you mean." Madeleine turned and looked at me, a touch of anger suddenly running across her face. "Are you trying to say that he kept something important from me?"

"No," I stalled.

"Well, he very probably did—a lot of important things." Madeleine ran on now, not looking for a precise answer to her original point. "And why not? I was never to be officially informed about his work. He told me what he thought he could, or what might be of joint interest. You know the sort of things. But I didn't know everything."

"Yes. I see that. It *was* all perfectly natural."

"Then what are you getting at?" She walked across the first-floor drawing room and looked out into the square.

"Simply that if I'm to help any, I think I'm going to have to go back through a lot of his life."

She turned decisively, smiling as if regretting her earlier anger and as though she had never suggested that Lindsay had ever kept one particular thing back from her.

"Yes. I see that. I've been doing it myself, too—and I'm very anxious to help you. The people from his office were doing the same thing, talking to me, going through some of his papers. But we didn't really get anywhere; we dragged through his papers just as we dragged through the loch." Madeleine sighed and looked back at the square. "I've gone through our life together, too, by myself. You know, trying to think of something in the past that might have led to this." She paused.

"And?" I said after a long moment.

"Well—and nothing," she said simply. "We were very happy. *We*, that is."

"Yes. Of course there was Eleanor."

Madeleine faced me again. "Yes, there was—and I thought of that. And certainly he talked a lot about her after it all happened, before we married, naturally: it was a frightful business, being married to someone, seeing her disintegrate in front of you, getting crazier day by day, poor woman, and then killing herself in Zagreb that day. It nearly killed him afterward. But that was forty years ago, I keep telling myself."

Madeleine looked through me now, her focus lost, quite caught up in those distant, terrible events in Lindsay's life about which I knew almost nothing. "Then there was Patrick, too," she said, with an effort. "I've thought about that as well—thirty years ago. That was just as bad—to have a wife and then a son go. And I've wondered if Lindsay might have suffered some sort of delayed reaction to these things, some kind of, I don't quite know—some kind of brainstorm. I spoke to Hunter—Gavin Hunter, the Service analyst about this, and he thought, well, he thought it *might* just be possible. But very unlikely."

"What?"

"That Lindsay might have killed himself—a long-delayed reaction: some guilt about these deaths that he'd repressed. Though God knows I don't think there was anything he could have done about either of them. Eleanor was that way, in any case. And Patrick went so quickly. It's true, it was just at the end of the war, early in 1945, and we couldn't get in touch with Lindsay—he was somewhere in Austria rounding up a lot of fascist Yugoslavs, and he didn't find out about Patrick's death until a week after it happened. But that wasn't his fault. *I* was the one who felt the guilt. I was responsible for Patrick after all—I was looking after him."

She didn't turn back from the window and I knew she must be feeling quite awful at that moment. I went to her and put my hand on her shoulder. She didn't turn; she was crying, I thought.

"Yes," I said. "I understand. But it isn't all a vale of tears. Believe me." I didn't believe that myself just then, but I had to say it. Lindsay's life at that moment—and Madeleine's too—suddenly seemed like one of the saddest stories ever told.

"You see, the trouble for me," I said, "is where do I begin? With Lindsay's life? I only came to know him in any adult way in the mid-fifties. Before that he was just a distant, miraculous uncle to me, someone I saw now and then during the war. I remember him in a smart uniform at Perth Station, or skating on the loch that Christmas morning it iced over—reading the lesson later like God, and giving us half-crowns wrapped up in silver paper afterward—and then disappearing the next day with Henty in a pony and trap, going back to the war again. There's a whole huge life about him that I never touched. I only really knew a child's version of him."

Madeleine turned from the window. I had moved away and given her time to recover, I think, with these memories of Lindsay, for her face had cleared again.

"Yes," she said. "I see that. But why—to find him—must you *know* all that life? I don't quite see. I'm willing to help, but I don't—"

"I don't quite know either, now I think about it. Except what else is there that the police and the others haven't tried? One has to take some new approach."

"I see that, but, Peter, if you think his disappearance was to do with his work, why bother so much with his personal affairs? Why not talk to his colleagues?"

"Because they wouldn't talk to me. For most of them I'm no more than a traitor, never properly cleared for that Egyptian business ten years ago. But the other point is this: I think he may have had some 'brainstorm,' as you put it, that Hunter might be right—and that's why he suddenly went,

93

a breakdown, not necessarily for personal reasons, though these may have helped. The pressures of this kind of clandestine work over—how many?—thirty, forty years impose tremendous strains, which you have to keep on bottling up. Well, one day the whole thing can just break wide open."

"Yes, I can see that—"

"Especially if you have no other outlet—"

"But that's the whole point," Madeleine broke in. "Lindsay *had* an outlet: his bees. He was with them whenever he got the slightest chance. Oh, I know what you mean, in his world, stuck in London, away from me, people can often take to drink or women, I realize that. But Lindsay didn't. He had his *bees*," she said vehemently, coming toward me and wringing her hands for emphasis. "They were everything to him—that, and the honey farm generally."

"Yes," I said, opening the lid of the little gold-plated music box without thinking; a military tune—"The Dashing White Sergeant" I think it was—suddenly sprung up into the warm room, startling us both.

"Yes, his bees," I said, closing the lid after a moment. We paused, and I thought about Lindsay's bees, and about the many rituals I'd seen him go through with them as a child. I remembered him stalking around the hives in the spring, with Billy, his bee manager. They'd looked like sinister divers, dressed in their thick white overalls and black veils, I'd thought then, as I watched them from the safety of the morning-room window. And I recalled seeing Lindsay, in a honey-smeared apron, out in the dark bee rooms that had been converted from the old coach house and stables. It was the end of the summer, and he was supervising the honey extraction; the pure heather honey had to be squeezed out laboriously by a wax press. This involved slowly turning a large screw at the top, while the thick white essence oozed out like toothpaste from a spigot beneath.

Madeleine was right: Lindsay did indeed have his bees. And I was reminded then that he had been in the middle of tending them when he had disappeared. I mentioned this to Madeleine.

"Yes," she said, "I've wondered about that too—why he went just then."

"Well, that's what I mean about the personal things in his life. His bees, for example—that's not something the police would have looked into."

Suddenly I was faced with the enormity of Lindsay's disappearance right under his wife's nose, on a fine day in spring, in the middle of what he was happiest at. It seemed if indeed he knew what he was doing, that he had acted with extraordinary cruelty toward his wife by choosing just that moment to get out of her life. Yet this idea was so out of character that I was forced to think of other reasons—that he had indeed been kidnapped or lost his memory. But here too I was confronted by the unlikelihood of the entire thing, considering the kind of man he was—the last person to suffer any mental vagaries; and the circumstances at Glenalyth were the least propitious in which to kidnap him.

But why, in any case, the bees? Did they have any special relevance? Why choose that moment—so intimate, so domestic—to disappear from life? The more I thought about it all, the fewer answers occurred to me. And yet, there was some definite reason for it all. Madeleine must have been having the same kind of thought at just that moment, too, for she said to me, "You know, on a quite objective level I'm truly appalled by the hideous lack of logic to any of this. If he'd disappeared overseas or in London or at a hundred and one other moments in his life I could have understood it. After all, he worked in the kind of world where such things happen to people. But at Glenalyth, at home, on his own doorstep..." She shook her head. "It's as if some huge hand had come down from the sky and picked him up while my back was turned."

I thought how just the same thing seemed to have happened to Pottinger opposite the British Museum. Yet there must be reasons there again, I reminded myself: some trick of light, perhaps, in Pottinger's case, or the fact that he'd run for a taxi while I wasn't looking. "You have a great need to know, don't you?" Fielding had said to me in the hotel.

But suddenly I felt that I didn't want to know about Lindsay at all: that my re-creation of his soul was surely not my business, that it was a matter inviolate and private to him or lay in the hands of some god. I saw my attempts at omniscience as dangerous impertinence—for what should I know of a world where people were scooped up by huge hands? It lay outside my normal competence, surely, to arrive at any fair understanding about his life. And why should I expect any inspired luck in re-creating the whole of him? If there was a reason for everything, perhaps there was, too, a reason why some things were better left unsaid.

On the other hand, it was clear that Madeleine was determined on the journey. It was her nature to think the best of people and she had obviously never thought a fraction less than this of her husband. She looked at me now with one of her forceful Crusader looks. "You know, Peter, I think if he is to be found you're the person who'll do it. And I think you're probably right. The reasons *are* in his past somewhere, if we can only put our hands on them. And I think you may do that—you who knew him, liked him, had a special sympathy with him."

I thought how closely her words paralleled Basil Fielding's; how he had said she would come to me of her own accord, asking my help, since I was an old friend, a dear friend. And, besides, one told things to friends that one didn't tell policemen. Yet I was a policeman, too, of a sort, although she didn't know that, and already I had betrayed her in a mild way. Such ways are an inevitable sickness in the world Lindsay and I had worked in, but they can become a general plague so that the truth dies everywhere before the game is finished. Yet Madeleine had made it impossible for me to back out. I was, indeed, close to her now and committed to her cause, an old friendship had rekindled between us in the warmth of that early summer morning in the gracious drawing room. But I was a friend with a shadow, even though she couldn't see it and I couldn't admit to it.

"I hope you're right," I said.

"I'm *sure* I am," she replied with feeling.

We heard Rachel clattering down from upstairs just then.

"Oh God, Oh Montreal!" she said, bursting into the room. "It's nearly eleven and I'm supposed to meet George and Max then—where, oh *where* is my music case?"

"In the hall—if it's not upstairs."

"Yes—it must be. But it never is."

Then Rachel stopped charging around the room and greeted me.

"Hello," she said. "You're back again. Good. What's been happening?"

"Brian has upped and gone off on a holiday suddenly," Madeleine said.

"So?" Rachel asked.

"Well, you know he said to Peter about Lindsay's going *back* to the Russians—"

"But that's just a nonsense," Rachel interrupted. "You know that. Brian is an old fool in his dotage. He'd tell you pigs could fly if he thought you'd like to hear it."

"Yes. But this wasn't something we *wanted* to hear."

"Oh God." Rachel sighed with elaborate exaggeration. "What on earth would Daddy want to go *back* to the Russians for? Just because he was in Intelligence and because of what happened to Philby and all those other wretches, you think it must have happened to him, that he was a KGB man or something. But, good Christ," she said vehemently, "you must know that most of the people in British Intelligence—the *vast* majority—are *not* double agents or KGB men. And Daddy certainly wasn't. Now—my music case." Then she stopped and looked at me. "Hey!" she said, "come with me. We've hardly said a word to each other. Come and bike with me and meet the others?"

"Bike?"

"Yes, you can use Mummy's—can't he?"

I'd not seen much of Rachel in the past thirty-six hours. She'd been upstairs a lot of the time, sleeping or recovering in some other way from her birthday evening. But now she seemed to be dancing back into life again, in a neat pair of blue cotton slacks, and a shawl-collared white shirt. She looked summery-fresh, while I felt like a decaying tailor's dummy.

"I should be getting back home," I said. "I need a change of clothes."

"Later, later," Rachel chanted. Then she paused in her skipping about and looked at me down her long straight nose. "You are still going to help us, aren't you? And come to Glenalyth next week? And not go on about old Brian Allcock?"

Madeleine had opened the bottom of the long sash window and a breath of warm air fluttered into the high room. Pigeons warbled deep in the green-leafed plane trees and a mower hummed over the grass in the square. Both women looked at me now.

"Yes," I said, not knowing where to begin helping them, or how.

Madeleine broke the silence. "Peter said it was a matter of going back through Lindsay's life, of looking through his papers."

"Maybe," Rachel said, adding impatiently, "*maybe*. But we have to live, too, meanwhile."

I thought at the time that she was trying to leave the thrall of her father behind her with these words, as she had been in her comments about the Professor. But now I see that she meant it was necessary, for her at least, to look toward the mysterious place where she believed he had hidden himself, whereas I would have to go back in time to discover him. She, who knew him so well in all that past, was sure that he could only lie ahead of her.

"Come on," she said quickly. "The bikes are in the back hall. And I must have left my music there as well, in the carrier basket."

A great contentment broke through me as we started off on our bicycles: that ease with another person that rarely comes, when one can be with them without having to speak, and yet is perfectly joined to them.

As we rode out of the square in the sunshine I tried to think when I had last been happy in this way with Rachel. The end of our time together, before I'd gone to Egypt and married Bridget in the mid-fifties, had been largely acrimonious. It must have been more than twenty years, I decided, since anything remotely enjoyable had happened between us. I was suddenly and uncomfortably aware that our real lives together, when we had been truly engaged with each other, had only existed in our childhood and adolescence, before we had set ourselves up alone outside our families.

8

Did you see the two of them, skipping about on those bloody bikes like lovers?" the young Special Branch detective said. "I thought we were going to run them down several times." The unmarked police car, which had been following some way behind the two cyclists since they had left Hyde Park Square, drove past the coffee shop now and on down Wigmore Street until it came to a halt just before John Bell & Croyden's, Chemists. The plain-clothes man next the driver got out onto the pavement before leaning back into the car and taking a copy of the *Express* from the glove compartment.

"Back you go then," his colleague told him brightly. "And don't eat too many Danish pastries. I'll let them know where you are."

"You do that," the other man remarked sourly. "And remember, I'm supposed to be off at one o'clock. So get the next crew up here at once, okay? I don't want to be chasing after this lot till midnight on my own."

The driver nodded before closing the door and picking up the radio mike from beneath the dashboard. Then he called from the window, "Don't worry, Jack. They'll probably go on for lunch at the Ritz—so you can do your trench-coat act with the headwaiter there. And don't forget to put it all down. Remember what they said: 'No expenses spared'—there's a fit on with these two, God knows why. They don't look like villains to me."

The plain-clothes man wandered back up Wigmore Street, shuffling his hands through his coat pockets like a disgruntled provincial up in town for the day, while the driver gave his call sign to headquarters and then the present location of the two cyclists: "Yes, the coffee shop, Miranda's or something, corner of Duke and Wigmore streets—you can't miss it . . . Yes, only Jack's with them now . . . and listen, he wants a replacement up here as soon as possible . . ."

MARCUS gazed thinly out at the bright spring sky over St. James's Park. A telephone rang on his broad, uncluttered desk.

"Well?" he said looking across at Basil Fielding, before picking up the phone. The Special Branch Chief at the other end gave him details of the present whereabouts of the two cyclists. "Thank you. Fine. Keep with them and let me know any changes."

"Well," Fielding said, repeating the word gently, sitting opposite Marcus in a red leather chair, looking grubby but not intimidated. "I accept your point, naturally: I work for your department, not the Prime Minister—"

"One might even say you worked for *me,* Fielding. Might one not?" Marcus looked at Basil with acid care.

"Of course. Though it's fair to point out, perhaps, that we *all* work for the PM, since he is nominally head of Intelligence services in this country. So to that extent my dealings with him were not, technically, any contravention of my contract with you."

"Hairsplitting, Fielding. And nonexistent hair, too. You can perfectly well see you cannot serve two masters in this matter. You must abide by the orders of those who have executive control over you, not nominal control. Fact is—and let me repeat it—for a variety of reasons we do *not* wish Phillips found, and if the PM wishes otherwise—"

"As he most certainly does—"

"Then he must employ you personally in the matter."

"Sir, with respect, that is patently ridiculous. The PM has given *you* direct orders in the matter of Phillips; my orders from him have been entirely indirect, mere confirmation of an action he supposes you are vigorously proceeding with."

"He has indeed, Fielding. But we do not invariably follow such orders, not to the letter, at least, which is what you are doing. We only go through the motions on some occasions, and this is one of them. You, on the other hand, are definitely taking your coat off in this matter. And that we don't want—"

"I might find him?"

"Marlow might find him. He has an awful knack that way. Amateurs often have. He found us the names of half the KGB men over here a few years back. As you know, I stopped your cash advance to Marlow yesterday. I wish now to have him stopped from any further meddling."

Fielding looked at Marcus, smiling wanly now—the sudden smile of an unexpected winner, a punter who has just seen his money romp home on a rank outsider. "I'm sure you know, as I do, from your own meeting with Marlow, that he intends to help the Phillips family in *any* case, whether we like it or not."

Marcus gripped the edge of the blotter in front of him. "*My* meeting with Marlow?"

Fielding nodded and Marcus didn't pursue the denial he had in mind. He relaxed his grip on the paper. "So Marlow told you?"

"No, as a matter of fact. I happened to drop into the club myself that lunchtime, when you met him. I saw you both at the bar."

"What?" Marcus began to rise and fill out like a little balloon.

"Yes. I was in the coffee room and glanced through the doorway. And there the two of you were. Oh, I'm a member," Fielding went on by way of easy explanation. "But if I may continue: I can't see how we can now prevent Marlow—in his private capacity—from helping the family. He's obviously doing just that already."

Marcus drummed his chubby fingers on the tabletop for an instant, a brief little drum roll, as though to herald some surprising and decisive action. "No," he said sharply. "Marlow hasn't begun to pick up any real threads. And that's what I want from you now, Fielding: a firm commitment to stop him before he does. And unless I have that from you—well, your days will be numbered in the House of the Lord. I want you to make it your personal business from now on to stop him."

Fielding looked into his lap, his hands cupped over his crotch, head to one side—a pained figure suddenly, midway along a via dolorosa. "I have no alternative, do I?" he said meekly, putting a finger to the knot of his grubby regimental tie.

"And keep clear of the PM while you're at it," Marcus added tartly.

"Right." Fielding stood up. "I'll do my best to dissuade Marlow." He paused and then said offhandedly. "There's really only one point—*why* is Phillips not to be found? I don't think I quite follow that."

Marcus looked at him maliciously. "When were you last given a positive security check, Fielding?"

"Oh, four, nearly five years ago."

"Time you had another session then. Keep you out of any more mischief. I'll make arrangements with the security people. And don't worry about Marlow. I'll have someone else attend to him. All right?"

"Very well," Fielding said, before turning and sloping out of the room like an underfed stable boy. But once outside in the corridor he hummed a jaunty little tune to himself, a smile touching his haggard face. "Every dog has his day," he said, half aloud, as he stopped by the lifts and pressed a button for the ground floor.

AN hour later Marcus was seated opposite the Prime Minister in the cabinet room of 10 Downing Street. On either side of the broad table, strategically placed both in opposition and in careful order of their own hierarchies, were a dozen other sharp-faced men, both military and civilian, dressed for the sober occasion in careful suits and uniforms. Without the new air-conditioning system, which still had not been made to function properly, the room was hot and oppressive in the bright spring sunshine that streamed through the long windows from the rose garden at the back of the building. Motes of dust rose from the carpet as a heavy woman—one of the Prime Minister's personal secretaries—clumped across the room pushing a trolley of coffee and biscuits.

This meeting of the inner cabinet, together with all the Security and Intelligence chiefs, had lasted for more than half an hour already. The Minister for Defence, sitting next to the PM, coughed once more, a harsh dry yack of a cough, a recalcitrant tickle in the bottom of his throat that had defied every lozenge and beaten back each breathy attack he had made upon it since the meeting had begun.

"I'm sorry, it's the dust."

The PM accepted a cup of coffee, then turned to the Secretary of the Cabinet seated two places away from him on his left, the vacant place between them kept for the Foreign Secretary who had not managed to turn up, his flight back from Rhodesia delayed by a sandstorm at Cairo Airport. "When will they do something about the air conditioning?" he asked the Cabinet Secretary.

"When the service engineers' pay demands are met," the old man replied.

"Surely we can fix it ourselves?"

"Do you mean you or I, Prime Minister? Or both of us?"

The PM turned away and sipped his coffee. He turned toward the opposition on the other side of the table, gazing at them, he hoped, with unconcealed distaste.

There was Marcus, head of D.I.6, whom he had trusted completely and now doubted; next to him, Lindsay Phillips's replacement as head of Section Nine, a man he didn't know at all, a young fellow from the north country called Jackson who had an unpleasant Border accent; beyond him, Sir Alan Maynard, who ran domestic security at D.I.5, and then Simon Bryant—another youngster, the PM thought—currently in charge of SIS's counterespionage section. They were all so young, the PM reminded himself once more—young men given their chance of rapid promotion through the appalling mistakes of their seniors during the past fifteen years, yet who now themselves had apparently allowed the unpardonable to happen.

The PM put aside his cup and looked again at his memoranda. Then, with a last tired glance around the room requesting silence, he commenced his performance again.

"I take it, then, that we none of us now are really in any doubt at all that Phillips is—or was—a major Soviet agent. And has been since the beginning of his career with the Diplomatic Service in the early thirties?"

No one dissented. A pin could have dropped.

"Bryant," the PM said roughly, "I think you, if anyone, had doubts?"

"Not after Petnički's depositions, I suppose, Prime Minister. I had doubts simply because I could not see how Phillips could have possibly survived so long: as I said before, it's been over forty years, and that's a long time. Half a dozen other Soviet or East European defectors have come and gone with information about doubles in our services meanwhile. Krevitsky, just before the war, for example, and Volkov in Ankara in 1948, who originally put us onto Burgess and Maclean—as well as Philby. And other sources, too. But none of them mentioned Phillips."

"Or rather," the PM interjected, "as you put it in your notes to me, one of them—surely Krevitsky at least—*did* spot Phillips. And we thought it was Maclean. There were, in fact, *two* 'upper-class, well-educated Scotsmen in the Foreign Office' who were Soviet agents, not one, as Krevitsky had thought. Isn't that it?"

"Yes, sir. Though of course all that was long before—"

"Yes, Bryant, 'long before your time.' I can see that." The PM glared at Marcus. "And before yours too, David," he added. "The fact is, once we found out about Maclean we didn't bother about any more well-bred intellectual Scots traitors." Again the PM looked pointedly at Marcus. "What is it about the Scots, David, that they should continue to be such devious thorns in our flesh?"

Marcus was very cool. "I hardly think such nationalistic innuendo is called for—"

The PM held up an arm. "No, no, of course not. It was beneath me. My apologies." He didn't mean a word of it.

"So we may confirm that point," the PM went on. "Phillips, more than Philby or any of the others, must have caused the real damage—to what exact extent it's impossible as yet to estimate—if it ever is. But put in the simplest terms, as far as Moscow was concerned Phillips took over where Philby left off—to the extent, even, of actually taking over Philby's old Soviet department, Section Nine. Which means that almost everything we've run against the Soviets, *after* as well as before 1952—up until about three months ago, in fact—has been run as a minor minus factor against us. Now what our allies are going to ask is, How was it possible"—the PM paused, genuinely amazed—"how was it *conceivably* possible for us to appoint *another* Soviet agent to replace Philby in his own section? How—more or less certain then, as we were, that Philby was a traitor—how could we have immediately promoted another in his place? You'll agree, it looks worse than carelessness. Finally, since at the time we combed right through that left-wing Cambridge generation in all our SIS staff, how could we possibly have failed to spot Phillips?"

Marcus answered very promptly, as though waiting a prearranged cue. "The answer is simple: Maclean, Burgess, Philby—they were all Cambridge men. But Phillips had no connection with them whatsoever. He was up at Oxford. And his left-wing associations there, so far as we can tell, were nonexistent."

"But so it was with Philby," the PM broke in. "He was never a card-carrier, a member of anything at Cambridge."

Marcus blinked rapidly several times, as though literally unable to believe in the Prime Minister's existence just at that moment. "The real issue," he said slowly, wishing to belabor the point, "was that Phillips was checked out in every possible way after the Philby business. And several times—three times in fact—since then; and he's had an absolutely clean bill each time. You have his security clearance sheets as an appendix to my report in front of you, sir."

The PM glanced down at his papers, fingering through them without really looking, for he knew exactly what his reply would be. He had been waiting for Marcus to give him the opportunity to make it. "Yes, I note your appendices. Interestingly enough—" He looked up, closing the file in front of him. "Interestingly enough, of course, I note that you personally, David, were the last person to give Phillips a positive vetting in 1970. And as you say yourself—an absolutely clean bill of health."

As the PM intended, a silence seemed to grow all over the room, spreading like a malign fungus. But Marcus was quite unworried by it. He looked detached, frustrated, annoyed even.

"I did indeed," Marcus said at last, as if he had willingly connived in the long silence, not in the least put out by its implications. "Prime Minister," he said suddenly, leaning forward, confronting the man opposite him like a bank manager dealing with a bad overdraft, "A Soviet agent—if such Phillips is—placed in British Intelligence from the very beginning, a man without definable left-wing connections at that time, will—unless he makes a mistake or there is some quite fortuitous luck involved—be impossible to detect subsequently. That's the nature of the game in a democracy such as ours. Phillips made no mistakes—and we had no luck with

105

him, until this Yugoslav defector, Petnički, arrived over here. Even then, apart from what Petnički actually told us, there was nothing in Phillips's record, when we went right through it, to confirm Petnički's statements about him—"

"'Nothing,' David? Nothing, that is, apart from NATO's new contingency plans in the event of a Soviet invasion of Yugoslavia. Only Phillips, apart from yourself, the Minister for Defence, the brigadier here, and myself were privy to those plans. 'Nothing' was quite a lot, wasn't it? And I have to explain what you call 'nothing' on Friday morning to the American Secretary of State and General Haig."

"I see several ways round your dilemma, sir," Marcus said coolly. "You may surely say to the Americans—since Phillips has not turned up anywhere yet—that these plans may have leaked from NATO headquarters itself, or from the French, for example," he added with a malicious smile. We don't, in fact—apart from Petnički's word—have as yet any *incontrovertible* evidence that Phillips actually passed these plans over to the Russians; nor do we have any *absolutely* firm evidence that Phillips *was* a Soviet agent. We merely hold strong suspicions, largely based on his sudden disappearance once he knew of Petnički's arrival here."

The PM response was eminently self-righteous. "Surprising as it may seem to you, I have no intention of covering up in the way you suggest, David. Our allies will have the truth as I see it. They will, once more, be rightly appalled at the performance of our Intelligence services, as am I. But I trust they will keep quiet about it. It is you, David, who is in the hot seat. I and my government would probably survive such public admissions of failure, but not you. On the other hand, if Phillips were to be *found* either dead or alive, we might save something from the disaster. With Phillips safely accounted for, either on trial or as a corpse, the effects of this appalling bungling could be minimized. I suggest you do everything in your power, you and the other special services"—the PM glanced at Marcus's companions—"to try and find the man. And this leads, gentlemen, to your final opinions of what you think has actually happened to this little Scotsman. Sir Alan?" The PM looked over at the head of D.I.5.

Maynard was overconfident. "It's my view that the man has gone over to Moscow. He could have gone with prearranged Soviet help, on that Russian trawler that left from Aberdeen. Or else he left entirely on his own: crossed over to the Continent by air on that Edinburgh-Paris flight the day after. We have a rough identification from the airport's emigration control of a man like Phillips traveling without very much luggage. He also could have left later in the week, by any one of a dozen ways. I don't hold with the suicide theory, or with a sudden loss of memory on his part—completely untypical of the man."

Simon Bryant, the bouncy head of Counterespionage, interrupted immediately, his eyes bright with righteous enthusiasm. "I agree, sir. The dates in the whole matter seem to me to be conclusive. Petnički came to us from the Yugoslav Embassy in Paris on March seventeenth. Now naturally, since this came very much within Phillips's own Slavs and Soviets' section, he was advised of Petnički's arrival here and of our impending interrogation of him. This had to be done in case, for example, Petnički had been some kind of a leg man in one of Phillips's circles in Yugoslavia. Yet outside our own counterespionage section—and apart from Chief of Service, of course"—Bryant glanced at Marcus—"*only* Phillips was notified."

Bryant consulted his notes. "That was on the eighteenth, in a personal meeting between Phillips and my deputy, Anderson. Phillips then confirmed that Petnički had no connection with any of our overseas Intelligence circles, and there was no form on him anywhere within Section Nine. Petnički was clean—he was 'real.' That established, we proceeded with our interrogation, and by the end of the week— on the twenty-first of March—Phillips, who had gone up to Scotland for the weekend, disappeared. It was late the day before—the twentieth, which was a Saturday—that Petnički first gave us a picture of this 'Scotsman' in SIS who he said he knew was working for the Soviets in Yugoslavia. It took us most of Sunday morning to get Central Registry on the ball, but by lunchtime that day we had narrowed it down to Phillips and two other Scotsmen, neither of whom had anything to do with Yugoslavia. As you know, we flew two men up to Perth on Sunday afternoon to question him—"

"Yes, I know the rest," interrupted the PM. "You were very quick, but not really quick enough. It's interesting, isn't it, how Phillips managed to get away, to 'disappear' about an hour before you arrived in Perth? One might almost think he'd been warned." The PM looked at Marcus.

Again Marcus was totally composed. "Yes, sir," he said, almost a cheeky tone in his voice. "It's possible. And there was—we know from his wife—a phone call Phillips took that Sunday, after lunch. She heard him say 'You have the wrong number.' So, of course, that may have been a warning. But we can't be sure. We can't, for example, be sure that the call came from London, which is where the warning would have had to come from, since the Phillipses' home number has been on a direct dialing system from London for over a year."

"You have it all so nicely balanced, David," the PM said. "'On the one hand: this. On the other: that. It could—and it couldn't: it might—and it mightn't.' Do you find it impossible to make your mind up in any way on this matter?"

"I'm afraid that in the absence of any conclusive evidence I must take that approach, Prime Minister," Marcus replied brightly. "This whole matter of Phillips is very much a matter of balance as far as I'm concerned, which in itself is typical of most Intelligence investigations. It's often, indeed, a matter of very fine balances." Marcus looked distantly at the PM. "Very fine indeed. If I may say so."

"Yes, I *know* all that, Marcus. I don't want a thesis on the art of espionage. I want your *opinion*, simply, as to where this man is or what's happened to him."

"I don't know, Prime Minister. I truly don't have a definite opinion. I can only offer you several alternatives."

The PM sighed delicately. "Let us bear with them then."

"My first thought—and I take it first only because it's the one all of you here seem most to favor—is that he has gone over to Moscow—"

"Thank you, David. At last. And it follows then, doesn't it, that Phillips was a major Soviet agent?"

"That *might* follow. Though not necessarily a major—"

"We can dispense with the 'Not necessarilys' I think. What if that *is* true? What's the Soviet move? When is he likely to surface?"

"With the others—Burgess and Philby—it took several years. They'll wait for a suitable occasion when they can make useful propaganda out of it before they uncover him. Or they may use him as a confidential bargaining counter, held against some advantage Brezhnev wants from the West. And that could be any time, next week or next year—"

"Splendid," the PM interjected. But this time it was Marcus who came very smartly back at him, holding up his hand like a traffic policeman. "If I may, Prime Minister. What I really have to say is this. We should continue to bear very much in mind my original point: we have as yet no absolutely conclusive evidence that he *has* gone over to Moscow. None of our sources over there, legal or illegal, have mentioned any rumors of him. And nor have the CIA. And he's been gone over two months. Thus we must continue seriously to consider the other alternatives: that he is still over here, dead or alive; that, for example, realizing we suspected his loyalty, he killed himself—drowned in that loch of his, perhaps. And there is a third alternative—one which we've not properly considered at all: that realizing we were on to him, he just upped and disappeared somewhere else, but not to the Soviet Union."

"Doubtful, isn't it?" the Defence Minister put in. "He took nothing with him—no luggage, passport, cash?"

Marcus allowed himself a pinched smile—a nasty grimace, it would have been, had it lasted more than a second. "Of course, Minister, he would have made detailed arrangements for such a move, long beforehand." Marcus returned to the PM. "What I'm suggesting is that Phillips, rather than going over to Russia and a drab life in the Moscow suburbs, may have gone to South America or some such place where we don't have any political extradition treaties. And he's waiting there for his wife to join him, before starting afresh."

"Surely not," the old Secretary of the Cabinet put in, aghast, unable to restrain himself. "From what I know of him, he'd too much at stake at home in Scotland: his house, his family, his bees. It's a very respected family, after all." He shook his head in righteous disbelief. "I really can't see someone like Lindsay ending up in a banana republic. That stretches fantasy too far."

"They have bees in South America," Marcus put in delicately. "And a lot of old and respected families out there, too, I understand. Phillips may not have seen Scotland and his distinguished ancestry as the be-all and end-all, you know, especially if he was a lifelong Communist, as must follow from your initial scenario that he was a Soviet agent."

"I think we've had enough of these disputatious theories, David. Though am I to gather from what you've just said that you now doubt that Phillips *is* a Soviet agent? I thought we were all agreed on that?" The PM gazed at Marcus malevolently.

"No, Prime Minister, I've not reached the stage of doubting anything yet. I'm still making my inquiries."

He gazed at the PM with the clear, cool eyes of an innocent child. The meeting closed shortly afterward—just long enough, in fact, for Marcus to confirm a narrow victory over the Prime Minister in the whole matter.

At lunch, though, which the PM took privately later with the Cabinet Secretary and the Minister, another card was brought into play.

"Of course it's useless," the Minister said, "using anyone in his own service for any kind of surveillance or confidential investigation on Marcus. He'd spot it at once. Besides, it's my reading that everyone that counts in the SIS is behind Marcus on this in any case. They're closing ranks, naturally."

"Naturally," the PM said, putting aside his half-finished plate of cold meat salad. "But I have someone within the SIS, although outside Marcus's ranks. He's a very senior chap, who has already voiced mild doubts about Marcus in any case. I'll brief him in the matter." The PM sipped a little water, lifting the glass a fraction as though toasting an equally small triumph.

"Is that wise?" asked the Cabinet Secretary, concerned at once by this devious approach. "Dividing loyalties in that way—can you trust this man?"

"Oh, I think so," the PM went on, basking confidently in the warmth of his illicit conceit. "At worst, this fellow is the Devil I know. Whereas with Marcus there's no question but that he's hiding something. Something I should know, therefore something serious. And I have to find out what."

"No question," put in the Minister.

"So either I fire him now, which is bolting the door with the horses gone, or I use this other fellow to try and find out what's going on. This whole Phillips situation couldn't be worse in any case. Might as well attack as sit back and wait for the chopper."

"Of course."

"Indeed."

The two men readily agreed.

"But this 'other fellow'?" the Cabinet Secretary queried innocently. "Who?"

"Better keep him under wraps, if you don't mind. For the time being. Don't want his cover blown. Fewer the better—you know the sort of thing." The PM looked at the other two with an amiable confidentiality and after they had left he put a call through to Basil Fielding.

"Don't use my name," the PM told the secretary before she rang. "Just put him on—if he's there."

Basil Fielding was there, back at his office in Holborn, and he recognized the Prime Minister's voice at once.

"Can you get round here, before three?"

"I'd like to," Fielding said. "Unfortunately, I have a security clearance meeting then."

"Well, hand it over to someone else."

"I'm afraid I'm the subject of this meeting."

"What? Who ordered this?"

"Head of Service, this morning. It rather takes me off active duty, I'm afraid," Fielding added sweetly.

"Never mind that. You get round here this evening on your own steam. Come by the garden entrance—say seven o'clock. All right?"

"Yes. Certainly. I'll be there."

Both men were pleased with the outcome of their conversation: the Prime Minister because it seemed to confirm his worst suspicions about Marcus, and Basil Fielding because, quite as an unexpected bonus, he had considerably enhanced his grip on the Prime Minister.

FEDOR Kudashkin had no idea who the man in the Professor's rooms had been; his clumsy method of trailing Kudashkin indicated that he could have come from some branch of British Security or Intelligence. The London KGB Resident might know. Kudashkin retained a clear image of the unexpected visitor that morning. A session with one of the embassy artists and an Identikit might well establish him.

But meanwhile, like some canny animal in a miracle of nature, Kudashkin had changed colors. His crumpled candy-striped summer suit was replaced by something much less conspicuous, a blue Dacron two-piece with a rather vulgar tie to go with it, made of the same false material. He carried a shiny black PVC briefcase with him into the lobby of the Londoner Hotel, together with a tartan zip bag in the same cheap style. His easy, windblown hair had been re-formed, mastered now with some sticky lotion that had set the strands over his skull like dried seaweed after a tide has left it. His cheeks were padded, and he had suddenly achieved a fashionable, if ridiculous, walrus mustache. His old spectacles had gone too, replaced by an ostentatious new pair, rimless, the glass cut in a smart hexagonal pattern. Overnight he had changed from a vague, Ivy League academic into an aggressive salesman from New Jersey.

The clerk gave him his key and he went straight up—to a small room at the back of the hotel in Marylebone. Once inside, he sat on the bed and dialed another room number in the same hotel. "Room thirty-two," he said, when a voice answered. "The third floor. Come straight over." Then he went to the window, gazing up over the grimy rooftops into a broad sweep of deep-blue sky, while waiting for the Croat policeman from Zagreb.

Ivo Vladović would not be easy to outwit, Kudashkin thought, reminding himself again, as the big man came into the bedroom, what a tough old bird this ex-partisan commander was: a great hulk of a man, with a light, belted raincoat draped over his shoulders, a face like badly chiseled rock, mottled cheeks hollowing with age, a drooping nose over a long chin, and hands that clasped a cigarette holder like the shaft of a spade.

Kudashkin had long since realized that, unlike the servile security or police chiefs with whom he'd dealt in the other Eastern bloc nations, this man, though nearly as orthodox as they in his Marxist politics, would brook a minimum of interference in his plans for unseating Tito and introducing a hard-line, Moscow-oriented regime in Yugoslavia. He and the other Yugoslav Cominformists were anxious for indirect Soviet support in their schemes—but for no more than that. When the day came that would see the end of Tito and his Marxist apostasy, it was Vladović who was determined to rule the roost and call the tune, Vladović who would run the country—in association with Moscow, yes, but an association hardly closer than that which existed between the two countries at present.

It was one of Kudashkin's responsibilities to prevent this happening, and to ensure a far more rigid control of Yugoslavia in these political eventualities—a task made the more difficult since he knew this Croatian police chief mistrusted him deeply already.

The two men shook hands, but hurriedly. Vladović turned then and without taking his coat off walked over to the other side of the room. Then he stood facing Kudashkin, like a tree.

"I've only two days in London," Vladović said formally. "I would like to have things settled by then." He spoke Russian well, but again in a hurry. There was a permanent impatience in his voice. For time was running out—his time, at least, and soon any changes in Yugoslavia would have to be left in the hands of younger men. Kudashkin had recognized this overanxious intent in the man before; it was a chink in his armor Kudashkin hoped to enlarge so that Vladović would overreach himself and find a place, with the others like him, in one of Tito's jails. For the Soviets had their own man in Yugoslavia, who was groomed for the succession after Tito, a younger and far more malleable Serb, already a member of the party's Central Committee in Belgrade. Vladović was an anachronism, though he retained much support, particularly among the exiled Yugoslav Cominformists of his own wartime generation. It was a matter of treading carefully, of using both carrot and stick with the man.

"I can't promise anything," Kudashkin said. "Not in that time."

"You promised Phillips—the British Intelligence officer. We handled his man Dearden for you, in Zagreb. And Phillips was supposed to come out, you said, to investigate. Well, he hasn't."

"He will," Kudashkin said confidently. "They've delayed him here. But he'll come—and then you can take him."

Vladović remained ill at ease, unconvinced. "It's *late*, though," he said angrily. "It puts every other arrangement out. I was supposed to arrest this Phillips weeks ago, shortly after Dearden was killed. The two events were meant to nearly coincide. Then I could have clearly proved Western interference in our internal affairs."

"You still can: he will come."

Vladović opened his arms, stretching his hands out in a hopeless gesture, so that his coat, opening around him like bat wings, nearly slipped to the floor. "You seem to forget our other agreements," he said viciously. "They *had* to happen in unison—"

"Not *exactly*. They couldn't, since we don't control everything. Phillips's movements, for example—"

"Look, the Croatian fascists, Radović and the others, in Munich and Brussels—you recall our plan?" Vladović said intently. Kudashkin nodded calmly. "We were to accuse Phillips of dealing with them, supporting them—showing how the West was anxious to create an alliance with these exiled nationalists, and was thus favoring a breakaway independent state of Croatia after Tito's death, which would give us the opportunity of clamping down and taking over."

"Yes, that was the plan."

"Well, as I forecast, Radović came to Zagreb three weeks ago, under cover, and we spotted him. But there was no Phillips, and no one else from British Intelligence there, either, to whom we could link Radović. I had to let him go. So we're back where we started. Radović won't come again for a long while, a year maybe."

Kudashkin smiled. "I remember all that. But Phillips will come—you can rely on it. And Radović can then be taken in Brussels and brought back into the country. You've done that before!"

"It's far more risky though—taking someone outside." Kudashkin was tart and officious now. "What you have to realize is that none of us can guarantee an exact date for Phillips's arrival; we never could. You are being inflexible: we had to allow for variations in our plans."

"I realize that. *Some* allowances. But it's three months since Dearden went—and every day Tito consolidates his succession. Flexibility, yes. But the time factor is even more important now. If we have to wait much longer it will be too late: Tito will have completed his plans for a collegiate leadership after his death. We must have action within the month—which means we must have Phillips. Or, if not him, then someone else from British or Western Intelligence whom we can pin these charges on."

"You shall have Phillips," Kudashkin said easily. "As I told you, I understand from our Resident here that he has simply been delayed with other work." He paused, a possibility forming in his mind. "Him—or someone else. We'll let you know who—as soon as our sources in British Intelligence tell us." Vladović left the room angry and unconvinced.

Alone again, Kudashkin considered his position. It was doubtful if Vladović would ever see Phillips in Yugoslavia now, he thought. Phillips seemed genuinely to have disappeared. Allcock had known nothing, apart from confirming that the family were neither hiding him nor, as far as he knew, privy to any British Intelligence ruse in which his disappearance had been intended. He had then packed the old man off to Amsterdam for a week or two as a precaution.

Now it was time to approach his other crucial source in the matter: Basil Fielding. He had a longstanding arrangement to meet him later that afternoon near the man's apartment in Kensington. Perhaps Fielding would have some fresh information, some new clues. Or, if not, perhaps together they might form some other plan which would both satisfy the impatient Croat and lead to his downfall.

THAT evening Fielding met the Prime Minister in Downing Street. After a few minutes he said, "I have an idea, I think. A way to test Marcus's loyalties. If you agree..."

The Prime Minister nodded, and then, overcome with some pent-up frustration, he said, "You know, it's inconceivable, surely, that Marcus should have warned Phillips that Sunday. If he did, it can only point to one thing—that he's tied up with the Soviets in some way. But I can't believe it."

Fielding raised his eyebrows, looking distantly into the shadows of the room, his wise face full of hard and secret responsibilities. "Well, somebody warned Phillips," he said gently, as though he was anxious, above all, to be fair to Marcus. "They must have done. But may I suggest what we might do?"

"Yes, tell me." The Prime Minister lit his pipe again.

"Well, to start with, if I may, to go back to the beginning. Has Marcus confirmed to you that Phillips never had any left-wing connections, as a student, for example?"

"Yes. At our meeting this morning. 'None, as far as we know,' he said."

Fielding smiled gingerly, licking his slightly purple lips. "Well, he couldn't have looked too hard. I have the evidence here." Fielding produced photocopies of several old-looking sheets of paper covered with messy typing, and handed them to the PM. "The minutes," he said, "of the Oxford University Labour Club, October 1932. I dug them out of the Bodleian Library."

The PM glanced through them; seeing nothing of import, he looked up at Fielding.

"At the end, sir—the faint handwriting at the end."

"Ah, yes, these names, I can hardly read them—Barton, McGinness, Phillips. Yes, 'Phillips—Merton.' And then some others—all with the letter 'R' bracketed after them."

"It either means 'Resignation' or 'Re-election,'" Fielding said. "It's the start of the academic year, and the minutes are about voting in the new officers of the club."

"'Phillips: R.'" The PM looked at the document closely

again. "Yes, I suppose it must. What do the earlier minutes say?"

"They're not in the Bodleian file, sir. Removed, possibly. I'm trying to get hold of other copies. But meanwhile we have that. It seems perfectly clear that Phillips *was* involved with the Socialists then. And if someone did remove the other minutes that mentioned him by name, they overlooked this one. The handwriting *is* very faint."

"So?" The PM looked eagerly at Fielding.

"Well, either Marcus is lying; or else he's made no real effort to check into Phillips's past at all. Now here's what I have in mind, as a test..."

"Yes?" The PM took up his pipe once more.

9

I never expected to spend that evening drinking with Rachel. We embarked on the long pub crawl shortly after they opened at five-thirty, when she'd finished her music session with George and Max in a rehearsal room at Wigmore Hall. She'd asked me to meet her again—alone—in the Dover Castle, a pub round the corner in a mews near Wigmore Street.

Rachel had never used drink in the old days. If her music had been going badly she took it out on other people, not herself, through straightforward bitchiness or nearly malicious jokes. Her excesses of willful energy in any case, diverted from her flute, never led her to the drinks cupboard. Yet she took to it then like long-lost sex, straightaway, when she came out of the evening sun in the mews and joined me on a stool in the corner of the bar where I'd been sipping a sherry.

"Me too," she said. "A large one."

"Difficult day?" It was like living with her again.

"No. Not very. But a nonsense day. A nonsense life I'm beginning to think, too."

She unbuttoned the loose-fitting cord safari jacket with huge pockets she had on now and took a silk scarf from her throat, rustling a hand through her short hair. She put the scarf on the edge of the counter; it began to slide off and I caught it, the fine silk wafer-thin in my hands, like a magician's prop that could be rolled up to the size of a marble. It smelled of something too, as I held it for a moment. And then I recognized it—a faint perfume, like warm plums. When I'd slept with her years before, she had smelled of just the same thing; that slight, fruity smell, almost gone by morning when we woke, but still just there, overlaid by other warmths that had bloomed during the night. No, Rachel hadn't drunk much then—and I had yet to find any real taste for sherry.

"A large one," I said to the barmaid. "Well?" I turned to Rachel, putting the scarf back on her knees, where she smoothed it out with her hands and started to stroke it sadly, pondering the fine material.

"You look tired," I said, continuing the role of pillow to lay her woes on—a familiar part for me; it was like Rachel in the old days entering one of her "unworthy" moods before recovering dramatically and biting my head off. Had Rachel not changed at all, I wondered, just grown older? Was everything still intact, all the imbalances of her temperament, the rage she brought to bear on life's dissatisfactions, the heart-stopping sorrows she found then, when, unable to beat the system, she lay meditating numbly like a penitent on the bed for hours afterward? Had she sorted out nothing in that ragbag mind of hers? I hoped she had. And yet I feared this hope. One comes to love people for their flaws, which they truly possess, mistrusting their virtues as something assumed, or forced upon them by circumstances.

"Tired?" She swallowed half the schooner of sherry. "Yes. Of George. And Max for that matter. What a pair of geniuses they are—oh, I know that. But somehow I can't feel them any more—or their musical on Dottie Parker."

"Musical on who?"

"Dorothy Parker. You know—the Catholic wit, the witty soak. It's called *Dottie*. We were working on it all afternoon, and next week we're supposed to do more, up in Scotland. They want some flute arrangements. It's a lovely idea, but I'm bored with it. Or them, rather. And George is so kind as well. And that's worse."

"George?" I queried. "Is he—?"

"Yes. Or he was. I was foolish enough to sleep with him

once. He's never forgiven me. You should never sleep with your manager, did you know that?"

She looked at me, narrowing her eyes—a twinkle in them, just a hint of a "come hither" look.

"Well—"

"Not if they're in love with you, I mean. That's the problem."

"Because you're not?"

"No." She pulled a thread from the seam of her cord jacket. "I loved George, the busy child. But with me he soon lost that, grew up and became terribly serious and responsible. Marriage was the next thing on his mind—dumping poor Marianne, and a manor for us in the Shires playing Schubert duets by candlelight. It was sad. Of course, I couldn't."

"My God," I said, "whenever I made a joke you used to think I was getting at you. You wanted me serious—"

"Yes—because you are serious, essentially. And George is really a child. What's wrong is when people try and change what they are."

"Ah," I said. "I *see*..." I smiled. "Sometimes they have to do that. The old person becomes a bore. You just said it yourself. A 'nonsense life,' you said you had."

"Oh, I *have* to change," she said briskly. "But I don't see why you people should. You haven't. People change worst of all 'in love,' of course. With George, it was dreadful, took all the stuffing out of him. Became bad opera. He ceased to be able to see himself—went all airy-fairy, like a hippo dancing."

Rachel hadn't lost her little cruelties. No love was good enough for Rachel, she treated every version offered her as suspect, since anyone who could love her must be a fool. Only one love did she believe in—the one she could not properly have, which would therefore never threaten the armor of her self-disgust.

"I'm sorry," I said. "About George."

"Yes—he's really extremely annoyed about you." She raised her glass again.

"He's no reason to be."

"The past. He's jealous of that. And the future. He thinks *he* knows what's best for me," Rachel added slowly.

I must have had an air of puritanical shock at that moment, for she started to laugh—a spluttering, childish laugh, air filling her cheeks and changing her face, that took me right back, past the woman I'd known to the girl she'd been

119

in our childhood. Rachel's childish nature still flew too readily to the surface. And yet it was an exciting quality for all that, a masterstroke against time—for one saw her just then as she had been when young; it was as if all her years were thrown off and she lived again as an eight-year-old once more, squabbling on the jungle gym or refusing to share a toy. There were times when Rachel could lay her whole life out for you, like a long, panoramic foldout in a book, and you could see all the main incidents at once—widely separated spires and domes pricking into the sky above a city—times when, through a mannerism, a change of expression, or a sudden new tone in her voice, she unlocked and released her past, destroying all the traditional processes of time, leaving one with a momentary vision of the complete life; no longer part of herself focused on a single moment, but the whole spread over all the years from the beginning.

"I hated you," she said. "And I can see why—"

"Yes, you had to live with me, not just imagine it all—like Lindsay. I was real—"

"Don't interrupt! If I didn't have much confidence about myself—well, you never helped."

"I wasn't your father."

"Fathead!"

"At twenty, one's looking for a little adult equality, not just nursery tea and sympathy. Well—he's gone. You'll have to grow up now."

There was a silence. Then, quite suddenly, she lifted my hand and put it to her cheek for an instant.

The silence returned. Her scarf fell again, this time to the floor, so that I had to bend right down to get it, and when I stood up to hand it back to her she was looking at me.

"Do you know what I think?" I said, suddenly tired of so many words and years talking to Rachel about her father. "I think it's all a lot of weak nonsense on your part. You should have sorted out your feelings about Lindsay years ago, not now, when it's a little late—and he's gone, and you feel like a widow. Is that what you wanted me here alone for? To hear this, to have it confirmed?"

"No." She was indecisive, looking at me closely.

"I mean, at twenty young girls sometimes still have that sort of crush on their handsome daddies in the Foreign Office. But twenty years later and to be still mooning around his coattails—it's like some bad old Scandinavian play."

I said my piece and lifted my glass like a satisfied bully. I suppose I still believed in shock therapy, as I had in the old days. It hadn't got me anywhere then, but one retains an awful fidelity to one's weaknesses: and that, after all, was exactly what Rachel had done with Lindsay.

"You can't lose him, not until you find yourself: is that all there is?" I asked, hammering a last nail in.

"No," she said gently.

She reached into her shoulder bag. "Here, I'll get the next one." She called the barmaid. "Two large sherries," she said to the girl.

"And I never saw you drink so much, Rachel."

She turned to me, looking pleased with herself. "You could never accept that I loved Lindsay without any problems."

The girl came with the sherry. The evening clatter was rising all around us, the happiness of drinkers embarking on a whole hot summer of beer. Only one man seemed alone in the entire bar, a bad-tempered-looking fellow reading the sports page of the *Express* in the far corner.

"You put a good front on it," I said, above the din.

"What?" She leaned forward, undoing the last button on her cord jacket.

"Nothing, really, except that with a few large sherries everything looks better, especially the past. But remember, I've seen you weep your eyes out about your father."

"Yes." She smiled hugely. "That's what's so nice: you know everything—and you're still annoyed."

I did remember, but I just sat there listening to her now, for she had suddenly found her stride, a perfect mix of alcohol and natural enthusiasm which might not last. "You see," she flew on, "my problem isn't that I was stupidly in love with Lindsay. It's just that I've suddenly come to remember almost everything I ever did with him. I see it so clearly now, as if things we'd shared had happened just yesterday—like photographs you take out of an old drawer which become so intense you can step into them and pick up your life at that very point and start living it again. That's what I feel. Do you see? I can just step back into all this other life, whole chunks of it, absolutely real: like climbing that big copper beech one afternoon, the one by the back drive, and watching Lindsay come down the hall steps with the oars and go down to the lake through the rhododendrons. Well, I remembered that to start with—and next I knew I was following him down the path—and this was quite a new memory. I mean, I seemed to be doing it for the first time—I was standing by the boathouse, actually *looking* at him out on the lake rowing. I could *see* the ripples, as though I could just walk into the water to him, and the water lilies all out by the island—so it was summer and I must have been about ten. And he waved at me. He wasn't too far out, because I could see the leather patches on his jacket. And I wasn't dreaming. Well, it's eerie—that all this comes back to me as something I'm actually experiencing *now* and not then. Just as if everything that ever happened to me had lost all its natural sequence and my whole life had become a simultaneous experience, like people are supposed to feel when they're dying. So you see that's why I can't think Lindsay's gone. I can see him so completely, so *absolutely*."

"Do other people come back to you in this way—your mother, for example?"

"Or you?" Rachel put in brightly.

"Or me, yes."

"Yes, they do. Once I've found Lindsay again at some exact spot in the past I can usually place you all in relation to him: you and Billy and Henty, Anna and Sally in the kitchen, everyone."

"Him and you—then all of us?"

"Yes. For example, that afternoon when he was out in the boat rowing—well, he was fishing too. I could see a line coming out from the back, trailing over the green stern. But something was wrong—he rarely went out on his own, always took one of us. And how could he fish and row at the same time? And then I saw what it was. Of course—Aunt Susan was with him! It was she who was fishing from the back, trawling for pike. And then the whole thing made sense: there she was—rather long and thin and brown—do you remember? Those brown cardigans and skirts she always wore? And dark stockings, so that we called her the Tree. Anyway, there she was crouched in the back of the boat in that straw Panama of hers. You remember? You must."

"Yes. Aunt Susan—you mean Eleanor's elder sister? Is she still alive?"

"Yes. She lives in their old house outside Dunkeld. Remember, she used to look after us when the others were away in London for something? She's about seventy. Mummy sees her now and then. But she never much liked Lindsay: thought he'd neglected Eleanor that time he was in Yugoslavia with her before the war, and she killed herself."

I nodded. Rachel's tiredness had been washed away in these memories and she had the excitement about her now of someone—herself, indeed—halfway through a performance of some great piece of music.

"But if they didn't like each other, what were they doing in the boat together?" I asked.

"I don't know. That was strange. But they were certainly in the boat together."

"Did he ever talk to you about Eleanor?" We'd stopped drinking now, and our heads were closer together the better to hear each other above the chatter, both of us intent now on Rachel's past.

"He never *didn't* speak to me about her—when I asked."

"What—"

"Oh, kind of heartbreaking: how fond he'd been—which was his way of saying 'in love with.' And I asked him what had been wrong with her, and he said, simply, that she'd gone dotty."

"In those words?"

"Yes: 'dotty.'"

"And?"

"And what?" Rachel looked puzzled, and began fiddling with her scarf again. "Well, he said Eleanor had started to spy on him, thought he was having affairs, which of course was absolutely ridiculous. Anyway, she became intensely possessive, jealous apparently. To the point of dementia. That's what he said."

"The point of...?"

"Well, of rushing out under that tram in Zagreb."

"It's strange, given his background, that he should have taken up with someone so uncontrolled like that, isn't it?" I looked at Rachel for confirmation. But now, taking up her sherry again, she was totally at ease once more, anxious, it seemed, to minimize these unexpected contradictions in her father's personality.

"Oh, yes—but don't forget, they were both hardly more than twenty when they married. And his background may have been stable, but it was a bit ghastly as well—that domineering father of his, the wicked old general. He'd do anything to get away from him and out of the house, I can see that—especially with someone sympathetic, which Eleanor was by every account, to begin with: sympathetic, and intelligent, too."

"Yes. But if Eleanor was so intelligent—"

"Well, she just didn't like the diplomatic life, when it came to it. She was a countrywoman—like Mummy. Paris, Rome, Vienna—that wasn't her style at all."

"No. I suppose not."

"Anyway," Rachel continued with even more conviction, changing the precise topic. "First marriages, too young, are often rather rotten. I know with Klaus and me."

"Did he love you too much?" I asked with some mischief.

"No. He just decided I didn't know who I was—and was never likely to learn. A bit German of him. But that wasn't his fault. Conductors are interpreters—and Klaus kept annoying himself by thinking I wasn't playing myself properly, wasn't hitting the right notes in my psyche."

"So why did you start with Klaus then?"

She let out a small shout of joy. "I wanted what I hadn't *got,* of course. And saw it in him. And you must know what that is by now, don't you?"

"Do I?"

"Order, security, straightforwardness, literalness, seriousness..." Rachel tolled each word lugubriously. "All that mousy bag of tricks." She was excited now, staring at me, her lips open, intent on some invisible fascination that had risen up and was there in the air, suspended between us, held by our gaze at each other.

"Yes, but *why,* Rachel? No one's life could have been more secure or loving than yours as a child. How did you come by all this insecurity, this craving for order?"

"Well, I can't understand that either. It's as if my early life *hadn't* in fact been all loving and wonderful at all."

"I see." But I didn't.

We looked at each other intently, mystified by what might have been, by what might have happened years before.

We walked out into the evening sun a few minutes afterward, the bar too smoky and crowded now. But outside the rush hour had cleared and the streets were nearly empty, the tall office blocks, catching the late sun high up like white cliff tops, had all drained away—the people gone home or settled in the many pubs along the route we took, just wandering, with nothing particular in mind, toward Marylebone High Street.

And then, crossing over the main road here, we lost ourselves in a string of narrow lines and passageways beyond. Rachel was a little ahead of me on the narrow broken pavement, swinging her leather shoulder bag in her hand like a sling, head down, thinking of something. She turned back at the entrance to a short street that led to the parking lot. "What shall we do? Pick up the bikes at the Hall? Or have another drink?"

There was a pub, I saw, on the other side of the road, a little way up, between a row of garages and small offices: a workers' bar with peeling brown paint and smudged windows, a simple boozer hidden away behind the smart streets of Marylebone like an old cloth-cap relative in a posh wedding photograph.

Rachel had stopped now right in the middle of the narrow street, and just then a car had turned the corner and came up behind her, quite fast, and she'd had to move quickly out of the way. She stared after it malevolently as it disappeared up toward Marylebone Road, still swinging her bag as if about to throw it.

"That man was in the pub with us," she said.

"Which man?"

"The man in that car, next the driver."

"Well, his friend must have come and picked him up. Or do you think he's following us?" I added.

"You should know. You're the spy, aren't you?" Rachel walked up to me, cocked her head, slinging the bag over her shoulder. I shrugged.

"Well, that's the other problem, isn't it? Let's have a drink and talk about it."

The lounge bar was a long, tatty room done in the same brown paint, with several pinball machines and a bad girlie calendar on one wall; some of last year's Christmas decorations still hung above the bar. A man sat in a wheelchair at one end, drinking a pint, leaning his hunched back up toward the counter, feeding himself carefully with his twisted fingers. A boy, who seemed under age, sat on a bench next him, sipping Coke from a can. The crowd were in the public bar across the way from us, men in shirt-sleeves and overalls playing darts, shouting between the concentrated silences and then moving in and out of the shafts of smoky sunlight.

"Just the place for a suspicious assignation," Rachel said, gazing at a half-nude girl fingering her boobs, as a man came up to us, wiping his hands on a bar rag. We had beer this time. The sherry had gone to my head, though Rachel showed no effects of it at all.

"You are a fool for a spy," she said when the man had gone. "That man in the car—that's the third time I've seen him today. He was following us this morning, in the same car, when we left Hyde Park Square."

"Well?" She was possibly right, I thought, remembering Marcus's warnings. He was probably keeping an eye on me. I wasn't very surprised. And I felt irresponsible just then, uncaring almost, with the heat and the sherry.

"Well—is it me, or you they're following?" Rachel repeated herself very precisely. The boy said something to the cripple at the end of the counter, about football. The barman joined them, and they started to argue. For some reason I couldn't stop listening to them, following obsessively their conflicting post-mortems.

"What?" I said.

"*Who* are they following?" Rachel said again.

"I don't know who the hell is following us, or which of us," I said abruptly. "Maybe they're keeping an eye on you, as his daughter. Or maybe me, because I worked for them once. Or maybe you're quite wrong and it's no one following anyone."

"I'm as tired as you are—of policemen." Rachel read my thoughts. "But—"

"Fine. I told Madeleine I'd help. I'll come up with you next week to Glenalyth. Start from there, from the beginning, lay out all the evidence, clues, papers, dates: a master plan. Then we'll see what turns up."

"The *beginning?*"

"It's there, isn't it? It must be—somewhere in his past, the things he did, the friends he knew, it's somewhere there." I felt angry then—angry at some long blindness I thought I detected in the two women that had finally allowed Lindsay to slip through their fingers. "For example, you thought it was perfectly natural for Lindsay to have married Eleanor. But I'm not so sure."

Rachel put her glass down and now she did look for a moment as if the drink had suddenly affected her.

"And then again, and more important maybe—*why* did Lindsay join British Intelligence in the first place? Wasn't like him at all, not the man I remember—lurking round back alleys and so on. He was just the opposite. So why?"

"He was—patriotic," Rachel said after a moment.

"Yes, exactly. Very upright and public-spirited. Very open. That's why it doesn't add up."

"I don't see—"

"You don't see the contradictions?"

"No, really. Not at all."

"Well, I do. And that's where I'd start looking for him: in his contradictions."

I could see that Rachel neither liked nor understood this line. But I pursued it.

"Well, he joined Intelligence because a close friend of his at Oxford did, in the early thirties. That's what I always heard. It was perfectly straightforward."

"A friend?"

"Yes. He's a don there still, I think. At Merton, Daddy's old college. John Wellcome—that's his name. He used to come and see us sometimes in London."

"He's left Intelligence then?"

"He must have, I suppose."

"That's exactly the sort of person I'd like to see."

"He'll hardly talk. It's all Official Secrets, isn't it?"

"Maybe. But I don't think there'd be anything wrong with getting your mother to speak to him. I'm trying to find out what happened to Lindsay, after all, not subvert the government."

Rachel didn't look too happy about this. I said, "Don't you want him found, if he is to be found?"

"Of course." But she was halfhearted somehow. "If you talk to John Wellcome, why not all the others? All the other people he's had to do with over the years?"

"Who, for example?"

"Oh, I don't know exactly. But there's MacAulay who was his CO during the war, in Argyll and Sutherland—"

"Not the whisky MacAulays?"

"Yes—in the big house, the Hall. They used to have juvenile dances."

"I remember. The wife always on the bottle. I didn't know he was Lindsay's CO though."

"And there's Parker. Willis Parker, a very old friend—went through the FO with Daddy before the war. He's in Brussels now. With the British delegation to the EEC. And there must be dozens of others. But what can they say?"

"We could find out," I said.

Later, when it got dark and we'd walked back toward Wigmore Street to collect our bikes, we ended up in a third bar, just off Marylebone High Street, an old-fashioned local this time, with gas lamps all gone electric, but with real aspidistras in the window. A few uncertain men from the service apartments nearby were listening to a fair-haired sailor boy playing an upright piano, glancing at him covertly.

"Hadn't we better eat?" I'd said.

"No. Later. I *like* this."

Her face was flushed now. She took off her loose cord jacket and stood there listening to the smooth piano for a minute, breathing deeply, embarking on some private performance of her own, as though she had joined an orchestra late and had just at that moment taken up her instrument but was already perfectly in tune with the others. She was fascinated, involved, like someone released from a long confinement or dull toil into a miraculous life. The sailor boy changed tempo—sliding into "Stranger in Paradise," I think, playing in a cocktail-hour manner, trilling expertly, syncopating the notes. It was all rather unreal—but we'd had seven drinks and it sounded fine.

"You see!" Rachel turned to me vehemently. "This is what I want." Her eyes were glassy—either with emotion or drink, I couldn't say which. "For years and years I was up on a pedestal being prim and musical—but never *this* music, *this* life!"

She looked round at the wan old bachelors, someone laughed raucously on the other side of the room, a fair-haired colonial rough, brandishing his arms, hammering some bad joke into the witless eyes of two young women next to him.

"This?" I asked. "Is *this* the life?"

"Yes."

I got the drinks. Rachel looked much younger now; the color in her cheeks and the unaccustomed alcohol had brought out a great vivacity in her—not a flirtatious thing, but a talent she had not known she possessed and which she played with then as with some glittering new toy.

"Didn't you do plenty of this with George?" I asked. "The 'hail-fellow-well met' stuff? I'd have thought that was very much his style: 'Knees up, Mother Brown' and six pints of bitter."

"Yes. We used to. Before he fell in love with me." Rachel

spoke as if of some great life before a tragic death. "After that, all he wanted to do was take me to Glyndebourne."

"I don't—"

"You won't fall in love with me again, will you?"

"No more cakes and ale?"

"Oh, that. Well, that's all right, isn't it? But love is like having a puncture. You suddenly can't go anywhere. You're stopped."

What she meant, I thought then, was that, deprived of the real object of her love, she would now preserve that emotion carefully, against her father's return. Rachel was a classic case of someone who must lie to maintain any foothold in dull reality; in love she was a conquistador who could only feel that emotion in face of an unattainable El Dorado.

"How shall we manage, then?" I asked lightly. "Less then lovers, more than friends?"

"Any way at all," she said. "As long as we're not what we were before. Anything, *anything* else," she went on earnestly, frowning now, looking at me in a way that years before I would have called passionate, yet which now was supposed to deny all such feelings.

So we stood there, getting quietly squiffy, melting into the warm room, "Begin the Beguine" dripping from the piano. A feeling of sweet carelessness had crept up on me all unawares—that cloudless confidence in the presence of a woman that seems to make going to bed with her only a matter of time. And then I thought—yes, even that she might offer, sirenlike, to deflect us from our purpose.

So I said, "What if I find myself wanting to sleep with you?"

She laughed and looked at me as though I was a dunderhead.

"'Found wanting' indeed! I should hope—"

And then, before she could properly reply, the velvet drapes across the door began to dance and shiver like a nursery ghost and George blundered into the bar, untimely to the dot, the water diviner in luck once more; the keen traveler, who would find Rachel over half the world, had made nothing of flushing her out of all the pubs in Marylebone.

"My God, my God, why hast thou forsaken us," Rachel said to him at once, mocking him, quite merry, offering him her beer glass.

George really played the role of jealous lover too close to

the bone that evening, so that the performance lacked objective style. It was full of ungoverned feeling, forceful yet painful, like a stage-struck amateur attempting Othello in a village hall.

"So here you are," he said shortly, without looking at me. He dried then, rooted to the spot, swaying slightly, out of breath, without managing another word. He'd forgotten his lines. I offered him a drink to fill the pause, turning back toward the bar and calling the barmaid, inserting some neat, impromptu stage business so that he might collect himself.

"We thought you were coming back for dinner," I heard him say at last to Rachel—not bluntly aggrieved but in the tones of a sad ringmaster who had inexplicably lost a valuable animal.

"Oh, do *relax*, George," she told him. "We were just talking about Lindsay."

I got George a pint of ale, a generous pint, and I thought how strange it was that this gregarious schoolboy of a man should so isolate himself in the toils of an operatically hopeless love, an illness without relief: prostrating himself at her feet, as at some Holy Grail, pleading for chamber music in the Shires and trips to view Chartres Cathedral on long weekends—with a half-crazed wife in the background, loneliness bleeding out of her like a wound.

It all seemed an unpleasant business then, naïve and cruel, something only a schoolboy could have contrived in his relationships. Or had it been Rachel's fault initially in leading him on, as she had once done with me before throwing me over, repeating the trick afterward with the German conductor? Rachel, who would punish every man for not being her father. That was as likely, I thought—and so much the more reason for her disbelief in love now that her father had gone, for I supposed she loved others only in Lindsay's presence, as it were, as a way of wounding and taking revenge on her father, and without him found no pleasure in the exercise.

"Yes—*Lindsay*," she repeated. "Trying to find him..."

I heard George grunt in annoyance. "Him again." I think George was coming to see Lindsay, as I did, as his real rival— a far greater shadow over his love than even I could cast.

Then suddenly, handing George his beer, I wanted to throw it at him. The whole business was ridiculous. I longed to turn on this big, willing bearlike man and clobber him for his abject, fruitless loving. But George preempted my anger, reversed it, by attacking me.

"How," he asked sarcastically, "do you expect to find Lindsay—if no one else has?"

I'm sure George saw my interest in Lindsay as nothing more than an excuse—a convenient and direct access to Rachel that I'd discovered, and that I would now patrol to his exclusion.

"Well," I said, "I thought I should try—"

"Peter did know him, after all," Rachel put in.

"So did I. But does that help?" George was sweating, his glasses clouded, so that he had to look over the gold rims at me.

"A long time ago, though." Rachel was trying to help me again. "There might be something in the past—"

"Oh, come on, Rachel—someone kidnapped him or bumped him off."

"Well, *who* then?" She turned on George. "I want to know—*who?*"

"All right, I don't know. But I can't see how Peter's going to be any more help."

"Well, he did work once in the same organization—British Intelligence," Rachel said carefully. "That might help."

This information came like an ace against George's meager hand. "Did you?" he asked me. And I nodded, feeling the cruelty of it all once more. One can summon limitless pity for the unloved in such circumstances and I tried to soften the blow. "Not that my work had anything to do with his," I said. "I was very junior."

But George would not be placated. I think he had suddenly decided just then that finding Lindsay was the key which would release Rachel to him once more. Like the two women, he believed in victory through love, against all odds. And although I knew that in Lindsay's world there were no such victories, and no room at all for such naïvely generous inquiries, his next words touched me all the same.

"Well, it may not be too difficult," he said with a sudden, kind authority.

"What?"

"Finding out what happened to Lindsay." George drank then, deeply, like a knight before battle.

"How?" Rachel asked.

"I've a friend in Intelligence here—I didn't tell you. I didn't think—"

"Who?"

"Fellow called Basil Fielding. Quite high up now, I think. I was in college with him after the war, knew him well then. I could ask him about it."

I looked at George as at someone who had just performed an astonishing trick—as indeed he had.

"Oh," was all I could say. It was my turn to forget my lines.

10

By the time I got back home to Oxfordshire the following afternoon I realized there was nothing to be done about George's unexpected friendship with Basil. In the pub, the night before, I'd not even bothered to advise him against renewing it. If he did this, Basil presumably—since he wished to maintain such secrecy in the whole matter—would not mention my involvement with him and would simply stall with George, play the great bear along.

In the end, as I drove home from the station, I was left only with a feeling of discomfort about the two of them in my mind—an additional mystery in a business already confused. These two together didn't fit into any plot that I could conceive. They were extra luggage, awkward, unwanted, characters who, denied a proper part in the proceedings might start to write their own dangerous lines.

I had a bath when I got in—and at last some fresh clothes, and then I poured a large sherry, Garvey's San Patricio. I still had a few bottles left of it, kept for special occasions or emergencies. It was six o'clock, my old rural cocktail hour, and I was happy to be alone again, leaning once more on the deep windowsill looking out on the side of the church where

133

the dying sun fell on it, and beyond that the empty evening hills, rolling away to the west beyond the village.

If the phone hadn't rung just then, I would have dug out my unfinished Egyptian typescript or got ready for a walk. It was Madeleine, from London, telling me she had finally managed to contact John Wellcome and that I should call him at his home outside Oxford for an appointment to see him. She gave me his number.

"You will be coming up with us next week, won't you?" she said as an afterthought before putting the phone down— and I remember looking at the weathercock on top of the old tithe barn down the road just then, and seeing it swing suddenly. I delayed a moment before saying, "Yes, I'll be coming."

But she noticed the pause in my voice and taking it for a doubt said, with just a touch of pique: "You don't have to, of course. You know that."

"No, no. I really want to. I was just looking at the weathercock on a barn opposite the cottage here. It suddenly changed direction."

"Well, why shouldn't it?"

"There isn't any wind, that's why. Or there wasn't when I came in."

We said good-bye and then I opened the window and put my head out into the warm evening—and there wasn't any wind, none at all, not a murmur. But the weathercock had definitely swung round by about 180 degrees.

It was nerves, I suppose; the tensions of the last three days. But it suddenly struck me that Marcus, with the connivance of the mad old major at the Manor, had put someone to watch over me in the tithe barn. An irrational thought, but it was enough to make me decide to call John Wellcome from outside my cottage, since if they had decided on such physical surveillance they would certainly have put a tap on my phone as well.

So I left the cottage and was halfway down the village street to the call box by the post office when I had the further thought: if they'd gone to the trouble of tapping my own private phone, they would surely have done the same with the village call box. I knew I was losing my head then, and I went back home and made the call from there—scowling forcefully all the same up at the arrow-slit windows of the barn as I passed it.

John Wellcome's voice was very unlike his name—excessively cold and businesslike. Without enthusiasm he told me he'd be watching cricket at the Oxford Parks the following day—the University Eleven against Surrey—and I could meet him on the far side of the ground, opposite the pavilion, by the scoreboard, at one o'clock the next day.

"I'm sure I can't help you," he added. "But of course, since Madeleine has asked me, I'll do what I can."

"I'm sure I can't help you." How often they say that, I thought, especially the ones who can.

JOHN Wellcome sat watching the cricket in a deck chair by the sight screen as I walked round the boundary line toward him. He was a minute fellow, his round tweed hat pulled down over his head like a pastry casing, wearing a jacket in the same rough greenish material, though the day was hot again, a hard blue sky running away over the playing fields to where the city murmured beyond the chestnut trees on the Parks Road. A girl sat next to him, his daughter I supposed, a thin, barefoot girl in a long, shapeless Indian print skirt, unkempt sun-bleached hair. A baby crawled in front of them, almost naked, gurgling and eating bits of grass as it made its way out toward the middle of the field.

"Do take him off, Caroline. He'll get hurt."

Wellcome spoke with pedantic care as I came up behind them and the girl called the child like a dog. "Here, Bonzo, come back, come on. Back, back!" She had an American accent—a pretty face, but worn, with hollow cheeks and the slightly bluish skin of an old woman. The *Guardian* book page lay open beneath her chair and the baby's feeding bottle had been discarded on top of it, along with some soiled paper diapers.

"Don't get up, please," I said, introducing myself. They didn't.

"Ah, Mr. Marlow. Here already?" the man said rather glumly, and I felt like a dull student with a duller essay arriving for my weekly tutorial. "My wife, Caroline." He gestured sharply toward the girl like a conductor bringing in a distant and unimportant instrument, and she looked up, gazing right through me with her tired eyes for an instant.

"Hi," she said before turning back to deal with her son, who had now crawled quite far out into the field.

"Goddamnit—that child." She got up and dragged him back over the boundary. The child started to cry and then, seeing me and believing I must be the cause of its restraint, it howled ever louder.

"I'm sorry to disturb you like this." There was nowhere for me to sit and I stood above them uncertainly, the child bellowing so loudly now that one of the umpires turned toward us in distant surprise.

"You'll have to take him away, Caroline." Wellcome spoke like a judge passing a death sentence. His wife got up and left us, carrying the protesting baby. But she chose a path right across the front of the sight screen, halfway through the bowler's run, so that the batsman at the far end held his arm up and the game came to a halt. The umpire turned again and now he gestured at us angrily.

"I *did* tell you, Caroline, *not* to do that when the bowler is running up. They can't see the ball if you do," Wellcome said.

"They must be blind then. I don't play this game, you know." She left us, flapping away in her Indian skirt, the child perched like a water jug on her shoulder, and I took her seat next the coldly irascible don.

"Well now—" Wellcome paused, taking up a pair of binoculars from his lap and looking out over the game, which had restarted. The batsman played and missed a ball. "There! That's Edrich all over—dabbing outside the off stump again. Lost him his England place."

"Did it? I'm not really very much in touch..."

Wellcome nodded without taking his eyes off the game. "So, you used to be with the old firm," he said.

"Well, nothing serious. I was in Information & Library—the old Mideast section. In Holborn."

"Oh yes. The Wogs and the Wops." Wellcome had small, rather piggy blue eyes and he shaded them now against the sun.

"Italians? I don't remember..."

"All from the same neck of the woods." He took out a packet of cheap cigars and lit one. "You don't smoke, do you?" he said, putting them away almost at once. "Oh, now this is interesting." He studied the game intently once more. There was a change of bowling. "Thought they'd bring him back for a spell before lunch. This is Ambler—our new opener: very fast."

The smoke from his cigar trailed back into my eyes, making them smart; the student called Ambler made a slow and thoughtful progress back to his mark quite near the boundary.

"He takes an awful long run," I said.

"Yes. But he's very pacey."

And so he was, so far as I could judge from his run, arms flailing round at a clamorous rate as he came into the crease before whipping the ball down—a bouncer that rose sharply over Edrich's head so that he nearly ducked into it.

"About Lindsay," I ventured again. "I wondered what you thought."

Wellcome didn't reply for a long moment, not until Ambler had turned and started his run again. "Absolute tragedy, that's what I think."

"You knew him well, didn't you? Here at Oxford? You joined the service together, I understand?" I decided not to waste any more time. But Wellcome was not so inclined.

"No. We didn't." There was silence again.

"Rachel, his daughter—"

"Oh, yes—I know her," Wellcome said at once, glad to suggest his willing cooperation over something, at least, in our conversation.

"She thought it was because of you that Lindsay joined Intelligence in the first place."

"Did she indeed. I wonder what gave her that idea?"

"No?" We had to wait for another ball before he said anything more.

"No, certainly not. That wasn't so." Wellcome twirled and pinched the dying cigar in his fingers. "I was already in the service—or about to be, rather."

"Yes—that's what she meant, I think—that he took after you."

Wellcome looked distressed suddenly. "'Took after' me?" he said.

"Well, you were older than him."

Wellcome shrugged his shoulders. "Yes. But not by much. I was in my last year at college when I met him, end of thirty-one, I think; he'd just come up. Or was it his second year? I forget. Yes, it may have been. I came back to college, you know—got a fellowship. I saw more of him then, I think."

"You didn't stay in Intelligence after you left college?"

Wellcome had picked up his field glasses and was looking at the game closely again. But I had the feeling he was listening to me carefully at last.

"No, I got a fellowship; I told you. I didn't take up Intelligence work again until the war started and I went to London. Worked with Dick Crossman in that black propaganda department. I didn't see Lindsay again until after the war, when he was back from the army, and I was back here in college. So I don't know where Rachel got the idea that Lindsay 'took after' me. Lindsay joined up entirely on his own, as far as I know."

"You mean, he was recruited by someone down here? Surely one doesn't just apply for a job like that?"

"Oh, I don't know." Wellcome was abrupt. "I've no idea—"

"But there must have been someone who approached—"

"You know I really can't go into all that. I simply can't: there's no thirty-year release clause as regards my Intelligence work, I'm afraid. It's still entirely confidential. I thought in any case you wanted my opinion about what had *happened* to Lindsay, not how he got into the job."

"Yes," I said. "Of course. But I think the two things may well be connected."

The players were coming off the field now, for the lunch interval. Wellcome stood up, wiping his brow with an old red hankie. I looked at him. He seemed flustered suddenly, as if he'd just undergone some sudden exertion, instead of being parked quietly on a deck chair for the last two hours. We started to walk round the boundary line toward the pavilion.

"How do you mean—the two things 'connected'?" Wellcome asked, with grudging interest now.

"Someone at that time must have specially encouraged Lindsay to join Intelligence. He wasn't the sort, was he? Very formal, open kind of person, very direct. Not cloak-and-dagger at all."

"Well, someone may have. But it wasn't me."

"Could he have been forced into it in some way?"

"Do you mean blackmailed? Never."

"No. I meant against his better judgment. You see, it doesn't add up to me—either his disappearance or his joining in the first place. Both seem quite unlike him."

We could see Caroline now, over by the tennis courts, watching two young men play, smashing the ball about with vigorous acrobatics. A shade of anxiety crossed Wellcome's face. He had lost touch with me again.

"You see, if I could find out how—and why—he joined

intelligence, I think I might get a line, at least, on *why* he disappeared."

But Wellcome appeared absorbed in his young wife now. The child, Bonzo, was scrabbling round the wire fence, rattling it, undoubtedly putting the players off their game.

"She really shouldn't..." I heard him mutter; his helpless, pained expression seemed a visible payment just then for this unlikely marriage of his. "I think Lindsay was recruited in a perfectly ordinary way," he said at last. "His disappearance, I grant you, remains a mystery. But you know, HQ must know why—and how—he joined them. All in the files. They must have gone into all that already."

"They won't tell me."

"Don't you trust them?"

"No."

"Well, I don't suppose you'll find out on your own—and I can't help you." Wellcome was almost sarcastic now. "It was all a long time ago, wasn't it? It's my view that he joined out of perfectly ordinary, patriotic reasons—because someone came down from London and asked him to, that's all. Why should there be any mystery about it? And as for his disappearance, well, he's not the first in that line of business, is he?"

"No, that's what struck me, of course. Do you think he was a double, that's he's gone back to Moscow?"

"Certainly not. Though I think it possible they may have killed him."

"And the body?"

"Dumped it in that loch of his, at Glenalyth."

"Were you ever up there?"

Wellcome smiled for the first time, as if he had at last got the whole business in hand. "No, no, I wasn't. You know, you make me out to be a much closer friend of Lindsay's than I was. We were colleagues for a short while, after the war, and shared the same staircase in Merton once, that's really all."

"Oh yes? Which staircase was that?" I asked with innocent interest. Wellcome had stalled with me ever since we'd met and I thought I'd try some shock tactics before he dismissed me. The child had seen his father, in any case, and seeing me as well had started to cry again. I didn't have long. But Wellcome halted in his walk, alert once more. "Oh—were you at Merton?"

"No. But I just thought that I might go round there now.

139

Maybe there's someone still there who remembers Lindsay, an old porter perhaps, or one of the college scouts. You see, if I could get some real impression of Lindsay in Oxford, that would help..."

I looked at Wellcome pointedly. He was blinking up at me, his small blue eyes startled in the sunlight. Then he laughed, an abrupt, grating laugh like a bad actor experimenting with a part. "I don't follow. It's forty-five-years ago. The scouts will all be dead. There won't be anyone there. Complete waste of time."

"It's worth a try. You see, someone, forty-five-years ago—someone from London you suggest—must have come down one day, by train probably, and talked to Lindsay, recruited him. Now, if I could find—"

"But that's nonsense—"

"Is it? You said that's how it must have happened, that it wasn't anyone in Oxford."

"Yes, but you don't really expect anyone to remember that, do you, even if they were alive?"

"No, possibly not. All the same..." I paused, thinking out the next step in my role. "Perhaps they had a drink in the Mitre," I went on enthusiastically. "Or the Eastgate. Or met at the Randolph for tea. I might go there and ask. Where would you meet a student in Oxford, if you wanted to recruit him for Intelligence, in the early thirties? They must have met somewhere."

"I find that an unbelievable approach. You must be out of your mind." Wellcome was worried now. I'd hit bottom at last and stumbled on something, I'd no idea what. But I felt Wellcome knew.

"It's just intuition," I said. "It's all I have to go on."

Wellcome looked at me with pitying animosity. "I shouldn't interfere, if I were you," he said. "Not like that."

"Why not? Isn't intuition—in Lindsay's world, and yours—often vital? The theories about English literature you profess—you can't actually prove them, can you? Or are you a Leavisite?"

I thought Wellcome was going to slap my face. Instead he looked at me in amazed horror for a moment before hurrying over to his wife, where he picked up the squealing Bonzo. Caroline trailed after them, casting backward glances at the gallant tennis players.

Was it a second marriage? I wondered. If so, it seemed

unlikely to turn out any better than his first. Wellcome was a liar—through omission, where the greatest untruths bloom. No marriage would survive that. Yet it seemed that Lindsay's had, or had he simply been more skillful than Wellcome in his evasions—perhaps because he had much more to hide?

11

I said, "There's something phony about Wellcome, that's all. I thought he was a close friend of Lindsay's, but he spent most of his time with me denying it."

Rachel stood in the big first-floor drawing room in Hyde Park Square, riffling through piles of old sheet music kept in the window seat there.

"Can't find the damn thing. Must be here: Telemann, Telemann, wherefore are thou?" She started to go through the dusty music once more.

Madeleine had gone up to Glenalyth by air the previous day; she couldn't stand British Rail. George and Max had already left too, traveling to Liverpool by car to see some new musical there prior to its London opening, before joining us at Glenalyth the next day, and Rachel and I were alone in the empty house, a huge white ship becalmed in the dazzling afternoon streets of Paddington.

"I'll have to buy another copy, that's all." Rachel let a pile of music fall with a thump on the floor, the dust rising up in sunlit motes.

"You don't mind going by train?" she said, still preoccupied.

"No." I stood up. "I was talking about Wellcome. He was hiding something."

"I'm not surprised. I told you you'd get nothing, rummaging through all Lindsay's old colleagues like that. Most of them are awful bores. MacAulay and Willis Parker for example: absolute stiffs."

Rachel seemed pleased by my lack of success in these inquiries.

"What *am* I going to do? With George and Max round the piano, with a toot and a flute for a whole week?"

"Yes. What *are* you doing? I wondered..."

"'Nearer, my God, to Thee,' I think. George likes the idea of having me under his eye for a while."

"It's unpleasant—"

"Oh, don't worry! Marianne, George's wife, is coming, and Max's wife, June. For the weekend. A real little house party. And you."

Rachel looked at me pleasantly and then, walking over from the window, put her hand on my shoulder for a second. But her eyes still roamed the room distractedly.

"I don't fancy playing the man between."

"George might bonk you one, you mean? Yes, he's a big fellow."

"Has he spoken to his old friend in British Intelligence yet? Fielding, wasn't it?"

Rachel had gone over to the mantelpiece and was tinkering with the silver music boxes there.

"Yes. He has, he says. He'll tell you all about it."

"What did he tell you?"

"The man was surprised to hear from him."

I thought again what a liar Basil was. Or had he genuinely forgotten George and their college days? But who could forget George? At college he was probably even more memorable, creating juvenile alarms at the debating society and frothing at the lips afterward in the local boozer. I wondered when anyone would ever start telling me the truth.

Rachel said, "George is just a Saint George. He believes in miracles. As if this old friend of his could help—he's probably never heard of Lindsay. But everyone wants to help, don't they? Especially George."

"Don't you want the help?"

"Lindsay will turn up—somewhere, sometime. I wonder if any of us can do much about it meanwhile."

She lifted the lid on one of the music boxes and a delicate tune emerged, a Viennese polka that spread through the warm air of the room, someone else's sweet memory invading the silence. I had never heard the tune before.

"All these music boxes were Eleanor's, you know. Daddy bought them for her before the war—there was a man in Zagreb who had a whole collection. Do you remember them?"

"No. They must have been kept down here. Not at Glenalyth."

Rachel nodded. "That's why Aunt Susan didn't get them. She took almost everything else of Eleanor's; she's got a sort of shrine of her things at Dunkeld."

"I never went to her house. We never did, I think."

"I hope we never have to—she's a vicious old party. I never really liked her: one of those 'not to' people when we were children. Full of revenge. I should have been Eleanor's child—and Patrick, her own nephew, was dead."

"Why did Lindsay ever have her at Glenalyth, then?"

"To be kind, that's all. Kind to everyone."

Rachel closed the music box decisively, killing all the past, the tune stopping halfway through a phrase.

"Come on—are you packed?"

"Yes."

"Country clothes? You can borrow Lindsay's gumboots."

"Hardly need them in this weather."

I looked out on the bright square. The grass was already browning slightly, even though the summer wasn't half over.

Rachel was wearing a white, tightly pleated cotton dress, and now she twirled round in it, the material opening like a fan for an instant, displaying a lacy petticoat beneath.

"You're worried. Why?" She looked down at me before starting to look through her shoulder bag. "Now—tickets, checkbook, pills, sunglasses, latchkey. All we need is the Telemann sonata and some food. There's no food on this night train, can you imagine? We'll have to buy some."

"What do I owe for the tickets?"

"Don't worry. I'm keeping a note. It's quite cheap anyway. I had to take a double sleeper, second class, you don't mind? The first-class ones were all full."

"No." I laughed. "But why—?"

Rachel stopped rummaging through her bag. "Why what?"

"I just wondered—going by the night train, that's all."

"Is that strange? I don't like airplanes—you know that."

"I'd forgotten. Of course, Lindsay always had a thing about trains and railways...all those toys in the attic at Glenalyth—lots of rails and great black clockwork engines."

"Don't start all that again."

"But it's true, isn't it? *You* like trains as well."

"What's wrong with that?" She smoothed the already very smooth pleats in her skirt.

Rachel was making this journey with me in memory of better times, I thought—of other travels with her father along this same route from London to Perth, secure in a first-class corner seat with him, flying past the ugly Midland towns, the dark railway sidings and slag heaps, clattering over the points, northward to the clean blue lakes and moors, even closer to that meeting with Henty in the big green Wolseley and the sudden magic of the highlands—the bright morning after the long sweet night. And now I was to play the same role for her. I thought how successfully Rachel had gratified herself, an ignoble envy rising in me again for her ability to discover and live in so many secret, self-sufficient worlds within herself, where time—and people too—could be changed about, shuffled and relived at will. I have rarely done better than to move rather slowly forward in my life.

"No—there's nothing wrong with going on trains," I said, with sudden enthusiasm. "It'll be great fun."

We picked up the Telemann sonata at Musica Rara in Great Marlborough Street, and the evening's goodies were packed into a big shopping bag for us at Robert Jackson's in Piccadilly. I chose a dry Aligote to go with the chef's terrine and the cold roast halves of wild duck. Rachel said there should be a good Beaujolais to follow with the slices of rare spiced silverside and the Normandy goat's cheese: she chose a Fleurie and then added a bottle of fresh orange juice for the next morning...

THE big electric engine throbbed quietly away at the end of a long line of blue-and-white coaches, a louder sonorous echo rising up into the stuffy night air. Though there was ten minutes to go before the train left, the platform was filled with an impatient bustle of passengers pushing and shoving all along its length. Rachel had hired a porter. "You could have taken one of those trolleys," I said. She didn't hear me.

With a face divorced from reality and too many magazines tucked under an arm, she had already started on her journey, her pace quickening unconsciously, drawn irrevocably into all the nervous magic of departure—checking her watch, her tickets, looking up at the coaches, searching out our number with the bright eye of a gambler at a fixed wheel who alone knows he must win.

"Here it is!" she called, like a lookout on a whaler, and we climbed up into a sleeper near the front of the train with only a parcel van between us and the engine.

I tipped the porter when he'd settled our bags and thought the compartment seemed rather small for two people—and then, right behind us, the sleeping-car attendant poked his nose through the door, a small pixie of a man with a very shiny bandleader's hair style, parted straight down the middle, an almost cheeky fellow with some deep Northern accent.

"Yoo tweo travelin' together?" He looked doubtfully at his booking sheet. "Mr. Marlow. Miss Phillips?"

I nodded. He remained doubtful. It was so long since I'd gone through any of this—years before in a hotel in Paris with Rachel, where they had never given a damn about such unlicensed relationships. But here, for a moment, I thought the man was about to separate us, invoking some old Northern Railway bylaw or Presbyterian canonical. I put my hand in my inside pocket, thinking to tip him at once, before I noticed Rachel's amused expression of patrician disdain. "My good man . . ." I fully expected her to say. But all that emerged from her firm lips was "Yes, we are together."

But then the attendant, still, I suppose, thinking me an interloper and smelling money somewhere, gave the game away.

"I cuid get you a sleeper in first class, madam—if ye wished. There's several available."

"No," Rachel said. "This will do. Thank you."

"Shall I make up the beds now then?" the bandleader asked.

"Later. We intend to dine first." She pointed to the Robert Jackson's bag on the seat. The Beaujolais bottle had slipped out, its dark neck thrusting along the couchette. The man noticed it.

"Will ye want a corkscrew?" he asked, without the slightest change in his dour expression.

"We have one, I think, thank you." Rachel looked at me and I nodded; the train gave a lurch and we were off.

"Well, call me if you need anything," the attendant said,

looking at me with a change in his eye now—either of envy or amusement, I couldn't say.

Rachel had kissed me firmly before the train had properly got out of the station. "Childish train fantasies indeed—and George," she said. "It never crossed your mind, did it? That it simply might be for you—traveling like this, just you."

It was almost too warm in the narrow compartment; Rachel at once took off her soiled cotton dress, keeping on just the lacy petticoat beneath. Then she picked up the Aligote.

"It won't be very nice," I said. "Not chilled at all."

"It'll do," Rachel said. "It'll do."

ONE doesn't expect love these days on night expresses—even in first-class sleepers—and I would have been surprised in any case by Rachel's sudden sweet affections.

I said later, "There were other more comfortable occasions—your flat upstairs in Hyde Park Square, or you could have come down to the cottage."

We were fingering our way through the first courses, the terrine and then the wild duck, licking our thumbs over the paper plates, sitting opposite each other in the corners of the bottom couchette, she with her feet up on it, a big hankie spread out over her petticoat. The train's movement had become firmer and faster some time before. And now, reaching its cruising speed, it settled into its long night's run with an immutable constancy—a huge metal necklace being dragged across the earth, which nothing now could ever impede and whose passengers, equally without appeal, shared the same sense of the inevitable.

"Why? Why not before?"

"Because we couldn't have got to Perth at the same time—that's why."

Rachel fluffed her dark curls and the smile was barely there, hiding nervously behind her too-straight nose. She started to eat the duck then, pulling a leg apart with her fingers, and her hands seemed to tremble. A Victorian miss in a frilly nightie, waiting for a story. Her other intents—whatever other adult schemes she nurtured just then—seemed far out of place with her present juvenile manner and dress.

She crunched into the leg of duck and then lifted the bottle

147

of Aligote and took a long swig. She handed the bottle across to me, wiping her lips with her bare arm.

"You used to be so meticulous," I said.

"About what?"

"About everything: wines, beds, napkins, life."

"I hated that ruined dump in Notting Hill—if that's what you mean. You always thought it was 'running home to Daddy' when I left. It was just I couldn't face the scum on the bath any more. Anyway, wouldn't it be awful if we all stayed the same? You just can't accept good fortune."

"Whose?"

"Ours." She took the wine back from me and drank once more. "I didn't tell you, but when I saw you at the flower show that morning, *you* were a new person, someone I wanted to be with."

"Why?"

"You'd finally stopped worrying about me."

"No risks with me, you mean, now, no broken hearts?" Just a jolly romp on a night express, I felt like adding, but didn't.

"I didn't say that."

Rachel, though she'd drunk about a third of the wine, was still nervous, holding back, like someone afraid of his good fortune. "We'd stopped fighting at last," she went on. "You can suddenly want someone then."

"I fought in the old days because I was worried about you."

"Exactly—a lot of people call that love. Shall we try the beef? The Fleurie must be getting cooked, too."

I picked up the bottle; I'd opened it earlier and put it next the hot vent on the floor. It had a faint yet rich flower smell, like old roses at the end of summer. It struck me that with a bit of steady drinking she and I need never really get to grips at all that night. And in truth I didn't feel I could touch her just then, since Rachel, for all her confident words, had the air of a child prostitute—falsely confident, nervous, even terrified.

I sat back, determined to relax. If I wasn't going to fight any more, I needn't worry about sex—or love for that matter, either, for the two had always gone together before with her, and I couldn't separate them now, even though that was apparently what she expected me to do. She would be disappointed perhaps, but the various vineyards should dull the pain, I thought.

"Try the Fleurie," I said. "It's perfect."

"I know what you're thinking." She took the bottle, balancing it in one hand, stroking it absent-mindedly with the other. "Enough of this. It wouldn't matter what we both felt or thought—your fighting and my wanting: neither problem would arise."

"I'm still something of a puritan."

"Yes."

"What did you expect? I've not changed as much as you. I wish I could."

She drank some of the wine now, upending it on her chin, Carmen-fashion. "Yes. Just as serious as ever, counting out your thoughts like an old Jewish moneylender and wondering how many you can afford to spare the next client. Most people would give their eyeteeth—" She bit into a slice of the silverside. "You're unreasonable," she went on, her mouth full.

"I loved you. That doesn't seem unreasonable. Even though it meant fighting. This is just going through the motions."

"'The more we are together, the happier we will be.'" She looked up at the ceiling, hopelessly. "Well, we're fighting all right now—good oh! You've had me in your way. Thanks."

"Yes," I said. "I love you—in that way."

"Yes—I know that."

"Let's try the goat," I said lightly, trying to ease the situation. And the goat, too, was good—a long barrel of cheese in waxed paper, just crisp on the outside, but chalky soft, with a faint tartness running into the center.

We ate in silence as the train clattered over the points of some hidden Midland junction, and we were suddenly strangers now, new passengers looking over the remains of a boozy picnic left by some previous and unaccountably lively travelers.

And then, when it seemed that nothing further could happen between us that night other than to climb distantly into our separate bunks—when we seemed dead to each other, when we'd tidied up the debris and put the empty bottles back in the shopping bag, when there was absolutely nothing else left to do—Rachel turned away from me and started to undress with the quite unconscious provocation of a preoccupied striptease artist. First the petticoat, pushing the straps off her shoulders, pulling it up her naked torso, over the hills of her small breasts, then a suspender belt and the seamed stockings, then her panties.

Finally she turned, her face untroubled, full of adult calm, no longer a child waiting for a story, but a woman who'd heard most stories in the world. She looked at me doubtfully for a moment—fully dressed on the other side of the compartment, wondering where to put the rubbish-filled shopping bag. Then she smiled, the full smile of someone perfectly and finally content in all her admissions.

"We can love each other in our separate ways, then—can't we?" she said.

And we did.

MORNING came, an early mist was beginning to clear, giving way to a pale-blue sky. The day had no heat in it yet; we climbed away into the highlands of Perthshire, up through dewy green fields dotted with cows, like black-and-white models in a child's farm.

Rachel had woken during an early stop, below me in her own bunk then, and had said something I couldn't hear, so that I'd leaned over and looked down on her.

"What?"

She looked up at me, half asleep, hair spilled over the pillow, just her hands peeking out above the sheet.

"It's *cold*." She pulled the sheet up further, to just beneath her nose, so that only her eyes smiled.

"It's the frozen north," I said. "Temperature drops out of sight in these parts. Very few people ever live to tell the tale." We need to tease each other more than we know, and love may come to depend on it.

I'd climbed down then and held her for a minute, that sweet warmth smelling of plums with me again, the sense of other mornings alive once more as the porters clattered trolleys in the half light beyond our curtained windows: the world in balance, time stopped, held between day and night for a moment, between travel and conclusion, briefly spellbound.

Time would start again, I knew now. Any moment the wheels would creak and roll once more.

Our coach moved forward a fraction, imperceptibly, without any noise, before the engine took up the slack with a soft roar and we were off again.

Later, after some long gulps of the fresh orange juice and a look at the misty Firth, I went on for a wash and brush-up in the gents' W.C.—the train rocketing through long curves and small defiles now, as we eased our way up into the hills. I brushed my teeth and shaved cautiously, looking in the swaying mirror of the small cubicle; the rattle of other home-comings in this way years before was a small ache of expectation in the pit of my stomach, the certainty of a warm day in the hills by a lake ahead of me. A return, even without Henty and the green car, to a house I had been happy in. I put my shaving things away and unlocked the door.

A man was waiting outside, blocking my path, right in front of me.

"Excuse me." I was carrying my toilet kit in one hand, and I was surprised when he didn't move but simply put his own hand out, as if to take it from me.

"I'm sorry." I tried to edge round him.

"Let's have a dekko then," he said. He had his hand on the bag now, looking at it intently. I thought he must be mad. He had that arrogant yet mystified look of the insane: a curly-headed, boyish fellow, thickset, with the body and Cockney accent of a builder's laborer. Yet he might have been Irish or lowland Scots originally, with his neat blue suit and coarse features that stuck out of his open collar. Perhaps, accompanied by his handler, he was on his way to some institution far north, out of harm's way.

"Give us a look then," he said again. But I wasn't in the mood to humor him and held on to my bag.

"Excuse me—I don't think—"

In a flash he'd moved his thick stubby fingers from the bag onto my wrist, and before I could do anything about it, had grasped it viciously and twisted my arm round, up behind into the small of my back, where he held it like a vise.

"Come on, my old cock," he murmured into my ear. "You were bloody long enough coming for a leak—been waiting for you all morning. We've not got a lot of time. *Move!*"

He jerked my arm and propelled me toward the swaying coach couplings beyond the lavatory which led into the parcels van next the engine. Once through the interconnecting doors he gave me a great shove so that I fell several yards away from him, into a great pile of Sunday newspaper color supplements stacked in the middle of the van. By the time I got to my feet he had closed the door and pushed a large box against it, below the level of the small window that I noticed was already covered with a sheet of cardboard. Now he was facing me with a gun.

"Just get back where you were—on the floor—that's right, right down."

I sat down again while he moved over to the big double loading doors of the van and started to unlock the triple bolts, top and bottom and the long safety bar across the middle. The pleasant ache in the pit of my stomach of a moment before had turned to one of ulcerous fear. But a fear that made me think furiously, too, after the first numbness had worn off.

He must be one of Marcus's hit men, I thought—caught up with me when I had least expected it, for I had never taken Marcus's threats seriously. If this were so, then he was unlikely to shoot me. The plan would obviously be to make it seem an accident—a man with a woman and too much wine, who had fallen out of the train in the early morning, hungover, making for the gents'.

My assailant had gloves on now—and the top and bottom bolts were free. But he was having trouble with the larger safety bar in the middle: it was stuck. I looked round the van, thinking I might edge toward him and push him out the door with my feet when he had it open. An unlikely ploy, I decided. And then I saw the beehives—half a dozen wooden hives on the other side of the van—not new but well seasoned, the bees obviously being moved up to some summer heather field in the highlands for a gathering of that specially rich, waxy white honey.

The lout had the doors open now. For a moment I didn't know what was intended: a huge, colorful hole had simply opened in the side of the van—an inconceivable error in railway management. Then I realized this hole was for me. The fresh morning air rushed in, the wheels clattered far more loudly now, and I saw the countryside beyond, a blurred vision of blue and spring green, with the sun just getting up properly, the mist all gone and the highlands rising up on the horizon beyond like a travel brochure.

I decided, in order to gain time and move back toward the hives, to play the coward—getting to my feet, cringing, yelping as I retreated, and indeed the role didn't take much acting.

"No! No!" I squealed as he came toward me.

"Come on, my old love. I got a job to do," the youth said offhandedly. He was a professional.

The train suddenly went into a cutting, granite rocks rearing up outside the open doors. I hated the idea of being cut open at speed on their razor edges. A surge of hatred, a feeling of gut survival rose in me, lending all the more force to my sudden kick at the first beehive on my right. The man was about two yards in front of me and, as I thought, he didn't shoot but rushed me instead, pinning both my arms in a bear hug—but not before I got in another successful kick, taking the roof off a second hive.

The lids were off both of them now, one hive completely on its side, with the honey frames in the whole top section spewed out over the floor. And the bees, stunned for a moment, were crawling about in great furry brown blobs as we struggled.

And struggle we did, closer to the open doors.

Luckily the first bee to strike chose my assailant—a vicious jab in some most tender place, for he relaxed his grip on me for a second with a shriek of pain. Our sweat and the smell of fear must have been an added infuriation to the already furious insects, for when they really started to sting it was with a voracious rapidity and energy. Soon the two of us were well apart, oblivious to each other, slapping our faces and necks and ears and scalps in hideous pain.

His gun had dropped to the floor behind the color supplements, but neither of us had a mind for it now, intent only on saving ourselves from the marauding bees. A man can die of beestings, I remembered—and two open hives of well-enraged bees, attacking in a confined space, is a likely death sentence. I had to get out of the van as quickly as possible. I picked up a big bundle of *Observer* supplements and threw them at the lout—and then another bundle, in his face, the wire ties cutting his cheek. He was down on the floor now, stunned, and I was able to get back to the interconnecting doors and move the packing case while he lay there.

Then the man crawled for his gun. But he never got to it. The bees must have got down his open collar and into his shirt by then; he started to writhe about in agony on the floor, twisting and turning in a frenzy, like a rank amateur on a bed of nails, a man with too few hands and too much skin to save himself.

There was no time to do anything but leave him there. I had the packing case aside now, pulling off the cardboard screen on the window, before moving into the next coach, and closing the door behind me. I looked back at him. He was like a human firecracker, exploding repeatedly as he jerked his body, still vainly swatting the bees—standing up now, swaying toward the open loading doors. There was no escape toward the engine and he had quite forgotten his gun. He could have pulled the communication cord, of course, but the thought didn't have time to cross his mind, I suppose; the bees had found their stride with him at that point, clustering round his head in a huge impenetrable cloud.

Then, suddenly, he disappeared and the van was empty. I didn't see him go.

I just heard a faint thunderous buzzing sound through the glass and saw the dense shadows of bees circling the van, some of them now beginning to swarm over the glass of the connecting door. But otherwise the space inside was empty. Some great hand had come down and plucked the man away.

I pulled the communication cord myself then, and the train eventually came to a halt in a long squeal of brakes. The next thing, Rachel was with me in the corridor, I remember—and behind her, running up, the guard from the other end of the train.

"I've had a little trouble with some bees," I told him, my face already puffing up in excruciating pain. But not as bad as his trouble or his pain, I thought, the moment before I fainted.

BOOK TWO

THE EVIDENCE

"Oh, the house?" I said. "Yes—I've not been there for twenty years, I suppose." My face was still like a burnt pumpkin. It was painful to talk, difficult even to think.

"It's a beautiful place," the detective inspector said soothingly, the two of us driving out alone that afternoon, up the lovely roads toward Glenalyth.

Though Rachel—and Madeleine who'd been at the station to meet us—had come to the hospital in Perth with me, they had gone home after a while, leaving me there for a few hours "under observation." And when I'd recovered the Inspector had come to see me, talking to me in a private room: Detective Inspector Carse, the contact Fielding had given me in Scotland, head of the Perthshire County CID who had been in charge of the original investigation into Lindsay's disappearance. I'd told him at once of the confidential nature of my visit to Glenalyth, and he'd confirmed that he had been asked to cooperate with me in what he took to be simply another, if more clandestine, attempt to discover what had happened to the laird of Glenalyth.

"I knew him, you see," I'd told Carse. "I used to stay with the family."

"Work in the same line of country, then?" he'd said.

"Yes."

"There'll be an inquest, of course, on that fellow."

"Well, I didn't push him out of the train."

"All the same, I don't see how I'll be able to keep you out of it."

"You may have to. We'll see what they say in London."

Carse was a genial Scotsman, a big, broad man with a veined, weatherbeaten face, more like a highland farmer than a detective, the canny, friendly sort who would nose out local crime through country intuitions and connections rather than through any police manual. He was obviously ill at ease in these distant, dangerous matters of espionage and national security. He looked unhappy now, fingering a lip thoughtfully as he drove with one hand up a long, straight hill that led past the famous hundred-foot-tall beech hedge just south of Blairgowrie—a well-remembered sign for me, in all the old years, that I was but minutes away from the small, granite-faced market town that lay beneath the moors and the winding single-track road that led up from there to the first of the white gates on the long drive into Glenalyth.

"Who was the fellow?" I asked. "Any idea?"

"Not yet. I'd say he was just a gangland hit man by the look of him. London address on his driving license, somewhere in the East End. But the Yard have confirmed that it's only a squat. No one there now. The whole street is coming down. You were lucky."

"Yes. He was—tougher."

"I thought most of you people carried guns." Carse smiled wanly. "You're going to need some protection if you're staying up here. I'll see what I can do."

And then Carse had pointed out the obvious to me. "Whoever it was, they knew you were going to be on that train. When did you know you were getting it? Who did you tell?"

"Only yesterday morning. And I told nobody. Just the girl, Rachel, knew."

"So he must have been following you, then. All yesterday, at the least."

"Yes."

I remembered the man in the Marylebone pub Rachel had said she'd seen twice before that day. We had been followed—we must have been, she had been right—ever since my meeting with David Marcus in that deserted apartment off the Edgware Road. So he must have put the contract out on me. Buy why? Because I'd said clearly I intended continuing to look for Lindsay. And it followed, therefore, that if Marcus was prepared to go to such extravagant lengths to prevent my finding him, he feared the discovery of Lindsay for some other reason than the rather tame one he had given me— about Lindsay's involvement in an already aborted right-wing SIS plot to unseat the Prime Minister. In any case, you didn't bump off outsiders on trains just to keep some inter-office strife tidily under the carpet in London; you didn't widen the potential retributive evidence against yourself in this way just for the sake of keeping your bureaucratic image clean. You employed hit men in Intelligence only as a very last resort, when your own skin was in jeopardy, or when not to do so would be to put a whole vital and elaborate operation at risk.

It was clear, too, that if Marcus was prepared to take these great risks it was only because he thought I *could* find Lindsay and therefore he, at least, thought—or knew—that he was still alive somewhere. In all, my finding Lindsay would either compromise Marcus himself in some fatal manner, or else would do the same for some operation that Marcus had set up with him, a scheme so clandestine, so important that it justified the appallingly cruel deceit that Lindsay had imposed on his family by disappearing without a word. I found it very difficult to believe that of Lindsay; it was much more likely Marcus was the fly in the ointment: he was with the KGB, for instance. But then it struck me that both of them could have been with Moscow. It didn't make easy sense. But it was possible. And if so, here was reason enough for getting rid of me, for if I discovered what had happened to Lindsay this might lead me to the evidence of their joint betrayal, that Lindsay and Marcus had been thieves together for a long time in the heart of the Citadel, for longer than Philby and the others—and more important than they. If this were so, then the hire of any number of hit men would be justified to prevent such explosive intelligence coming to light. I suddenly didn't care for my future.

"Yes," Carse went on. "Someone must have stuck to you like a leech the last few days. The KGB I suppose?" he said. "Must have been them—working through some five-hundred-quid lout. There's plenty about, these days."

"I suppose so," I said, lying. "The KGB, yes."

"Well, that's your business. But I'd get back to London. Back among your colleagues. They can help—give you the sort of cover I can't very easily manage up here for you."

"Yes," I said. "When I've seen round Glenalyth—thought out what may have happened to Lindsay that afternoon—then I'll go back."

I spoke with a decisiveness, even a bravery, that I didn't feel just then. I was no real match for hit men. It was simply that I had given my word to Rachel and Madeleine and was determined to keep it. I suppose, too, I didn't want to fail them again, or be part of a failure, as I had been with them twenty years before.

We stopped talking then, going through Blairgowrie, past the white stucco of the Angus Hotel on the corner—opposite the small triangular, railed park, with its soldier war memorial and the round cattle trough facing the bridge that led out of the town again, going northwards over the burbling stream of the Ericht. When we went in the trap from Glenalyth to Blairgowrie, almost a day's trip there and back during the war, the cob would be tethered to those same railings, next the trough. After the war we had sped through or to the town in the green Wolseley, and Blairgowrie had become less distinct to me, a place that had shrunk since the years of early childhood and become simply a brief anchorage without any thrall or excitement in it.

But now, so many years later, seeing it all from the peak of some kind of maturity, the town had become mysterious once more, something vastly remote and tempting, where I felt that if I'd left the car just then I might have walked straight into my childhood again.

We crossed the bridge and soon had turned off the main road and were rising steeply through heavy trees. Suddenly we were out of the shade, on top of a first rise into the bright light. The whole moorland stretched ahead of us. On the higher ground several miles away, I could see the great green spread of the pine forest, a few puffy white clouds running away above the sylvan fortress of Glenalyth.

Glenalyth, originally the site of a medieval chieftain's castle, had been completely rebuilt in the mid-eighteenth century as a fort house, a domestic stronghold in an early Georgian mood, one of the very few of its kind in the British Isles, with walls four feet thick, a dry moat that ran beneath the huge Doric-columned portico and all the original windows on the ground floor placed high above the level of the lawns, so that invaders, however intrepid or skilled with their muskets on the lower slopes, could never do much better than smash the gilded ceilings and the stucco cherubs holding up the corners of the rooms inside.

A renowned ancestor of Lindsay's—a warlike and romantic Highlander who had survived Culloden—had built this new Glenalyth, this perfect mix of the impregnable and the beautiful, from the plans of an ambitious Edinburgh architect then developing that city in its Georgian phase. He had faced the house southward down the moors, toward the border, still hoping for the sounds of battle drums from that quarter.

We came round the hill of Alyth, the highest point in the area, and then for an instant I could see the four tall gray chimneys of the house, sticking up like the funnels of a ship in a green sea, before they dipped back into the trees again as we went down the other side of the hill. The bare moorland gave way to forest a mile further on, where the road turned sharp right and ran along the edge of the estate. But we drove straight on here, through the first of the white gates. The avenue sloped gradually down toward the loch after this, edging past a reed-fringed corner of it where little soapy waves flapped against the shore. We climbed then, passing through another gate and along a rhododendron-bordered lane, until finally the house reared up ahead of us, the parkland opening up around it suddenly like a fan, huge copper beeches dotting the meadow. The tallest of them by the path down to the loch was still there. It was this tree Rachel had told me about in London, the tree she'd climbed when she was seven or eight, perched somewhere high up in its smooth branches, from where she'd seen her father leaving the house alone that day with the oars on his way down to the loch, only to find him later—in her memory at least—trawling for pike with Aunt Susan. Rachel had such a clear recall of these things, so many more years and memories of this house than I had, that I felt an interloper, a distant cousin pretending to a great intimacy with affairs which, in reality, I had never had much to do with at all.

Then I saw her. Hearing the car, she had come out onto the steps and was jumping up and down like an impatient child. And for that moment I shared her recall, seeing her waiting for me as the car crunched round onto the gravel forecourt. I felt I'd come home again then, not at that instant as the car drew up, but thirty years before.

Madeleine had come out into the porch behind Rachel. There was no sign of the other house guests, George and Max, but they'd arrived: I could hear the sound of a furious piano somewhere in the background, the music stopping and starting abruptly—with anger almost, I thought, at my arrival. Miss Dorothy Parker, in the uncertain fits and starts of the lady herself, was edging her way into a musical reincarnation.

The two women looked at me silently for a moment—my face must have been a swollen horror. Then Rachel, in lieu of any more intimate contact, touched my shoulder briefly with a finger—that way of hers of expressing more emotion than she dared show made conveniently appropriate now by my tender condition. And I thought, for the first time in years, is this what love is like?

Everyone started to talk at once then, and we trooped inside to the big square hall, which in the summer, and when there was a large party staying, served as the drawing room. And I caught that unique smell, a whiff that had always been at the heart of the house for me, of sun-warmed flagstones, of old books and wax polish and of long-burned logs from the huge grate on the far side of the room: the dry, ageless smell of ancient content.

"You're in the flower room." Rachel had come up behind me. I turned and had to smile at her—though it was agony—for she had her own two cheeks puffed out in a huge breath, which she held for a moment, her eyes little ink spots now in what had become a great puffball of flesh.

She came with me upstairs while Madeleine exchanged civilities with Carse before tea.

Turning from the window of the best guest room that gave out onto the flower garden to the side of the house, she said, "You're not going to get yourself killed looking for Lindsay, you know. You mustn't."

I had started to unpack. "No," I said.

"We'll have to stop it. It's ridiculous."

"What?"

"Someone doesn't want you involved with us—it's obvious."

"Who? George, do you think?" I said lightly. "Do you think

he hired the lout?" I tried to smile but couldn't manage it this time.

"Be serious."

"Well, he didn't exactly welcome me with open arms just now. It must be him."

I put my pajamas out on the bed and was going to put on a clean pair of socks, but found a big hole in the toe of one of them. I suddenly realized how few decent clothes I had.

"Don't worry about George." Rachel picked up the sock, put a finger through the hole and then dropped it from on high, like a bomb, into a wastepaper basket by the bed. "We can get you some new ones. There's a shop in Gowrie that has some great wools and tweeds and things." She went back to the window again. The garden was a rage of warm color, wafts of heat shimmering over the rosebushes; the bedroom seemed to have known years of summer. It was as dry as an oven, smelling of sun-baked linen. Rachel went to the open window and we heard the piano again, coming from the study downstairs at the back of the house, the same half-formed tune hardly more developed, a repetitive, questioning phrase.

"Part of the overture—and one of the main songs," Rachel said, leaning out on the sill. "Parker's 'Prologue to a Saga'— know the poem?"

"I only know her one about not making passes at girls who wear glasses." Rachel turned and gave the words to the intermittent music beneath us:

"Maidens, gather not the yew,
    Leave the glossy myrtle sleeping;
Any lad was born untrue,
    Never a one is fit your weeping.

Pretty dears, your tumult cease;
    Love's a fardel, burthening double.
Clear your hearts, and have you peace—
    Gangway, girls: I'll show you trouble!"

"Sounds a winner all the way," I said. "If they can get the music right. It'll suit Max, too—Miss Parker has already done all the lyrics for him, I'd say: that speechless fellow."

"They're all right, don't worry about them. They've sworn to lock themselves up six hours a day—that's why they weren't out to meet you. Drinks at six. That's when they stop. You'll see them then."

"Thanks. Are they casting yet? Dottie had a lot of lovers, didn't she? Maybe they could fit me in."

"Why not just get along with them, Peter?"

"Yes." I went on rummaging in my case. "I can't find my toilet kit—all that expensive after-shave I brought up. I must have left it on the train."

Reminded thus of the morning horrors, Rachel took up her first theme again. "Exactly—that's what I've been trying to tell you: will you try and forget Lindsay for a while? Can you? Just get better, be here and do nothing. Do you understand?"

"Not really. I came here to help—"

"Peter."

Rachel walked over to me quietly, with a kind of tiptoeing concern—as light and warm as the sunny room, so much a part of it and of the house, a dark-topped flower born and nurtured here and flourishing now in her own native soil, where she alone knew best, where all things could be ordered to the good, if only I would listen.

"No. I don't understand," I said.

"I meant the hell with helping for a bit," she said vehemently. "Just live here. Be with, do things with us. Not the past any more or the future, but just now for a while. Don't you see the chance? Half of life is done with for us. But can't we start filling the rest of it well now? Haven't both of us just been thinking about getting by for too long? About not losing, just hanging on. Well, I'm tired of that. I want to win for a bit. Don't you? Do you see? Because we can. We've given up the will to win and I'm fed up—" She gestured toward the huge landscape outside. "I want to go out *there*, to the lakes and woods, and walk and walk—or drink or swim or talk. Or anything. And you too—and let George and Max work those ivories to the bone if they want. I'm done with music for a bit and people trying to kill each other. This morning, you know, when you fainted in the corridor of that train, I thought you'd died—just like that. Someone else gone for no possible reason. And when you weren't dead I knew we had to be *bright*—we have to be very bright before it's too late."

"Yes," I said. I had a pair of underpants in my hand. I didn't know quite what to do with them now. Rachel opened a drawer for me. The piano started up again downstairs and someone—George, it must have been—let out a roar, of approval it seemed. "They've got it right at last," I said. "What was that line of Parker's? 'Love's a fardel, something double. Gangway, girls—I'll show you trouble!'"

"Well, will you?"

"Be bright? Yes." I closed the drawer and turned and ran a finger down Rachel's cheek. "Yes, I'll try."

Now I knew what Rachel had meant when she'd insisted that love slowed you up: the finest thing to share was brightness. Love wouldn't matter then, for it would be implicit, already achieved and could be put away as ballast for the happy voyage. Yet there was, I felt even then, quite another side to Rachel's bright proposals. In taking up the good life with her, I might the more readily forget Lindsay's pain, Lindsay's absence, which was something—I was certain now— that for some reason she wanted me to forget.

"SO what did your friend Fielding say?" I asked George when we had a moment together that evening during the six o'clock drinks, sipping tumblers of a fine malt whisky and water, Lindsay's special tipple, decanted from a small barrel he had had sent from one of the Western Islands, and which he always kept in his study.

"He said he knew you vaguely," George said shortly. He was dressed in what he must have thought appropriate country clothes for someone who yet wished to maintain a few hints of the bohemian life: a pair of blue-and-white striped linen trousers that were far too tight round his bum and a T-shirt with a portrait of Beethoven die-stamped on it. He had an ever-boyish face, came out hugely around the middle, and tapered sharply at both ends. Had he worn a cap, he would have been the image of Tweedledum. His friend, Max, was Tweedledee on the other side of the hall: minutely smooth in perfectly creased tropicals, a gold chain rattling beneath a cuff and a look of princely boredom on his sallow features. He was talking to Tommy MacAulay, of the whisky MacAulays—the elderly brigadier and neighbor of Lindsay's who had been his CO during the war, and had come round with some others, to share drinks with us that evening. He was a sharp old dodderer, whose wife, Rachel told me, had crossed Jordan in an alcoholic stupor some time before, freeing him to fight a happy rearguard action on the near bank.

The big double hall doors were open in the evening heat and George and I took our drinks out onto the porch, from where I could still see a slight shimmer in the air above the loch and the grass beginning to wilt in the long meadow. They'd make hay from it any moment, I thought, as they had in the old days—or would life go on at all here as it had before, without Lindsay's directions and energies? Since we had no evidence of his death, it was still possible to stand on the porch then and wonder if he might come up the drive at any moment to join the party, a late guest, delayed three months for some perfectly explicable reason—come, as he had so often before, suddenly, out of the blue in a green car, home from the wars or from some canceled event in London.

It was then that Rachel's offer struck me as unreal. It proposed only one truth, and that entirely at the expense of another: she took her brightness from Lindsay's absence, while I at that moment, standing on the porch of his house and drinking his whisky, was suddenly aware of his presence—here, quite close to us possibly, so that the hair prickled on the back of my neck as I thought about it. I turned involuntarily, as if Lindsay himself had just come up behind me. Instead I saw his dog, the little terrier Ratty, who just at that moment had come out from the hall and was standing on the threshold of the house, looking up at me quizzically, unaccountably shivering.

"Yes," I said, turning back to George, "I knew Basil Fielding a bit. He was in my section, Mideast Intelligence. Did he help any?"

"Not much. Said in fact you'd be more help—especially as you were coming up here."

"Did he indeed?"

George looked at me, carefully avoiding my swollen face. "Yes, he said you'd be the one to find him. That you were clever that way. Rather you than I, after what happened this morning. In the sleeper," he added derisively.

I could see that it had crossed George's mind that his suit with Rachel might soon prosper again, for if someone had gone so far as to try and evict me from a speeding train, other more certain, less exotic attempts on my life must surely be in the cards.

This was a point taken up by the bibulous brigadier when I talked to him later. Tommy was enjoying his whisky, and it struck me I might turn his thirst to my advantage. He had already heard of the morning's adventures—and heard, too, from Madeleine I suppose, that I had once worked with British Intelligence.

"Don't you fellows carry any weapons?" he asked brightly. "Trained, I suppose? Small arms and all that. I should have seen that chap off pretty quick in my day: always carried a little 'un inside my jacket, as well as the Service .45."

"I'm afraid I've no skills there. I only worked for Intelligence Research—going through a lot of old Arab newspapers."

"Well, you're in the front line now. It's interesting: someone doesn't want poor Lindsay found, it seems." The brigadier sneezed then, a great bluster of a sneeze. "High pollen count," he said after he'd wiped himself up with a hankie, glancing round the hall, seeking some floral reason for his nasal discomfort. There was a big vase of fresh lavender on a table near us. "Might be that," I said. "Shall we go outside?" We moved out onto the porch.

"Yes," I said, in the relative quiet. "I can't think who would want to prevent him being found. I offered to help—"

"It's an outrage," the brigadier interrupted angrily. "Intelligence chappies in London told Madeleine he'd probably just lost his memory and wandered off somewhere—some cock-and-bull story. Lindsay would never have done that. He was abducted, kidnapped—and it must have been the Russians."

"Yes?"

"Well, who else? Of course Lindsay was involved with them. Never really spoke about it. But one knew. A messy business. He should have stayed in the army: he was a fine officer, first-rate—never knew why he went back to Whitehall after the war, all that cloak-and-dagger nonsense. And now look what's happened. Never could follow it—chap like Lindsay tied up in all that backdoor politics. Not like him at all, doesn't add up. He was the most straightforward man I think I ever knew. Only once heard him tell a lie. But we all had to lie then."

"Oh, when was that?" I asked innocently.

"After Monte Cassino, when we'd got up into the Po valley, Tolmezzo, and then into southern Austria. Just at the end of the war."

"What happened?"

"Had a lot of fascist Croats on our hands. Pavelić's ragtag army, must have been three or four hundred thousand of them, who'd come over the Yugoslav border, chased by the partisans—landed up in a little town called Bleiburg, just at

166

the edge of our command, on the frontier. Unpleasant business." The brigadier drank again and smacked his lips, his faint blue eyes looking out over the loch, but narrowing now over some indelible memory from his past.

"Yes?"

"Well—" The brigadier turned and humphed and I could tell now that he was the kind of old soldier who bloomed in front of an attentive audience. "Well, the war had just ended, two or three days before—but this was the worst thing in my war. You see, these Croat fellows, and their families too, women and children—close to half a million of them in all—well, knowing they'd get the chop in the biggest way if Tito's chaps ever got their hands on them, they made hell for leather across the border, ostensibly to surrender to us, but looking simply for our protection in fact. Sort of mass emigration of the whole province. Said they could never live under the Commies. True enough as it turned out. They didn't."

He paused, brushed his lips with a handkerchief, remembering carefully now, going back through the outlines of the story into the precise facts of the time, living them again. "Well, there we were, a little to the north in the Drau valley, with thirty thousand fully armed Cossacks on our hands whom we didn't know what to do with either—except we knew they'd eventually have to be sent back to Russia under the Yalta agreements, which didn't apply to the Yugoslavs. So then this other crowd cropped up, fifteen miles south in Bleiburg, and we couldn't spare more than a platoon or so to deal with them. An impossible situation. Anyway, I went down there, taking Lindsay with me, of course, since he was fluent in the Croat lingo.

"Well, they were camped out all over the village and all the hills for miles around. And just across the border in Yugoslavia was a whole assault division of the partisans getting ready to come over and slaughter them. Lindsay managed to bluff our way out of that little holocaust. We met the two rival commanders separately, insisted on fair play and all that, got the thing off the boil. And then we received precise instructions from HQ to repatriate all the Croats. Every one of them. Tito was our ally now, after all, and these others had fought with the Germans. So we had to do that—packed them all into cattle wagons and sent them back over the frontier. No one knows *exactly* what happened to them—so they say now." The brigadier laughed dryly. "But I needn't tell you—

they were put to the sword in the next few weeks and months, we heard the news afterward, we were still in the area—upwards of half a million of them; throats cut, machine-gunned into mass graves, dumped in rivers, forced marches—the lot. Unbelievable. No one talks about it these days, least of all the Yugoslavs. But it was the biggest slaughter of the war, after the Jews and Poles."

The brigadier finished his whisky abruptly, as if to wash away the unpleasant memory.

"But Lindsay," I said. "You said something about his lying?"

"We all lied. That's when I had to use the little 'un, inside my jacket."

"What—"

"Lindsay and I were down by the wagons one morning, seeing them in. We tried to make it all as pleasant as possible, though you can imagine what I felt like when I got home and saw those Nazi transports en route to the camps on the news-reels. Of course it wasn't pleasant at all. It couldn't be: we had to lie to them, telling them they were all going off to Italy, else we'd never have got any of them near the damn wagons. Anyway, that morning one of these Croats, with his wife and child, broke ranks and came up to Lindsay, recognized him apparently. He'd been a friend of Lindsay's when he lived in Zagreb before the war. And this chap knew they were all being sent back into Yugoslavia and that Lindsay had been lying to everyone. The two of them started to argue on the siding. And then this fellow took out a revolver he must have hidden somehow, and I thought: the bugger's going to shoot Lindsay. Well, he wasn't, Lindsay told me afterward. He was going to kill *himself* and his family—sooner dead than red, you know. Anyway, I got in a shot at him first—and I missed—can you imagine? But my sergeant was onto him in a flash. Lindsay just stood there, frozen, couldn't do a thing. We put them on a later transport—I dealt with it. Lindsay couldn't face the man again, naturally enough, I suppose. It was all a disgraceful business. But we had absolutely no alternative. Orders from the top—all in aid of jollying along Stalin and the rest of his bloody crew, which, of course, included Tito then."

"What happened to the man?" I asked.

"Who?"

"The Croat who knew Lindsay."

"Expect he ended up in a lime quarry. The big cement works outside Maribor took a lot of them, we heard."

"You don't remember his name, I suppose."

"No idea. Lindsay said he was a teacher of some sort, at some university. Why?"

"I'm still hoping to find out what happened to Lindsay. Perhaps that man survived. He'd certainly bear Lindsay a grudge."

"Yes. I see. But it's unlikely—they all got the chop."

"Not everyone, surely? There were survivors even in the worst of the Nazi death camps."

"Perhaps—but it's a hell of a long shot. Wish you luck. It's my view the Russians took Lindsay—and Whitehall doesn't want to make a fuss about it for some political reason; it's just like Stalin and those poor bloody Croats."

Rachel came out soon after and we dropped the subject. I asked her when they were going to cut the hay in the long meadow below us.

"Cut it with me tomorrow, if you like. There's a small tractor you could drive, and we could bale it. It might be fun."

"Need a gallon or two of ale for that job, if this weather keeps up," the brigadier said, looking up at the cloudless evening sky.

"Why not?" I said, going along with Rachel's brightness.

The heat had died at last. The shimmer had gone from above the loch, and the water had become a darker, plummier blue, while the tall copper beeches began to reach across the meadow, filling it with long shadows. The guests were ready to leave, bumping about with good-byes on the porch. Ratty stood among them curling his lip and whining slightly, jumping up and down in front of Madeleine, pleading for an evening walk.

I went off with her and Ratty when they'd all left and Rachel had gone inside to see to supper.

"I won't take you along the Oak Walk," she said. "That's where the bees are."

"No, let's go that way. I'd like to see where...The bees will have gone to sleep." And so we set off across the croquet court and into the first of the woods, where the evening had arrived earlier than elsewhere, with swarms of midges and pools of warm shadow.

"There. He was dealing with that second hive—you can

see it clearly from the morning room, where I was. That's where I last saw him."

The hive was between two oak trees and there was a small stone wall behind them that gave onto the vegetable garden. The Oak Walk ran away westward for about a quarter of a mile before the pine forest started, and we took this course now. But Ratty was disinclined to follow us, stopping before the first of the beehives and looking back anxiously toward the house.

"He doesn't like the bees," Madeleine said. "He always hangs back here. Come on, Ratty," she called.

"Was he with Lindsay that afternoon?"

"He wasn't with me. But, as I say, he's never liked the bees. He was probably nearby, though. Ratty was crazy about Lindsay, of course. He was his dog."

"That's interesting—he'd have followed him, you mean?"

"He usually did—everywhere. Inside and out."

The dog had taken evasive action now, going behind the row of beehives and running along by the garden wall. Suddenly he stopped, putting his front paws up on it, as if trying to climb over. Again, my spine prickled all the way down my back.

Madeleine turned to me, quickly, her face sharp with pain. "How could a dog tell, Peter—three months afterwards—where anyone went?"

"Dogs have memories. If he could speak, he would tell us."

Instead Ratty simply barked at the gathering night, his shrill yelps piercing the empty garden, floating away into the emptier forest beyond.

2

The fine weather never really broke that summer. But around the heights of Glenalyth, at least, the heat was spiced with pine and cooled with water. Rachel and I—and sometimes Madeleine—often walked up the long, dry corridors through the pine forest, or bathed from the small island in the loch, while George and Max, before their wives broke up the party that weekend, remained tied to their repetitive themes and variations in the study. Madeleine gave me directions to all Lindsay's old papers, stored in the morning room or in trunks and boxes up in the long attics that ran almost the length of the house, and in tiny, whitewashed bedrooms beneath them under the eaves: rooms like dog kennels, filled with lime dust and dead butterflies, that had been servants' quarters in other times.

But each day's vivid brightness had its shadowy counterpart every evening when I went back into Lindsay's past, shuffling through his papers, making notes—names from old letters or faded carbon memoranda; sifting through inexplicable loose sheets of paper that had long since come adrift from their original context—letters that began halfway through some vital or casual event: "...and wasn't it *unbe-*

lievable that he should have behaved in that way..."—with nothing left of who he was or what he had done; thumbing through a forgotten address book I found curled up from the attic heat and that contained a whole gallery of distant people between the pages—dead, or perhaps still living down the road or in another country. They must have been early friends or perhaps just acquaintances of Lindsay's, written clearly here in his neat hand. Someone called simply "Maria," with the address: "32 Reisnerstrasse, Vienna 3." "Miles McGough, 12 Smith Street, London, S.W.3"; "Sally Haughton—SLOane 2798." No address, but the old Chelsea telephone exchange proposing itself brightly once more, after a lapse of more than forty years—a temptation come to life again now in the dry attic: "Shall I phone her? Shall I not?"... I could almost hear the young Lindsay speaking. The meager little address book with its stained, bent covers was in fact the key to an empire, the world of Lindsay's youth.

These long evening investigations resembled playing Scrabble in an unknown language, or trying to finish a huge jigsaw puzzle that might never, in fact, have had any picture imprinted on it. Some of the pieces in front of me—a railway ticket or a negative in a yellowing Kodak folder—could be vital clues to the puzzle; other bits and pieces, an ornately die-stamped bill from a *pensione* in Florence in 1934 or a bank statement from the same year, might be irrelevant. For the moment I had no way of distinguishing between them, of giving this detritus any exact hierarchy of importance in Lindsay's life. At times I gave up any attempt to establish a precise chronology or location to the events in some folder or suitcase and simply trusted to luck, hovering like a necromancer among the dusty cobwebs, my hands spread out over the papers, selecting them quite arbitrarily, as in some elaborate card trick, hoping that so chancy a method would release the kind of lucky magic I knew I needed if I was to find anything that bore on Lindsay's disappearance in all this mass of ancient material.

Thus a day would start in the sun, with a Glenalyth honey breakfast on the porch, hay-bailing until midday, and afternoons in the limpid water. But each evening would bring me back into some prewar Continental darkness, for I soon realized that it was here, in the violent thirties, that the events which had formed Lindsay's life lay—events that had given it a far more complex and contradictory character than I had ever imagined. It was an existence light years away from that of the traditional Scots laird walking his grouse moors and patronizing the annual Highland Games—which was how I had seen much of Lindsay's essential life in the old days.

But the evidence I got together over the first two or three evenings pointed to some very different, if entirely conflicting, political absorptions; in the first instance, an apparently deep and sympathetic involvement with all the socialist tragedies in Europe between the wars—and on the other and far larger hand, an almost outright condemnation of those same socialists and all their doings throughout the same period.

Here was something I couldn't follow at all—this far earlier confirmation of something Marcus and Fielding had told me a week before in London: that Lindsay had been both left and right wing at the same time, information which I had taken then as no more than part of some bureaucratic trickery toward me in London. But here was the evidence, from Lindsay's pen itself, of the apparent truth of their statements to me. At least, at that moment, I saw no other way of interpreting some of his papers that appeared to be quite contradictory in their political enthusiasms. This was most notable in two sets of letters I discovered in different attic rooms: one collection written to Lindsay's mother at Glenalyth, and the other (only one letter, in fact) addressed to Eleanor before Lindsay married her. It had obviously been while he was a junior secretary in the Diplomatic Service and she was still at Oxford in her last year, apparently reading Modern Languages. This latter note, though it was without date or heading, I could place and date fairly readily: it must have been February 1934, in Vienna, for it dealt with the outbreak of brief civil war there. Chancellor Dollfuss, together with the fascist bully boys in the Heimwehr militia, had started shelling the workers' apartments in the suburbs of the city, killing off hundreds of people who had been trapped in their fine new municipal estates. February 1934—a classic date in the destruction of European democracy and the rise of the dictators.

...we knew something was up, because I could see from the legation window that two trams had come to a stop, blocking the junction out to the Schwarzenberger Platz—and that, of course, was the agreed sign for a general strike throughout the

city—and a sign for the Schutzbunders, too, to take up their hidden arms. So I hung about in the legation most of the morning, doing nothing, trying to phone people. I was mad with frustration by lunchtime, and though H. E. had told us to keep indoors I crept out by the chauffeur's exit and just as I got outside I heard what sounded like thunder from the east, sort of drum rolls which shook slightly over the inner city. And then I knew—but I couldn't believe it! They were shelling the workers—howitzers and trench mortars as we learnt afterward: no small-arms fire at all—just a massacre. There were Heimwehr and police all over the inner city but just a few shots here and there, nothing serious. Obviously they were intent on flattening the workers' blocks and leaving it at that— and I was determined to get out to Floridsdorf or Ottakring where we heard the worst of the fighting was, and see for myself what was going on, and I did that evening. Of course the British press will say how the workers started it all—stabbing poor little Dollfuss in the back just as he was establishing some sort of Austrian independence from the Nazis. But that is just untrue. Must run now. I'll finish this later . . .

Yet in a subsequent letter to his mother, a week or so after these bloody events, he had taken quite a different line:

. . . the fighting was severe out in the workers' suburbs. But it didn't last long, and the bark was worse than the bite—for the damage, as I saw myself afterwards, was mostly just to the masonry of their great fortresslike blocks of flats, which the workers originally built, of course, as military redoubts from which, when the time was ripe, they could sally forth to impose their own socialist dictatorship—something which, thankfully, little Dollfuss has prevented them doing—indefinitely, I should say . . .

There were other letters and notes for some official memoranda, all in the same vein. They condemned the socialists throughout Europe for rocking the boat, and proposed that Herr Hitler's activities, if not entirely justified, were of an understandable nature and that, when all else was said against him, he did appear to be the only bulwark left against a fast encroaching Red peril—a line which almost exactly followed British official foreign policy at the time. Yet it was only, I discovered, in his one letter to Eleanor that Lindsay showed himself to be clearly socialist. Someone was being lied to, but who and, above all, why? And then it struck me that of course it was Eleanor, his girl friend, with whom he had shared the truth; for the others he had put up a front. And if this were the case then she too must have had socialist inclinations. That made sense: a whole generation of Oxford and Cambridge undergraduates had gone pink, if not bright red, during the thirties. But why the need to lie about his beliefs to his mother and his other friends? Presumably it had simply been a means of securing entry and maintaining his position in the Foreign Office. Yet if this were so Lindsay had been working for them under very false colors, for they would certainly never have employed any acknowledged left-winger in the sensitive positions he afterwards came to occupy for them. And the answer here seemed clear to me as well: Lindsay must have intentionally misled the Foreign Office, joining it either to subvert its policies, or—like his contemporaries Philby, Burgess and Maclean—on behalf of the Soviets as a spy. My experience the week before with old Professor Allcock and his mysterious American visitor now formed a natural part of this elaborate ploy. In sum, I was left with a vague confirmation of my earlier conclusion—that Lindsay had been working for the KGB for most of his life.

Yet I couldn't really believe that Lindsay could be such a traitor. Surely, I thought, climbing down the narrow attic stairs that evening, his sympathy with the Viennese workers could be put down to nothing more than a well-developed Scots social conscience. Or perhaps Lindsay, like so many others of his generation, had momentarily shared the sweet dream of Marx, all the bright socialist fevers of the time, but had not been smitten with either illusion permanently. Yet I remembered how they'd thought just the same things about so many others in British Intelligence over the years—such true fellows, all of them, trusted like Philby and Maclean—until they had turned up in Moscow one day. Was Lindsay the last of their mold, caught out fifteen years after them, the man who had stayed the course longer than any, and who had now, at last, been helped on his way home over many borders? I was left with the entirely unsatisfactory conclusion that Lindsay's likely innocence was exactly balanced by his probable guilt.

* * *

RACHEL didn't care for my grubbing around the attics in this way each evening. Yet she stifled the complaints I'm sure she would otherwise have made, since we so fully shared the days together. I was left curious only by George's sudden lack of interest in our close association: he had quite given up the role of jealous lover. It struck me that this might have been because of something that had passed between him and Basil Fielding when they'd been in touch in London, some hint about my future Basil had dropped; or perhaps, as I've said, it was simply that George clearly saw my end in view if I persisted, as I appeared to be doing, in looking for Lindsay. For whatever reason, George regarded me almost with condescension, as if rivalry with me was something entirely wasted—I, who would not be long for this world.

But here, to forestall such unhappy ends, I had taken secret steps myself. I remembered that Lindsay's father, the old general, had been presented once with a small, ivory-handled, silver-plated .22 revolver, kept in a gilt morocco presentation case. I had once seen this fabulous toy as a child in Glenalyth; it had been brought out one day by Lindsay to show a visiting army colleague, and I knew exactly where it had been kept: the middle compartment at the back of his rolltop desk in the morning room—which was where I found it on my second evening, using Madeleine's keys. I got it out, replaced the box and locked the little door again. It was a beautiful object, small enough to hide almost entirely in the palm of one hand, in a breast pocket, which was where I kept it—but with sufficient weight and exquisite balance, I thought, to make it a completely effective weapon. I looked along the chased silver barrel, eased the trigger a fraction, saw the chamber turn and felt the satisfying pressure. A drop of oil and some ammunition was all it needed—and the shells I took from Billy's office in the yard where the guns were kept, opening the gun cupboard with the same bunch of keys, the next day when he had gone out for the afternoon.

WE were rowing one afternoon on the loch, Rachel and I, making for the small island at the far end, where we sometimes bathed, out of sight of the boathouse. "Water Lily Island," we called it, for in summer it was surrounded by a thick carpet of these creamy flowers, their crimson-streaked petal cups nestling in leaves like huge green plates that left only a sandy channel between them, giving access to a small wooden pier.

The island had been created in the late nineteenth century by Lindsay's grandfather, an amateur horticulturist and eminent Indian administrator, who had hammered a large circle of stakes into this shallow part of the loch, filled it in with stones and soil and then planted it out with exotic trees and flowering shrubs, which he had brought back from his sunny travels. The place was a miniature botanical garden and arboretum in this sheltered, hidden part of the water, set a hundred yards or so from the lakeshore and protected from the northerly winds by the huge, pine-clad hump of Kintyre Hill immediately behind it.

That afternoon it stood up out of the still, heat-hazed water like a deserted tropical island, a thick, silent clump of exotic greenery from some South Sea adventure tale, where an outcast might already be watching us through a deep filigree of leaves as Rachel took us toward it, rowing in a floppy linen hat and a swimsuit—her skin more bronzed than ever from this long heat wave, and looking like someone from the South Seas herself—while I sat in the stern with a pair of binoculars, scanning the shoreline every now and then, and looking at the huge green pine hill behind us.

She stopped rowing. I had the glasses raised, looking at a forester's hut halfway up the hill, and all I could hear was the slow dripping from the oar tips and the dying slap of water under the bows as the boat gradually came to a halt. The heat settled down on us, seeming to suck up all the air around as the small breeze of movement died in our faces. I put the glasses down.

"What have you found?" She leaned on the oars, holding them together with one hand, while she rubbed some insect off her nose with the other.

"Nothing. Just a forester's hut—empty, I think."

"Yes, they were here in the spring. But I meant in the attics."

"I thought we weren't talking about that."

"Well, you've taken no notice—when I told you not to bother looking for Lindsay. So why not?" She took off the floppy hat and wiped her brow with it. "You're going to go on looking for him then?"

"Obviously."

"I should be more gracious, shouldn't I? He was my father, after all."

"Yes. Why aren't you? Recently," I went on, "I've felt you didn't want him found, somehow."

"Recently, I've had you. And didn't want you killed." She looked at me candidly, inspecting me, almost, down the length of her long, straight nose, her big, inky-dark eyes calm beneath the loose hair, her arms resting easily, professionally on the oars. She was like some deft warrior heading a flotilla of tribal catamarans, waiting for a sign, about to lay waste some rivals on a tropic isle.

"That's nice," I said. "But is it really that simple?"

"Yes, it is." She smiled now. "You've lived so long alone you've forgotten how very simple some things are, Peter." With that she stood up on the seat, poised herself for an instant, and just before the boat started to tip, dived over the side into the greeny-blue depths, her body rippling just under the top of the water for twenty yards like a great fish, before she surfaced and swam off toward the island. I thought then how common a longing for simplicity was, and how, since it was so rare a thing, we were usually in the end forced to invent it.

She was lying naked, soaking up the sun, a little way up from the jetty on a sliver of grass between the trees, when I got to the island and had tied up the boat—stretched right out with her eyes closed, her swimsuit dispensed with, drying beside her, a dark ornament in the sunlight. The thick greenery spread all around and above her, forming a seemingly impenetrable barrier to the center of the island and leaning right round over the water on either side of us, enclosing this small area where we'd come to picnic as children, inviolate then as it was now.

"So?" I asked.

"'So, so—break off this last lamenting kiss, which sucks two souls and vapours both away.'" She quoted the lines abruptly, with her eyes closed.

There was silence then, a dead silence filled with heat. The world had gone to sleep for the afternoon. I sat on the wooden pier with my feet trailing in the water.

"I was thinking," she said after a minute, "of how much people want to be together—yet how really very bad they are at it. A complete conflict, somehow."

"To be bonded yet free—the old irreconcilables." I looked

out over the water. "We should have brought some fishing things—trolled for pike."

"Not in this heat—there'd be nothing. In the evening perhaps."

I turned back to her. She was sitting up now, playing with a twirl of bark, chin on her knees, looking through me vacantly.

"You remember," I said, "when you told me about Eleanor—how she didn't like the diplomatic life with Lindsay, that she was a countrywoman at heart? Were you suggesting they had irreconcilable attitudes?"

"No—I was thinking of us. When we lived together."

"Oh, we just had juvenile rows. But what about Eleanor?"

"What about her? I never knew her—"

"Was she left-wing, socialist in any way?"

"I don't know. You found something in the attic?"

"Yes. A letter Lindsay wrote from Vienna years ago, sympathizing with the workers there."

"Well, Lindsay wasn't socialist, you know," she said firmly. "As for Eleanor—well, Aunt Susan might know."

"I'll try and see her."

"If you have to. I won't."

"I'll swim," I said. "I'm baking." And I pushed myself slowly down from the jetty into the water, which swallowed me up gently, curling over my skin like warm mercury.

I swam out to the first clump of water lilies, where I could still just put my feet on the bottom, and ducked my head under them, watching the rising lily stems sway vaguely in the opalescent water; above them the green hats of their leaves shading the sun but ringed with halves of dazzling light, so that when I swum forward underwater, pushing between these long green tendrils, the sun burst down in glittering shafts, illuminating the sandy bottom before it sloped away sharply, out into deeper, darker water.

After a while I surfaced and swam out toward the middle of the loch before stopping a hundred yards or so from the island and turning back, treading water for a minute, letting my feet sink into the chillier layers beneath me while the sun baked my forehead. Rachel had stood up on the jetty and was holding something. It was only after I'd swum halfway back and she had moved her hand so that something flashed brightly in the sun that I realized she had found the little silver revolver I'd left in my trouser pocket. She was pointing it at me.

I'd put half a dozen shells, wedged in an empty matchbox, into my pocket as well, and I assumed she hadn't touched these and was simply playing the fool—starting some devious maneuver, some childish game of the kind we'd both played together on this same island thirty years before.

But then she fired the thing.

A small fountain burst from the water twenty yards ahead and to my right, and with it came a sound like a stick breaking—a sharp, minute echo over the water between us, bringing an awful change to the miracle of the afternoon. Rachel must indeed be playing some game, I thought, and so kept on swimming toward her, annoyed but not really alarmed.

"Don't be stupid, Rachel. Put the gun down. Never *ever* play with guns." But she took no notice and instead raised the revolver at me once more, like an executioner in the dazzling light.

She's gone mad, I thought suddenly, and ducked underwater, going down deep this time and making for the nearest clump of water lilies that would give me cover. And now I was really annoyed, and frightened too, for the water was suddenly cold. I wondered if my breath would keep—and quite simply I knew I didn't want to die.

But when I surfaced very carefully, underneath a lily pad still some distance from the island, she'd disappeared from the jetty and only a slight stirring in the thick greenery behind showed where she must have gone.

"Rachel? Come out for goodness' sakes!" I shouted, my nose only just above water. I waited there a minute but there was no reply. The loch was quite still and nothing moved now on the island. The afternoon had died again in the heat.

Instead of landing at the jetty, which I thought she might be covering with the gun from some hiding place behind the trees, I swam round to the other side of the island, bobbing in and out among the water lilies, ready at any moment to duck back into the water again. But the whole green clump was quite still, and when I got out of the water on the far side, pulling myself delicately ashore along the branch of an overhanging tree, I realized that if I ventured into the center of the island, disturbing the thick undergrowth, I would immediately become the hunted once more—unless I could crouch down and move inch by inch without a sound.

I thought how preposterous the whole thing was, that I shouldn't lend myself to this mad game any more, stalking someone—someone loved—like an Indian on all fours; I should simply call out to her in a calm voice and ask her to put down her gun. But I had already done that without result—and it was anger that came then and made me move forward, inch by inch, without a sound—anger and a need to know what I thought at last I could learn in this instance: why twice in a week someone should want to kill me. So I crawled off on my knees, upward through the bushes, testing every move ahead with my hands, clearing away any noisy twigs—determined to hunt myself now, and do it properly.

About five minutes passed, with several false alarms, before I suddenly saw her ankles several yards ahead of me, my own face almost touching the ground at this point. She was standing beyond a thick, sweet-smelling mock-orange-blossom bush—standing quite still to begin with, her two feet like the remains of some discarded surrealist statuary in the greenery. And then, as I froze for a long minute, she began to circle round the bush, as if she'd heard something, but wasn't quite sure where. Finally, making her mind up, she walked straight toward me.

It was a lucky break. She couldn't have expected me to come up at her out of the earth as I did, grabbing her by the ankles first and then pulling them both viciously so that she collapsed like a ninepin in a cloud of white flowers. I straddled her, pinning her down, the two of us flaying about in the hot, confined space that suddenly smelled like a hairdresser's shop.

She didn't seem to have the gun with her now. But she struggled like fury in my arms for a minute, saying nothing, looking up at me with a fierce smile that annoyed me all the more; eventually, I pinched one of her wrists in fury.

"Ouch! Don't hurt." She spoke at last, aggrieved now, like a child losing a struggle with an older companion, sensing a dangerous viciousness in the other which they know they can no longer deal with. "Can't you play without hurting?"

She tried to lift her head up but I forced her back against the broken branches of the bush. *"Du calme, du calme,"* she said then, accepting matters, her heart beating furiously, making her small breasts jump in strange spasms.

"Yes," I said. *"Du* bloody *calme* indeed—with live ammunition!"

"It was a game. I left the gun on the jetty for you—didn't you see it?"

"I came round the other way. I knew you'd say it was an accident or a game. But how do I *really* know?"

I began bending her arm. "What on earth do you think you're bloody well doing, firing guns at people, you bitch?"

"Please—you're hurting!"

"I mean to. So tell me the truth, go on." I twisted the arm a little more. "Why? Why try and kill me?"

She turned her face away and the smile had long gone.

"I—*wasn't!*" she screeched. "I was terrified myself when the thing went off. I was just playing with it. I found it in your pocket—"

"And why don't you want Lindsay found—or for me to go and see Aunt Susan? Why have you been lying—?"

"I haven't."

"No? Well, not telling me the truth then." I gave another twist. "That's worse than lying, when I'm trying to help. It's all too serious now. You better tell me!"

I was furious. But I knew I'd really hurt her if I kept on turning her arm. So I relaxed my grip a fraction. And taking this as a first sign of my relenting, Rachel started to cry suddenly and I let her go entirely as streams of anguished sound filled the afternoon, a well of some terrible emotion breaking out as she lay covering her eyes, trying to wipe them with one arm, the other lying numbed beside her.

And then, as in the past when some blazing row had finally released each to the other, we found the threads once more that held us together, quicker now than before, when several days might pass without a word. Anger became a key to peace in a matter of minutes here, and I wondered if we might be growing up at last.

"I'm frightened," she said eventually, sitting up brushing the petals off her belly.

"I can see that—drinking that way in London, letting off revolvers at me. Buy why?" I touched the tip of her nose, then ran my thumb gently down from the corner of her eye, taking the last moisture away.

"I suppose I wanted to find Lindsay on my own. And when you turned up, I knew I couldn't."

"Yes, but *why?*"

She licked her lips in the dry heat. "In the past," she said.

"It must have been when you started talking about Aunt Susan, just before you swam off."

"That was why you fired at me?"

"I told you I didn't mean it. It scared me much more . . ."

She looked at me vacantly. I could sense that at any moment she might stall, go back on the truths that I felt were just about to emerge from her.

"Come on, Rachel. It must be more than an accident. You told me in London how you had this terrible sense of insecurity and didn't know why—"

"I *still* don't know!"

"But you were close to it—just then, before I swam out, when I mentioned seeing Aunt Susan."

"Yes—yes, I was," she admitted.

"You have such recall about other things. But not this. The classic case of a block."

She nodded. But then she said, "A block?"

"Yes. I was talking about fishing, you remember—about our trolling for pike, and you said it was too hot? And before that we'd talked about people being incompatible, even though they so wanted to be together. And then I mentioned Susan. That was the sequence: affairs going wrong, pike fishing, and then Aunt Susan." And I rushed on now, certain that I had isolated something important. "And remember in London—that day you told me about. You were up in the copper beech and you saw your father going down to the loch and you followed him and saw him—alone—trolling for pike. But afterwards, you saw Aunt Susan with him in the back of the boat. It was *she* who was fishing for pike, and it suddenly all made sense to you, because Lindsay never went out fishing alone. You saw all this in your mind afterwards, didn't you?"

"Yes," she said doubtfully.

"Well—*yes*—so it's because of something to do with Aunt Susan that you don't want Lindsay found. Or at least, you don't want him found in any way *through her*. That's what it amounts to: she knows something—and you know it too, unconsciously—to Lindsay's disadvantage. And I know all this, too—or sense it at least—which is why you felt like shooting me just now."

"I didn't! It just went off!"

I thought I was losing her then, that she had become afraid of the truths she felt rising in her. I leaned forward to kiss her, as if to rescue the truth in this way before it drowned again, to draw it out, once and for all, from that darkness she had maintained for so long about her father.

And she kissed me, too—putting her arms about me so that we both fell into the broken orange bush.

Afterwards, when we'd pushed our way back through the undergrowth to the jetty and she was putting on her swimsuit, while I was untying the boat, she said, "When you first kissed me then I had such a surprise, such a strange feeling..."

"The earth sinking?..."

"No. When you kissed me, I saw—" She stopped. "Can you fasten this up for me? I can't—"

I came up and fixed the straps at the back of her suit and then she said, "Of course, it all became clear when you kissed me: it was *Aunt Susan* who was being kissed. That's what I saw when I went down to the lake that afternoon as a child—it's what Lindsay was doing, there—in the boat."

She turned and we both looked with surprised disbelief at the old green rowing boat. It had drifted out a little from the island while our backs were turned, as if inhabited by some life of its own now, or by some other life, moving gently away across the water.

I picked the little revolver up from the jetty and opened the chamber. She had only put one shell in. Had she really wanted to kill me, I thought, she would surely have filled the chamber, waited until I'd swum nearer the island, and then had six shots at me. I had to suppose, in the event, that she'd told me the truth, that it had been an accident—or a game—taken from childhood and spiced here with a more elaborate, adult danger: a charade we had finally defused, and whose message we had interpreted at last in the shape of Aunt Susan being kissed in a boat thirty years before. Yet there remained, for all that, some ambiguous residue about the events of the afternoon—a matter left still undecided, some unresolved notion or frustration on Rachel's part, a kind of madness our renewed loving hadn't cured.

3

All the same, Rachel took up the search for Lindsay again, there and then. At least, she came with me up to the attics that evening and together we sorted through more of her father's papers.

"It's funny," I said, as we made our way through the minute, whitewashed maid's rooms before going up the narrow staircase into the attics themselves, "Lindsay used to keep his old train sets up here—all those wonderful big black clockwork engines and yellow coaches. But there aren't any around at all now. Just a few rails." I prodded a rusty example lying on the floor. "And a broken signal."

"They must be somewhere about."

"No. I've looked."

"In some cupboard, then. The house if full of cupboards."

We'd come up into the first of the attics, where I'd put a box aside containing one or two things I thought might be important. "This is the only railway thing I found—this membership card." I showed it to Rachel. "You see: 'The Oxford and Cambridge Model Railway Society, 17, The Rise, Bow Brickhill, Bletchley, Buckinghamshire.' With Lindsay's name. And the date at the bottom: 1932. I don't follow it."

"What is there to follow?"

"Why is the Society in such an out-of-the-way place? Why not in either Oxford or Cambridge itself? And why was there such a club in the first place? For children, yes. But for undergraduates?"

"Daddy was always mad about trains. And I suppose the two universities joined together—there wouldn't have been enough members otherwise."

"But why in Bletchley?"

"Why not? Maybe it was halfway between Oxford and Cambridge. Buckinghamshire, isn't it?"

"Yes, of course." I suddenly saw the reason for this unlikely site of the club. "It must have been on the old Oxford-to-Cambridge line, so the members could get to it equally well from either university."

"Probably."

"That explains it." Yet there was something about this club that bothered me. "Even so, it must have been quite a trip to make just for a club evening. A train journey each time you wanted to play with your model engines."

"Part of the fun, surely, if you were train-mad."

Afterwards we started going through some more old boxes and suitcases, squatting on the rough wood, a single light bulb above us. I'd been looking, without success, for evidence of the Yugoslav in the brigadier's tale, of the Croat who had tried to kill himself on the rail siding in Austria just after the war: Lindsay's friend from his time at the Zagreb consulate in the thirties, a teacher, the brigadier had thought. But there had been no sign of him anywhere, not even in a case full of Yugoslav papers, and I'd given up trying to identify him.

But then I came on some old folders packed tight with papers dealing with Lindsay's beekeeping activities before the war—Ministry of Agriculture pamphlets and other advisory texts for the most part, together with a number of catalogues from bee suppliers in the home counties. And it was while thumbing quickly through one of these that the letter dropped out—a neatly folded but badly typed letter, in English, with the heading "Croatian National University" and dated April 1936.

It was written to Lindsay in his official capacity at the consulate—a formally polite inquiry asking him if he could send the address in London of the appropriate library or ministry where the writer could obtain some beekeeping information he needed not then available in Yugoslavia. The letter was signed "Dr. Ivo Kovačić, Assistant Lecturer in English at Zagreb University." Here, I thought, must be the Croat whom Lindsay had betrayed on the rail siding more than thirty years before—who'd then been sent packing, back over the border into the merciless arms of Tito's partisans. There was nothing else on him, however. Rachel had never heard of him and I had to assume the brigadier had probably been correct: this old Croat nationalist had died in a lime quarry.

Throughout our searches that evening we were looking, too, for some evidence of Lindsay's apparently close relationship with Susan.

"It may have been nothing more than a friendly peck on the cheek you saw in the boat that afternoon," I said, as we went on through the boxes.

"But they *weren't* friends—that's the whole point. She always loathed Daddy. I can remember the silences when they were together, like ice."

Rachel wiped the sweat off her hands. We were kneeling close together, perched under the baking eaves, and the long day's heat had made it oppressive. "We thought Susan an old dame, all dressed in brown like a stick," Rachel went on. "But that's only because *we* were very young then. In fact, she can't have been more than forty—she was only a year or so older than Eleanor. To an adult she would have seemed quite young and attractive."

"You think she had some affair with Lindsay, that he dropped her—and that's why she was so cold with him?"

"Might explain the awful unease I felt at the time, some sort of great stress in the household."

"Don't forget Patrick died at the end of the war."

"This was before Patrick died, I'm sure."

"The kissing in the boat?"

"Yes."

"Which means Lindsay must have been up here on leave—which means, if they had any sort of relationship or affair, it must have started *before* the war."

"Yes," Rachel said decisively.

"I'm not so sure I believe it, you know. Much more likely just a placatory offering, that kiss. Not important. Or you've got it mixed up and it was Madeleine you saw in the boat that afternoon."

187

Rachel eased herself on the bare floorboards and folded her hands in her lap. "You think I've invented Susan as a rival for Lindsay's affections, don't you? In order to justify what you see as my own insatiable love for him: that I've set Susan up as a wicked temptress taking Lindsay away from me."

"You've put it better than I could, I think."

"Well, who can tell?" Rachel looked as if she truly couldn't. "But I don't think I've done that," she went on.

Certainly there was no documentary evidence in the attics to substantiate Rachel's claim. I don't know that we seriously thought there would be. What did we expect? Old love letters, a diary? Certainly there was nothing of the kind. There was only one particular photograph in a trunk, among a lot of others in old yellow Kodak folders—the leftover snaps of three or four decades that hadn't made it into the family albums downstairs in the drawing room. I'd looked through this trunk quickly before. But now, with Rachel with me, I studied the photographs more carefully, helped this time by her comments and interpretations.

The photograph was on its own, not part of any sequence, as though it had slipped from a folder or had been sent to the family as a holiday memento by some outsider who had taken it. It showed Lindsay as a young man (his hair combed sideways and quite dark, while I had always known it straight back and half white) with two women on the deck of a river steamer. It looked like the Rhine Valley, for there were steeply rising hills, crisscrossed with vineyards, on either side of the water.

"Yes," Rachel said. "That's Lindsay. With Eleanor and Susan."

The two women were sitting at a table, with Lindsay standing between in a Fair Isle sweater and a baggy pair of pants that looked like cricket flannels, his hands lightly on the women's shoulders, bending down toward the camera with a confident, almost cheeky smile.

"Some jolly holiday down the Rhine, that's all," I said. "Mid-thirties by the clothes."

"So they had the opportunity. Didn't they?" Rachel looked up at me inquiringly. "Just the three of them." She had changed subtly, I thought, from being her father's supporter to being his prosecutor. And so I reversed my own role and became his advocate.

"How do you know? There were probably four of them—the person who took the snap as well. A friend of Susan's."

Rachel picked up the photo again and I leaned over her shoulder, the yellow light above us illuminating this forty-year-old holiday more sharply. The two women looked remarkably alike without somehow giving the impression of any similar temperament. They seemed divided, each in her own world—as Lindsay divided them physically, standing between them. Eleanor was smiling slightly, while Susan's face remained severe. Both of them wore long cardigans and rather full-bodiced dresses, dark hair parted precisely in the middle; nonetheless they seemed to come from different worlds, as if the figures for rain and shine in a weather house had both come out at the same moment.

Behind them I could just see a man in uniform, standing against the ship's rail. He wore a tightly belted jacket with a single line of braid around the collar and a steeply raked, peaked cap. It might have been an SS officer's outfit, I thought. And then I wondered what these three were doing holidaying in Germany at this time, especially Lindsay and Eleanor with their apparently strong socialist sympathies. It must have been about 1935, only a year after the fascist atrocities in Vienna Lindsay had described in his letters to Eleanor. And if Eleanor was a serious socialist at that time, what of Susan? Was she socialist too? I asked Rachel.

"Just the opposite, I'd say. Tory to her bones. She was very fond of Eleanor. But they were quite different."

"You can sense that in the photo—they *feel* different."

"Susan didn't hold much with gadding about the place. She was very much the vicarage girl, the stay-at-home potential Lady Bountiful of the manor. I'm sure she'd have been pro-Hitler then, at least to begin with—until Chamberlain said we'd have to fight him. She thought Eleanor was going to the dogs with her university life: quite the wrong thing. They were chalk and cheese."

"Then what were they all doing on that boat together, in the middle of Nazi Germany?"

"Trips down the Rhine would have been all right for her. And the Dutch tulip fields. And she'd have gone with Eleanor. She had this thing about saving her."

"From Lindsay? Surely he'd have represented every fine Tory, landowning virtue for her—the laird of Glenalyth?"

"No—saving her from, well—I don't know." Rachel looked

genuinely blank. "The perils of thought, I suppose; and perhaps you're right—perhaps Eleanor was left-wing at college. And Susan would certainly have been annoyed by that."

"When were they married—Lindsay and Eleanor?"

"End of 1935, I think. Or 1936. Patrick was born at the beginning of 1937—the same year Eleanor died—"

"So when that snap was taken they weren't married?"

"No, I don't think so."

"I wonder if your kissing in the boat on the lake doesn't make some sense now," I said.

"Why?"

"You said Susan was a potential Lady Bountiful of the manor. It's possible, isn't it, that that's why she wanted to be with Lindsay. You said she was keen on 'saving' Eleanor: well, that's what she may have been trying to do—going down the Rhine, saving her from Lindsay, so that she might marry him. And hence her sour look in the photo—she obviously wasn't succeeding."

"She's rather a formal old party, you know. She'd never have thought of marrying Lindsay unless he'd given her grounds for thinking it possible."

"Perhaps he did. And perhaps unwittingly. There's often that sort of trouble between a man and two sisters."

And then it suddenly struck me what might have happened: Susan and Eleanor were alike in their striking, if rather severe, good looks, yet quite opposite, it seemed, in their political views. If Lindsay, as I'd established, seemed to have embraced both the left and right wings at this time, what more natural than that each of these sisters should have become attracted by these quite separate parts of his personality—Eleanor reaching out for what was socialist in him, while Susan had taken to all the Tory elements in his nature? Yet there remained a startling flaw in this proposal: what person, by nature, can embrace two utterly opposed political dogmas at the same time? By nature—and especially given Lindsay's formal dispositions here—holding such political faiths simultaneously was surely as impossible as actually making love to two women at the same time. It followed, of course, that Lindsay had assumed one of these faiths, and that only one was natural to him. But which one? And which of the two sisters, given the truth of Rachel's memory of the boat, had fallen for the genuine article? Aunt Susan herself was the only person who might help me to a closer view of the truth.

SUSAN Bailey's father had been the Church of Scotland vicar of a parish outside the small cathedral town of Dunkeld, some twenty miles west of Glenalyth. And though, as Madeleine had told me, the living there had long since withered and died and the church had become a partial ruin, Susan still lived in the old rectory there—a small Georgian house, surrounded by rook-infested trees on a rise above the Tay, looking out over the railway bridge down the valley where it crossed the big river, taking the main line northwards.

I'd phoned her the day before and she remembered me at once; her crisp voice gave me precise directions as to how to find her. And I thought then how unlikely it was that she would tell me anything about Lindsay, so that I mentioned nothing about him on the phone, hoping to have my chance when we met in person.

Apart from some daily help from the woman in the gate lodge she lived entirely on her own, but not without money and with two Scots terriers, one black, the other a Highland white, just like the whisky advertisements. All three of them came out of the glass porch to meet me as I drew up in the black Volvo station wagon. The rooks cackled fearfully in the upper branches of the tall chestnuts, and the terriers barked loudly.

We shook hands. The photograph I'd taken from the attic was burning a hole in my inside pocket, but she took my hand in both of hers with an unexpected warmth and a smile that was affectionate as well as simply cordial.

"Peter!—here you are: twenty years to the month since I last saw you. I was looking in my diary. Nineteen fifty-six—that summer you were up here, you'd broken your heel, it was all in plaster—do you remember? It's so nice of you to have come and seen me. Come in, come in. Or shall we walk?"

She was over seventy. But something—exercise and the moorland life—had kept her young. And though the dark hair of the old photograph had turned quite white, the rest of her appearance was that of a woman at least ten years younger. She had an extraordinarily good complexion for someone her age—fine and pale, the skin barely wrinkled, apart from vague indentations at the corners of her eyes and mouth, the mere tracings of age. Whatever pain and disappointment she'd suffered was not apparent here, so that once more I began to doubt my earlier deductions about her and Lindsay. No hurt seemed to lie behind her calm, faint blue eyes; a refined and courteous confidence marked her long, straight face. Human aberration seemed a complete stranger in this self-sufficient, sensible, attractive old lady.

She took a blackthorn walking stick from the porch and put on another of the straw hats that I'd remembered her in, and together we walked away from the house, a small breeze running up from the Tay valley beneath us, just sharpening the hot afternoon, stirring the huge chestnuts, leaving minute sighs in their branches. We went down the back drive, exchanging news and small talk, until we came to a box-hedged path that led to the old parish church, a cracked steeple and yew trees looming up ahead of us, the dogs worrying at imaginary rabbits in the thick undergrowth, but startling nothing in the drowsy heat of this enclosed space where the breeze had died.

"Lindsay's dog, Ratty," I said casually. "He's an extraordinary creature. Almost speaks to you."

She took no notice of this casual introduction to Lindsay, replying, without any change of tone, "Terriers do, some of them. Uncanny."

I opened an old wicket gate and the dark granite church came clearly into view ahead of us. We looked at the dilapidated building. Slates had fallen from the steep roof and a crack in the stone was about to bisect the square belfry.

"I wanted it repaired," she said, waving her stick at it. "But the estimates were preposterous. And the commissioners weren't interested. I didn't want it to fall down."

The dogs joined us, and we walked toward the vestry door. Then she said quite casually, so that I thought she had sensed all along the real reasons behind my visit, "Lindsay and Eleanor were married here, you know. Christmas 1935. I always thought it such bad luck—having a wedding and Christmas almost together. Well, that was one reason for keeping it up. The dead will have to look after themselves, don't you think?" She waved her stick at the old tombstones in the long summer grass, poppies and huge white daisies rearing up here and there, the whole place gone to seed in waves of bright color.

"But there's something living about a marriage that you've shared in that makes you want to keep the building where it happened." She spoke in so sensible a tone that sentimentality could be no part of her thought. "So much sadness about churches," she went on, "except for people marrying in them. Worth preserving for that—for Lindsay and Eleanor's sake." I remembered Rachel telling me how Susan had made a shrine at the rectory out of Eleanor's things. It seemed true—and yet a surprising thing for such an apparently sensible old woman to do.

She went on ahead of me now, picking her way confidently through the overgrown tombs toward the vestry door, which she opened with a key, and we walked out of the heat into a musty damp, the smell of many winters' ruin. There was a pile of hymn books and psalters on a bench and a lot of mouse droppings in all the corners.

"It's what you came to talk about, I imagine—Lindsay. And us," she said, without looking up.

"Well—"

"Why not? The others won't. Apart from a few words from Madeleine I've heard nothing." She opened a cupboard now and took out a large, leather-bound book, putting it up on a small vestry lectern before thumbing through the pages. It was the church's marriage register.

"There," she said, as I came to her shoulder. She pointed to the signatures. Lindsay's hand I recognized at once; clear and precise. Eleanor's was quite different: a sprawling, unformed signature, flowery almost. The date was December 18, 1935.

The vestry door was open and I could feel the wafts of heat coming in from the shimmering afternoon outside. One of the terriers was flat out, panting on the threshold, while the other, the younger white one, looked outside, whimpering slightly, still anxious to play. The world stopped just then. Again, as in that moment on the porch at Glenalyth while I was talking to the old brigadier and Ratty had come behind us, I had the clear impression that Lindsay was in the room; that, through looking at these faded signatures, I had gained access to the exact moment in time when he and Eleanor had made them; a feeling that wasn't eerie at all, since it was so clear that I was in the presence of Lindsay and his first wife—who were there, in all but a material sense, in that small musty room.

"It snowed all day. Like a fairy tale." Susan broke the silence. "Half the guests never got here. And most that did had to stay the night, strewn all over the hall and drawing room." She smiled at the memory. But again it was simply in amusement.

"There was snow, was there?"

A bumblebee flew in and droned about for a moment, before swinging away out into the warm air again.

"They should have put it off until spring." Susan closed the register and put it away. "But Lindsay was going to have been abroad then. So it was all held in a snowstorm. Just cleared a bit during the reception, I remember. The sun came out then and the champagne was too cold."

She pulled the tattered vestry curtain aside and we went into the chancel of the church.

"I know you don't think I can tell you where Lindsay is," she said, walking up to the old mahogany altar rails and looking at the stained-glass east window above them—Christ in the pre-Raphaelite style, with the Lamb of God in his arms, and a lot of very woolly sheep beneath on a green hill. "So you must want something else." She gazed vacantly up at the bleeding crown of thorns that seemed so inappropriate an addition to this otherwise placid Victorian agricultural scene.

"You didn't like Lindsay, did you? I wondered why." I thought the time had come to be honest with her.

"I liked Eleanor."

She turned and came down the chancel steps, walking past me rather slowly and regally, her face set now with a purpose that it had lacked before, a kind of brave disappointment. She was like a bride, stood up at the very last moment, returning from the altar alone but determined to go forth and make the best of things.

She walked down the nave now and stopped in front of another stained-glass window halfway along the south wall. Here was a more recent design, a portrait in the overliteral style of the thirties, of a dark-haired woman set against a background of rhododendrons in full flower. At first I took it to be Mary Magdalen depicted in some Scottish grove. But on looking more closely I was surprised by the legend beneath: "In Memoriam: Eleanor Phillips. 1912–1937. When the day breaks and the shadows flee away." There was no other comfort added, just the plain statement of memory, of birth and mortality, embedded in the yellow-and-green glass. And now I was aware of a great emptiness in the church, of present life alone in the musty building: no longer the extraordinarily vibrant sense of Lindsay and his first wife that had so clearly been about me in the vestry, but the feeling that, without knowing anything of their life in between, I had experienced both their marriage and their death in the space of a few minutes.

She said, "Rachel has been talking to you. I was so sorry you two didn't marry. That was when you last came up here —in '56. I thought you should have. But Lindsay said you had no prospects, that you were too young. Yet he was only twenty-five when he married."

"It was hardly his fault. Though with a bit of encouragement from him, Rachel might have changed her mind at that point."

"Exactly. But that was the problem, wasn't it? He wanted her for himself. He was such a possessive man, without knowing it. And, of course, no one else suspected it. He wouldn't let her go. It was as simple as that. And I told him so."

"Yes—I've said the same thing to Rachel. But it never did any good. People set on a course—"

"Oh yes, I know—just like Eleanor." Susan chuckled almost, waving her stick at the window portrait. "Eleanor would never see the same thing—that polite ruthlessness of Lindsay's. But I did. Which was probably why we never married in the end."

"I'd no idea—"

The church suddenly started to fill again: another door had opened into the past—into other times and people and fevers then, filing into the building now like a late congregation.

"Oh, I wanted to," Susan went on, much more brightly now. "In many other ways, and for other reasons." She paused and came closer to the picture of her sister, inspecting it minutely as if searching out some invisible mark or sign known only to her.

"I never knew that."

"Why should you? No one did. Not even Eleanor." She spoke to the picture now. "But now that he's gone—why not? One gets so tired of living with omissions all one's life." She leaned forward and rubbed at what I saw now was a speck of bird dropping on the glass. "My father had this window put up as a reminder—since she was buried so far away. It isn't very good."

"In—Zagreb, was it?"

"Yes. In a huge, heavy, Viennese sort of cemetery: you know—angels playing granite violins. Went to see her grave once."

"I never really heard what happened out there," I said gently, still thinking that Susan might suddenly decide to dry up on all this uncomfortable past and start talking about the weather and the crops. But she didn't.

"She ran out the front door of the Palace Hotel one morning—straight under a tram," Susan said shortly.

"Yes. I knew that—"

"Do you think what happened between them then has something to do with Lindsay's disappearance now?" Susan turned from the glass and looked at me rather carefully.

"It—yes, it may have."

"Very well then. I'll tell you, because I think you may be right."

We left the church, and walked toward the formal pleasure gardens at the far side of the rectory, the dogs recovered now after their shady siesta, off after imaginary rabbits once more.

"I was a little older than Lindsay after all," she said, picking up a basket and pruning shears from a wooden wheelbarrow and walking to the rosebushes. "And Eleanor was several years younger. Makes a difference when one is young. He and I were in our late teens. Eleanor was still almost a child. My father had been padre in one of the general's regiments during the Great War, so we were accepted neighbors of the Phillipses'. Spent whole days over at Glenalyth, as Lindsay did over here."

"With just you two girls?"

"Yes, but he fished, you see: fly-fishing—trout and salmon on the Tay here. There was none of that on the loch at Glenalyth. So we got to see quite a lot of him during the holidays. It wasn't difficult—" She stopped, bending down over a recalcitrant thorny bloom, trying to cut it firmly, and yet at an angle, at its base.

"Yes?" I said.

"Well, things were excessively formal in those days, you know. Especially among families like ours. Nonetheless, suitable marriages were pondered on, well ahead of time. He and I were not discouraged, shall I say. And Lindsay was 'suitable' to put it mildly. Besides, I liked him a lot."

Susan moved on to another rosebush, a delicate, crimsonpetaled flower whose perfume, even in the heat, was clear as a bell. "He was rather a diffident, withdrawn person, an only child who never got on well with his father, the rough old general. And I liked that side of him. But he knew what he wanted, too. There was a kind of frustrated confidence about him. In short, we took to each other. That was the end of his first year at Oxford—the summer of 1929 or '30."

Having taken a dozen fragrant roses in the basket, we moved back now to a long wooden greenhouse at the top of the garden, where Susan inspected a small nectarine tree that was feebly trying to climb up one wall, with fruit the size of a marble. "Looks like leaf curl, I'm afraid, " she said and I thought once more she was going to die on me.

"You said he had a ruthless streak," I reminded her.

"Yes." She turned from the little tree, rubbing one of the diseased leaves to dust in her fingers. "I first noticed it in silly things—in games. Tennis or croquet, that sort of thing." She smiled now at the memory. "Lindsay was really a very bad loser—terrible. Though he hid this well, too. He'd even cheat if things went badly against him. Very hard to spot, but I saw it several times: calling a ball out on the line more than once, you know?" She turned to me, suddenly gesturing with her hands, and saying briskly, "You see, he desperately wanted to win. A sort of insecurity in the shadow of his warlike Papa, I suppose. And I quite understood that. But then, well, one day—it was up there by that sundial." She waved her stick through the door at a broken marble column in the middle of the pleasure garden. "We were standing there and I asked him why he did this—why he cheated in small things. He denied it point-blank. And we never talked about it again."

We left the baking greenhouse and went down through the pleasure garden to a little summerhouse, where we took wicker chairs, and the two dogs lapped thirstily at bowls of water Susan poured for them out of a watering can before filling an old vase on the table and starting to arrange the roses in it.

"The next summer he asked me to marry him. We were alone, he and I, most of that summer. Eleanor had gone to a crammer's in Edinburgh. She had a chance of a place in Lady Margaret Hall that September. Well, I was very cool-headed about his offer. All the same, I said yes, though we didn't tell either of our parents—which must show that either he or I had some sort of doubt about it all. That was 1932. Well, he went back to Oxford then, and we wrote to each other—rather careful letters. But the style of the times, I suppose. I was in Edinburgh trying to be a secretary—had rooms just next the Lyceum theater with an old cousin. We saw each other over Christmas and all seemed well. And then in his New Year letters he started talking about socialism—about Marx and about completely changing society and all that—and about Eleanor. He was seeing quite a lot of her in Oxford by then. And that's when it all started going downhill between us."

I had picked up an old croquet mallet from an open box beside me and was letting it swing gently between my knees. One of the terriers had got up anxiously, thinking I was about to start a game. I put the mallet down.

"He had obviously convinced Eleanor of his ideas." Susan finished her rose flower arrangement. "But I'm afraid he never persuaded me."

"But surely," I said tactfully, "that wasn't at all uncommon then. So many young people, especially undergraduates, went left in the thirties. It was a bad time—"

"Oh yes, I know all that." Susan looked at me as if I were being intentionally obtuse. "I was something of a reformer myself by then. Not socialist, but decidedly liberal, if you like."

"So why did it go wrong between you?"

"Because I became convinced that Lindsay's socialism—his communism even, for that's what it was—was a complete fraud. He didn't mean it, which is what came to infuriate me about him and Eleanor: that he made *her* believe in it all, hook, line and sinker—without believing in it himself. It was a lie."

I was amazed by this ready confirmation of my own thoughts about Lindsay. "But how did you become convinced that he was lying about his beliefs?"

"Perhaps it was my interest in crosswords and puzzle games and clues generally. I should have been a mystery writer." She smiled, putting down the roses and straightening her fingers as if they'd been too long at a typewriter. "I used to be very sharp—too sharp—about what people said, the way they contradicted themselves." She paused now, as if considering a new and risky thought and was wondering whether to voice it. "You see, the one thing Lindsay was never very interested in was verse. Well, I was, in a quiet way. It was when he came up here—that would be the summer of '33—and started quoting all the moderns then, Auden and Day Lewis and the others. That's when I first had my suspicions. I remember particularly walking over the moors at Glenalyth one afternoon—Eleanor was with us—and Lindsay began to quote one of those apocalyptic socialist millennia poems, something from Auden about 'giving away all the farms,' I remember. And he said that this would mean giving up all the tenanted farms on the Glenalyth estate which he was going to own. Well, I knew this was ridiculous, that he was saying something he didn't really believe at all. Lindsay was very land-conscious, you know. And I told him so afterwards—that he was cheating again, or at least playing games. And we didn't talk about getting married after that. There was a coldness..."

Susan looked out onto the sun-filled lawn, living that coldness again, her pale face absolutely immobile.

"The funny thing was," she went on, "that by next year, when he'd left Oxford and was cramming for the F.O. exams—before he was posted to Vienna—he'd completely given up all his left-wing business and taken just the opposite course: became very reactionary, never stopped running the socialists down and blackguarding Ramsay MacDonald—which was a sore temptation then, I'll admit.

"But surely that was a fairly common process at the time? Simply a flirtation with Marx, and then over to the other side? Why should the whole thing have been fraudulent? Lindsay was growing up, after all, in Oxford, which was full of extreme views; but they were temporary ones. I don't find that unusual—his trying things out."

"Yes, I've thought of that, of course. But the fact is Lindsay had no extreme views in politics. The pro-Hitler line he took in the mid-thirties was as false as his earlier socialist enthusiasms. I'm sure of that."

"But how can you be sure?"

She stood up, taking the basket impatiently from the table, while the dogs came to a canine alert behind her.

"If you've spent a great part of your childhood with someone, growing up together—if you've been close to them—you *know*. And I know: Lindsay was never more than a simple patriot at heart."

"But does one ever really know what happens inside someone else? I grew up with Rachel—just like you and Lindsay. Yet now I feel I never got to grips with the real person."

Susan shrugged her shoulders. "Simply because Lindsay prevented you—kept her in thrall. I was luckier. Lindsay didn't fool me. It was Eleanor who suffered. Of course, what I'd like to know is why in the first place he pretended to all these things he didn't believe in. Come, let's have some tea."

The dogs were allowed a saucer of cooled milky tea each, dispensed from an elegant Georgian silver teapot, while Susan and I ate some thin tomato sandwiches and crumbly oatcakes prepared for us by the woman in the gate lodge. The drawing room was bright and cheerful, with two large windows at each angle looking southwards down the tree-lined valley. There was a steady table in the middle, comfortable chintz armchairs, some good Scottish watercolors on the well-papered walls, and what looked like an engraving of Byron to one side of the fine red marble mantelpiece, on which I saw a number of delicately carved wooden and enameled music boxes—half a dozen perhaps; more, certainly, than the remainder of this collection that I had seen in the drawing room in Hyde Park Square. Yet there was no sense of any shrine here—unless it were a most tactful one to the bad Lord B. himself. The room was as gracious and carefully composed as the woman who occupied it.

"You see, what I can't understand," Susan said, "was why, not believing in all this socialist business himself, he then encouraged Eleanor in it. That was the dishonest thing—and the cruelest. For it was she who suffered as a result, long before he did, wherever he is." She looked out the window dismissively, as though Lindsay had gone down the valley into some well-merited exile in a distant country.

"You think her suicide came as a result of her believing in him—in their shared socialism, which he then denied?"

"More than possible—that that was part of it."

"There were other parts?"

"I—don't know." She spoke more carefully now, I thought. "I wasn't there at the time. Though I'd been in Zagreb that summer before she died. The four of us. We'd just come back from a motor trip through Slovenia."

"Four of you?"

"Of course. Zlatko was with us."

"Who?"

"Zlatko Rabernak—Lindsay's Yugoslav friend."

"Not a university teacher?"

"No. Zlatko was from Zagreb. He was a musicologist and collector." She pointed to the row of music boxes on the mantelpiece. "All those. He was a great collector of them. They bought a few from him, but most he gave her."

"Of course, the music boxes. There are some in London. But I'd not heard of him."

"He was a dear friend." Susan refilled my cup. The tea was some delicious mix of Indian and China. "We'd taken holidays together several times before," she continued lightly.

"Down the Rhine?"

"Yes. How did you know?"

I produced the old photograph from my pocket. "I found it in one of the attics at Glenalyth."

Susan became quite animated. "I have some rather better ones than that." She stood up, went over to a bureau near the fireplace, and took out an album, bringing it back for me to look at.

"There," she said, finding a page in the middle of the book. And now I saw a much fuller and more exact representation of that forty-year-old holiday in Germany: some dozens of photographs of the three of them and the man Zlatko—a small-faced, bright-eyed, impish fellow with shiny dark hair combed straight back from his forehead. They were shown sitting on benches at a riverbank inn, picnicking by a car on a roadside or moving along narrow mountain paths in the sunny Rhineland of 1935. And I noticed how Susan's expression here, unlike her gloomy mood in my own photograph, was almost invariably happy—especially in the snaps where she and Zlatko appeared together.

Suddenly the question in the back of my mind occurred to me clearly, but somehow I couldn't voice it. It seemed impertinent to broach so private a thing. And it might not have been true, in any case. But here, surely, was one possible answer. Of course, as I had said to Rachel, there had been four of them on that prewar summer holiday in Germany—floating down the great river and cruising Hitler's new autobahns in a Sunbeam Talbot. And since Lindsay and Eleanor were clearly spoken for at that time, Zlatko must have been Susan's particular friend and companion. And if this were so, had there—as I sensed—been some trouble between the two of them then?

Susan had just described him as a "dear friend," hers,

presumably, as well as of the other two. Had Zlatko thrown Susan over in some way? And I remembered the music boxes and Susan's slightly tart comment: "They bought a few . . . but most he gave her." And I thought, too, how Rachel had told me that Susan had insisted on taking all these little music boxes back after Eleanor's death. Had she done this not to create any kind of shrine to Eleanor—and indeed there was no evidence of such in the house—but in order to take subsequently gifts which she had hoped to receive from Zlatko then? Failing with Lindsay, had she fallen in love with one of his friends, only to find that he, too, was engaged elsewhere? Had Zlatko, like Lindsay, taken first to her but then to her younger sister? Still I couldn't put these questions in any direct way to Susan. They seemed too dense and complex, with the implication of appalling emotion, to survive an entry or clarification in this calm drawing room. Yet I had to broach the topic in some way.

"Is Zlatko still alive?" I asked easily, without looking up from the album.

"No idea, really."

"You don't hear from him ever?"

"No. Why?"

"You mentioned that he was a dear friend," I said uneasily.

"I see what you mean." And now Susan for the first time that afternoon, became the Aunt Susan she had been to Rachel and me in our childhood: a rather formidable, bossy lady in a long brown cardigan, someone difficult to appease whom one therefore tried to avoid. "I was very fond of Zlatko, that's all—if that's what you mean," she said shortly, closing the album.

I knew then that I had passed over the line between polite adult inquiry and childish impertinence; that I had prised open a private memory, an ancient wound.

"I didn't want to pry—"

"How could you?" she said, angrily. "You weren't even born then. Did you find something else in the attic?"

"No."

She became calm again after this short outburst. "It's so ridiculous, that one should be upset, so long afterwards. I'm sorry." She bent down and picked up the two saucers the dogs had emptied.

"No, it's not ridiculous. We spend so much of our lives

avoiding the truth. You said so yourself—in the church: 'living so long with omissions.'"

Susan said nothing; both hands lay quietly on the table in front of her, as if she were about to play something on a piano.

"I've always prided myself on being sensible," she said at last. "Even the most difficult clue had an answer, a meaning somewhere. But I never understood their lives, no matter how I've tried. Perhaps Lindsay was simply mesmerized," Susan said, more to herself than to me. "Standing there doing nothing, while Zlatko took over his wife."

"I see," I said. "That's what happened?"

"Yes. He simply let her go."

"Did she *want* to go?"

"I don't know. I could never make the least sense out of it. It defied all reason."

"These sort of things usually do."

The older dog moved over to the cold fireplace now, and lay down, while the Highland terrier started to whine, anxious to be let out. "Oh, do be quiet, Tomkins!" Susan said. But I got up and went to the door, the dog following.

"Of course, Lindsay may have wanted her away because he no longer shared her politics. She may have become an embarrassment to him and his FO career." I opened the door. But the dog wouldn't go out now; it just sat there on the threshold, looking up at me expectantly.

"Yes," Susan said. "I've thought of that. And if it's true it's quite appalling. Let him stay if he wants," she added. I closed the door and the dog followed me back to my seat. "Give him a bit of oatcake," Susan said. "That's exactly what I meant," she went on, "when I told you how it was Eleanor who suffered for her beliefs, not Lindsay, who never held them."

"It's a terrible tale. If it's true—"

"It *is* true. I saw it happen. And Zlatko told me himself—how he'd become involved with Eleanor, which is why I left that summer before she died."

"What did he say?"

"He was totally vague about it—they all were: said it was just something that 'happened'—and that Eleanor was unhappy with Lindsay in any case. Well, I knew that. But I told him he shouldn't *let* it happen—"

She paused now, as though aware of the element of personal bias she had allowed into her description.

"And Lindsay?" I said, covering the silence. "How did he explain it all afterwards to you?"

"He never did—other than once ascribing Eleanor's behavior to a kind of madness."

"Well, there may have been that in it, too. There often is. How did you know Eleanor was unhappy with Lindsay?"

"She talked to me about it. She was unhappy for the same reasons as I'd been, I think, though she wouldn't admit it. She felt there was something basically false in him."

"Living a lie?"

"Yes."

"You know that Lindsay was really working for British Intelligence for most of his career?"

"Yes. At least, I learned that only after the war."

"And that perhaps wives in such cases don't always know what their husbands are really up to? It may, in any case, have been necessary for Lindsay to lead a double life, especially if Eleanor had all these socialist sympathies. You could see the whole thing that way, couldn't you? That Lindsay married Eleanor in good faith but subsequently his work required him to—to withhold things from her, even to lie to her."

Susan didn't answer at once.

"If you looked at the whole business quite without bias," I went on, "entirely objectively, it could make sense that way, couldn't it?"

"Yes, it could," Susan admitted at last.

"And Zlatko was right. These things—I mean he and Eleanor—they do just 'happen.'"

The little white dog started to whine again, looking toward the door, and this time I got up and put him firmly outside.

"What you say makes objective sense, maybe," Susan said when I'd got back. "But you didn't know the people involved, weren't actually there. Subjectively the whole thing was a fearful mess."

"As it would be, because you were closely involved. I was simply trying to be fair to Lindsay."

"I see that," she said reasonably. "And perhaps you're right. But it still doesn't explain my feeling—" She stopped, as though she'd quite lost the feeling. "My certainty almost, that all these political involvements of Lindsay's were a charade. Simply wasn't him."

"No, indeed, because British Intelligence could well have *required* him, from the start, to take up these fronts."

"Simply carrying out orders, you mean? Well, doesn't that make it worse?" Susan was firmly dismissive now. "If that's so—and let's say we agree that his socialism was all a pose—why did he encourage Eleanor in it initially? Share it with her, and then, forced into the opposite, reactionary extreme by his bosses, deceive Eleanor about this new course? Why did he carry her along with him, marry her? He should have dropped her long before if he felt he couldn't share *anything* in his professional life with her. Instead, he held on to her, he lied and he manipulated her."

It was my turn for silence now. "Well?" she asked.

"Yes, I agree. It does seem . . . strange."

"Cruel, surely—cheating of the worst sort."

"It's putting country above people, of course. You said he was really a simple patriot at heart."

"Yes, a patriot. But not a fool. He knew right from wrong in personal affairs. You're suggesting he was a moral simpleton. That wasn't so. He was a perfectly aware person, as well."

Susan finished her little biography with some vehemence. It had a precision and feeling that smacked of the truth, of her direct experience of it and her sad disgust with the man himself.

"But," I said, "you told me you thought all this business with Eleanor had to do with his disappearance. How?"

"I simply meant that anyone who behaved as he did then—so illogically and unfeelingly—well, one day it was bound to catch up with him."

"Isn't that just the revenge of myth? In reality, don't the worst rogues always go unhanged?"

"You admit it, then?"

"No. Well, I don't know. I've often wondered: does cause and effect really operate like that—so far apart in time?"

"Yes—if you go on living your lies long enough."

Susan looked at me critically.

"You're right," I said. "But I thought you might have meant something more precise—"

"That Zlatko bumped him off, you mean? Forty years later? No." She smiled minutely and I was reminded again of the other Yugoslav in Zagreb—Ivo Kovačić, the beekeeper and university professor whose letter to Lindsay I had found in the attic. I asked Susan if she'd known him.

"Yes—a big man, very forthcoming, very nationalistic about Croatia, talked endlessly. We used to meet at that café in Zagreb on the main square, the Gradska something. And you're right—he kept bees. We had some of his honey, I remember. And Lindsay rented his house when he first came to the consulate in Zagreb. Yes—it was up in a nice park above the town. Why?"

"They were quite close friends, then?"

"Yes, I'm sure they were. Lindsay had a lot of friends out there at the time. They were very kind..." She let the sentence die away, seeming to remember that time indecisively, warily almost.

I had one further, and under the circumstances, most difficult point to try and raise with Susan: Rachel's vision of her and Lindsay in the boat that afternoon, ten years after the tragedy in Zagreb. In the light of what Susan had just told me, it seemed more than ever an unlikely view.

"Rachel—" I said, "I wanted to ask you. She's told me of feeling some sort of terrible unease as a child in Glenalyth, during and just after the war. Well, you were often there then, you remember—you came over to look after us sometimes. I wondered why you did this, feeling about Lindsay as you did?"

"I helped out because I was—still part of the family," she said firmly, shades of Aunt Susan beginning to move over her face again.

"Even after all you'd been through with Eleanor and Lindsay?"

"With Lindsay? No. It was the family. As I say. Not Lindsay." She spoke abruptly now, her words reflecting some uncontrolled staccato in her thoughts. "It was you. And Patrick. And Rachel."

"Yes, it was Rachel who felt this unease. She told me yesterday she suddenly thought she knew why: a sense of antagonism between you and Lindsay—"

"Well, there was that."

"But then she says—and it may be nonsense—she says she saw you in the boat one afternoon together. She was hiding on the shore somewhere. And...there didn't seem to be any antagonism at all."

Susan stood up and went over to the mantelpiece; she took a pair of spectacles out of a case and put them on before turning back to me. She now seemed the image of her former self, the rather bitter schoolmarm that I remembered. But when she spoke her voice was quite calm.

"Poor Rachel. She was so insecure then."

"Yes, but why?"

"Because of Patrick. Have you found out something in the attics? I can't think—"

"No, what?"

"Patrick was our son—Lindsay's and mine; not Eleanor's," she said quite simply. "That's why I was at Glenalyth, looking after you all quite a lot." She moved over to the open window where the bees were loudly sampling a cotoneaster bush just outside. "No one knew. Except Eleanor, and then she died. And no one knows now. And he's dead, too."

"I'm—sorry."

Susan turned from the window. "It wasn't the done thing, you see, in those days. And now it's all so irrelevant, with none of them left."

"All the same, I'm terribly..." But there was nothing more I could say. The chasm was too deep, had no bottom to it.

"It doesn't square at all, does it, about what I've told you about being sensible. Well, it never has to me either." She walked over to the mantelpiece again and now I recognized one of the watercolors above it as the loch at Glenalyth. Susan glanced at it. "Oh, yes, Rachel probably did see us in the boat that afternoon." She stopped, before continuing forcibly. "I detest the expression 'love—hate.' It seems so pat and unreal. But it wasn't."

She turned and said, "Where is Lindsay, do you think?" a minute hope, I thought, in her voice. A few hours before, she had been so calm, a woman untouched by human aberration. But now her expression was that of someone who has suffered every horror in the book.

"I don't know," I said. "I'm trying to find out."

The indecisive dog started to scratch at the door again, and I got up once more to let him in.

4

June and Marianne arrived the following day from London, in clothes as unsuited to the country as their husbands' had been. Their mood was awkward, too—as strangers in an already well-developed house party who had perhaps missed more than half the fun. Marianne drank too much whisky the first evening, while June kept to her room until lunchtime on Saturday. The house was uneasy that weekend.

I'd described my visit with Susan to Madeleine and Rachel at breakfast in no more than social terms, avoiding any depths and denying that she'd helped in any real way over Lindsay—a deception that wasn't difficult, since neither showed any great interest in my meeting the previous day. I was surprised by this. It was as if, for some reason, the matter of Lindsay and all his doings had ceased to interest the household. Or perhaps, I thought, it had simply come to obsess me.

Marianne alone, perhaps due to the careless euphoria and impertinence that comes with a hangover, appeared interested in the problem that had brought me to Glenalyth. Before she burst in on me, I was in the study at the back of the house where most of the books were kept, looking for some detailed map of the Home Counties that might have the old Oxford-Cambridge railway lines on it, when something else caught my eye—a German book that had fallen behind a bottom shelf where the prewar ordnance survey maps were, with a vaguely familiar name on the spine: Maria von Karlinberg. Maria? And then I rememberd her—could it have been the same person? "Maria" had been a name in the youthful address book of Lindsay's that I'd brought down from the attic. I imagined her to be an aristocratic old Viennese lady, living on a pittance in some decrepit Hapsburg *Schloss*. But she must have been someone rather younger, I thought now, almost a contemporary of Lindsay's, for the book, so far as I could judge from my rusty German, had been issued without a printer's or publisher's name and therefore perhaps clandestinely. It appeared to be an account, in the form of a "comrade's diary," of all the bloody events that had led up to the demise of Austrian democracy, beginning with Dollfuss's massacre of the workers in their model estates in February 1934—the same violent events that Lindsay had witnessed when he had first been posted to Vienna, and about which he had written home in such a two-faced manner.

There was a printed dedication in German: "To the Fat Man in the Blue Bar at Sacher's"—was how I translated it, a message that intrigued me, since this expensive Viennese hotel seemed an unlikely place for any "comrade" to drink, then or now. The book, apart from the dust and cobwebs, was in mint condition, seemingly unopened. I put it aside for later reading, as a possible pointer to something, although I'd no idea what.

"Oh, I'm sorry," Marianne said, when she disturbed me, looking haggard but purposeful in a pair of sky-blue nylon ski pants and fashionable knee-length Cossack boots, unlikely accessories given the weather outside, where the sun was beating down as usual on a tinder-dry world. I'd just found what I wanted, an old ordnance survey map kept with a host of others on a bottom shelf. I didn't stop what I was doing, trying to identify and trace the branch line between Oxford and Cambridge. She came up to me.

"Going on a journey?"

It was impossible to be even vaguely rude to Marianne, her brashness was so assumed and she herself so essentially vulnerable. "Yes. I mean, no. I was looking for an old railway line." And then I spotted it, quite clearly, a branch track that wound east to west between Cambridge and Oxford, across Buckinghamshire, through Bedford and Bletchley, with the station at Bow Brickhill just about midway between the two universities.

"There, there it is," I said involuntarily.

"Just what *is* going on—will you tell me?" Marianne was abruptly rude. "George tells me nothing. What games are you all playing?"

"I—we, we were looking for Lindsay—"

"Down that old railway line?"

"Maybe."

"I'm not quite such a fool, you know." I looked up. Her rather unruly fair hair had been crimped back against the sides of her skull with tortoiseshell combs; her cheeks were flushed and the whites of her eyes streaked with crimson lines. I could see the neat Scotch the previous night had affected her badly.

"Of course you're not." And she wasn't a fool, I realized again, except in one way—in allowing herself to be so consistently hurt in her long and hopeless love for George. "I didn't know you wanted to know about Lindsay."

She sighed, rather dramatically. "I want to know about George—what the hell he's up to. He never says."

"Oh?"

"I don't see why he should get mixed up in all this cloak-and-dagger nonsense."

"Is he?"

"Yes. Phoning and seeing people all last week, before he came up here. He's a musician, not a private eye," she added abruptly.

"Who—"

"I was so annoyed I went to see Fielding myself." She was almost stamping round the study now. "His bloody friend Fielding," she went on. "Well, I know Basil from the old days at college: just a soak—but a dangerous soak. And George shouldn't be involved."

I didn't look up too quickly from my map. Indeed something had just struck me that seemed of even more interest than what Marianne had just said. But I forgot it in this new and unexpected intelligence.

"You went to see him?"

"Yes."

"What for?"

210

Marianne stopped walking about and stood, both hands on her hips, legs apart, like a stable girl about to lose patience with a nag.

"Did you know Fielding was with the Russians?" She spoke with the slurred, cheeky confidence that results from a bad hangover.

"The *Russians?* How do you know?"

"Well, working for someone he shouldn't. I didn't phone him, you see. Just went around, rang the bell. He wasn't in. But someone else opened the door—"

"When was this?"

"Friday. Yesterday. Anyway, it was the police, you see, or the special branch or whoever they are. They were in the flat. The whole place was upside down and they more or less pounced on me: Who was I? What was I doing—and I didn't have many good answers as I'd not made an appointment and hadn't seen Basil for years. They thought I was a contact of his. Anyway, they eventually realized I wasn't, and let me go. But it was quite obvious they were onto Basil in a bad way. So he must have done something pretty wrong. Defected or something," she added professionally.

"Yes? What?"

"Well, I don't know. But I don't want George involved. It's none of his business, looking for Lindsay Phillips," she added very tartly.

"Did you tell George?"

"Of course. He said it wasn't important."

What was George up to? Why suddenly was none of all this important to anyone any more?

"So Basil has decamped," Marianne went on with authority. "And you only do that if you're working for the other side, don't you?"

"I suppose so." I was fairly stunned.

"Well, can't we do something?"

"What?"

"Because they're coming up here, they said so, to talk to George about his phone calls and about his seeing Basil just before he disappeared. You see, I had to tell them about why I was there—because George was up to something with him. And I suppose they'd been watching his flat and tapping the phone as well."

"Coming here? No one's said anything."

"Well, they said they were. And I don't like it. Basil is

211

probably another Philby all over again. And now George is going to be involved in it all."

It was her mentioning Philby that brought me back to the map and the old railway line. Philby, Burgess, and Maclean—of course. All Cambridge men, the same college, same generation. And hadn't we always wondered who had recruited them, how they'd managed their initial involvement with the Russians who were then in England? Someone already at Cambridge, some don there, it had often been thought. But why only at Cambridge? The undergraduates at Oxford must have offered the Soviets almost as rich a potential in recruits. Had the KGB tried and failed there, or had they tried and succeeded without anyone ever knowing?

How, I thought, as a Soviet Intelligence recruiter, might you best minister to both universities in this matter, while at the same time giving the recruits from each equal cover in their early clandestine activities? Might you not situate yourself midway between the two universities—say half an hour's train ride either way—in order to spot prospective traitors? And might not those clients—apprentices now in the NKVD—put the process into reverse, and under the guise of attending meetings of a model railway club, make their reports to this first link in the Soviet Intelligence chain—either to the man who ran the "Oxford and Cambridge Model Railway Club" or to someone from London, a member of it himself, who came up to engage his new recruits under cover of this innocuous hobby, talking to them afterwards in the village pub or as they walked back to the real railway station? Was this how Lindsay had first become a part of Soviet Intelligence—through his model railway trains?

It was a theory, at least, with only one obvious flaw: the clients of such a Soviet controller or contact could never have all visited Bow Brickhill at the same time, or even actually used the place as a club together, since their identity as Soviet recruits would then have become known among themselves. On the other hand, the place might have been used only individually by its members, one at a time, with instructions never to divulge their involvement with the club. Or again, it might simply have been used as a message drop or as a contact only in emergencies. Finally, of course, my theories could have been pure fantasy; the club could have been entirely bona fide. *Have* been? Perhaps it still existed.

"Well?" Marianne said.

"Wait and see. What else?"

We didn't have long. The phone rang at midday. It was for George, and the whole business emerged over lunch. I must say George handled it very well. "A matter of no importance," he'd said. *"Pas de problème,"* he added—one of his favorite phrases. George was in a confident, garrulous mood: the impresario about to make a killing. And apparently his music with Rachel had gone well that morning—Dottie Parker was being shoved along at a gallop. The others seemed to agree with George's diagnosis of the events in London.

"Just a fellow I knew years ago." He started to round off the topic. "Thought he might be able to help over Lindsay. Of course I can't tell them anything about him; wonder they're bothering to come up all this way." George was almost witty about it now. "Old Basil's probably done a bunk to Moscow. Sly fellow he always was anyway. Little half-pint man." George quaffed at a larger pewter mug of beer—a refreshment he'd provided himself with each lunch time since the start of the week—and cracked some unsuitable joke about life in a *dacha* in the Moscow woods.

It didn't really strike me as very funny at all. Almost everyone I'd come across in my inquiries about Lindsay had gone the same way, or worse: first McKnight in the Wren church, then the lout on the train; then Allcock and his American friend, and now Basil. Even Professor Wellcome in Oxford had tried to run a mile from me when I'd taxed him on the matter. Lindsay's friends appeared a remarkably unstable lot. As for Basil—who could tell? Had Marcus framed him, just, as I suspected, he'd tried to get rid of me? And what of Basil's friend the Prime Minister? Perhaps he'd be the next to go.

"When are they coming to see you?" I asked George.

George looked up from his tankard mischievously. "This afternoon," he said. "On their way now—flying up to Perth."

A rush job, I thought. But I was more surprised still when, right after lunch, David Marcus got out of the car, followed by Inspector Carse and another man.

Marcus barely introduced himself and it was obvious that Carse had no idea who he really was. His colleague from London—a D.I. 5 man by the heavy-footed look of him—took George to the morning room, while Marcus led me off tactfully into the study.

"Yes," I said at once. "I wanted to see you..."

"I warned you, Marlow—"

"Yes, that lout on the train was warning enough. But I've not taken it."

"He was nothing to do with me, that man."

"Of course not, 'I got a job to do,' he told me. And he certainly wasn't looking for my wristwatch."

"You're in the firing line, Marlow. But they're not my guns."

"You're lying. Or do you suppose the Russkies are after me? That *they* don't want Lindsay found?"

Marcus made a gesture of impatience. "Believe what you will. It's no matter—"

"Dead bodies never did matter to you. All right. You don't want Lindsay found. But you won't tell me why, will you? Not really why. Just a lot of cock about his being a right-winger on the make in your Service, which is a pretty poor excuse for the mayhem you're setting up—"

"Believe what you will. You want to find Lindsay? Well, go ahead. But don't say you weren't warned."

"Oh yes, I'm being warned all the time. Everyone's doing it."

"You're not progressing, then?"

"Why should I tell you? Was that what you came all this way for, a progress report?"

"It interests me, naturally."

"Naturally. But you could have sent a junior up to talk to me. Whatever's going on, you want to keep it entirely to yourself. So it's bigger than some right-wing conspiracy, isn't it, Marcus?"

"I came to talk to you about Basil Fielding," Marcus said wearily.

"What is there to say? Fielding—and the PM—wanted Lindsay found. You don't. So I suppose you did Basil in, and the PM is next on your list. But you surely can't do away with everyone who wants to see Lindsay again. Or can you?"

"Do stop this fantasizing, Marlow. Matters have changed. Fielding, it now seems clear, was with Moscow—"

"Shouldn't have been too difficult for you to fake things that way for him—"

"*Listen* for once, will you?" Marcus said fiercely. "I faked nothing for him. A routine security check put us onto him. He was being followed and he met a man who was nothing to do with us. We don't know who he was—"

"Where was this?"

"Hampstead. By the pond there, last Sunday, pretending to look at the model boats."

"You followed the other man too, of course."

"Yes. But we lost him. We think he must have been with the Soviets, though, up the road from the Highgate compound."

"Well, all it simply means is that *you* don't want Lindsay found, but the KGB do. Ergo: he's one of theirs, probably has been all along. And that would embarrass you, Marcus, which is why you're shutting the shop up tight on Lindsay Phillips and pretending he never existed, or better still, praying he's at the bottom of the loch down there and won't turn up in a month or so at the Moscow press club, telling how he pulled the wool over all your eyes for forty years. That's what all this amounts to. After Philby and the others, you'd do anything to stop another really big scandal. And this would be one, no doubt. They'd really have your head on a plate then, Marcus."

"They would, if it were true. But it isn't." Marcus fingered his pearly tie. "It's more complicated than that."

"It always is."

"You're no longer a member of the Service. I can't give you all the details. I warned you, simply—"

"Good God, Marcus, I told you in London—these people are my friends. That's why I'm looking for Lindsay. I don't give a tinker's curse for the rest of it—whether he was left, right or center. So tell me—what have you really come to see me about?"

"About Fielding, as I said. Did he ever say anything else to you, when he briefed you about Lindsay, that might have made you think he was with the KGB?"

"That won't wash, Marcus. You don't really want to know that. Your men in London could get all that sort of information for you. You've come all the way up here for something else. And I can't for the life of me think what it is."

There was silence then, a neat impasse. Marcus looked across at me with a kind of amused confidence. "No?" he said. "Well, don't worry. You go on looking for him, if you must."

Marcus and I parted amicably enough in the hall. Madeleine had offered him tea but he'd declined, pleading urgent affairs elsewhere.

"What's up with George?" I asked. He was still closeted

215

in the morning room. Marcus shifted about uneasily by the dead fireplace before going back to see what had happened to them all.

Marianne was with us, shades of unhappy worry everywhere about her face. "What *can* they be up to? George knows nothing about that fool."

The morning-room door opened at last, and we heard the heavy tramp of feet coming toward us—and George's voice protesting about something, the rather high-pitched undergraduate tones arguing the toss in the college debating society, but now with a really serious edge to it: "It's ridiculous," we heard him say as the group came along the back corridor. "There's no question! You can't possibly..."

They all came into the hall. George stooped by the door, surrounded now by the three much smaller men.

"They're arresting me," he said, loudly, incredulously, addressing all of us, his great face shining, expanding with anger and amazement.

"Not arresting, sir," the Special Branch man put in. "Further questioning, that's all."

George took no notice of him. "They're taking me down to London!" he declaimed, like some great nationalist orator betrayed. Then he looked at me, walking toward me. "You. You must know what's going on—"

"Yes, he does!" Marianne almost shrieked, rushing over to George, taking him by the arm, then turning so that they both confronted me. But George took no notice of her. "You set this up," he said vehemently. I thought he was going to hit me as he took another step nearer. I retreated.

"What—"

And he would have hit me if Carse and the others hadn't held on to him just then like a tug-of-war team. "You set it up, all of it. To get me out of the way," he added.

I couldn't think what he was getting at. And then I saw him looking at Rachel bitterly and I knew. It was pure farce and I couldn't prevent a smile, which, of course, infuriated George still more. He made another lunge at me, struggling like a great bear caught in a trap.

"I've no idea," I said, retreating once more. "Marcus! What is going on?"

But none of them replied. George was told to pack a bag, and Marianne went upstairs with him. Fifteen minutes later the two of them were bundled into the car and they all disappeared down the drive. We stood on the porch watching them go. Max and June had arrived from somewhere during the fracas.

"Well, there goes Dottie Parker," Max said, before turning and looking at me with distaste. "'Gangway, girls: I'll show you trouble,'" he added. I scowled back at him in return. "You don't know what you're talking about," I said. "It was nothing to do with me." Then I noticed both Rachel and Madeleine looking at me questioningly. I shook my head in disbelief.

"You don't really want Lindsay found, do you?"

"Well..." Madeleine paused. "If it leads to all this trouble..."

And then I realized that this was exactly why they'd taken George: to *cause* that trouble, so that I would be forced, or at least asked to stop looking for Lindsay. And what would happen when I told them, as I now felt I must, that Lindsay had probably been a traitor most of his life? No doubt they would see that as simply another piece of mischief on my part.

We were in the hall after supper. June and Max had left the three of us alone. Indeed, they were upstairs packing, having decided to return to London the next morning. The house party had rather collapsed.

"You asked me to help," I said. "I don't see how we can possibly stop now."

Madeleine sat perfectly still in one corner of the sofa, looking into some middle distance, while Rachel fidgeted on the edge of a chair opposite. Our coffee was getting cold. They said nothing.

"How *can* you?" I asked, almost roughly.

"I begin to feel somehow that he's not to be found," Madeleine said eventually.

"David Marcus doesn't *want* him found, that's all, because he thinks Lindsay was with the Russians. It would be an embarrassment for him if he turned up. But we can't just do nothing."

"What can we do?" Rachel asked briskly. "If what you say is true, then he must have gone over there. Are you suggesting a trip to Moscow?"

"Do *you* think he's been with them all this time?" Madeleine asked.

"Yes, I think it's quite possible that he was with Moscow." I looked at her firmly. She laughed, unnaturally, I thought, bent forward with the spasm. "It doesn't sound like him, Peter. It really doesn't."

"In his world it's perfectly possible."

"His world was mine too." I remembered Susan's bitter comments on Lindsay's earlier betrayals with Eleanor.

"He wouldn't have told you," was all I could say.

"But I knew him for nearly forty years. I *knew* him. He wouldn't have done that." Madeleine looked at me with absolute certainty in her eyes: the glowing, clear look of the totally innocent, and thus possibly the most deceived. "I *knew* him," she said again, repeating that great confidence in knowledge that comes of a long love. But Susan had "known" him in this way, too, earlier in his life; Susan who had grown up with him and loved him as well—and borne his child into the bargain. Yet she had been proved wrong and been deceived in the end. I feared for Madeleine. She "knew" him too—but had never known that Patrick wasn't Eleanor's child and had thus been equally ignorant of the real reasons for all that pain in Zagreb forty years before. Madeleine, it seemed, knew quite a different man.

"If he's worked for the Russians all his life I'll eat my hat," Rachel said, using the old slang, a schoolgirl now again herself and as full of belief as her mother in a man they had lived with and loved most of their lives. As I had suspected, it was I whom they viewed now as a presumptuous interloper come to disrupt and deny their familial affections, a messenger of darkness here to put out the light. I think at that moment they wished they'd never set eyes on me at the Chelsea Flower Show. Yet the fact remained, which they could not deny, that Lindsay had upped and disappeared one fine spring afternoon without leaving a word for them. If not to Moscow, then where? They might deny he was a traitor and be right, but if so, they were left with an even deeper mystery. For what husband and father, unblemished politically, would impose such a cruelty on his family? And for what reason?

As it turned out, to their unbelievable joy, the postman on Monday morning seemed to prove them right, in their initial belief at least.

"There—you see! He hasn't gone to Moscow," were Madeleine's first words to me, tears streaking her cheeks, after she had read the letter. It was typewritten, with a heading in capitals: HRVATSKA SLOBODAN!, the words divided by a flaming sword, the envelope postmarked Munich on the

Tuesday of the previous week.

My darling Tika and dearest Rachel,
  I can't describe the horrors of being out of touch with you these past three months and knowing how desperately you must have been worrying. Of course, as you will understand, it was none of my doing. I was taken and am being held (in considerable comfort, I may add) by the "Free Croatia" organization who are allowing me this letter to you both—which I am dictating since my arm was injured (not badly, so please don't worry). I am being held against demands which this group is rightly making for the release of Croatian nationalists and liberators now imprisoned throughout Europe. I am sure that, in this respect, our government will now liberate Stephan Vlada, the Croat patriot, unjustly held by them in Durham prison. When they have done that, I will be freed.

After this political spiel the letter continued in an entirely personal vein:

  I don't know when this will be, but soon I hope, and I long for that. In the meantime you will be brave and happy as you can be, both of you, until I see you again. I know you will be. We have been through worse things, after all, and survived—you and I and Rachel. Patrick I'm thinking of, and the war too. Wear the silver bracelet and be well till I see you again. And tell Billy I'm thinking of him and the honey. With this marvelous weather there should be a bumper yield this year. I'm sure I will be able to write again. My dearest love to you both, Chokis.

The mysterious signature alone was in ink: not in Lindsay's usual hand but a close approximation of it, I thought. All the same I played the devil's advocate for a moment.
  "Could it be forgery?"
  "How could it? He hardly ever called me 'Tika.' It's an old nickname from before the war," Madeleine said.
  "And 'Chokis'?" I asked. "What's that?"
  "Another reason it must be genuine," Madeleine raced on. "I sometimes called him 'Chokis'—*tjockis* means 'Fatso' in Swedish. We all went there once. Before the war. Lindsay apparently was rather plump when he was young and the name stuck among some of his intimates. But I didn't like

219

it. So I translated it—'Chokis'—a mixture of chocolates and kisses."

"And that silver bracelet," Rachel added. "You got that in Sweden too, didn't you?"

"Yes. It's very precious—I only wear it on special occasions. Who else could know all this—and about Patrick and Billy? And it's his style too. I can feel it. My God, he's alive," she added, turning away, restraining further tears and patting Ratty, who jumped for joy at her feet.

"He's alive." Rachel repeated the words calmly, a fine light in her eyes. She was not looking at either of us, though, but through the open hall door, her gaze fixed somewhere on the great summer outside.

"To the Fat Man in the Blue Bar at Sacher's" was all I could think of just then—the dedication in the *Comrade's Diary* by Maria von Karlinberg. Who, then, *was* Maria?

THE small village of Bow Brickhill in Buckinghamshire lay just a few miles off the M1 motorway, so it was an easy detour on our car journey to London two days later. "The Rise," given as the address of "The Oxford and Cambridge Model Railway Society," was no more than a narrow track leading steeply up from the single village street, soon to lose itself above us in the thick beech woods at the back of the Woburn estate that covered all the top of the hills. No. 17 was a fairly large, pink-bricked, recently restored cottage halfway up, on a small plateau of land. It looked down over the whole village, with a station and railway just beyond it—a line that was still operational, from Bedford to the new town of Milton Keynes, I presumed, for just as I got out of the Volvo a commuter train clattered toward us along the valley in the bright sunlight.

The cottage was a natural bastion and vantage point, I thought, with clear views all around for miles, except for the thick woods immediately behind it, which instead formed an ideal retreat or bolt hole. There was no bell, so I knocked on the handsome teak door with its inset of bottle-glass panes. A baby squealed bitterly from somewhere in a garden at the back.

I knocked again and a few moments later an elderly ruffle-haired man, half of a cheap cheroot burning in his mouth, in shorts and a colored shirt, opened the door. It was Professor John Wellcome.

220

He didn't recognize me at first. "Yes?" he asked abruptly. "I'm sorry, but the scenic railway is by appointment only." It was Madeleine he saw then, behind me, just getting out of the car. And in the instant he recognized her, he remembered me, and his face became still and canny before turning into a mask of welcome.

"Goodness gracious, John! I never knew you lived out here," Madeleine said when our surprised greetings were over and we were all inside the low-beamed drawing room. The dreadful baby, Bonzo, had come in from the garden now; seeing us all as usurpers of his ground and likely to delay his lunch, he started to scream. The American girl, Caroline, in a crocheted wool bikini, petulantly took him away to the kitchen.

"Oh yes." Wellcome clapped his hands in what struck me as an assumed joy, though the other two women were quite at ease. "Yes, indeed. This was my father's old house. We use it as a country cottage now. How splendid to see you both. Let me get you all a sherry—or even better, I've got some cold wine in the fridge . . . This weather!"

"We were just on our way down from Glenalyth. We've heard from Lindsay! Can you imagine—a letter yesterday. Some awful Yugoslavs are holding him somewhere . . ."

"Good God!" Wellcome drew the words out in genuine astonishment. "I'll get the wine and then you must tell me all about it." But then something struck him forcibly. "How did you get down here, Madeleine? We're hardly ever here—the place is usually let. How did you know—?"

"Oh, Peter here. He found an old membership card in the attics at Glenalyth—'The Oxford and Cambridge Model Railway Society' or something. And it had Lindsay's name on the bottom. Peter wanted to check and see if the society was still here: thought it might have had something to do with Lindsay's disappearance."

Wellcome turned and looked at me before drawing heavily on his cheroot and humphing like a stage clubman. "Still playing the detective, are you?" He spoke lightly, but the malice was there, just under the surface, I felt.

"Well, it *is* rather surprising, isn't it, John?" Madeleine said. "Finding you in this place—and Lindsay apparently involved as well. He must have often been out here in the old days. But he never mentioned it."

"Oh, it was nothing. He's probably forgotten it. Just an

undergraduate hobby we had then. My father was a great model-railway enthusiast. You remember Lindsay's interest in all that? We came out here once or twice in those days; my father had started a whole layout upstairs. Still there, in fact. People come to see it sometimes, by appointment—one of the best scenic model railways in England apparently. But let me get you some wine."

He left us then, Bonzo screamed in the kitchen and Caroline shouted at him and it was very hot in the small room. "How strange," Madeleine said, leaning back in a rocking chair that for some reason didn't rock. "Lindsay's never mentioning that John had a place out here."

"Or John himself never telling us," Rachel added.

In the next room the child threw something violently on the floor.

"We mustn't stay long," Madeleine said, getting up from her awkward chair. But when the wine—an already opened flagon of supermarket Italian plonk—was finished, Wellcome insisted that we should all see the model railway before we left.

He led us upstairs and into an extension of the cottage at the back, a large, dark, windowless room where, when he went to a corner and operated a switchboard, we were confronted with a sensational little miracle, a toy to end all toys.

The whole area, apart from slightly raised viewing duckboards running down the middle of the room, was given over to the most elaborately realistic multitrack model railway layout, every item of station furnishing, rolling stock and incidental decor exactly in the period of some prewar golden age of the railways. Half a dozen passenger and goods trains went streaking along over viaducts and into tunnels, going in opposite directions, passing each other at small suburban stations with old Virol advertisements, before running off into an idealized English countryside through fields with sheep and shepherds and tractors that actually moved.

All the trains eventually ended up at a large city terminus by the switchboard, complete with miniature passengers and a marshaling yard just outside it, where Wellcome would rearrange the travel patterns, setting off the whole magic circus once more. We watched, spellbound. The illusion was so complete and inviting that one wanted to climb over the barrier and enter the dream, certain that we, like the models, would then become smaller than the smallest child.

"Now watch!" Wellcome said. "The night sequences."

The lights in the room began to dim slowly and the minute table lamps in the yellow Pullman carriages came on, and the trains sped through a soft darkness growing over all the land. In the towns and villages pub windows lit up and cinema signs came on. Model cars shone weak beams on level-crossing gates; signals fell from red to green as boat-train expresses fled into the farthest corners of the room, while a small rail car came to a halt at a country junction, the platform lit by weak oil light, waiting for the night mail to pass. Wellcome lurked in the shadows some distance away, hunched over the switchboard, ministering to his toys with the concentration of the obsessed.

It was then that a freight car he was shunting back over a set of points in front of Rachel came off the rails.

"Can you pick it up?" he asked her. "Just put it back on—it won't bite." Rachel leaned over the barrier and set the car to rights again, and Wellcome brought up the little shunting engine to it once more, pushing it over the points and onto a separate track that led up to where I was standing.

"Watch this!" Wellcome said, now altogether the totally absorbed child. "There's a small down gradient here—together with a wagon vise: it's a way of marshaling goods traffic. There's a shoe brake on either side of the rails—just there—that holds each truck as it runs off the incoming feed train. Then when you release the vise blocks, the truck free-wheels down the slope and onto those points where you can turn it off into any one of those three lines, making up a new combination of goods traffic."

He released the little metal coal car and it came gently down the slope toward me. But again, when it met the points that were supposed to divert it, it came off the rails just in front of me.

"Damn. Something must be wrong with the wagon wheels. Try it once more. Put it back on again, will you?" Wellcome called across to me. I put my hand over the barrier and picked up the car and when I set it back on the rails the dark room was filled with a terrible scream. After a second I realized it came from me.

My height may have saved me, since, unlike Rachel, in leaning over the barrier, I had not needed to take my rubber-soled boots off the floor. Nonetheless I was badly stunned, my whole arm throbbing with pinpricks all along the skin, while inside it felt as if someone had just rammed a huge needle right up my arteries, from wrist to shoulder blade. I held myself fiercely with my good arm, rubbing my elbow, clamping it to my side in a sort of cold agony. My head seemed to have come off my shoulders and be floating around above me.

Wellcome fussed abominably, muttering about a short circuit, while Rachel said in amazement, "But why didn't it happen when *I* picked the damn thing up?" I knew enough to realize that the layout entailed probably half a dozen quite separate tracks, each with its own electrical circuit, any one of which could have been isolated from the others and charged with a far higher voltage at the drop of a switch. On the other hand, I didn't know enough to prove there and then that Wellcome had intentionally activated such a charge. In so complex a layout, it might have been a genuine fault. But it was easy to doubt this.

"I am so fearfully sorry," Wellcome said. "I really am. Come downstairs and I'll get you a brandy."

In the circumstances, I declined the offer. The Italian plonk had been bad enough and this might have been a genuinely poisoned chalice. I looked once more over the suddenly stilled landscape—the little carriages and engines all marooned at inappropriate places, an express stalled at a level crossing, the night mail halfway into a tunnel. A sleep had come over all the game; some evil genius had gripped this magic world and made the boyish sport malign. Tears before bedtime, I thought—and all the delicious canary-colored coaches and boot-black engines struck me suddenly as an emblem of childhood betrayed. Or was Lindsay himself somewhere here, I wondered, rising up out of the old trains he had played with so long ago, forbidding me, across all the years, access to some vital secret somewhere there in the layout in front of me, a truth I had nearly touched before another hand in the ether had stretched out to protect his innocence—or guilt?

BOOK THREE

THE SEARCH

I

We met in my London club once more. But this time privately, in the empty gilt-and-blue library upstairs, where Marcus was pretending to an interest in some recent literary donations that lay on a table by the window.

Marcus had seen the Yugoslav letter and spoken with Madeleine too, which was why I had craved an appointment with the clever little man, for he had been unable to offer her any real help.

"Oh, it's quite genuine, I think," he said, thumbing through a large new quarto edition of *The Water Babies*—vilely illustrated by one of our younger members. "Rackham would have done it so much better," Marcus added.

"He has, Marcus. He has. The letter—"

"Yes, genuine I'd say." He looked up brightly, the pearl tie pin in place, the confident jeweler's smile swelling out gently from the fatty jowls. "They always put their logo on the top. It's King Tomislav's sword—did you know that? Tenth century. First king of an independent Croatia. And that's what they want again, of course; to get out of Tito's mob."

"I gathered that."

"*Hrvatska Slobodan,* Marlow." Marcus pronounced the phrase with relish and in probably the right accents. He had obviously been well briefed by experts in the last few days. "'Free Croatia,'" he continued. "That's the name of the game from now on." He said this with pleasure, as though he had at last learned that Lindsay had simply been picked up by some old friends who were halfway through an elaborate practical joke with him. Something had happened to Lindsay that Marcus, at least, viewed with relief.

"The letter: what did your people—"

"Oh, yes. Our handwriting fellow says it's almost certainly Lindsay's signature. But not fluent. So he may have damaged his arm somewhere along the way. The trouble is, as I told Mrs. Phillips, we can't release this Croat terrorist. The PM is adamant. Hijacked one of our planes last year. But more than that, it would queer our pitch with the Marshal entirely. So that's out, I'm afraid."

"Marcus, now you know who has Lindsay, where he is, you're going to have to make every effort to get him back in any case, aren't you? Whatever Tito thinks."

"Yes, Marlow. But I don't think you know very much about these exiled Croat extremists, do you? That's the whole point, you see: we *don't* know where Lindsay is. Could be anywhere in Europe. These fellows live all over the place. Particularly in Munich and Brussels. But also in Paris, Zurich, Vienna. And there are at least two separate front-line terrorist groups involved: the Croatian Revolutionary Brotherhood as well as Free Croatia, with several splinter groups such as Matika thrown in. Needle-in-the-haystack department, I'm afraid."

"Yes—but this group: it's the one we know." Marcus was trying to blind me with science. "Where do they operate?"

"Anywhere. They've worked out of both Brussels and Munich before. But that doesn't mean they have in Lindsay's case."

"Even with a Munich postmark?"

"Almost certainly a blind."

"You could try Brussels, then."

"We could. We will. Through Interpol, though, and the local chaps. So it'll take time. What will you do, Marlow?"

"We could start with Brussels too, I think. And maybe it won't take us so long."

Marcus clasped his hands together, lowering his head and frowning meekly like a penitent come to his vengeful God at last. "You really don't know these Croat nationalists, do you, Marlow?" He leaned forward, the sunlight touching his silken-smooth, gray-flecked hair.

"How should I?"

"They put the IRA provos in the shade." Marcus warmed to his bad news. "They've had forty years' experience starting with the assassination of King Alexander in Marseilles in '34 and they've been successfully gun-thugging their way around Europe ever since. And nasty with it—even the resident SS men in Yugoslavia couldn't stomach their methods during the war, ran home to Adolf. I don't think you want to get involved."

"I'm not going to start gunning for them, just dealing with them. Once they know you aren't going to release their man, we can probably deal. The Phillipses aren't poor. I've talked it over with Mrs. Phillips. They could probably use thirty or forty thousand. Well, you can't put an offer like that to them, can you? Tito would be upset."

"True. It's a possibility." But Marcus couldn't keep a touch of doubt out of his voice.

"You still don't really want Lindsay back, do you?" I said. "That's why you took George."

"Who?"

"Willoughby-Hughes. You remember." Marcus looked annoyed now, returning to unpleasant memory. "George and Basil and the Russians, Marcus," I went on. "There's still all that. You seem to have forgotten about it."

"This Mr. Wallaby-Hughes is simply helping us with our inquiries. A lot of what he said about himself and Fielding didn't add up."

"You've got it wrong: *Willoughby*-Hughes—and George is simply a romantic old fool. Nothing to do with Moscow. He went to see Basil to try and help the family, just as I'm doing. And you don't want that, so you took him to cause trouble. But it won't work. When you told Mrs. Phillips about this Croat over here, she agreed with me: that we should tactfully look for these Free Croatia people and offer them a deal. Are you going to try and stop us?"

Marcus shook his head slowly, incredulously, with the expression of a diamond merchant being offered paste.

"Marlow, you're a free agent. Our hands are tied, as I say. You must do as you think fit. But I've told you about these Croats. They bite, to say the least."

"What about Basil Fielding and the PM?"

"An unfortunate case of misplaced trust. The PM is being suitably advised now. So you have no authority whatsoever—from him or us—to concern yourself in this business any more." Marcus stood up, looking at me dismissively. Our meeting was over. It was clear that he was relieved at the course events had taken. These dangerous Croats would absolve him from much further work in the matter. His hands were comfortably tied. As far as he was concerned, Lindsay Phillips was out of harm's way.

Madeleine and Rachel, on the other hand, were filled with hope and anxious for all sorts of careful activity. The letter had transformed their lives. These words out of the blue had brought the man before them again in a hundred familiar images: he existed somewhere; he slept, woke, and thought of them and they could believe in him once more. These reciprocal thoughts ran like a magic lifeline in the air between them, a line they could now follow up materially across the Continent, and which must lead them to him eventually. Lindsay, in effect, had been dead for nearly three months; now they shared in his miraculous resurrection. There but remained the journey to the hidden tomb where he waited for them.

I spent the afternoon at Thomas Cook's in Berkeley Street making the travel arrangements, while Madeleine telephoned Willis Parker, Lindsay's old friend in Brussels, now a senior diplomat with the British EEC delegation there. He was to expect us the next day, and had made arrangements for us to stay at the Amigo Hotel in the center of the city.

Early next morning I took the big black Volvo station wagon southwards out of London, making for the Dover-Ostend car ferry: the beginning of things, I thought, surrounded by an air of happy confidence in the powerfully singing car, the windows open to the dazzling weather, the luggage well packed and all arrangements made. The journey started like a holiday, coming back from school to Scotland years before. Though now it was I, and not Henty in the old green Wolseley, who was going to meet Lindsay. A sense of family had come strongly among us once more. And in the bright, clear light that morning all that we had lost seemed already very nearly made good.

* * *

MADELEINE sat in the front seat next to me as we edged our way out of Ostend early that afternoon. The clamor of the quayside, the bustle of the holiday corniche dying behind us as the big green-and-yellow motorway signs loomed up ahead. She had, quite simply, become young again in the past few days, as if someone had just fallen in love with her. The nightmare had died in her eyes and she no longer had to be brave, so that for the first time since we'd met again her expression became as I remembered it from years before: a quite different face now, with different shapes and colors in it; a portrait not just restored but one where a whole new line and texture is revealed beneath, the original conception again brilliantly displayed. She was the bright crusader once more, struck by some visionary cause, moving toward it now with that huge happiness found in the renewal of a lost faith.

Rachel, in the back, had collapsed with the heat, her legs sprawled along the whole width of the seat, one arm stretched out on top of it. I could just see the side of her face in the rear mirror, curls bobbing in the warm breeze from my window.

"Look!" she said as we passed by a market garden on the outskirts. "Just look at those *beautiful* flowers in all those *awful* rows and rows."

"The Belgians grow them for money. Not for fun. We're in Europe now," I said. She put her hand on my shoulder and squeezed it and said, "I'd prefer to be poor."

"Something of a rhetorical statement," I told her. But still she kept her hand where it was. We could tease each other once more, I realized; the little shafts of pleasurable enmity had grown up between us again in the last few days, that wordless connection we had possessed before, in her father's time, when he was always there, a sure and certain presence at the edge of her vision, just beyond that part of her life which she gave me—and which, should I fail her, she could return to. And so it was once more, mentally she could give herself to me again because he was there, somewhere just over the horizon—a placatory, advising, all-embracing spirit that supported our love, on which, indeed, it depended. And though in the past I had hated this tie, this continual proviso to the success of our relationship, I accepted it now, not simply as the lesser of two evils but as one of the effective compromises that, if we're lucky, time brings to love.

We glided across those flat lowlands of Flanders, laid out like a perfect exercise in agrarian geometry, lines of polder dykes and ruled canals and arrow-sharp poplar trees dipping into a huge sky: a vision I had seen before only in dull geography books or on weary school trips through provincial art galleries as a child, so that this reality, seen for the first time, struck me now with the sudden, intense pleasure of great art.

Madeleine gazed down a long perspective of trees and water away to our left, her profile like part of the picture as I glanced at her for an instant.

"I'd better tell you about Willis," she said without turning.

"Yes. I was going to ask you," I said. "Presumably he'll have contacts, or at least know someone who can get us onto these Croats."

"Yes, I'm sure he will. But apart from that—well, he's always rather had a thing about me, in the nicest possible way. But I thought I'd tell you in case you wondered—"

"In case you thought Maurice Chevalier had risen from the tomb," Rachel put in brightly. "Willis is the Don Juan of the diplomatic corps. The biggest old roué you ever saw," she added. "Sort of permanent Edwardian bachelor, chasing skirts all his life. That's all Mummy wanted to tell you."

"Well, that's a little harsh—"

"But it's *true*."

"He did want to marry me though. I met Lindsay through him." Madeleine turned to me. "So don't be surprised—"

"No, indeed! He never gives up hope. He's marvelous. But I suppose he's sad."

He didn't sound too sad to me and I said so.

"It's only sad because I think he really *did* want to marry me," Madeleine added thoughtfully. And we left it at that, determined to keep the sadness out of our lives from then on.

The Amigo, a discreet luxury hotel, lay hidden on a quiet side street behind the rebuilt neo-Gothic excrescences of the Town Hall, which gave onto the Grand' Place, a huge medieval market space, filled with spiritless tourists and great slabs of shadow from the high gilded buildings as we circled it late that afternoon, trying vainly to get out of an endless one-way system.

When we finally found the hotel there on the steps was Willis Parker, waving at us excitedly, a hungry-looking little Santa Claus of a man with a ring of white hair like a halo circling a bald pate, dressed in immaculate linen tropicals and some kind of old boy's tie. Even before the car stopped

I noticed his eyes—merry, dark blackberries in a cherubic face, and yes, dancing bedroom eyes, I thought, yet of someone unlikely ever to truly make it in that direction. But it was his energetic joy that came across at once: an air of tremendous excitement and expectancy, as if he found the world really too much of a good thing altogether and could not restrain the kind of continual orgasm he made in its direction.

He must have been in his sixties, but he waved his arms and danced about like a young clown in a bad circus, giving directions to one porter about the luggage and to another man who then quite unexpectedly took over the wheel of the car, so that I thought we were about to lose it.

"No! No! He's only taking it downstairs for you. There's an underground parking lot. Leads directly up into the hotel. Very convenient, what?" He glanced at me with a touch of roguishness I didn't understand. "Now, come along in, all of you. I've arranged everything with the manager—an old friend. I perched here myself when we were trying to get into the Common Market. Come on in!"

The day's heat still danced up from the concrete and my pockets were so sticky after the drive I couldn't reach for any small change to tip the men. We'd been traveling for ten hours and I was glad of Willis Parker.

"You look done in," he said, holding the door open for me, while I was still reaching for coins and passport, holding a damp hankie in the other hand. "Now don't you worry about any of that, it's all seen to. Come straight in—a shower, change of togs, you'll be a new man. And I've one or two things fixed up for this evening I think you'll enjoy." Again the slightly risqué look, some mild conspiracy among the men, before the big glass doors closed behind me.

We were in a large, cool, flagstoned hall, sparsely but richly furnished in the Empire style—high-backed, flock-covered armchairs grouped in twos and threes for subtle conversation around the dressed stone walls, which were hung with expensively imitated Gobelin tapestries and what might have been a genuine Aubusson that led like an exotic royal train to the banks of elevators. The rooms, I noted, were close on fifty pounds a night. But it was not this that really worried me; I had a chunk of Basil's money with me—or rather, as it now seemed, the KGB's—and was using that, though Madeleine had tried to insist that she pay all the expenses. No, it had suddenly struck me that this wasn't my world at all.

Mine lay years back, it seemed, in a cloudy, country past: a world of sparse dry sherries and a small cottage lost in the wolds. I had taken on a cause not beyond my competency, perhaps, but certainly far from my ease now, in this frigid, air-conditioned hotel, sealed from the real world. So far I had moved among familiar places in my search for Lindsay, places where he had lived himself. But now I felt the enormity, the stupidity even, of the task I had proposed. Lindsay had been everywhere at Glenalyth, in the country hats and coats and old mackintoshes in the back hall, in his books and bees. But here, how could he be anywhere here, in this antiseptic room or in any anonymous continuation of it throughout the Continent? His fingerprints, all the previous clues to his whereabouts, had been erased once he'd crossed the Channel. I had lost faith in Lindsay somehow.

And then, after I'd turned the shower off, I heard Rachel playing the flute through the bathroom wall in the room next to mine—a flurry of high notes followed by a repeated diminuendo, something from Gluck's *Orpheus* I thought, anyway certainly a tune remembered from our days together twenty years ago in Notting Hill. And I saw then that I had some sort of a past, however failed and tenuous, that I could remember and return to, a past that was nearby—right there, in fact, in the next room. What of a man like Lindsay—so richly endowed with wife and family, friends and memories—who could not return to this wealth because he was dead? Suddenly that seemed the worse loss—not the cessation of life but of memory. And I felt for Lindsay once more then, in that arid room, and hoped he was alive somewhere—still attached to his reminiscences.

When I got some clothes on I went in to see Rachel. She had turned the air conditioning off and was playing near the open window, half dressed, a huge bowl of late June roses on a table in front of her.

"I didn't know you'd brought the flute. That was nice," I said when she'd finished.

"Yes." She stood up before putting it away. "It's work. Apart from all the other things. All you really need: 'Work and love.'" She snapped the flute-case shut. "As Freud said."

She touched the crimson roses now, rearranging them so that their disturbed scent came to me across the warm room. She had already unpacked everything and strewn all her things about the place—hankies and tennis shoes, fine summer cottons, a bikini, and all the other balms of travel: the place looked as though she'd lived in it a week.

Seeing my glance over the confusion she said, "Yes, I couldn't bear it otherwise, the emptiness, without me in it. Oh, I don't mean *me* the body—or the suitcases or skirts or these flowers Willis sent up. I mean something really mine, made by me—so I played a tune. And now I belong here, suddenly." She smiled, yawned hugely and then lifted both her arms straight up in the air, as though stretching from a trapeze, the muscles in her stomach curving inwards, hips rising free of the rim of her thin panties for a moment. "The work you can depend on," she said at last. "The other—rarely. It's usually 'either/or,' isn't it?"

"Yes. You told me. All your real feelings go into your work. You'll be back to your concerts soon."

"No. I'm just going to play for myself, if all this comes out right."

"If Lindsay turns up?"

"Yes." She looked calmly at me, yet with a kind of tired intensity. "You've put too many feelings into your life," she said. "I've put too few. I've seen most things in terms of being alone on a platform. Just the music—with my father as the only really needed emotion." She stood up, started to undress, moving toward the bathroom. "You were right, I suppose," she called over her shoulder. "About Lindsay. I always said you weren't. But only because I resented your resenting my dependency on him."

"A lot of what we think is love is just weakness," I said. "I wasn't free of that either."

She turned, holding her panties in her hand. "I could be a great concert flautist, I think—but then the music would simply go on saying all the things I didn't dare tell my father, just as it used to. I was really loving him through my music. Maybe that's why he disappeared—he couldn't take the emotion. And that's what I mean: feelings like that, expressed in that way, are all too charged, too manic. If we find him, then I'll love him in an ordinary way. And if I do that, my music won't be extraordinary any more, just a pleasant thing, a hobby. I'd have a life then and not just a career. Don't you think I'm right?"

It all seemed so reasonable I had to say yes, especially since she came over and kissed me just then. But I realized that her change of heart had been dictated by her father's

234

letter, her renewed faith in his life somewhere. What if, in the end, he failed her? Her arms would slip away from me then—just as they held me now, only through her renewed belief now in his existence.

Several bells started to chime somewhere in the Grand' Place—thin, melodious bells, the sort accompanied by archaic figures emerging from a hole before hesitantly circling a clockface. I looked over Rachel's ear, out into the yellow evening; a great streak of sun, like a spotlight, was dying dramatically on some pink gargoyles at the back of the Town Hall. The day had a softness to it now, a calm before the trumpets of the evening, for there was an invitation in the air, and a hint of drama as well.

It seemed like the moment before the curtain went up, making me say suddenly, "You can't give up your music like that—twenty-five years of work."

"We have to be able to change. To take on other lives."

She held me lightly in her arms, then stepped away from me, holding my shoulders instead, rocking them gently for emphasis.

"If—we—didn't—fight," she said. Then she paused.

"We could take each other on again?" I asked.

"I love you, if that's what you mean," she said.

"Me too, if that's what you want."

We smiled. It all seemed too simple just then. But it was surely the great difficulties between us that had gone before, I felt, that made me uneasy. We were gingerly trying the ice, that was all—a few first footsteps, and it hadn't broken.

"You can't spend the rest of your life just us together, without your music," I said. "You'll have to face the public again."

"An audience of one is more important."

She turned away and started to run the shower in the bathroom, the water hissing briskly. Then she came out for a moment to look for some shampoo, dabbling among her crowded things on the bed, her familiar bronzed body stretching easily as she searched. This was all her, her essential being—a nakedness that had survived through twenty years, from a room in Notting Hill and hotel beds in Paris. We had come through an age apart and found something vital in each other again, in yet another foreign bedroom, full of the impermanent knickknacks of travel. But now the lotions and travel-sickness pills had a future; the sun-tan cream and paper handkerchiefs were things held in common once more. This was what love was like.

WILLIS was so full of bubbling pleasure when he met us again that evening, and drove us out to a restaurant on the outskirts of the city bordering the great forest at Soignes, that it was hard to think of the grim work ahead of us with Lindsay, and not give ourselves over completely to the sense of happiness together—four people on holiday, suddenly more than fond of each other.

We sat at the Chalet de la Forêt over a crisp pink table-cloth, the color warmed to gold by candles down the middle of the table, each one sunk in a cluster of fern leaves. We sat on an open terrace looking out over the dark woods on the other side of the forest road.

"It's not actually the *best* restaurant in Brussels," Willis said with pedantic care. "But I think it's by far the nicest." He smiled now, looking at Madeleine, seated exactly opposite him, with some ancient tenderness.

Rachel finished a last spoonful of cold Vichyssoise before she moved her face out of my vision and into the halo of candle flame that separated us. "It's the *nicest* restaurant I've ever been to," she said decisively, leaning across to Willis. "Thank you," she added gently. Then she moved the little candelabra of ferns to one side, the more readily to see me; there was a slight, questioning look in her glance, seeking some wordless confirmation of her mood in me. We stared at each other for a second—a time when all is well lost beyond two people—and then I raised my glass to Willis. "Thank you." I wasn't really thinking of him, though, but of how you could come to need someone, perhaps for a lifetime, while doing no more than look at them for an instant over a res-taurant table. There is a moment in every affair when there is no turning back; it must have occurred once before between Rachel and me, at some time, somewhere, in London or Glen-alyth. Would I forget this moment too?

It was Willis's turn to offer a toast. "To Lindsay—and to you, Madeleine," he said, generously enough, perhaps, in the circumstances. For Lindsay, I realized, was not just a silent fifth at our feast that night but a more constant shadow over all of us, wherever we went, whatever we thought, each hour of the day. I hated this absent proviso he cast over our lives just then. I wanted our future settled, wanted him dead or alive suddenly, so that I broke the gentle mood, taking advantage of Willis's toast, and said, "What do you think, Willis? Where is he? Who should we talk to?"

Willis was taken aback. He gulped at his wine too eagerly. "I'm sure he'll turn up," he said at last, a little unwillingly, I thought, as though Lindsay was a difficult dog we were well rid of, did we but know it.

"Yes. But where should we begin? Do you have any ideas?"

"Of course. I'm sorry." Willis began to pay attention. I could see that he, like the others, had hoped to enjoy dinner first, before broaching the topic, but it was too late now. I was tired of dancing endless attendance on this dictatorial wraith.

"I've been talking to a friend in the Belgian Home Office here." Willis embarked on his progress report without enthusiasm, the evening's pleasurable excitement draining from his face as he spoke. "The man you may need lives quite near here. Just the other side of the road, in fact, over there, in the suburb of Ucckle." Willis gestured behind him, toward the city. "Fellow called Radović, an old Croat nationalist, been living here for years. But he was a colonel in Pavelić's puppet army during the war, friend of all the top Nazis in Yugoslavia at the time—which is why he was sentenced to death *in absentia* by the partisan courts afterwards. And that's the trouble—Tito's police have been out to get him ever since, especially recently with this upsurge of Croat terrorism —so that he's impossible to see. Lives in a barbed-wire protected villa surrounded by bodyguards: he sees no one, speaks to nobody, doesn't reply to any letters—at least none that have anything to do with Yugoslavia. He says, with some truth, that he's a naturalized Belgian businessman now, with absolutely no connections with his old country. In fact, he is certainly the money man and most likely the brains behind at least one of these exiled Croat extremist groups: the Croatian Revolutionary Brotherhood, as well as perhaps the Free Croatia group, which is the one you want. I'm told the only way of meeting him is to be a member of the Cercle Sportif here. He rides with them. He and his cronies go out most mornings with their horses. Out there." Willis pointed into the deep woods behind the restaurant.

"On the other hand, even if you *did* get to meet him, I'm not certain it would do the least good. He's never going to admit he has anything whatsoever to do with these exiled groups. And he's certainly not going to be interested in money. He's a very wealthy man."

The waiter came with our second course, and we all looked at Willis, saying nothing. We had ordered a saddle of lamb and it smelled delicious, the big dish circled with mushrooms and covered in fresh herbs. But none of us felt like starting it now. Willis picked up the wine bottle and filled our glasses. "I'm sorry," he said. "It's not encouraging."

"No," I agreed.

"You see the difficulty?" Willis went on. "You really need to get in touch with someone much further down the line in this organization. The field commanders, the activists. But we don't have their names, and the top dogs certainly won't give them to you. Surely you'll have to leave it to Interpol and the local police?"

"We have talked to them about it," I interrupted. "But they'll take a year. We can move far quicker."

"I don't see how, without some initial contact."

"I wonder if your friend in the Home Office here has heard of a Yugoslav called Ivo Kovačić," I said. "He was a friend of Lindsay's before the war in Zagreb—something of a Croat nationalist. He taught at the university there and kept bees."

Willis had started to serve the lamb now. "He certainly didn't mention him. But there are thousands of Croats in and about the city. Quite a few of them live down by the railway near here in a pinched little suburb called St. Job."

"Why do you ask about this man?" said Madeleine.

"The brigadier told me about an unpleasant business between him and Lindsay, at the end of the war in Austria: Kovačić tried to kill himself just as Lindsay was packing him onto a transport to send him back into the hands of Tito's partisans. Well, I thought he might have survived and ended up here."

"Yes. Lindsay did once tell me something about that. I'd forgotten. You think this man may have had to do with kidnapping him?"

"I wondered. It's just possible."

"If he's here," Willis said, "I could find out. He'd be listed in the aliens registration files."

"You never came across any Croats with Lindsay when you worked with him?"

"No. Don't remember any. But I only really worked with Lindsay at the start of his career, in Vienna," Willis said.

238

"And once, of course, when we crossed embassies in Paris for a few months. That was 1938, wasn't it?" He looked over at Madeleine, who smiled at him, readily.

"Yes, Willis—the summer of '38, when you had your wallet pinched at the Brasserie Lipp and they refused to let us do the dishes. You were so furious over both setbacks." Madeleine turned to me, explaining: "That's how I met Lindsay. The Parkers—" She paused then, fiddling with her food, as if uncertain over something in that meeting. "The Parkers were great London friends of my family," she went on. But she didn't add any more to the history—simply, I thought, because the story was so far from our present concerns.

"How are things in Hyde Park Square?" Willis asked her lightly, apropos of nothing, it seemed. Yet I had the sudden sensation of eavesdropping on the distant, muted chatterings of family skeletons, rattling at their cupboard doors, seeking release. There was a slight, but very definite, tension in the air.

"How can you afford to keep the place on?"

"We can't. We're going to sell it as soon as Lindsay retires."

Lindsay, I noticed, was again firmly inhabiting a present tense.

"Selling it, are you?" Willis had found some of his natural gusto once more. "I'm finishing this year, too. Thought of a place back in London. Might you consider selling it to me?"

"Oh, Willis, it'd be *miles* too big for you." Madeleine was dismissive. "It's a ridiculous idea. What *would* you do there?" She laughed.

Willis's face fell then, became meek and unhappy just for an instant, as though he had been some pet animal unjustly reprimanded. But he recovered at once. "I'd put it into flats. Give me an income. Besides, I've always been very fond of the place. You remember those children's parties your parents gave—and the lemon water ices? That Italian they had every year, complete with his little ice-cream cart and straw boater, serving them out in the hall?"

"Yes! I *do* remember." Madeleine was radiant now. The moment's unease I'd felt between them had gone. "Giovanni something, with a droopy mustache, just like my Crimean grandfather."

The two of them shared their happy reminiscences with vigor. Their early relationship appeared uncannily like my own with Rachel, I thought, twenty-five years later in the

239

same house. And the result, too, seemed to have been identical: Willis and I had both lost out to the same man—Lindsay. Wherever either of us had turned, in these two generations of the same family, Lindsay was always there, waiting to preempt our happy destiny. And I was annoyed once more at Lindsay then, so that when a lull came in their conversation I took the opportunity of mentioning something possibly embarrassing or even discreditable about him.

"I found a book stuffed down the back of a shelf in Glenalyth the other day," I said innocently. "A diary about Dollfuss and the civil war in Vienna in 1934—written by some Austrian woman called Maria von Karlinberg. A 'comrade's diary.' I wondered if you'd ever heard of her, Willis, when you were out there with Lindsay?"

Willis paused, his fork halfway to his mouth. He put it down and drank some wine instead. Then, having given himself time to think, he said, "Yes, I *do* remember her. At legation receptions in the Metternichstrasse. We had to invite her, because she was a very rich and well-connected woman; she'd turned socialist, worked as a reporter on one of the Red papers they had out there before Dollfuss put an end to them all. Her father had been something like Minister of Posts and Telegraphs under the old Franz Josef. He had a grand *Schloss* somewhere in Hungary, or was it Slovakia? In any event, I remember there was a lot of complaint about how they'd lost all their property after the Versailles Conference, with the daughter saying it was all a very good thing. Quite a little to-do one night at the legation, sort of family row. I remember that..."

Willis embarked on a witty social history of the family and their times in Vienna, but without mentioning the daughter again, so that I had to bring her back into the conversation. "But Lindsay knew this woman, Maria, did he?" Willis didn't reply. "I suppose he must have," I went on, "if she sent him her book."

"Yes. Lindsay did know her," Willis said at last. "But only vaguely, I think. As I did. Lindsay handled what passed for 'Information' in the legation then, so she came to see him about that: what Ramsay MacDonald was up to with the miners and so on."

Willis steered the topic to an end in some good humor, as did Madeleine. "Before my time," she said. "I never heard of this Maria. One of Lindsay's old flames was she, Willis?"

Willis chuckled deprecatingly. "Hardly, Madeleine. Hardly. Why, Lindsay was engaged to Eleanor at the time. She came out and joined him that spring, as I remember. Yes, just after the February battles: spring of '34."

I was pretty certain now that Willis was lying; a white lie of some sort, a tactful evasion in order to save Madeleine's face: Maria von Karlinberg had been something more to Lindsay than just an importunate socialist newspaper reporter, I felt. And I was almost certain, too, that her diary had been dedicated to Lindsay: "To the Fat Man in the Blue Bar at Sacher's." What was new was the information that Eleanor had been in Vienna at the same time. It seemed more and more as if Lindsay, not Willis, had been the inveterate philanderer all his life. Yet Willis—for Madeleine's sake, I supposed—was protecting him, forty years after the events. It was an act of love or charity toward her which brought him no comfort, however, for he looked awkwardly across the table at us both just then, like a schoolboy who has got away with a whopping lie right in front of matron but who knows he will not succeed in the same with the headmaster. Willis was suddenly an unhappy man.

Yet the evening recovered, with talk about other purely happy topics and the splendid food and more good wine passed around the gold-lit tablecloth. By the end of it I felt ashamed that I had raised my awkward queries. And yet, I thought, why else were we all here, if not to discover Lindsay? Was it my fault that, in aiding the search, his devious soul was coming to light rather than his body: I supposed it was. I was the wrong person to help look for him; I bore him a grudge. Though perhaps a grudge, like love, is among the few things that ever lead us to anyone in the end. It keeps him in our mind, at least.

The maid had turned Rachel's bed down and closed the windows and tidied up the chaos when we got back to her room that night, the shadowed lamplight falling tactfully over the renewed order.

"I'm sorry for Willis," I said. "I don't think he's a happy man at all."

Rachel opened the window. The muggy summer air warmed the slightly chill room at once; a car hooted somewhere out in the silent streets. Rachel kicked her shoes off, sitting by the window table, and then started to fiddle with the red roses once more, counting them aimlessly.

"The maid's pinched one!" she said suddenly. "There were a dozen here before, I'm sure." She took all the roses out of the bowl to count them properly, and as she did so a small card fell from between the stalks onto the table. She picked it up.

"Oh God! I know why Willis wasn't very happy this evening. Look! The flowers weren't for me at all. They were for Mummy. They put them in the wrong room, so she never mentioned them to him, and I didn't, either."

I looked at the damp little visiting card with its now almost indecipherable message: "Madeleine, with love. Willis."

"God, how he must have felt snubbed by her. Poor Willis. How *awful*."

"It wasn't your fault. Or Madeleine's. You can explain it tomorrow. Or I can, when I see him at his office."

"Shall I call him at home?"

"It's midnight. I wouldn't bother. Get Madeleine to call him first thing."

"I don't have his home number anyway. How dreadful of us."

Rachel stood up and started to undress. "Poor Willis," she said again, grieved.

"Don't," I said, touching her shoulder. "There's nothing to be done."

She stood back, looking at me. "A bowl of roses," she said at last. "'I sent a letter to my love, and on the way I dropped it. One of you has picked it up, and put it in your pocket...'"

As she spoke she took her clothes off piece by piece, and flung them all around her, willfully pitching everything away as she recited the nursery rhyme.

"'It wasn't you, it wasn't you, it wasn't you—but it was YOU!'"

Finally she said, "I'm not tired. It's funny."

"You slept in the car."

"Sleep with me, won't you?"

I did. But before we slept, pulling her face away from mine on the pillow, she said, "You need never be like Willis now, with me, you know that. Never ever."

2

Poor Willis—he was poorer than any of us thought. At first I wondered if, in awful revenge, he'd hoped Madeleine alone might find him, when she got to his apartment for the lunch date she had arranged with him the previous evening. Or had he counted on my getting there, as I did, before the police, and learning something crucial from the chaos on the floor? All the letters, photographs, memorabilia, as it seemed, of his hopeless love for Madeleine, that was now strewn about the front room of the rather grand bachelor apartment he had on the rue Washington just off the Avenue Louise.

There had been no reply when Madeleine had rung him first thing with her apologies that morning. The two women had then gone shopping while I had taken a taxi to the British EEC delegation's offices in the Place Schumann, where Willis was to have let me know the results of his inquiries about Ivo Kovačić. But he never turned up. His secretary wasn't really worried until she'd called him twice and had no reply. I said I'd go and see what might have happened to him myself—told her it was personal business in any case.

I was happy that morning coming out into the sunlight of the great ugly Place—happy in a way I'd thought never to feel again. I had a future in love—which made the sight of Willis himself when I got to him, curled up on his sofa like a baby, all the more unhappy. Here was no Lothario, but a far too single-minded heart, whose constancy had never brought him anything. Willis, as he lay there next the remnants of pills and an empty whisky bottle, was like a government warning against infidelity. And I feared for my own future with Rachel, which seemed founded on just the same drug.

At first, when I'd discovered the porter and we had opened his door, I thought Willis had simply been burgled through a fire escape or window after he'd left for work, for he was nowhere to be seen in the shadowy apartment. It was a minute or two before we came on him, his small body wreathed voluptuously in cushions, embedded in a long white sofa by the picture window. The porter opened the curtains. They swished across on their silken pulleys and sun filled the room, illuminating Willis like a corpse found in the library at the start of some Agatha Christie drama.

The body was surrounded by old letters and photographs. The photographs of Madeleine weren't particularly special. Again, as in the ones in the attics of Glenalyth, where Lindsay, Eleanor, and Susan had figured, here were prewar holiday snaps featuring another variation in Lindsay's stable. He and Madeleine and Willis were in Paris this time, and leapfrogging on the cabined beach of what might have been Le Touquet. But Willis's letters to Madeleine were another matter. I had to revise my view of him as the lovelorn swain entirely. There were some dozens of them, carbon copies, some in pencil but mostly typewritten, going back many years— addressed from various foreign capitals, and a few on military stationery, written to her during the war—and other quite recent letters, judging from the freshness of the paper. I glanced through several while the porter phoned and we waited for the police. One was addressed from Stockholm, dated June 1938.

Dear Madeleine,

It was so nice having your letter. You hardly have to thank me—much more the other way around: thank you for sharing your holiday with me. It was a wonderful gesture of you all coming over here in the first place. I won't forget it—and of course I wish you both much happiness, it couldn't be other-

wise. I'm glad you like Lindsay's bracelet. The silverwork over here is so simple, without any of that vulgar ornamentation on modern jewelry found everywhere else in Europe now ... Dearest Madeleine, it's a fine feeling now to know that you are happy—entirely positive—and you must never think of me in the future as leaning over your shoulder regretfully or any other nonsense of that sort ...

As far as I could see none of the letters echoed the dashing philanderer in Willis. On the contrary, they suggested a completely adult relationship between him and Madeleine, with nothing clandestine to it. The words were quite innocent in their friendly love, without apparent stress, reflecting familial concerns. Here was a perfectly natural intimacy. Why, then, had Willis apparently killed himself over it?

But where were the replies, I suddenly thought—Madeleine's letters back? I looked through the mess of paper. There was nothing from her. A vital piece of the puzzle was missing. Had she never written to him? It seemed inconceivable. Had he destroyed her letters? And, if so, why? I no longer saw Willis then as a pathetic figure, the victim of some naïve passion, but as a perfectly sensible man who for some obscure reason had become involved in what seemed an entirely one-sided relationship. Willis appeared to have entered some kind of fraud in his dealings with Madeleine—and perhaps with Lindsay, too—that had finally, in the snubs of the previous evening, become too much for him, and he had terminated the agreement. And here only Madeleine herself could help me.

I was sorry in a way that she didn't have to see Willis; I thought perhaps that, as in a medieval judgment, confronted with the actual corpse, her guilt or innocence in the matter might automatically emerge. As it was, the embassy took everything off our hands, while the police did no more than get my name and address before I left the sad apartment on the rue Washington.

The others were back at the hotel when I returned there at midday—Madeleine in a breezy summer hat about to set off for her *déjeuner intime*. There were a few bad minutes in the lobby when I told her the news, but she fought it well before Rachel took her up to her room. I thought they'd be gone for some time, but they appeared again ten minutes later, and Madeleine said she'd like a drink in the shadowy cocktail bar at the back of the lobby.

It was quiet and nearly empty, apart from two Germans munching peanuts loudly up at the bar. We sat in a corner, nursing brandies. As I'd always known, Madeleine—in the grip of a particular enthusiasm or when faced with a special difficulty—took on the sudden force of a crusader. And Willis's demise, I supposed, might bring the best out in her. It did, to begin with. She listened to me with a sharp, businesslike attention as I elaborated on the morning's events; it was as though death were essentially a matter of balancing figures in a ledger. My talk of Willis's letters to her, however, she took less confidently, as though unsure now of her earlier addition.

"Of course," I said, "a snub by itself surely isn't enough for someone to kill himself." I didn't look at her directly but I had her in the corner of my eye nonetheless. "And I can't understand why he had all his letters to you around him, but none of your answers," I went on.

Madeleine interrupted me with her answer, as though the better to underline its truth. "He must have destroyed them. Of course I wrote to him. We were great friends."

"Of course. But why destroy your letters and so religiously keep copies of all his own?"

She must have been expecting this question and she accepted its implications now with sudden resignation.

"Willis was protecting me, I suppose," she said. "I can't think of anything else."

Rachel and I said nothing, but Madeleine must have read our thoughts. "Oh, no, it wasn't any indiscretion of that sort. Willis and I were very fond of each other but it was never anything more. No, it was about Lindsay. I sometimes wrote to Willis about things I didn't understand. He never replied to me directly about this, just sent ordinary letters back. We talked when we met, in London mostly. That's what we were going to do today at lunch." She paused and sighed before gathering herself. "I'm sure he destroyed the letters: I told him to. He was very loyal about Lindsay. He helped me a lot."

"But why? What was it about Daddy?" Rachel leaned forward eagerly.

"At times I felt I didn't know him. No, that's too simple. I felt I was looking through him, through the person I knew

246

so well and into someone I didn't know at all." She gestured impatiently. "Of course, it's such a cliché—I know we all have to have our privacies. But with Lindsay sometimes..." She stopped, looking at us both searchingly, as if we possessed the knowledge that would complete her sentence.

I said, "In Lindsay's case sometimes the person you didn't know at all took over?"

"No. Just once or twice I thought the second person was all there really was of him, and that the man I knew was a front."

"You never mentioned any of this," I said tactfully. "It might have helped." At last this woman admits a crack in the armor of her love, I thought, and I felt for her suddenly, as for someone who might, in the end, become entirely bankrupt in her affections.

"It was all a long time ago," she replied, easily. "And Willis reassured me in any case—said it was the sort of tricky work Lindsay did. It came not to matter. Anyway, that was all I wrote to Willis about."

"Hardly enough for him to kill himself, Mummy."

She turned to Rachel briskly. "You don't have to tell me. I can't say why he did it. I really can't."

"Surely he wanted to marry you—and the news of Daddy's existence again, together with the snubs?"

"Perhaps," Madeleine said. But she was being optimistic, I thought. Willis seemed basically sensible, not really suicide material at all. And I said as much. And then it struck me: "I wonder if someone killed him?" I asked. "And the letters were strewn round everywhere to make it look like a romantic suicide?"

They both looked astonished. "But why? Who?"

"I don't know." I saw Willis's death now as one with a real future in it—for I believed in Madeleine's innocence then.

As sometimes happens, the door that became closed to us, with Willis's death, seemed to release the locks on another with barely any effort on our part whatsoever. I'd picked up the Brussels phone book before lunch. Radović wasn't there. He must have been unlisted. I turned back to the letter K, idly looking for Kovačić—and there he was, suddenly jumping out of the page at me: Kovačić, Dr. Ivo, the only one listed, at an address in the suburb of St. Job on the outskirts of the city. The phone was no use—he could have put me off, denied ever knowing Lindsay. I had to confront him and take the chance that he was the right man, the University lecturer, Lindsay's old beekeeping friend from Zagreb. I bought a map and had a cab drop me near the area late that afternoon.

The rue de Ham wasn't a slum but it hovered on the brink of poverty. A row of small terraced houses in the English manner, with whitewashed doorsteps and cheap curtains facing outwards, led up a hill from the dusty square of St. Job. Evening commuter trains rattled through a cutting behind the terrace while trams ground slowly up the incline in front. The area had a pinched gentility, a forgotten nineteenth-century suburb condemned now to be always on the roads to somewhere better.

I walked past Kovačić's doorway on the other side of the road—crossed over higher up and then came down the hill back to it. The place looked innocent enough and I was certain no one had followed me.

A thin-faced man, dressed in a too-smart shirt and a Henry the Fifth hairstyle, opened the door. I heard a typewriter clattering away in the background. The youth smiled slightly, as though I were expected. "*Oui?*"

"*Monsieur Kovačić? Je voudrais parler avec lui. S'était possible...*"

The typewriter stopped and an older voice, with a permanent frog in the throat, shouted, "*Qui est là?*"

"*Sais pas. Quelqu'un pour vous.*" The wiry, sad-faced man spoke French perfectly, yet he didn't look French. He looked queer, if anything. But he looked tough as well.

"I'm Peter Marlow—"

"*C'est un Anglais,*" he called back, and then a man like a great tired bear ambled out in slippers from a room to the side of the hall—bushy eyebrows beneath a tangle of graying hair, as broad as he was big, in a fine blue silk shirt buttoned meticulously at each wrist, the face not yet collapsed with age but close to it, the rather sensuous flesh about the nose and lips about to fall away forever.

"Mr. Kovačić?..."

"Yes—you came about private lessons?" He spoke slowly but in almost perfectly accented English, as if he'd been listening to the BBC World Service for many years.

"No, I—"

"You should have made an appointment." There was something of the pedant in his attitude.

"No, I came to see you—about something else. Can I come in?"

Kovačić gestured to his friend, who closed the door with a thump behind me.

"Yes. About what?"

"About Lindsay Phillips." I was trapped now between the two men.

"Who?" Kovačić straightened his cuffs impatiently.

"Lindsay Phillips—an old friend of yours." It sounded an unlikely description of their relationship, given its latter development. But I had to start somewhere.

"*Lindsay?* Lindsay Phillips?" Kovačić spoke now in angry astonishment, the skin tightening all over his old face. "Didi—see if he's alone."

The man by the door opened it again a fraction and looked carefully up and down the street. They spoke rapidly in Serbo-Croat.

"I'm alone. This is entirely private," I said to Kovačić, before his friend came up behind me and frisked me from top to bottom. There was nothing. I'd left the little .22 revolver at the hotel.

"Come in then," Kovačić said at last. "This is Didi." We didn't shake hands.

The little front room might have been that of some poor scholars in a provincial town forty years before. Apart from a frozen winter landscape in the naïve Croatian style above a tiny fireplace, books filled all the available spaces between floor and ceiling. There were two battered easy chairs with a primus stove in between, and what must have been an old church lectern at one end with a typewriter sloped down across it. Kovačić went up and leaned on this now, looking at me accusingly, like some hellfire priest. The room had a dusty, remote quality. It was not part of the city; it smelled of exile, of chalk, and old textbooks, and methylated spirits.

"A friend of Lindsay's?" Kovačić asked. "I can't say you are very welcome."

"No. I'm sorry. I realize that."

"Did Lindsay send you? Or British Intelligence?"

"No. Lindsay has disappeared. Three months ago. I came on behalf of the family—entirely a personal matter. I found your name in the directory."

Kovačić grunted. A train suddenly clattered past, loudly, almost in the next room it seemed. The house must have looked directly over the railway cutting at the back. And I'd had enough of trains just then. Didi was standing aggressively by the doorway. I realized I was thumping with fear.

"I understand your feelings," I said brazenly. "You had some trouble with Lindsay. Just after the war. I know. But I thought you might be able to help. Apparently he's been kidnapped by some exiled Croats—"

"Has he, indeed? I'm not surprised." Kovačić came out from behind the lectern now. He was pleased with what I'd just said. The atmosphere relaxed a fraction.

"Yes. His family have had a letter from him. The Free Croatia group."

"I wonder they've not executed him already. Some 'trouble' you say I had with him. You know why I can't sit down? Why I have to use this stupid church desk all the time? They broke my back. That's because of him—because of what the partisans did to me when he sent us all back over the border in May '45. My wife didn't survive at all, nor several hundred thousand others like us. Didi and me—we were among the few lucky ones. Trouble? Lindsay Phillips and his friends created a holocaust for us all."

"Yes. I heard that. I know what happened at Bleiburg. I'm very sorry."

Kovačić threw up his hands abruptly. "Well, you're too young to have been involved. But if you know about it all, you'll understand that I'm the last person to want to help. Don't you think?"

"I suppose he was acting under orders then—"

"Of course. But you don't know the whole story. Some British officers actually *helped* many of us Croats escape—let us run away into Austria or Italy. But not Lindsay, who could have done that so easily in our case. After all—"

"You were friends, I know."

Kovačić nodded. "Yes. We were. He rented my house in Zagreb before the war, you know. Oh, dear me!" Kovačić put a hand to his brow, covering his eyes, so that for a moment I thought he was crying. But when he looked up I saw he was simply trying to hide some ghastly rictus of laughter. "Yes, we were friends: in Zagreb before the war—he and his wife Eleanor. And her sister, Susan. I remember them all. Many good times at the Gradski Kavana...And the bees we kept together behind my house up in Tuškanac park." Kovačić wandered round the small room now as if he were trying to find an escape from it, back into some reasonable emotion, an understandable life.

"But why didn't he help you?" I asked.

He stopped his perambulations and went over to a shelf, picking out a drum-shaped bottle from among the books—plum brandy, I saw. He poured himself a stiff glass, downed it and then shook his head at me. "What naïveté! I told his commanding officer in Bleiburg at the time—"

"A man called MacAulay?"

"Yes, the brigadier there. You see, Lindsay wanted me out of the way. I knew by then he wasn't the man he said he was—a British diplomat. He was an agent for the Soviets, the Comintern or the NKVD before the war. That's why he made sure I was sent back over the border into Yugoslavia, knowing I was very unlikely to survive."

"But how could you have possibly found that out?"

"From his wife. From Eleanor."

"Who killed herself—"

"I never believed the suicide story. Lindsay killed her." Kovačić started to walk again. "I was away from Zagreb just then. But I knew the hall porter at the Palace Hotel. He said there was something funny about it all. He saw it happen."

"I was told she ran out under a tram, just in front of the hotel."

"Yes, she did. But Lindsay was right next to her. The porter thought he pushed her." Kovačić drank again, considering the past as though turning over the pages of an old diary in his mind. "She didn't die at once, apparently. Just lay on the tramlines with her eyes open."

"Died in hospital, I suppose?"

"I wasn't there. But yes, that evening or the next morning. There was an inquest of sorts."

"What do you mean?"

"It wasn't very thorough. Something was being covered up. The porter was never called as a witness, for example. I'm sure Lindsay killed her."

"But how did you learn he was with the Russians?"

"Eleanor told me. That's why he got rid of her, she'd found out about him. They were having terrible fights in those days. She was very unhappy, but not suicidal. She just wanted to leave him, get away from everything." Kovačić walked back behind the lectern. "That was the other problem: Lindsay had been unfaithful to her," he said sharply, the archaic term

251

exactly reflecting the period he was describing. "You knew that, I suppose? With Susan, her sister. The year before. The child was born in Zagreb that spring, I remember: in 1937 a few months before Eleanor died. But it wasn't her child. It was Susan's. They arranged to pretend otherwise—the British taste for decorum in everything."

"Yes, I know. Susan told me. But wasn't Eleanor pretty left-wing herself? Why should she complain if she'd found out Lindsay was with the Russians then? Many people were. It was a very common allegiance in the thirties."

"I asked her that myself. We'd had arguments before, she and I, about left and right." Kovačić rubbed his chin and picked at his ear, crinkling up his eyes as though the better to see into the past, into a time which, in his long exile, had obviously never ceased to concern or perhaps obsess him. "I was up at my house one morning when Eleanor and Lindsay were renting it; Lindsay was at the consulate. I had some books I wanted to pick up." He moved out from behind the lectern now, and suddenly he was gesturing vehemently, like a frustrated hot-gospeler. "She said he was cheating! That he'd lied to her, first about Susan and now about his politics. You see, Lindsay always made such a point of being very right-wing in those days. But she found him out. I remember exactly when it was, one day in that same spring—Eleanor was out on the terrace at the back of our house, wearing just a thin dressing gown. She was sitting at the little bamboo table we had—doodling, you know?" Kovačić looked at me; but really he was looking through me, the exact details of that morning nearly forty years ago forming a drama in his eyes. "She was making circles on a newspaper, staring at the cherry trees at the end of the garden. She was—numb. But she insisted on staying outside and we had some coffee, sitting there in the wind, the blossom falling everywhere—it was like a pink snowstorm up on the hill that day—and she said, 'Lindsay is a Soviet agent'—just like that."

"How did she know?"

"She'd had suspicions for some time. And then she'd caught him, she said, with his Soviet contact—walked straight into the two of them quite by chance in Strossmayer Square the previous afternoon. He was a Russian, she told me, pretending to be a friend of Lindsay's, a Viennese businessman. But Eleanor wasn't a fool. She spoke German perfectly, some Russian too—said his accent was all wrong for a Viennese.

252

But because of Susan she'd come to realize Lindsay was a liar in any case. I was very sorry for her. I'd liked them both, you see."

"But she may have been wrong about the man—just suspicious about everything then, since she'd found out about Susan."

"Exactly what I told her. But she insisted she was right, that it was something she'd felt about him for some time—that he was living a big lie, in his work as well as with her. He wasn't 'coming clean'—that was the phrase she used."

"Even so, you'd no real proof."

"No, no code books or anything like that. But aren't people's feelings some kind of proof? Strong feelings. And Eleanor was a very honest person. Very uncompromising. Besides, Zlatko, who knew her far better than me, told me the same thing."

"Zlatko?"

"Rabernak—a friend of theirs. An antique dealer in Zagreb—"

"Of course. Susan mentioned him. He sort of took over Eleanor then."

"Why not? Lindsay had left her in every way. Well, I'd been up in Ljubljana lecturing that summer; after I came back, I heard she'd died and spoke to the porter at the Palace Hotel, and then I believed what she'd said about Lindsay, and told him so. He denied it all, of course. I didn't see him again until I got over the border in Bleiburg eight years later. So you can see now why he didn't help me."

"And Zlatko—what happened to him?"

"He went back to Vienna immediately after she died. He had his main family shop there. I never saw him again. I should think he died in the war."

"Did you ever tell anyone about Lindsay later?"

Kovačić shook his head ironically. "Who would have believed me? I was a displaced person—discredited too, since the allies believed, wrongly, that all Croats had been pro-Nazi. I had difficulties enough getting myself established in this small teaching job here. You don't get involved with the authorities in such a position. I did nothing. But"—Kovačić spread his hands out wide, signifying not mercy but an appropriate fate—"I'm not surprised he's been picked up by my Croatian compatriots. Slow justice. But justice all the same. I know you think we are all just violent extremists, and why should you worry about us—a lot of Croats who fought on the wrong side because they believed in their country? Well, we worry. We still do. And though I'm not one myself I understand those extremists very well. Our nation was put to the sword in May 1945—and Lindsay, my friend Lindsay, was one of the instruments of that massacre."

"Yes, I see that." There was silence. There was little more I felt I could say. I was saddened by this awful account of someone I had admired, who had been a friend of mine, too—and more than that, who had long been for me an emblem of the good life, a man of honor, as I and many others had thought, of great loyalty, sanity and familial affection. Kovačić's story utterly contradicted all these known qualities. Yet it had a ring of truth in it; indeed much of what he'd told me was simply a confirmation of what I'd heard from Susan in Dunkeld a week before.

As if sensing my thoughts, Kovačić said, "You're not a relation of Lindsay's?"

"No. Just a friend of the family."

"I'm sorry. I should have offered you a slivovitz."

"I said I'd try and help them—his second wife and daughter."

Kovačić laughed, pouring me a small glass from the drum-shaped bottle. "He married again, of course." He turned away, still smiling. "Stanka, my wife—she was pushed into a lime quarry near Maribor. So was my son. Didi here, he's not my real son. His father was killed too—killed at Maribor," he said with finality, as if describing some honorable battle and not a massacre. "We look after each other now."

Kovačić left it at that. The evening sun had slanted and the room was cut in half by a deep shadow. The warm air smelled of plum brandy—something like the perfume Rachel used. Another tram started its long grind up the hill outside, laden with homecomers returning to these drab, forgotten suburbs. How many other lives, besides Kovačić's, were lived out in quiet desperation here? Yet perhaps his was the worst, I thought. A fine house in a park on a hill, with cherry trees surrounded by beehives, the spring singing with insects, infested with blossom, full of sweet purpose, good friends, and merry evenings at the Gradski Kavana: and it had all come to this—a primus stove, an orphan, memories in a bottle of plum brandy. This was what the war had led to—as it never had for Lindsay; this was what Europe in the previous generation was all about: immeasurable losses that we knew nothing of, in our grand hotel down in the city or in those offices in Whitehall where Marcus still plotted, covering up some deeper plot of Lindsay's. It all ended here, in an impoverished room on a dingy suburban street—in my disgust.

"Will they kill him?" I said at last.

"I wouldn't blame them if they do."

"No." I paused. "We thought we might make a deal with them. With a man here called Radović?" I added halfheartedly, and indeed I had no more appetite at all now for the search.

Kovačić shook his head. "He'll never see you. I should just go home." He slumped once more over the lectern. His back must have been hurting him. "You understand?" he asked.

"Yes. I understand." I stood up, finishing the warm slivovitz. But I realized when I got outside and walked away into the summer evening that I didn't really understand it all—not yet.

A first secretary from the embassy, a Mr. Huxley, was with the two women in the lobby when I got back to the hotel. He was a careful man, pale-faced, nervously alert, with a very soft voice that made him appear all the more guarded. He spoke as if he was in a small room with a sick child. He said, "We've had confirmation from your farm manager in Scotland. There's been another letter this morning from your husband, postmarked Munich again. They have the text on the embassy telex—if you'd like to come with me?"

The letter was shorter this time and Lindsay's signature was in a much firmer hand.

Am still well. But hoping very much that H.M. Government will proceed with arrangements as outlined in previous letter. Please have them indicate willingness to cooperate by placing notice to "Janko" in personal column of Times, *with phone number.*

Again, the last part of the message was briefly but tellingly personal:

Do hope I may be released in time for honey crop.
                                        All love, Lindsay.

Huxley was distantly kind but quite unhelpful. "Of course, we're working on it all the time," he said, his voice dropping almost to a whisper. "Problem is, as you know, we can't release this man they want in the UK. But at least we can make contact with them now. We'll put a notice in the personal column, of course, and perhaps come to some other arrangement with them. Who knows?" Huxley was expert in leaving things in the air. And he left himself soon afterward. I wished he'd stayed—it would have postponed the difficult task ahead of explaining to Rachel and Madeleine what Ivo Kovačić had told me an hour before in the unhappy little room in the rue de Ham. Unlike Susan's information, it was not something I could entirely hold back from them any more.

We ate in the formal hotel dining room, on high-backed chairs; there was too much napery and cutlery. I should have liked a simpler meal but the women felt disinclined to go out. And after all, it was a meal from their kind of world, I thought, rather unfairly, realizing how far my loyalties had become divided. It wasn't their fault that they were rich; and neither of them had sent men to their doom in cattle wagons or pushed someone under a tram.

I told them about Bleiburg and the massacre outside Maribor first. And Madeleine's reply was expected: "But he was only carrying out orders. He told me. How could Lindsay have saved them in any case, and let the others go?"

"Some of the other British officers there at the time did just that apparently," I said. "Saved as many as they could. And after all, this man Kovačić was a close friend..."

"That's ridiculous. None of us were there. How do we know what the circumstances were exactly? It may have been quite impossible for Lindsay to have done anything about it." Madeleine spoke easily, without any rancor at my devil's advocacy.

"I'm only telling you what Kovačić said."

"Go on then." I felt like a witness in some nightmare trial, forced to speak of events in a country and in a time none of which I had ever experienced. Rachel and Madeleine stared across the table at me with cold interest. As I had suspected, we had at last come to a showdown between their intuitive love for the man and my knowledge of the dirty world he worked in, that business of endless deceit which could not but infect the men who proposed and manipulated the deceptions. For the sake of whatever he'd believed in, Lindsay had betrayed those nearest to him from the very start of his career—perhaps without realizing it—by the very act of joining a world he could not share with them. The two women had believed in the promotion of a definable truth, through love—a love that unbolts the dark; whereas all his life Lindsay had been intent on keeping that door firmly shut. Lindsay's way—and my way too—of looking at things was simply not possible for them, since, apart from the calculated dishonesty, they could never have seen the usefulness of it. And indeed there was none; which was why they looked at me now with so little enthusiasm. They sensed in me what Lindsay had always managed to hide from them: a dissembling nature.

So I decided not to tell them anything of any importance. Why should I tar them with the same brush of dissension and betrayal—the horrors Lindsay and I had either perpetrated or suffered in the world of Intelligence? If Kovačić's dingy little room was the fag-end evidence of a European holocaust, one in which Lindsay had had a hand, did that mean they had to share it? Why shouldn't some people remain untainted? And God knows, I thought, Kovačić, who bore such a grudge against Lindsay, could well have been a very unreliable witness, and the hall porter at the Palace Hotel even worse. And Susan? Well, she could have been in the same boat with them: possessed by some ancient jealousy that had worked its way into her heart so that she had come to believe what was not true: that Lindsay had been her lover and Patrick her son. Why did I so readily believe the possible fantasies of these distant people, and not the factual experience of the two women—my friends—in front of me? Because, like others in my world, I had formed over the years a kind of loyalty toward betrayal. It was so much the expected thing. So I said, "Kovačić didn't say much more other than that they'd obviously taken Lindsay because of what happened at Bleiburg—a kind of revenge. That follows. But he has no connection with any of these terrorist groups."

"What did he say we should do?" Madeleine asked.

"He said we should just go home."

Madeleine's eyes flashed with annoyance. "That's nonsense. There's lots we can do. I'll go and see him myself. I should have come with you. We could go now—"

"I don't think so."

"Why not?"

"Because I've just seen him," I stalled.

"You were gone long enough. Was that all he told you—just to go home?" Rachel asked indignantly. I'd moved from the witness box into the dock.

"No. We talked about the time when Lindsay lived in Zagreb in the old days."

"So you talked about Eleanor then?" Rachel put in with the enthusiasm of a prosecutor.

"Yes." And then I went on, avoiding the topic of Eleanor, "And about the bees he and Lindsay kept together at the back of his house there, somewhere in a park above the city."

Madeleine looked at me intently, as though seeing in me something of her husband, some fascinating aspect of the man before she'd ever met him—as if I had experienced him before she had. And indeed in a way I had, for I'd come to see that moment when Kovačić had found Eleanor out on the terrace very clearly—the wind blowing the cherry blossom about, the little bamboo table and the dark-haired woman, like the girl I'd seen in the stained-glass window at Dunkeld, doodling on a newspaper and staring out numbly into the pink trees saying, "Lindsay is a Russian agent."

And it was as if Madeleine saw some faint image of these same pictures in my mind as she watched me, so that she said, without any sarcasm, "Why don't you tell us really what happened between you and this man?"

I put down my fork; the food was getting cold in any case. "Kovačić thought Lindsay was working for the Russians. He met Eleanor one morning. She told him." I explained the background to this discovery. They laughed.

"Is that all?" Rachel asked defiantly. "That old chestnut?"

"No." I was getting annoyed. "He said something else. He thought there was something funny about Eleanor's death."

I looked at the two women. They were almost relaxed now, a touch of sympathy for me in their eyes.

"Funny peculiar or funny ha-ha?" Rachel asked.

"Peculiar," I said slowly, seriously.

"How would this man know?"

"He was there—or at least he talked to the hall porter at the hotel afterwards. The man thought she'd been pushed under the tram—"

"By Daddy, of course," Rachel put in, in her lightest mood. But she was angry beneath it.

"Yes."

"Well, that's nonsense, isn't it?" Madeleine said easily, relieved now to hear that the worst was so mild a thing.

"I don't know. It's what he said."

"Poor man. He bears a grudge, doesn't he?" Madeleine spoke quietly.

"Yes. His wife and son were both killed after they were sent back into Yugoslavia."

"Well, that explains it," Rachel said brightly. "Doesn't it?" She looked at me tartly.

"I don't—"

"Whose side are you on anyway?"

"I'm not on sides. I'm simply trying—"

"You know Daddy. Do you really think he could have pushed his wife under a bus—"

"A tram—"

"Or do you still secretly resent him?" Rachel ran on in a kind of sudden panic. "Because of my affection for him? Are you really like this man Kovačić too—bearing him a grudge?"

"No—"

"I've told you so often: it wasn't Daddy that took me away from you in Notting Hill, it was that bloody dirty bath and the broken windows. I don't understand you—you always seem to want to see the bad in him."

The two women looked at me now—both with the same question in their eyes, though Madeleine had left it unsaid.

"No, that's not true. I've only wanted to find him. And as I explained to you both, to do that meant looking into his past."

"Where you enjoy coming up with a lot of mud," Rachel said vindictively. "You—horror!"

"That's not true, so don't try and browbeat me."

Madeleine entered now, referee-like. "For goodness' sake, don't squabble like children."

And, indeed, it was an apt image. Rachel, having been angry, now took on the expression of a hurt schoolgirl, a child betrayed in some wretched boarding school who had expected a parent to come and take her out for the day, a guardian angel who would not now arrive. And I was that person, I suddenly realized—not Lindsay, who had never failed her. Again I was the man who had let her down, who had been unable to shield her from uncomfortable reality—from broken windows, scum on the bathtub, a woman under a tram. Loving her was not enough; I had to lie to her as well, which

259

I could not do. I couldn't do what Lindsay had obviously done so well for her—give her that blind peace and security without which she couldn't love, so that she had loved only him. Instead of replacing him as her god I had once more questioned his divinity. She would return to him now, I felt, as a prodigal daughter, a penitent, searching for him all the more passionately, blindly—as one must look for a god who is not there.

How tiresome her petulant and immature nature could be: Yet I loved her for it, for all her flaws—and I was well able to understand what I had lost as her face crinkled in tears and she got up from the table without a word and walked away. She had been what love was like, I thought.

3

I had slept badly—and alone. Yet my fatigue was more than physical next morning as I stood in the hotel lobby after breakfast, the bright sun streaming in from the summer streets outside. Rachel wasn't up yet—she'd gone to ground, as she so often had in the old days after some setback with me or her father. Madeleine apologized for her and I had tried to be bright about things in return. "We must be very bright," Rachel had said a week before in Glenalyth. But she had failed. The past had crept up on her again—uncertain images which were not bright and darker feelings even less resolved. And suddenly I had no more heart for it all. I wanted a rest. You could go on looking for something or someone too long, like a child crying for a lost ball, something dearly loved, which he finally has to admit he will not see again.

I was tired of Lindsay's loss—the pain and anger he could still bring about, the deceptions that surrounded his disappearance. And I didn't care now who had deceived whom, or when or why. I wanted to go out alone into the summer, have coffee somewhere or a beer, and think about something else. A trip to the national gallery perhaps, or better, up into those woods on the edge of the city, near that restaurant where we'd been happy.

I said to Madeleine, "There's only one other possible contact here. This man Radović. I'll try and see him," I lied.

"How?"

"He goes riding every morning in the forest—you remember, Willis told us."

"And you're going to get on a horse too?"

"No. I'll take a bike. Why not?"

"You're mad. How will you recognize him? It's a huge forest."

"All right! I just want to go out by myself, into the air, and *think*."

The porter told me of a shop in the city where I could hire a bicycle. But just as I was leaving he came up and said he thought one of the kitchen staff had a bike he might lend me. It was a rather flashy racing machine with dropped handlebars, which the man seemed unwilling to part with until I left him a few thousand francs on deposit. I hadn't realized how desperate I was to be away from everyone that morning.

But still I was held up. Just as I was tucking my trousers into my socks Rachel rushed up to us, bright again, happy, so that I thought she'd forgiven me.

"I've suddenly had an idea," she said. "We could all go on to Munich, where the last letter came from. Klaus would help." She stood there in the slight breeze, her curls dancing round her eyes, smiling with hope.

"Klaus?" I said dully.

"My ex-husband."

"Of course." I'd forgotten Rachel's marriage, let alone remembering the name of her husband. Lindsay had absorbed too much of me, damn him—and here was his daughter, happy once more, in pursuit of him. I had made no real difference to her; it was Lindsay she wanted. Yet what was the point? I foresaw nothing but more lies and evasions ahead of us in our search for him; Lindsay was unobtainable. But I didn't argue.

"Why not?" I said. "Who knows? He might well come up with something."

We were fooling ourselves, I thought, as I rode off into the sunlight. And then at the corner, as I waited for the traffic to pass, I looked back and saw the two women standing outside the hotel. Madeleine waved, a little abrupt gesture. She had probably read my thoughts. But then, since she was no fool, I decided she'd surely had the same thoughts already.

She and I were pretending there were still useful pursuits ahead of us. In fact we were as lost as Lindsay was. Only Rachel believed otherwise, caught up once more in those ecstasies of anticipation, that blind optimism which was her father's ever-available gift to her in the old days, when I had failed her.

My journey was slightly uphill, all along the length of the Avenue Louise and then through into the Bois de la Cambre before I finally came to the beginnings of the forest. It was nearly twelve o'clock before I got there, too late in the day under the huge sun for anyone to be out riding, I thought. I was wrong.

The heat died suddenly under the immense copper beech trees, whose darkly bronzed leaves blotted out the sun and left great cool spaces beneath. Hoof-pitted rides and walks and a few asphalt paths crisscrossed each other, running away for miles into the distance, down slopes, over little wooden bridges and round, dank ponds. A few minutes after I'd left the roar of traffic on the main road that ran along one side of the forest, I found myself in the midst of an extreme silence—a world lit by faint colors, mistlike blues and golds shimmering in the long vertical distances between the trees, the sunken valleys shot through with light here and there, and flocks of bluebells, like strange seaweed, stirring slightly in the breeze thrusting up from the floor of what seemed a cavernous ocean.

Yet I wasn't alone. After ten minutes' ride deeper into the woods I suddenly seemed surrounded by people. First another cyclist, in shorts and a yellow jersey, his head well down over a racing machine like mine, sped past me, going down toward a small lake to my right; approaching me, just about to cross a little bridge, I saw three other men on huge horses, the one in the middle seemingly hedged in by his two companions, who appeared to be protecting him.

The cyclist coasted rapidly down the hill. He's going to crash, I thought, there surely wasn't enough room to pass the riders. But he slid to a halt twenty yards or so away from them and I saw him lift out one of the metal water bottles from a rack on his handlebars, as if to drink from it. But then, in a flash, he threw the thing expertly, like a grenade, the canister soaring up over the horsemen before landing in the middle of them.

It exploded on impact in a fan of light and a great smudge of dirty smoke. Then he threw the second water bottle and an immense cracking sound spread up from the little valley beneath me. When the air cleared I saw that half the bridge had disintegrated. One of the horses was floundering about in the shallow water while the other two, both riderless now, lay across the remaining planks like carcasses in a butcher's shop. Of the three men only one seemed to have survived the explosion—and I saw him fighting for his life, taking cover by the water's edge from the spurts of automatic fire that were now coming from both sides of the lake. Looking across the valley, I saw that a second cyclist had come down the hill from the far side, joining his companion in the mayhem. The big man in the water, though I now could see that he was armed, didn't have a chance. Caught in a fearful pincer of fire fore and aft, he keeled over like some aquatic animal, his head tipping back neatly in a reverse dive before he fell into the muddy shallows, just his stomach and part of his face remaining above water.

In the end only one of the horses remained alive, wounded and neighing atrociously. The first cyclist crossed the bridge, carrying his bike, putting the beast out of its misery on the way over. Then the two men pedaled away at surprising speed, disappearing up the hill on the other side of the lake.

By the time I got down to the water's edge nothing moved. There was silence again. The light still fell in magic beams through the high canopy of leaves above and there were calm blue visions in the long distances once more. But the carnage in front of me spoiled the view: some terrible fault had occurred in nature, as if a volcano had risen from the earth a minute before. Horses and bodies lay half in, half out of the water. One man's head lolled in the mud like a piece of broken statuary, the eyes gazing up appalled; the bleeding hind-quarters of an animal dripped over the parapet. And there was a sickly warmth in the little valley, and an acrid smell of flesh crushed, bleeding in the heat, singed by fire. I couldn't stomach it. I turned and bicycled furiously up the hill, making for the center of the forest where the trees soon hid me and the flocks of bluebells waved me on deeper into the woods.

I THOUGHT how quick the police had been when I got back to the hotel—downhill all the way—half an hour later. Two plain-clothes men were in the lobby with Madeleine waiting for me. I was about to mention the battle in the forest but the smaller man, as if in a great hurry, got in first. He was a neat, precise little detective whose English was good enough, in an old-fashioned way, to suggest a senior position in the service.

"Inspector Payenne," he said. "Welcome. But I must tell you that we have discovered suspicious circumstances, in the death of your compatriot, Mr. Willis Parker—"

"They think it wasn't suicide at all," Madeleine put in wearily, "just as you did—"

"Oh," Payenne interrupted, like a man trained in the old school. "You thought *before* it was not suicide, did you, Mr. Marlow?"

"I thought he wasn't the kind to kill himself, that's all," I said sharply. "What have you found?"

"The post-mortem shows few traces of alcohol in the system, and none at all of any barbiturates."

"The pills and whisky may have been a plant, then?"

"We think so."

"So what does the post-mortem show?"

"Heart failure—perhaps."

"Is that enough to constitute 'suspicious circumstances'?"

"It may be. Your embassy records show that Mr. Parker had no history of any cardiac trouble."

"You've been in touch with them?"

"Yes, with a Mr. Huxley."

Of course, I thought, Huxley would have helped them, the soft-tongued conspirator finding a role at last. It was then that I first suspected we were about to be framed. "Well, heart failure," I said. "What can one do? A tragedy."

"He may still have been poisoned or killed in some other way," Payenne said, holding up a neat, stubby finger like a cricket umpire. "Our laboratory is considering that. And also one of your own Home Office pathologists who has come over. I must ask you all to remain here until we have completed the results."

"He thinks one of us killed him," Madeleine said mockingly.

"I did not *say* that, Madame Phillips—"

"You think it, though."

"You were the last people to see him alive. Naturally... We

265

must await our conclusions," Payenne added in his formal English. Perhaps Kovačić had once taught him, I thought—after hours, in his language college downtown. Certainly Inspector Payenne was pursuing a traditional line—straight out of Agatha Christie, with its talk of poisons, pathologists, post-mortems, and three equally suspect murderers. It was quite unreal. Yet it was just as I'd forecast: Willis's death had a future in it now—a future in which, with Huxley's connivance (and therefore also with Marcus's) we were to be framed. Once more, I thought, Marcus had leaned out over the Channel to forestall our journey toward Lindsay.

"For the moment I would like you all to keep yourselves in the hotel. I would be most obliged," Payenne said. And when he left I saw that at least one of his colleagues had remained behind, lurking now outside the big glass doors in the sunshine. What more severe incarceration would ensue, I wondered, when Payenne discovered the news in the forest—and learned that I had been up there myself, on a racing bike, at the same time? He didn't know this now, but I was sure the hall porter or the kitchen hand would be pleased to tell him. It was a good moment to leave—but how? And why should the two women agree?

Rachel, who had been on the phone in her room, came downstairs just then in high good spirits. "I got through to Klaus—at last! He's on tour with the Bavarian State Orchestra. They're in Heidelberg now. Not far from here. But listen! He's been trying to get in touch with *us:* someone approached him in Munich yesterday, saying they know about Daddy—where he is, and would the family care to make a deal. Isn't it extraordinary?" She smiled hugely. I wished I could have made her so abundantly happy.

"Who?" I asked. "Who called him?"

"Someone from the Free Croatia people, of course. Who else? The man said so. Klaus said for us to come on down to Heidelberg at once. They're giving a concert tonight in the castle, but he'll be free afterwards and we can stay with him. He's borrowed a house there."

"It won't be so easy," Madeleine said. We explained the news about Willis. But Rachel laughed it off at once. "Well, we didn't kill him. We were all in bed here." She looked at me briefly. "It's ridiculous. Of course we can leave. We *must!*"

"There's someone outside the hotel door right now," I said. "And probably there are others. Anyway, if we did get out,

266

they'd stop us at the border very easily. Remember, Heidelberg is in Germany."

"Excuse me butting in," a pleasant American voice said suddenly from nowhere. And then a man in a candy-striped summer suit stood up from behind a group of high-backed chairs next to us. He came over, smiling, apologetic—a nice, old-fashioned American, I thought, at first not recognizing him. "I couldn't help overhearing your conversation. But I'm going down to that concert in Heidelberg myself this afternoon—I could take you with me. I don't know if you remember me, Mr. Marlow?" He smiled across to me, his hand on the chair above Rachel. Of course, it was Pottinger. Art Pottinger—Professor Allcock's American academic friend who had disappeared in front of my eyes so successfully a few weeks before opposite the British Museum. I introduced him. "Ah—Rachel Phillips," he said in a slow admiring way. "We spoke about you—Mr. Marlow and I—when we last met. Are you playing over here on tour?... I'd love to hear—"

"No. We're looking for my father," she said abruptly.

"Sit down, do," Madeleine said, by way of apology.

The candy-striped linen suit had been pressed recently and Pottinger had now become a well-groomed academic—if that's what he was at all. But I didn't question his bona fides just then.

"You seem to be in some trouble," he said. "I couldn't help overhearing... you must forgive me. I've been over on the Continent a few weeks—in Amsterdam with the Professor, and now I'm staying here. Sort of sabbatical tour of the music festivals, among other things. I was going to take in this concert tonight in any case, then on to Salzburg. So if I can help?..."

"What's happened to Brian?" Madeleine asked.

"Oh, the Professor? He went on back to London, as far as I know. And I came down here. I don't want to interfere, but I do have a car in the underground garage."

"So have we," Rachel said. "But we can't use it."

"Thank you, but we really couldn't," Madeleine said. "We wouldn't want to get you involved—"

"Why not, Mummy?"

"Rachel—"

"No, no, that's quite all right. I'd be very pleased to be of help. Your father, you say—he's disappeared? The Professor didn't mention it—but then I'm not that close a friend. And now they say you've murdered someone!" Pottinger smiled slowly. "You don't any of you look the type."

We explained the position to Pottinger then, and I must say I saw no real reason not to trust him. He'd hardly have presented himself to us if he had been with the CIA or the KGB—and his whole attitude seemed so much more straightforward than anyone else's I'd come across in the past few days. "What do you suggest?" I said.

"I suggest you come out with me in my car. They won't have their eye on that. And if they do spot us, well, I'll just say you asked me for a lift uptown."

"And the border crossing?" I asked. "They'll check our passports there. They'll be looking for us by then."

Pottinger smiled once more, with a lazy, archaic American confidence. "Oh, I know this part of the world pretty well. I did some research at the University of Louvain over here a few years back. There are half a dozen small roads to the east where we can get over. No checkpoints. I did it quite often when I was here."

"But the whole thing's entirely illegal," Madeleine said, perturbed.

"Do they have a warrant to keep you under house arrest?" Pottinger asked, leaning forward incisively, like a small-town attorney. He was a big man, I noticed again now; there was something of the wrestler in him—apart from the face, which might have belonged to someone else altogether, with its sharp-featured intelligence and mobility.

"No. There was no warrant or anything."

"So it's not illegal. And if they catch us at the border—well, we'll just say we strayed over. Lots of people do. It's not an indictable offense, Mrs. Phillips—leaving your hotel."

"But why take the risk on our behalf? No—we couldn't."

It was a point that had crossed my mind too. But Pottinger smiled once more—a smile of genuine concern. "Mrs. Phillips—any friend of the Professor's—well, I needn't say. Besides I was *going* to Heidelberg anyways—so why not help out? Listen, put a few things into some overnight bags after lunch, then take the lift down to the basement garage. I'll be waiting for you. It couldn't be simpler."

He stood up, beaming. He was an easy man to like.

"What about the hotel bills?" I asked. "They'll have warned them about us."

Pottinger shrugged. "You'll be coming back here. So when

you get over the border just phone and ask them to keep your rooms—say you decided to take in this Heidelberg concert on the spur of the moment."

"Oh, Mummy—we really ought to get down there. Any way we can." Rachel was eager again, the idea of action making her face glow.

Half an hour later we left our rooms. I shared a small holdall with Rachel, emptying the contents of my brief case into it—a change of pants and socks, my Baedekers and Maria von Karlinberg's diary, which I hadn't yet read properly—and we took the lift down, one by one, to the underground garage without anyone noticing us. Pottinger was waiting for us like a chauffeur, in a hired Peugeot. By two o'clock we were out in the lovely afternoon, on the motorway, going eastwards toward Louvain.

Pottinger drove easily, only one hand on the wheel, and we were free once more, gliding across the flat green countryside with its geometric fields and small white farms and distant church spires—free of Huxley and Payenne, and the little holocaust in the forest, which I hadn't mentioned. But, of course, I should have remembered it. There was a queue of cars at a roadblock some miles outside the city and we were trapped in it before we could turn back.

"Stay calm. They can't have gotten all this show together, in so short a time, just for you people. It has to be for something else." Pottinger was admirable, taking off his linen jacket casually as we waited in the burning heat.

We showed our passports, they checked the trunk. "Just tourists, going to see Louvain," Pottinger said in response to the inquiry. "What's happened?"

"Rien. Rien du tout," the patrolman said, waving us through. But there was a radio in the car and Pottinger turned it on. "That's a full-scale alert," he said. "Something big has happened." Then I told them what had happened that morning, in the forest. I could hardly do otherwise. And ten minutes afterward a news bulletin confirmed it. What I didn't know was that it was Radović, the exiled Croatian army officer, the man I'd gone to see, who had been the principal victim in the killings.

"I'm sorry," I said. "I should have told you."

Pottinger turned to me, shaking his head in disbelief. "And you were on a racing bike too?" he asked.

"Yes, I borrowed it from one of the hotel staff. But I didn't kill him."

"No. I shouldn't think you did. I know something of the background to this Croat business. That man Radović—the SB, Tito's secret police—they've been gunning for him for years. He's the top man of one of those exiled Croat groups."

"Yes," I said. "That's why I was trying to see him."

"We didn't tell you," Madeleine interrupted from the back. "It's one of these Croatian terrorist groups who've taken Lindsay. We've had letters from him, one from Munich, in fact. The 'Free' something or other."

"Free Croatia—'Hrvatska Slobodan'?" Pottinger asked, turning off the motorway now, following an exit sign for Louvain.

"Yes, those are the people."

"I see." Pottinger nodded his head carefully. "I see how it is," he said, as if he'd found the answer to a lifetime's search. "Well, that does make it all a little more difficult. But tell me, your husband, Mrs. Phillips, you say he was in the British Foreign Office, and that you've had these letters from him for some time? Well, are you looking for him entirely on your own? Surely your own people at the embassy or your Intelligence services are helping you?"

Pottinger looked straight ahead, concentrating on the road.

"I'm afraid we've not had a lot of help from them," Madeleine said.

"None at all. They're trying to stop us, if anything," Rachel added. "I'm pretty sure they're trying to frame us—blame our friend's death on us. It's all crazy. They don't want to be involved."

"But why? Your father had an important position—"

"They say they can't deal with these Croat terrorists; it would upset Tito," Madeleine said shortly. "That's more important than all my husband's work."

"I see. It's a bad business—"

Madeleine leaned forward. "Why don't we go back? We can go back," she said apologetically. "Just see Louvain and go back. Wouldn't that be best?"

"If someone saw you—or knows you were on that racing machine, Mr. Marlow—going back would be out of the frying pan into the fire. On, on, I'd say: never apologize, never explain."

Pottinger enjoyed his idioms, I noticed, like someone who'd just learned a language—and I was tempted once more to try and confirm his bona fides. "It's a pity we haven't got time to see Louvain," I said. "Were you there long?"

"Just a semester. There," he said, pointing to a spire on the horizon, sticking up beyond some dull suburbs. We were taking a circular road around the town. "That spire—that's the Louvain University Library, the one the Germans burnt down in World War One. But the town hall is more interesting; it's one of the finest examples of late Gothic in Belgium, if you like that sort of thing. Personally I found the whole place rather provincial."

"What were you researching? I thought you specialized in Soviet studies. I saw that typescript of yours in the Professor's rooms."

"A paper on the history of the Reformed Church in Prussia. That's East Germany now: Louvain has the best collection of books on that topic in Europe."

"The Reformed Church? Surely Louvain is a Catholic foundation?"

"Indeed. But they keep all the texts on their enemies, Mr. Marlow. Complete files, you might say." He smiled easily. "And what do you do?" he asked, neatly turning the tables.

"Oh, I write histories too," I said. "About Egypt. I was a teacher there years ago."

Pottinger nodded politely. "Were you? That must have been quite something. Do I know your books? Do you write under your own name?"

"No, I'm afraid they've not been published yet."

After Louvain we took a secondary road for Hasselt and then Maastricht, a small town near the German border. From the map it seemed we were going too far north to hit the Cologne-Heidelberg autobahn. But Pottinger obviously knew his way.

"What sort of road are you going across on?" I asked. "A track? I thought the Germans were very efficient—checkpoints everywhere."

"There are tracks. But even better, there's a few miles of old turnpike—a motorway they never completed. It's not used. Leads right up to the German border, between Visé and Eisden. Stops at a farm this side. There's a track across from there on. It'll be hard as rock in this heat. I've used it before."

"You make a habit of illegal entry and exit?" I smiled.

Again, as outside the British Museum, I sensed a too clever will-o'-the-wisp in Pottinger, a man who could appear and disappear with a skill that was more than academic.

"No," he said deprecatingly, "I just used it once to see what would happen. Hell, it's all one Europe now anyway. Same as state lines. What's the odds?" He spoke like a cattle rustler from the New World.

The land rose gradually as we neared the border, turning south now through Tongres, and soon a few hills began to appear, at last a break in the long, flat land. But by the time we got to Visé the countryside had sloped again; it was rougher now, marshy in places.

"Here's the river Meuse," Pottinger said, as we crossed over the wide expanse of water before passing through the small market town of Visé. "The old motorway is next. It's as swampy as hell round here—floods in the winter. That's why they never completed it."

Beyond Visé we turned north again and now there were rows of pine trees on either side of us, small plantations running up the side of the valley. The sun was behind us, slanting a little and shadowed here and there by the greenery. But it was still hot, and we'd been traveling for more than two hours.

"I could do with a break," Rachel said.

"So could I. But I don't know if it's the right moment." Pottinger was looking up into the rear mirror now. There was a car following us, a good way behind. But it was there, on this isolated, empty road. We turned a corner and the trees hid us. Pottinger increased speed and by the time we saw the car again it was a long way behind.

"Nothing. Just some farmer." Pottinger shrugged.

"If they are following us they don't have to go fast," I said. "There doesn't seem to be any turn off this road, not till we get to Bereneau."

"There isn't—except the motorway."

Another corner hid us and again we picked up speed, imperceptibly almost, as though Pottinger were anxious not to alarm us. But we were alarmed.

Then, to our left, in a clearing in the plantation, we saw the entrance to the old motorway. It was neatly walled up. Yet we made straight for it, fast.

I hadn't seen the gap at one side of the wall—an old contractors' path that sloped down through the woods. Pottinger swerved onto it expertly, the car suddenly thudding on the hard, sun-beaten earth. He swung the wheel round, following the curve in the trees like a rally driver late for a checkpoint. Half a minute later we were out in the sunlight again, bumping over stony ground, along one side of a V that merged with the shoulder of the motorway rising ahead of us. We hit it at fifty miles an hour and suddenly it was wonderfully smooth as the thumping stopped and the wheels bit sharply into the asphalt. "Jesus!" Pottinger said. He was excited, like a small boy.

The motorway was divided down the middle by a rusty central barrier and we were traveling up it now on the wrong side, which made our speed all the more unnerving. The surface was broken here and there with great potholes; although Pottinger swerved quite often, he still hit some of them, since he was keeping an eye on the rear mirror, too. It was a fairly hair-raising journey.

Then we saw the other car again. There it was suddenly, a black speck in the rear mirror, gaining on us steadily. But it wasn't exactly behind us, we soon saw. It was traveling on the right-hand carriageway, separated from us by the steel barrier. And then I saw that it was a British car, a Rover or an Austin Princess, with its lines raked up toward the back.

Pottinger remarked on this too. "It's not the police. Crazy fools. They've got themselves on the wrong track."

"Surely we're on the wrong side," I said.

"Yes—intentionally. That side doesn't lead anywhere. We come off the motorway down another builder's track, on our side about a mile ahead. But he can't get off it. There's no hard shoulder—the road just ends, a hundred feet above the ground."

The other car was racing us now, coming level almost, and I saw a man waving from the near window, pointing at someone or something in our car, then gesturing us to stop. I didn't recognize him for a moment, he was so low down in the seat. Then I saw it was Huxley, the minute little conspirator from the embassy in Brussels.

I opened my own window and waved back furiously, pointing ahead of their car, trying to warn them. "Slow down," I turned, shouting at Pottinger. But it was just then that we pulled sharply to the left onto the hard shoulder before dipping away very quickly on a steep track running down the embankment, so that we were hidden from the other car.

The supporting pillars of the motorway ran along to our right now for about a hundred yards before they stopped abruptly at the edge of a small valley. And it was into this valley that we saw the bottom of the car, high above our heads now, curving gracefully in a gentle arc at first before the car lost momentum and plummeted nose first into the ground. And for the second time that day I was faced with a world of fire as the car crumpled, turned on its side and the gas tank exploded in a great sheath of flame.

"Jesus!" Pottinger said again, but no longer in the tones of some happy schoolboy. We stopped and got out and walked toward the flames. But there was nothing we could do. Madeleine was appalled. "We must get the police," she shouted.

Pottinger wiped his face. He was sweating badly. But his nerve was far from gone. "The police? It's too late for them. Come on. They'll be here soon enough anyway." He looked up at the pall of dirty smoke rising into the clear summer sky. Then he hurriedly shepherded us all back into the car and we hit the track through the edge of the farm. Within five minutes we were out on some minor road—in Germany.

What the hell had Huxley been up to, I wondered? It was a thought Rachel, identifying him, echoed from the back of the car.

"One of your embassy men, was he?" Pottinger asked.

"Yes."

"I wonder what he wanted to say to you."

"I wonder how he managed to follow us."

"He must have been hanging around outside the Amigo all the time."

"Yes, he must."

Pottinger said, "I don't understand. You tell me your official friends aren't being any use to you. They're being unhelpful. Yet here they are keeping tabs on you all the time."

"They don't want Lindsay found," Rachel said. "We told you."

"It doesn't follow, though, does it? Risking their lives like that just to stop you finding your father."

"It does follow," I said. "If the game is big enough."

Pottinger looked at me in surprise. "What game?" he asked.

"I wish I knew," I said. But I was lying. For I thought for a second that I did know what was going on just then. The puzzle became clear for an instant and was then entirely lost to me. I had somehow touched the answer, but it had slipped from my grasp: an answer that had to do with two groups of people looking for the same thing—Lindsay, perhaps?—but for different reasons. Looking for Lindsay? ... But the thought was gone, lost in the furor somewhere of that bright summer afternoon.

We got to the Cologne-Frankfurt autobahn an hour later, and by six o'clock we were halfway to Heidelberg.

4

The castle at Heidelberg reared up high above us on the other bank of the river as we drove through the narrow streets of the old town—a dream of Gothic towers and broken battlements, floodlit already, streaked in golden light against a velvet evening sky. It was after eight o'clock, and Klaus's concert must have started already. It had been impossible to park near the castle itself, so we'd walked up the steeply winding road in the shadowy twilight, the old medieval bridge below us now, lights winking on the river and pale stars coming out over the wooded valley.

The air was still and warm, faint trails of perfume lingered from the crowds of expensive people who had walked this way a little earlier. The music came to us from a distance—a burst of trembling strings interrupted suddenly by a sweet fanfare that died and then was repeated, more loudly this time.

"Strauss," Rachel said, her face excited now, alive in the shadows—a different woman who was about to forget the recent past and go back into her own, her real life.

"Johann?"

"No. Richard." She strode away from us, like an addict

sniffing opium on the wind. "I hope he's left the tickets for us," she called over her shoulder.

Pottinger had his ticket in his hand—that at least was real, I thought; he'd bought it in Brussels. And he was once more the academic, not the cattle rustler—his face set with pleasure, full of intelligent purpose. We were all of us free then, as if the violent events of the day had happened in some afternoon movie we'd seen before leaving Brussels. Our journey down had passed entirely without incident. We were ordinary people once more—because we so much wanted to be that. We'd pressed our luck and won and now it was time to retreat into anonymity.

Our tickets had been left for us and we found our seats halfway down the courtyard, with Pottinger somewhere behind us by himself—and there was nothing to do then but sit back and enjoy Richard Strauss. But he wasn't a composer I liked, and my attention soon drifted away from the music. Though Rachel was so close to me on the small chairs, I had lost her again. She had been polite, almost formally distant toward me since the evening before and now she had gone back entirely into her music, into that world where for so long she had lived alone, and to which she could now return. And the sounds that I heard then, despite all their artistry, were like those in Notting Hill, when Rachel had played the flute behind the bathroom door—a prelude to loss and departure, when she'd run back to her father from the scum and the dirty bathtub. Perhaps Klaus might take her on again, I thought—the big man with his back to us now. He was extremely broad-shouldered, with long strands of luxuriant jet-black hair flying about his ears as he took the orchestra through the complex score: big-boned yet with delicate movements. When he turned you could see his features were somewhat Italianate, almost Gypsy-like—it was a face resembling a solid, handsome watch that would never go wrong. Surely Rachel needed that—and not my kind of truth, my time-telling, which would always be at variance with hers? And yet I didn't want to lose her.

I thought of Huxley instead, the music beginning to crash distantly in my ears, visions of the ruined motorway that afternoon taking its place—and the bottom of a car that had circled over our heads, soundlessly, like a great silver bullet in a surrealist dream, before it touched the earth and rose again in flames. What had he been trying to signal so vehemently, so desperately, as he raced along beside us? He had been pointing at Pottinger and me in the front seat, not at the women. And since presumably he knew all about me by then—from Marcus in London—he could only have been trying to tell me something about Pottinger.

Then it dawned on me—or rather, dawned again: I'd been avoiding the evidence for the sake of a convenient escape out of Brussels. Of course, as I'd felt ever since that morning in Bloomsbury, Pottinger wasn't just an academic. He was with Intelligence—with the Americans, or possibly with Moscow. One of Huxley's minions, keeping tabs on us, had spotted him with us in the hotel perhaps, and identified him, and Huxley had then followed us, assuming we'd been taken in some kidnap. Of course, I thought, eastwards: they must have thought we were headed for East Germany and Moscow. That was it. Pottinger was in that camp. But why on earth had he run the risk of openly attaching himself to us, if he was with the KGB? Why, because of course he wanted to know as badly as we did what had become of Lindsay—one of his men who hadn't come back home to Mummy. And now we'd told Pottinger that the Croatians had taken Lindsay. Thus, if my theories were right, he would no longer have any more use for us.

I turned around. I could see Pottinger's seat ten rows back on the aisle. It was empty. And then way behind, at the entrance where we'd come in, I saw a figure in a candy-striped jacket pushing quickly past the little tent that housed the box office.

I was in an aisle seat myself and was up after him in a second, running back down the courtyard and out past the attendants onto the floodlit causeway. But its one-hundred-yard length was deserted, the broken battlements casting a huge jagged shadow all down one side. I went over to the wall. There was a drop of about a hundred feet: no one could have made it—and no one, in such a short time, could have run so fast as to have disappeared at the far end of the causeway. Pottinger had again found himself some great hand to scoop him out of thin air. But this time I was determined to find him.

I saw there were only two ways he could have gone—to the right or left of the entrance tent, crawling along part of the broken battlements before dropping back into the castle forecourt a little further on along either side. I chose the right-hand path, leaping up onto the battlement and making my way along it for a few yards without looking down into the moat far beneath me. I was soon able to drop down onto the far side, behind another tent this time, which hid me from the audience. Pulling aside the flap I found myself facing an old woman, knitting by a small card table. I was in one of the women's cloakrooms.

"Keine Herren!" she shouted at me. She pointed further along in the direction I'd been taking. I backed out and moved on round the edge of the courtyard, the music getting louder as I circled slowly toward the podium. There was another tent now and again I was behind it, wedged between it and the castle wall. I could hear someone peeing almost straight in front of me, a foot or so beyond the canvas. It must have been the gents'. But there was no flap I could open this time to get inside.

"Pottinger?" I said, shouting into the canvas without much hope. The peeing stopped abruptly and a German voice, greatly shocked, said suddenly, *"Ja? Mein Gott! Was ist das?"*

I was trapped behind the latrine now. Pottinger, I supposed, must have taken the other direction and gone around the castle battlements. He was gone anyway. The music came to a rowdy climax beyond me and there was a great cannonade of applause—applause for Pottinger, it seemed, as I fought my way out from behind the guy ropes and folds of canvas back into the forecourt.

After the concert we walked all the way down the hill again, to where we'd parked the car, halfway along an old street by the river. The space was empty. But there, placed neatly together on the pavement, were Rachel's holdall and Madeleine's overnight bag. Pottinger being considerate to the end, I thought. But then I realized that he'd want to help us; he was as anxious for Lindsay as we were. I looked around the dark street, into the shadowy archways. Pottinger had disappeared.

"Where's he gone?" Madeleine asked. The two women were astounded.

"God knows."

But I felt that he, or his colleagues from Moscow, would be with us from now on—eavesdropping on us, following us, as I was sure Marcus had done and would continue to do, in ways we would never know. We were three Pied Pipers now, leading all the others on a grim dance. I opened Rachel's holdall. My things were still there: Maria von Karlinberg's diary and the little silver revolver and matchbox of ammunition. I put the gun and matchbox in my pocket this time. I'd keep them with me from now on.

KLAUS had borrowed an appallingly contemporary studio from some friend—a "bijou" apartment decorated in the most clinical modern style, with one long room full of mirrored tabletops and chrome armchairs, which looked out over the whole valley, twinkling in the night beneath us.

He had taken his tailcoat off and was in a starched shirt and cummerbund now, busying himself first with a tray of drinks and then with the curtains at one end of the long picture window. He started to close them, but stopped halfway.

"No," he said decisively, as though reconsidering a vital piece of stage management. "Let us look at the night." He left the curtains as they were, then stood back, admiring his work briefly. He turned, rubbing his hands. *"Quelle histoire,"* he said to himself. I presumed he was commenting on our story, which we had all of us fed to him by degrees since the concert had finished. "No," he went on, picking up an earlier question. "They obviously got in touch with me because I'd been married to you." He went over to Rachel and put his arm around her for a second. "There is a syphon of soda in the kitchen," he told her, towering above her from a great height. "They might like it." She left willingly. They might have been still married, I thought, Rachel operating so meekly in his shadow, the compliant hausfrau almost, who had never left him that day years before.

Madeleine was perched on one of the sharp chrome chairs; I was over by the window, staring vacantly out at the night. And now he came up to me, looking at me generously. It wasn't that he was patronizing, I felt, but rather that he was the famous conductor, someone from whom precise directions about every aspect of life were to be expected. I felt extremely unnecessary and didn't mind a bit. He offered me a large cut-glass tumbler of expensive whisky.

"Good," he said. "Very good," he added, as I took a first taste of it.

"Thank you. I think I'd like some soda."

"And you shall have some soda. Rachel?" He turned and smiled as just then she came back into the room with a big

280

colored syphon. He took it from her and brought it over to me ceremoniously. "Say when." He squeezed the lever.

"When." Klaus went on round the room, conducting an elaborate ritual with the drinks. I suppose he thought whisky and soda was something every true English person still required after ten o'clock at night.

He sat down at last, taking off his watch first, then his cuff links and finally rolling up his sleeves.

"Now," he said. "First things first. About this man who called me." He picked up a large engagement book from the mirror-topped table in front of him. "Here's what he said—"

"Did he speak German? Can we call him now?" Madeleine interrupted eagerly.

"Yes, German. But you can't call him now. He didn't leave any number—obviously. He's going to call you at the Schwarzenberg Palace Hotel in Vienna. Between nine and nine-fifteen two nights from now, on Wednesday. I made the arrangements. You can stay at this hotel. I know the owners."

"But why Vienna?" I asked.

"Obviously they have Lindsay down there somewhere." Klaus took off his cummerbund. He was disrobing gradually. "The man didn't explain. But you must go there, to the hotel, and wait for him to call. See for yourself."

"Go there? But how?" Madeleine was tired. "This foolish American...All our things are back in Brussels. Besides, we shouldn't really be here at all. We left illegally—and they're bound to be looking for us at the next frontier—"

"Nonsense, Madeleine." Klaus stood up and went over to her, kneeling down rather formally and taking her hand, as though rehearsing a scene from some grand opera. "Nonsense. You *must* go on and find Lindsay. You must go on, not look back."

"But—"

"With *me*, Madeleine. We are all going on to Vienna tomorrow morning. We have a concert there the day after. It couldn't be simpler. You can come in the musicians' coach. They rarely check all the orchestra against their passports in any case. But if you stop now—well, you may lose him."

Klaus stood up and came over to me again. "Peter," he said. "You tell her. You've brought them here so far. You shouldn't stop now." He turned back toward Madeleine as though waiting impatiently for a tardy musician to pick up his cue.

"Yes," I said. "Why not? A sheep as a lamb," I added. I hardly cared any more, I was so tired just then. After Vienna, if nothing happened, we could pack up the whole business and go home. Home? Well, back to a summer of cool, dry sherries at least, lost in the Cotswolds, and the remains of a book about the British in the Nile valley. It wasn't much—but they were surer things than anything in Lindsay's life, it seemed.

"All right, let's go on." Madeleine had revived once more.

"There. You see, I knew it was the right thing. You can all come with me. And stop worrying. Let me change my things and I'll come downtown with you. We'll have some food, and you can all camp with me here on the sofas. No need to sign any hotel registers. Okay?" He turned and smiled at Rachel.

"You're marvelous," she said. "Absolutely marvelous."

"Ah," he said, putting an arm around her shoulders again. "There is nothing really difficult. It's all in the *mind*—where we have no limitations!"

Klaus was a godsend for Rachel, I could see—and he knew it.

THE huge coach was air-conditioned, which was just as well. Although the day had started early with a cool, thin mist over the river, swirling on the water by the old bridge, by nine o'clock it had given way to a heavy blue sky, the heat already shimmering on the twisting valley road that led eastward down the romantic river Neckar.

I had taken Maria von Karlinberg's diary out of Rachel's bag as well as Lindsay's old address book, which I still had with me, and I turned to the letter M. There she was: "Maria—Reisnerstrasse 32, Vienna 3." The same woman, I wondered? The socialist journalist of forty years before trying to get a foot in the legation door? Lindsay's friend—or something more? Willis had been just fractionally hesitant about her. Well, we were going to Vienna now. She might be still around, might help. I could but try. Kovačić, after all, had clarified many things and he'd turned up out of a phone directory. Perhaps more elderly people in Europe had survived the war than I had imagined.

Klaus came with us in the coach for the first part of the journey—down the Danube valley, to Passau, where we were to have lunch. He sat in front of Madeleine and me now, talking with Rachel, introducing her to some of the musicians. I saw her fingering a flute belonging to one of them, examining it with love. She was at home again. What nonsense it had been for her to suggest a future with me, "an audience of one," as she had in Brussels a few days before. That had been a convenient dream of hers, far from her real nature. Rachel had become "unworthy" once more, either of me or of life. She bloomed in a crowd, among the attention of many, as she did now, her skin glowing in the bright morning light, playing a few delicately phrased notes that floated back down the coach like the tentative theme for a life renewed.

After some thermoses of coffee had been passed round I got out the diary and started to look through it. Madeleine glanced at the cover. "That's the book by Lindsay's friend in Vienna?"

"Yes. I wish I understood more German."

I was able to translate only a little of the text, a passage here and there, and part of one long account of a train journey the woman had made with an unnamed man to visit socialist prisoners in a small Austrian town. There was a lot of talk about someone called Koloman Wallisch, a socialist martyr of the times, apparently, whom the authorities had executed in the provinces after the Vienna risings of February 1934.

Later, when Klaus came down to see us, I asked him to take a look at the passage. "An old friend of Lindsay's," I told him. "What does she say?"

Klaus stood in the aisle a minute, holding the luggage rack, swaying a little. Then he read from the diary, translating it fluently, in almost dramatic tones:

We traveled all night in that uncomfortable third-class compartment, the snow falling all the time. Do you remember? The first of our wedding snows. And the hills were all covered with it next morning. But the town was gay and springlike with fruit and vegetable stalls, and we had that small front room in the Gasthaus facing the street with all those fine baroque houses and the great market cross—and beyond, the mountains, still streaked with snow. But Wallisch had died and was buried here in the cold cemetery down by the river. And there was nothing left but our love then. Our snow love, which was not yet cold.

* * *

Klaus looked up, surprised. "Poetic," he said. "In very simple German, almost like a children's story." He looked puzzled. "But this Wallisch—he was a socialist agitator." He glanced through some more pages. "Yet it's a love story," he said, "from what I can make out. A socialist love story." He turned back to the beginning of the book, looking at the dedication. "'To the Fat Man in the Blue Bar of Sacher's',," he read out. "What does that mean? Is the woman still alive?"

"I don't know."

"The 'Fat one'?" Madeleine asked. "Could that have been Lindsay? People used to call him Fatso."

"I wondered just that myself," I said.

"This Maria must have been an old flame then—though Willis denied it, tactfully enough."

But had Madeleine really followed all the implications? "If it's dedicated to him," I said gently, "and it's a love story, well, Lindsay must have been its subject. The man she's talking about traveling with in that train all night and in the hotel next morning—that must be Lindsay, don't you think?"

"Possibly. Why? Is that strange? He was young enough. I'm sure he had girl friends out there then."

"Yes. But at that time he was supposed to be with Eleanor. You remember? She was with him in Vienna then."

Madeleine shrugged. "Who knows all the exact dates? And what does it matter anyway? It was forty-five years ago."

But I felt it did matter, though I couldn't say why. And then it struck me: "What was that phrase exactly?" I asked Klaus. "Our 'snow love'?"

Klaus went back to the passage. "'The first of our wedding snows,'" he read out. "Or 'wedding of snow' you might translate it."

And then I remembered Aunt Susan standing in the empty summer church at Dunkeld, telling me of Lindsay's Christmas wedding to Eleanor in 1935, when it had snowed all day, "like a fairy tale," except for part of the reception, "when the sun had come out and the champagne was too cold."

"And here?" I asked Klaus again, pointing to the end of the passage. "'Our snow love'?"

"'Which was not yet cold,'" Klaus finished.

I looked at the date on the flyleaf: 1937—the year of the breakup between Lindsay and Eleanor, according to Kovačić and Aunt Susan. I turned to Madeleine. "Eleanor studied German at Oxford, didn't she?"

"I don't know. I think so. Modern languages. Why?"

"This diary was written by her, I'm sure of it. She wrote it sometime before she died. It's the story of her time with Lindsay in Vienna in 1934."

Madeleine smiled sympathetically. She took the book from me and glanced through it. "But, Peter, why would she have bothered to write it all in *German*? And why did Lindsay never tell me about it? He had nothing to hide. I didn't know him then, after all."

"I don't know, but I'm somehow sure of it," I said.

"Well, that's as may be," Madeleine gave the book back. "But even if you're right, how will it help to find Lindsay now?"

She turned away and started to doze then, the sunlight touching her ash-gold hair through the big window. Klaus went back to the front of the coach, and I sat there remembering clearly the little church at Dunkeld, and that pale debutante's face in the stained-glass-window—oval-shaped, dark-haired, serene: "In Memoriam: Eleanor Phillips. 1912-1937"—the woman who had married there in a snowstorm.

"Poetic—like a children's story," Klaus had said. "A socialist love story." But why, indeed—if it be true—had Eleanor gone to all the trouble of telling it in German, and publishing it under an assumed name the year she died? And I felt the scent of the chase blowing about me once more, a strange pricking at the back of my neck, just as I had that afternoon in the ruined church, as though I were once again in the presence of these two people, long ago married and parted—and one, if not both, of them dead now. Yet for a moment they lived again in the dry air of the coach as fully as they ever had together in life; real people joined once more, refilling all the shapes of passion and anger which they had created then, released now in a book that I felt certain commemorated them.

And again I wanted to discover Lindsay, to complete my vision of his life in some way—a life that appeared to me now as something vastly strange and contradictory.

Madeleine dozed next to me, oblivious of my thoughts. And I thought: What peace she has with Lindsay. Alive or dead, guilty or innocent, it didn't matter to her. I looked at her face, sweet and calm in the light. She had that gift of total belief. Whatever happened she could not be wrong about her husband. And he? What had he done to deserve this faith in him?

The border with Austria came just after Passau. There were a few bad moments. But there were many other cars and dozens of tourists lining up against the passport counters, and, since we were the Bavarian State Symphony Orchestra, they took all the passports in a bunch, stamped them, and returned them without taking a head count, just as Klaus had predicted. We three had mingled with the crowds, apart from the musicians, our own passports at the ready, but no one noticed us and we climbed back onto the coach with the others. It was all extremely simple. I was surprised, since I assumed that the Belgian police would have found Huxley's car by now and, having checked back through the embassy, would almost certainly have discovered that he had been following us—we, who had jumped our house arrest at the Amigo Hotel. I could only suppose that either the Belgian or the German frontier police were being inefficient or that the orchestra had given us perfect cover. Or were we, I thought for a moment, because of some other ploy contrived by someone—Marcus perhaps, with the connivance of Interpol—being allowed to cross the frontier unhindered so that we might lead them to Lindsay? Perhaps we were too precious as pathfinders to be stopped, no matter how many corpses littered our way.

I sat by Rachel afterwards. We had drunk some wine with our lunch and she was tired now, the blinding afternoon sun streaking through the big coach window, touching her bronzed skin with fire. We had chatted about nothing and now she closed her eyes. She seemed to be sleeping.

I said gently, "You remember in Glenalyth, what you told me in the flower room: that we had to win, to try and win in our life, you and I, and not always settle for less: that we had to be *bright?*"

"Yes," she said after several seconds, almost inaudibly.

"Now it's my turn—to tell you the same thing."

She opened one eye sleepily. "Yes," she said again, without looking at me. "But I seem to have lost confidence in us. You make me look back. We're never really new people to each other. And there's too much in the past..."

"That you won't accept?"

"No doubt, no doubt." She was sarcastic now. She took out a handkerchief and wiped her forehead.

We were fighting again, the one thing we'd always been truly expert in. Our relationship, at heart, was still full of nursery antagonisms, exaggerated feelings. We had no middle way. We had to be either enemies or lovers.

I said, "You're going back into being terrified of the truth. That's not winning in life."

"Do stop talking about terror and winning and things. You said you thought Lindsay had killed Eleanor—*that's* the problem, or one of them. The truth can hurt too much to be worth it," she added severely, as if from the depths of some unquestionable knowledge.

We were coming toward Linz, the old Danube fortress town in the middle of the huge river. Narrow bridges straddled either side, one of them crossing over to the far bank and onto the Salzburg-Vienna motorway. Rachel turned away from me and looked at the view of spires and baroque cupolas, glittering in the late afternoon light, rising up ahead of us.

I put my hand on hers. "I love you," I said.

She turned on me brightly. "And I love my father. Is there anything to be ashamed of in that?"

She spoke loudly, with harshness almost, and her eyes were bright with anger and with fear.

"No," I said. But I knew she was adrift again now, tremulous, terrified—and yet excited by the venture, the daring cause she had taken on once more: a cause that lay in some hurt or unsatisfied longing in childhood and had formed her real search ever since, a need for reassurance so deep that it was impossible to assuage through the mechanics of real life. It could only be satisfied now, as in the past, by that fictional relationship she had maintained with Lindsay— where, like a warm toy or a perfect character in a child's book, he could be made to rise from some nursery world, day or night, and bring her an incredible comfort, a joy not subject to change or decay, wondrous and freely imagined. She could be an artist with her father, dealing in inspiration, miracles. With me, she knew, the fiction would run out after a while: rain would fall all day on a cracked windowpane somewhere and there would be scum round the edge of the bath.

I squeezed her hand and tried to be bright. But I was not bright at all.

5

We arrived in Vienna in the evening, running down the long slopes of the Salzburg motorway into a huge flat valley that lay beneath us like a plum-colored sea, with a pale, blue-velvet haze all over it, pricked everywhere with light.

The coach had been largely silent for the last hour, its passengers dazed with heat or half asleep after the long day. But now they stirred in mild anticipation, gathering their bits and pieces carefully about them—newspapers, cameras, and summer hats—like tidy little animals clearing up before venturing out into an exciting dark.

Most of the orchestra were staying at the Hilton next the air terminal, a little to the east of the city. From there, having seen them off for the evening, Klaus took a taxi back to the inner city with us, and then up Schwarzenbergstrasse and finally out onto a huge, ruined square with a glittering fountain rising up in the middle.

"Schwarzenbergplatz," Klaus said. "And the new metro." Spotlights illuminated great stacks of girders and piles of sand, with little builder's huts perched everywhere among the debris. The earth thudded with underground drills and the oven of summer air was thick with dust. But soon, circling this battlefield, we drove up into a darker street away from the city, swinging round into some thick bushes where there was a dim light above a small sign: SCHWARZENBERG-PALAIS HOTEL. Beyond this a short drive circled round to a gravel forecourt where a silver Mercedes lurked in the porch light from a low, two-storied building, the yellow stucco crumbling slightly between the tall shuttered windows.

"Come." Klaus gestured from the porch; we had stood there in the forecourt, looking around uncertainly at the clumps of bushes and the ghostly umber-colored building in front of us.

"This is the west wing of the palace. The family still live in the rest of it. Over there." Klaus pointed beyond the undergrowth to where we could just see a much larger edifice looming up in the shadows.

"Come on in. I've made all the arrangements."

I thought of Willis Parker a week before in Brussels, standing outside the Amigo in a similarly welcoming attitude, and I wondered when our luck—or Klaus's—was going to run out.

Inside, the illusion of being in a guest wing of a country house was almost complete. Taste predominated in the beautiful eighteenth-century furnishings in the narrow hallway. Huge bowls of orchids and other hothouse flowers were everywhere, with ugly modern facilities hardly in evidence at all, though I noticed a telex behind the reception desk, where a young man in a dark coat and pin-striped trousers welcomed Klaus like a courtier.

"Herr Fischer—how nice to see you." He spoke in English, as if in deference to Klaus's guests, whom he had already tactfully surmised came from those parts. He didn't glance at our passports as we filled in the reservation cards. Such vulgar modern actions, he seemed to suggest, were hardly necessary in these charmed circles to which, through Klaus, we had already achieved automatic entry. A retainer took our bags upstairs.

The bath in my room was as big as a tomb, circled in dark mahogany; the double bed was curtained, Indian fashion, by thin muslin drapes from the rest of what was a drawingroom and not a bedroom at all, with a tapestry along one wall, Louis Quinze armchairs, a rosewood escritoire and long, double-glazed windows that gave out over the formal, statue-strewn gardens at the back. A vague, clotted smell of flowers floated up on the air when I opened the windows, a perfume sun-warmed all day long and cooled now, a faint sweetness in the night. I was surprised to see a telephone by my bed. It seemed entirely out of place. Rachel and Madeleine had rooms immediately next to mine, with Klaus a little further down the corridor.

I didn't bother going in to see Rachel this time and since she no longer had her flute with her, there was no music. But I could hear someone talking to her, through the open window, half an hour later, when I'd had a bath and was just going downstairs for dinner. Leaning out I could just distinguish Klaus's voice. "I'm glad you like it," I heard him say. Their voices came right up to the open window now and I stepped back. Klaus spoke again. "There—you can just see one of the statues. They form a semicircle. Spring, I think that one is. Vivaldi's supposed to have written *The Four Seasons* here." I hated Klaus mildly then.

Downstairs over dinner Klaus was even more informative. "We can, of course, go to the police and tell them about the phone call tomorrow night. But why not deal with it ourselves? We can even record it here. I can make arrangements. Chances are the Viennese police may have your name. But remember, in any case, you yourselves came out here to offer these Yugoslavs a financial deal. So why not leave it that way?" He sipped the light, chilled wine, a Grinzinger from the Wiener Wald. "The concert we're giving tomorrow night—it's going to be over there, in the Belvedere Park." Klaus pointed beyond our own garden outside the dining room and up to the left. "All this central part round here is really just one big garden. Schwarzenberg, Belvedere, the Botanical Gardens: it's extraordinary—"

"I wonder how far away we are from Reisnerstrasse," I said, tactlessly.

"Reisnerstrasse?" Madeleine asked. Her face was happy in the candlelight. Klaus had been good for her too.

"Where that woman, Maria, lived, the one who wrote the book."

"Did she? How do you know that?"

"From an old address book of Lindsay's I found up in the attics in Glenalyth. Didn't I tell you?"

"No." Madeleine was less happy now. "I didn't know—"

"Oh, yes. 32 Reisnerstrasse. And of course, as I say, I think Maria was, in fact, Eleanor."

"What's the point—even if she was? It can't help now. It's nothing to do with this Yugoslav and the phone call—"

"This is where Lindsay and Eleanor lived, you know. Forty-five years ago—here, in Vienna. Right here." I felt the others were betraying their memory. There was silence. Rachel toyed with her food.

"I still don't see," Madeleine said at last. I had become an unwelcome outsider at the feast.

"They shot all the workers," I said with bitter enthusiasm. "They used mortars and howitzers—killed them in all their fine new model estates, the Karl Marx Hof and so on, on the outskirts of the city. Lindsay was here at the legation; Eleanor came out and joined him. They *lived* here together, in 1934. Willis told us that Lindsay knew this Maria von Karlinberg, that she was a socialist journalist, daughter of some great Hapsburg family here. Well, I don't think she was; she was Eleanor. Isn't that all worth finding out about?"

"No," Rachel said firmly.

"Why?" Madeleine asked me, more sensibly.

"Because I think it has something to do with why Lindsay disappeared."

"But he was taken by these Yugoslavs as a revenge for what's supposed to have happened on the border with all those Croats just after the war. That's what you said."

"Yes. But I'm not convinced. I can't see, for example, how they got Lindsay all the way down from Glenalyth to Vienna—over the Channel and across half a dozen borders. How do you do that? You can't drug a man for that long. Had we thought of that?" I looked round the table.

"He's not here at all—is that what you mean?"

"No, not necessarily." But I had suggested an element of doubt and they were not pleased. "I just think that while we're here in Vienna, waiting for this call...Well, I'll go round there myself tomorrow and see. You never know..." I left the uncertain future hanging in the warm air.

Klaus broke the unease. "Well, why not?" he said. He raised his glass. "If Peter believes it..."

I suspected that Klaus was encouraging me to do something the others found unpleasant, that I might the more alienate myself from them, to his advantage.

"Reisnerstrasse is just around the corner. It's an old street," he went on, "full of Hapsburg apartments. One of my music professors lived there. Runs from the Heumarkt to

Rennweg—past the present British Embassy, in fact, halfway along. Go round by Schwarzenbergplatz and you can't miss it."

Madeleine sighed. She shook her head. "I don't know what you expect to find forty-five years later," she said. "Even if Eleanor did live there once..."

"He expects to find trouble," Rachel said shortly.

"No," I said. "Not trouble. If anything, only the truth."

"You talk like a third-rate lawyer. Lindsay isn't on trial, you know," Rachel said.

"No," I lied. For to my mind, that was exactly the case. I slept uneasily that night and had a guilty dream in which, while naked and making love to Rachel in some great, ornately gilded bed, I tried to strangle her. It seemed such a classically obvious dream, in this city of Freud, that I smiled when I woke and remembered it next morning, opening the big windows and looking out on the twisted statuary, the gardens ablaze already in the white summer light.

The women didn't come down for breakfast. But Klaus was already in the dining room, reading through a musical score, so I had to join him over the fresh orange juice, coffee and pastries. I was surprised by his warmth toward me. He sympathized over my rebuff the previous night, and with my problems in helping the family.

"They're not easy people to do things for—or to live with." His face fell as though he genuinely regretted his failure with Rachel. "It was good of you to take on the—" He paused. "Their cause," he added at last. Klaus lived amid an allenveloping caul of drama. Almost every aspect of life was like great music to him, I felt. It had to be shaped and phrased carefully and then given out fortissimo. And I sensed that he enjoyed—even thrived on—the drama that had unexpectedly come to him through us. The whole business with Lindsay was something of an opera for him, the libretto being created there and then, right in front of him, and he was setting it to music, conducting it already in his mind's eye.

Klaus drained his coffee and stood up. "I'll arrange for Karl Hauptmann, our recording engineer, to come round and fix up a tape recorder in Madeleine's room for tonight. I won't be here, so I'll leave it with you. All right?"

We shook hands, rather formally. I liked him a little better now. Perhaps, I thought, the truth wasn't so important after all.

Reisnerstrasse wasn't too far: round the edge of the great square, splitting with noise and fire that morning, and then into the broad Rennweg that led south out of the city. My street was a few hundred yards up this boulevard to the left. But it was a long street, and No. 32 seemed to be right down at the end, so that I was sweating when I got to the arched doorway of the tall, grimy nineteenth-century apartment block. Coaches had entered a covered forecourt here in better days, picking up their evening-gowned and jeweled charges for a night at the opera. But now, when I turned the huge handle, the great doors creaked with untended age and I was confronted with gloom and decay. Inside was a tall, vaulted space, lit only by a few beams of dusty sunlight coming from a window high up in a back wall. The plaster was damp and cracked on either side, where two doors gave onto stairways and a row of metal mailboxes stood against the far end.

I walked over and looked at the names in the little slots, some of them barely visible in the gloom. There was no Von Karlinberg. I had hardly suspected such luck. I was just about to leave when I saw the firm capital letters. I lit a match to make sure. It said simply RABERNAK, and indicated an apartment on the fourth floor.

I was dizzy for a moment, but dizzy from excitement as much as anything. I'd found something better than Von Karlinberg. This must have been Zlatko Rabernak, the Zagreb antique dealer—or his family. Kovačić had told me that Zlatko had had a shop in Zagreb. It had been Zlatko Rabernak who'd collected music boxes and given so many of them to Eleanor; who had taken Eleanor away from Lindsay that spring in Zagreb when the cherry blossoms had fallen like snow in the park above the city.

I decided to take a chance there and then. The mailbox said RABERNAK. Somebody, at least, of that family still lived there. And so I climbed the shallow wooden stairway, past great tarnished mirrors at each landing, seeing myself framed in the decaying gilt as I rose upwards in my summer suit, an avenging angel or a fool—I couldn't say which.

On the fourth floor I rang a bell that pinged cheaply right behind the door, so that I jumped badly. It was opened almost at once by a fresh-faced young woman, large-boned and wide-eyed, with a very toothy smile, like some Coke ad from an old *National Geographic* magazine. She was in a dressing-

293

gown and smelled of soap; her hair was twirled up in a towel. I sensed she was American. She was.

"Yes?" she said. "Can I help you?" A pleasant Southern drawl. I was in luck. I hadn't expected my kitchen German to get me too far.

"Forgive me, I'm looking for Mr. or Mrs. Rabernak." I explained my business, briefly, tactfully. "We were friends of the Rabernak family—years ago. We were just passing through Vienna..."

"Well, come in then. I'm Clare. I just have a room with Mrs. Rabernak. There's only one. Mr. Rabernak died years ago, I think. Mrs. Irena Rabernak. She's nearly eighty—and not up yet. But I'll tell her—she likes to meet old friends. Come on in."

The hall was dark, paneled in plaster with gilt bas-reliefs, and there was a huge portrait of what looked like the old Emperor Franz Josef himself along the back wall.

"I'm studying at the conservatory here," Clare said brightly, as we walked across a thick carpet. The hall smelled of shampoo. Through an open doorway I saw a small bathroom, still steaming and with a line of underwear drying on a string.

"Oh yes," I said. "That's nice. There's a concert here tomorrow night we hope to get to, at the Belvedere Gardens."

"Yes. They do a few of the popular Viennese ones for the annual Vienna Festival. *Die Fledermaus*—that sort of thing."

"Opera—at this time of year?"

"Yes. They do a few of the popular Viennese ones for the annual Vienna Festival. *Die Fledermaus*—that sort of thing."

She had led me into a large, heavily furnished salon looking out over the street. The walls and shelves were filled with turn-of-the-century ornaments, chocolate-box portraits, old plate photographs and many potted plants. The big double windows were closed against the vague sounds of the street below, and the heavy velvet curtains, running all the way down to the floor from gilded rods right up against the ceiling, added to the sense of being in an almost soundless, brown-colored aquarium. It was a little Hapsburg museum, with its bits and pieces from the Belle Époque and earlier scattered everywhere—an inkstand shaped like a water-lily pond on a huge, dark desk; a small mirror with a languorous, half-clad maiden forming one side of the pewter frame, her arm leaning over the top, dangling a bunch of grapes. The place reeked of nineteenth-century certainty and long-settled virtue. Freud and Hitler had never been to this city—nor the Crown Prince begun to dally with Marie Vetsera up in the Hofburg.

The only modern thing in the room was a vulgar chrome tea trolley with silver bowls of old paper-wrapped chocolates on the bottom shelf, an empty ice bucket and a dusty, quarter-filled red vermouth bottle on top. Clare left me, and I could hear voices in some distant room. I picked up one of the chocolates from the trolley. It crumbled in my fingers.

It was quite some time before Mrs. Rabernak arrived. She was a small, fine-faced, slightly nervous woman with straggly gray hair, but dressed in a smart red pantsuit and neat pearl necklace, so that she didn't immediately look her age at all. She was heavily made up, her mouth forming a startling red gash right across her face. Only her hands properly revealed the years: arthritic and bony, the thin fingers were weighed down with old rings; they tended to slip, and she nursed them all the while with the other hand, moving them up and down nervously, like beads on an abacus.

She looked at me intently but uncertainly, as though I was someone with whom she had made an important appointment which she had afterwards forgotten about. Clare stood behind her in a bright, sleeveless summer dress, her pretty, unformed face surrounded by long corn-colored hair which she had now combed out so thoroughly that it shone even in the dull light. They were almost like Grant Wood's famous painting, standing beside each other, suggesting a relationship not unnatural but unfathomable.

"Mrs. Rabernak, you must excuse me for butting in like this..." I made my explanations, mentioning the Palais Schwarzenberg Hotel as a bona fide.

She held up a hand. "My English," she said, "is no very good. But Clare"—she turned to her, smiling—"Clare will help." We all sat down, huddling round the tea trolley and the dusty vermouth bottle in the middle of the huge room.

I had brought both Maria von Karlinberg's diary and Lindsay's address book with me. Having explained about looking for this Maria, I showed both books to Mrs. Rabernak. She looked through the diary carefully, turning the pages one by one, then skipping to the middle and stopping over a passage, reading it out in German in a low voice, intently, unaware of us. Her face withdrew into itself, the lines of age splitting the makeup and crinkling about her neck and cheeks as she sucked her breath in. I heard the name "Koloman Wallisch" faintly, derisively, on her lips.

At last she turned back to the front cover, jabbing a finger at it. Then she looked at me oddly. "Is not Maria von Karlinberg," she said hoarsely. "Is an Englishwoman who is living here before the war." She turned and spoke to Clare in German. I heard the name "Eleanor" and then "Biley," and I could suddenly hear my heart thumping in the quiet room.

Clare translated. "Mrs. Rabernak says it was written by a young woman called Eleanor Bally—or Bailey, I think. The Rabernaks had a much larger apartment in this same block then, and she lived with them for several months in—" Clare turned back. But the old woman had already understood.

"In 1934. Before they killed Dollfuss. In those bad times." She rattled her rings. She had a confidence now that had been lacking earlier—a gossip suddenly confronted by a juicy scandal.

"Is this the woman you've been looking for?" Clare asked.

"Yes. I'm a friend of the families. But how did she come to be here?" I asked the old lady. Again she didn't seem to understand, so I started off in German.

"No, no—I have understood you," she said helpfully. "How was she here? I will tell you." Her face was tense now, even angry. "She was a friend of a cousin of our Rabernaks, here in Wien. A distant cousin." She emphasized the distance by waving her arm in the air southwards. "The Zagreb Rabernaks. Of little Zlatko's," she added icily.

"Of course," I nodded. "He had an antique shop here in Vienna as well."

"No," Mrs. Rabernak said firmly. "Zat shop was my husband's. In Kohlmarkt." She spoke in German again to Clare.

"She says that everything these Zagreb Rabernaks ever collected was rubbish. How do you say it? Knickknacks?"

"Yes," I said. "Knickknacks. Music boxes?"

Mrs. Rabernak nodded her head vigorously. "That is it!" she said happily. "Just rubbish, music boxes." Again there was a flow of German addressed to the American girl.

Clare looked at her curiously before translating. "She says, well—" She hesitated. "That her father—that's Mrs. Rabernak's father—was a minister here under the old regime, with the emperor—"

"Minister of *Post und Telegraph*," Mrs. Rabernak said very precisely.

"I see," I said, not seeing the relevance at all. "And what happened to this Eleanor Bailey?"

Mrs. Rabernak put the diary back on the trolley. "We do not talk about her," she said.

"I'm sorry—"

"It must be that book," Clare added.

"She vas a socialist," Mrs. Rabernak broke in unexpectedly. "A Communist!" Then she spoke in German once more.

"Mrs. Rabernak says this woman lived here wrongly—no"—Clare fiddled for the word—"no—under 'false colors'? Mrs. Rabernak thought she was a woman of—" Again she searched for the word.

"A girl of good family," Mrs. Rabernak said shortly. Her English was better than she admitted. But again she lapsed into her own tongue.

"But they found she was a Communist," Clare said.

"And little Zlatko too," Mrs. Rabernak came in again like a cheeky bird. "He betray us all. Ve speak no more of him. Or of his wife."

"His *wife?*" I asked in surprise. My hair prickled all round the back of my skull. "Zlatko married this woman?"

Mrs. Rabernak nodded. "So ve have hert. Ve understood such. But ve do not speak of it. They are Communists."

"You mean this woman is still alive?" But Mrs. Rabernak didn't follow me this time. "Vat does he speak?" She turned to Clare. Clare started to translate, but awkwardly. She was beginning to get confused.

"Oh yes," Mrs. Rabernak broke in again. "They live, I think. In communism Yugoslavia. In Zagreb still." She lapsed into German once more.

At the end Clare said, "As far as she *knows,* they are both still alive, in Yugoslavia. If her cousin Zlatko had died, she says, she would have heard. So she assumes he's still living. But she hasn't seen or heard from him since before the war."

"But this woman Eleanor and he—they *married,* she knows that?"

"Oh yes—they marry," Mrs. Rabernak broke in derisively again. "At least, they have the children. I have heard that. Though as Communists maybe they do not marry," she added with even more scorn. "But ve forget them, these Communists and socialists," she ended triumphantly.

Then she picked up the diary and wagged it at me. "They are *bad* people," she started up again, enjoying this character assassination, her old eyes glittering with ancient enmity. "They make—how you say?" She turned to Clare, talking to her rapidly in German. I heard the name Von Karlinberg mentioned.

"She says this woman Eleanor made fun of the family," Clare said at last. "Mrs. Rabernak's father that she mentioned—the minister—well, he was a Von Karlinberg, a great friend of the Emperor Franz Josef. And this Eleanor Bailey—" She turned to Mrs. Rabernak, as if uncertain of something.

"Yes, yes!" Mrs. Rabernak nodded her head impatiently.

"She used her father's name on this diary."

"She make bad jokes with my family name," Mrs. Rabernak said icily, almost rising from the high-backed armchair. Finally, unable to restrain herself any longer, she got up and started to hunt round the room for something, muttering the while in German. Clare looked at me uneasily. Eventually Mrs. Rabernak found an old packet of Marlboros. She lit a cigarette shakily before coming back to us.

"I'm sorry," I said. "But I don't understand. Why would she use your father's name on this diary?"

"Because she make fun of all Wiener nobility," Mrs. Rabernak said, exhaling a cloud of smoke. "And all rich people, because she is a Communist! I hope she is not friend of you."

"No. I didn't know her. Just a friend of this other family."

"She was a journalist then, you know." Mrs. Rabernak looked at me suspiciously. "She is writing for all the Red papers here in Wien—and using my father's name for meeting important people. You are a journalist too?"

"No, no," I said. "Just a friend of the family. But tell me, I wonder if you ever met another friend of Eleanor Bailey's here: a young Englishman, he was at the British Embassy here then. Lindsay Phillips?"

Mrs. Rabernak looked puzzled. "Young Englishman. Phipps—"

"No. *Phill*ips."

"Never," Mrs. Rabernak said decisively. "No other man was ever here. Only Zlatko, who brought her here. *Mein Gott!* To think—" She turned once more to Clare.

"To harbor a Communist, she says—in those days. If she had known, how quickly she would have thrown her out of the house."

"Underground!" Mrs. Rabernak broke in quickly, pointing to the floor. "Like rats—that is how they lived! In the sewers. After Dollfuss had got rid of them in Floridsdorf and Ottakring!" She was triumphant once more, but nervously triumphant, as if those Communist rats might still be there, lurking beneath the floorboards, about to rise again, so that she could do battle with them with the Belle Époque inkstand and the great gilded curtain rods.

"I see," I said. "So how did she find out that this woman was a Communist?"

Mrs. Rabernak sat down, leaning forward confidentially. She picked up the diary again. "This," she said, whispering. I looked at the now rather grubby cover of the *Comrade's Diary*. She turned to Clare once more. After a while I had my translation. "They were talking about it in all the cafés," Clare said. "In 1937. How could a Von Karlinberg have written such stuff? It was printed clandestinely—in Prague, she thinks—and copies were distributed illegally, among the socialists here in Vienna. It was extremely embarrassing—and the risk of being connected with the diary in this way was dangerous for the Rabernaks. But in the end everyone realized it was only some anonymous joke."

"A very bad joke," Mrs. Rabernak added haughtily. And I supposed it must have been, with the fascists already in control of Vienna and Hitler with his Anschluss only just around the corner. Yet in a way I liked the cheek of it, biting the hands of a decayed and preposterous Viennese nobility like this—a class that had outlawed what Eleanor had apparently held most dear, the socialists in the city, and had driven them underground into the sewers and ruined their dream estates with howitzers. This diary seemed a just revenge, in a way—which had probably been exactly Eleanor's intention.

"I'm sorry," I said. "For all your trouble. It seems a bad business." I stood up then. There seemed nothing more to say, and Mrs. Rabernak was showing signs of overexcitement and fatigue. "I'm really most grateful to you both for all your help..." I shook Mrs. Rabernak's hand; one of the loose rings very nearly came away in my grip.

"I hope it may be some use," Clare said as she showed me to the door. "Your friend seems to have been quite strange. Really!"

"Yes," I agreed. "Very strange." I thanked Clare, who was

so very ordinary and open and obliging, another lodger in this house. I wondered that Mrs. Rabernak risked having guests at all after the betrayals of forty-five years before. I glanced at the huge portrait of the emperor in the hall as I left: authoritarian, portentous. But the cracked gilt frames and discolored glass of the huge landing mirrors on my way downstairs gave the lie to all these former glories. Old, impoverished families in Vienna—a city thrust deep into the throat of Communist Europe, where the rats might one day come again—took lodgers where they could these days, I supposed.

Outside in the street the sun hit me like a hot plate. It was nearly midday. I looked round at the tall, overdecorated apartment blocks. Eleanor Bailey had looked out on more or less exactly the same view, I thought, leaving this very apartment by the huge archway when she lived here. She'd probably have turned to the left, making for some rendezvous with Lindsay in the city: at the Blue Bar, no doubt, in Sacher's. I took the same course myself now, walking as it were in her footsteps, back into the Schwarzenbergplatz and toward the inner city, nearing something clandestine, just as Eleanor must have done in those prewar years when the city was on fire and Dollfuss was shelling the workers out in Floridsdorf. But what appointment?

What kind of woman had Eleanor really been? The news that morning gave her a character very different from that which Aunt Susan had described, and different, too, from that cool, sad image in the stained-glass window in the ruined church outside Dunkeld. She seemed rather a wicked prankster, as well as a Communist. There were still further contradictions in that it was she, indubitably now, who had written that "socialist" love story about her time with Lindsay in Vienna: "To the Fat One in the Blue Bar at Sacher's."

Yet Zlatko Rabernak had apparently been her friend in those days as well, long before she'd got to Zagreb three years later. The only explanation was that she and Lindsay and Zlatko had been conspirators of some sort together in Vienna in that early spring of 1934, all helping the Communist cause, I supposed, and all with perfect cover: Lindsay up at the embassy and the other two lying low in that heavy, impeccably bourgeois apartment down the street. It all fitted together. Sometime later Eleanor had written an account of it in this diary, under cover of the German language but still unable to resist a stab at her previous hosts by using the pseudonym.

And I saw then why Willis Parker had told such a tactful lie about Maria von Karlinberg in the restaurant in Brussels. After all, he had worked in the Vienna legation with Lindsay, and must have known that the journalist Von Karlinberg had, in fact, been Eleanor. But why, so long afterwards, should he bother to tell such elaborate fibs about it, since it was all something so much in the past? The woman herself was dead. And then I realized that, as Mrs. Rabernak had suggested, Eleanor Phillips was *not* dead. Chances were she was still alive in Zagreb, with Zlatko. And Willis had lied because he knew this, which meant that British Intelligence, or at least David Marcus, knew it too: which was why they had killed Willis—he had known too much. But again—about what? That Eleanor, long the ex-wife of a British agent, had been a Communist prankster and had written an indiscreet diary over forty years before? That wouldn't have been sufficient reason to kill Willis. There had to be some more vital secret at stake to justify his silence. The answer, I thought, might lie a little farther south: in Zagreb, with some woman who was not in a graveyard there but probably lived in an old house, in a park above the city ... And perhaps there were cherry trees in the garden, and beehives; the sweet charm of a music box drifting into the garden on summer-evening celebrations, or when old friends called ...

Old friends? More: another long-lived life somewhere in Zagreb—a life with music and fine antiques—and children, apparently, presided over by a woman now in her mid-sixties—some willful, rather extraordinary lady who forty years before had been killed under a tram outside the Palace Hotel and buried in the local cemetery. Was it possible? The idea was so preposterous that it came full circle, back into the realm of truth. And in doing so, it led to another proposition: that Lindsay had perhaps returned to this woman, his first wife.

But no; I'd forgotten Lindsay until that moment: Lindsay, who was probably lurking nearby, in a basement room, at the mercy of some louts—and another man who would call Madeleine that evening at nine o'clock. For the moment there was still a quite separate scenario to follow through with

Lindsay. Our immediate appointment lay in the Schwarzen-berg-Palais Hotel that night, in a bedroom by a telephone. I decided meanwhile to tell the women as little as possible about my morning with Mrs. Rabernak.

6

It wasn't difficult to postpone my account of the meeting. Neither of them was at the hotel when I got back there at lunchtime. It was six o'clock—I'd spent the afternoon looking at the seductive Klimts and Schieles in the Belvedere Gallery—before I met them again, in the foyer of the hotel. They were with Karl, the recording engineer, who had just come from the orchestra, who were setting up their concert in the Belvedere Gardens beyond our hotel.

Rachel more or less looked straight through me. Madeleine asked how I'd been. "Hot," I said. "I'll tell you about it later. I need a shower."

Karl went upstairs with the two women, taking his equipment to Madeleine's bedroom. I cooled off in a shower and went for a beer in the hotel bar before I joined them all again in Madeleine's room an hour later.

Karl, a dexterous little Münchener, explained the equipment to me, before he left to supervise a recording of the concert. He'd attached an expensive fifteen-inch-per-second Nagra machine to the bedside telephone, together with an automatic activator line that started the recorder the moment the handset was picked up. We tested it from the phone in my bedroom. It worked perfectly; the definition was uncannily high.

"That was a house call," Karl explained. "An outside call may not be so clear."

I came downstairs with Karl and saw him out. I didn't want to lurk about with the two women. Instead I took a walk into the deeply scented twilight of our gardens, moving down the crisp gravel paths and among the twisted statuary and baroque ornaments. And then, at eight-thirty, I heard Klaus's concert begin, over the wall in the Belvedere Gardens. It wasn't German music this time, but something lighter—ethereal, yet precisely phrased in quickly varying tempi: balletic almost. Gounod's *Faust,* I thought afterwards. I wished I could have stayed outside and listened to it, the air filled now with every kind of sweetness. But at five to nine I was up in Madeleine's room, the windows closed against the night, waiting for the phone to ring.

It rang at exactly five past. I checked the time against my watch. Rachel and I looked at Madeleine as she held the receiver.

"Yes?" she said. "Madeleine Phillips speaking." And then she listened for a bit. "Yes, of course," she went on. And then there was silence for half a minute. "Yes, I've got that," Madeleine spoke again. "You are prepared—two-hundred-and-fifty thousand dollars. Yes. We have less than twenty-four hours. And you'll call me again at three o'clock tomorrow afternoon. Yes." She put the handset down. "Well, they have him. He's alive anyway," she said, shaken but thankful. "Though how we get hold of two-hundred-and-fifty-thousand dollars out here, I don't know."

I played the conversation back. It was a young voice, exceptionally clear, a little nervous I thought, speaking good English, but with German rather than any Balkan or Yugoslav overtones. The man explained that the Free Croatia group were holding Lindsay and since the British government were not prepared to release the Croat in Durham Jail, they would exchange him for $250,000 in cash. We had less than twenty-four hours to consider the proposition and agree to make a first payment. He would call again after three o'clock the following day.

Despite Madeleine's interjections, the man appeared not so much to talk into the phone as to read something prepared or memorized. "He hardly pauses—do you hear?" Madeleine said.

"Yes. As if he's reading a statement. And in a hurry, too. In case the police trace the call. He spoke for hardly more than a minute. Any longer and they can trace it, I suppose."

We played the conversation back once more. I turned the volume up slightly.

"What's that noise?" Rachel asked. "There—just after the start. There's another voice, isn't there? Someone singing."

I played it back again, turning the volume up and the tone to a sharper level. And now we could just hear a second voice and then, quite clearly, faint music and what sounded like a chorus of voices. Then silence, and then, very faintly, what seemed a duet of voices singing in German.

"What is it?" Rachel asked.

"Just a radio or something in the background," Madeleine said.

It wasn't until much later that evening, when Klaus's concert was finished and we had gone round with the tape to meet him in the Belvedere Gardens, that we discovered exactly what the music was. We'd met Karl in the Bavarian Radio van that had accompanied the orchestra from Munich. He sat in front of a big multitrack recording console, faced with a variety of levers and switches—fade-ups, mixers, baffles, top and bottom cut-outs. He put our tape on a vertical spool above him and fiddled carefully with the machine, consulting a colleague next to him. Klaus stood behind him with Rachel. The van was air-cooled and smelled of nail varnish. It was Rachel who had insisted that there was something strange going on in the background of the tape. I wondered what the use of all this technology was.

And then, under Max's careful ministrations, when the tape began to play once more we heard the voices and the music in the background quite clearly. It was distorted, as the man's voice-over had become deep and growly, but recognizable, at least by Klaus.

"Der Zigeunerbaron," Klaus said at once. "There, listen: it's the duet in the second act. 'Wer uns getraut,' between Saffi and Barinkay. No question."

He turned to Rachel. She nodded. Karl played the tape back once more. "Yes—it is!" Rachel said.

"What is it?" I asked sourly.

"The Gypsy Baron—Viennese light opera."

"So?" Madeleine asked. She was as mystified as I.

Klaus was speaking to Max in German now. Afterwards he turned to us.

"So it's just a radio," I said. "On in the background."

Klaus was smiling. "No. Max thinks it's almost certainly not a radio—or from a turntable. He thinks it's probably the real voices."

Karl stood up from the console just then and went to look among some papers on a desk at the top of the van. He came back with a *What's On in Vienna* guide for the week. Flicking through the pages he stopped in the middle and said decisively, "Yes—I am right." He gave the booklet to Klaus, pointing to a column.

Klaus showed it to Rachel. "There—at the Staatsoper. Tonight, and a matinee tomorrow afternoon: *Der Zigeunerbaron*. It's just on for the Festival of Vienna. Two performances, for the tourists."

"I still don't follow." Madeleine leaned over Klaus's shoulder.

Klaus turned to her triumphantly, loving the drama. "The man who called you this evening almost certainly was phoning from the Staatsoper." He turned back to Max. "Have you a copy of any daily paper? Check the radio column." Max looked about the van. There wasn't one. But one of the truck drivers outside had a copy. They looked down the radio listings for that day. "No," Klaus said. "There was no radio relay from the Staatsoper this evening. So you see! He must have been calling from the Opera House."

"Why?" I asked. "It still might have been a record of *The Gypsy Baron*."

"It's just possible. But don't you see? The man said he'd call again tomorrow *afternoon*. After three o'clock. That's about halfway through the matinee. It fits. He's using a public phone—backstage somewhere probably. Yes," Klaus ran on, "and maybe he's not onstage at that moment and can just step out for a minute. You see, if the police had been monitoring the call—and he doesn't know that they haven't been, and even if they managed to trace it back to a call box in the Staatsoper—well, there are probably a hundred people backstage at any one time there. How could they isolate any single person? Especially if he'd gone back onstage immediately afterwards."

"All rather far-fetched," I said, suspecting Klaus's Sherlock Holmes act had been done more to impress Rachel and Madeleine than as a pointer to any actual truth.

Klaus turned to Madeleine. "Well, we've heard it now ourselves: as you say, the man is reading or memorizing the statement. He's an *actor:* that well-modulated voice, exaggerated too, just as an actor would do it—disguising it, in case anyone tried to identify him afterwards in that way. Probably a bit player—there are lots of them in *The Gypsy Baron.* Crowds of Gypsies—"

"And hussars too," Rachel put in.

"Of course. They come right after the *Dompfaff* duet—the arrival of Graf Homonay and his troop of hussars. Of course! They interrupt the lovers. That's why the man stops so short on the call. He's onstage in the next scene. It's my guess that he's one of the hussars. Perfect cover."

Klaus was very pleased with himself. I really didn't know if he had a point or not. One flaw struck me. "But why," I said, "should these Croatians go to all the trouble and risk of getting a Viennese bit-part actor to read the message when they could do it themselves?"

"Who knows?" Klaus said expressively. "Maybe they don't speak English or German too well. Or this actor may be a sympathizer—one of the Red Brigade or some such."

"I think it's just a recording in the background," I said. I disliked Klaus's confident deductions. "It's all too unlikely," I said again.

"Well, we can find out, can't we? We can be backstage at the Staatsoper when he calls tomorrow afternoon."

"We should give the tape to the police," Madeleine said steadily. "And let them handle it."

"You can," Klaus replied forcefully. "But you run the risk that they know about you all in Vienna by now. They may just pick you up and keep you on ice—and that will be the end of it. The Viennese police aren't going to interest themselves in arresting bit players at the Staatsoper on your behalf. Besides, it'll be too late then. The performances will be over." He turned to Madeleine. "You wait in your room at three o'clock and I'll take Peter with me to the Staatsoper and we'll watch tomorrow afternoon, backstage. I can easily pretend I'm auditioning for some singers or musicians. They know me well there in any case."

There was silence in the big van. It was nearly midnight. We were all tired. "Well, why not?" I said limply, giving in

307

once more to Klaus's proposals, sure that I was simply placating him and his wild ideas and allowing us to get home to bed.

All the same, Klaus was right about the Viennese police. He spoke to me next morning at breakfast, sipping his orange juice, a confident mischievousness about his face, the day so bright once more.

He said, "The manager told me privately this morning: he's had a routine inquiry from the city police—purely routine, a list they send out round all the hotels and guest houses every week, lost tourists, credit-card thieves and so on. All three of you are on it. By name. I told him it wasn't important—some family row in England. Lawyers chasing you. So he's agreed to say nothing about it for a day or so. But he'll have to report it by the end of the week. So, you can't go to the police. We'll go to the Staatsoper this afternoon instead."

"Why take all these risks, Klaus?" I asked.

"Risks? Where are the risks? You are all innocent, are you not? And what are old friends for? It's a matter of *action,* Peter. Never wait until things happen to you!"

"It's dangerous. These Croatians—"

"It's more dangerous just to wait for them. We must take the advantage here. See if we can identify this man, follow him."

"But we're not the police. We've no—"

"No. But you were the police, were you not, in a way? With British Intelligence. This is really your kind of job, is it not?" he added formally, almost coldly.

I could see that Rachel had been telling him about me. I was a man with a tradition of derring-do behind me, though they weren't to know my bravery had not extended much beyond culling through the Arab press on damp Monday mornings in the Holborn office ten years before. Rachel had probably told him as well that I had a little ivory-handled .22 revolver with me. I had it on me now. Klaus looked at me circumspectly, waiting for me to agree or refuse the challenge.

Was it conceivable that he viewed me as a rival, as in some romantic operetta, and was now contriving a match between us to test my honor? I didn't like the idea at all. But I could see it would appear cowardly of me to turn him down. Besides, it was all probably safe enough—for I doubted the truth of Klaus's musical deductions: the clear-voiced terrorist in the Staatsoper phone booth was almost certainly pure fiction. So I went with Klaus that morning, down into the blazing city, to spy out the land.

The opera house, a black, grimy building, straddled the Opernring and Kärntner Ring like some grim barracks in the crowded sunshine. Tourists queued for last-minute seats, straggling round the theater, which seemed to have half a dozen stage doors. But Klaus knew his way about and soon he was talking to one of the stage-door men—someone he knew only vaguely, but a man who remembered him precisely. The greetings were effusive.

"Ja, Herr Fischer . . . Nein, Herr Fischer. Danke schön, Herr Fischer . . ."

The little man in the braided cap nodded his head up and down with furious willingness. In the background we could hear music, an orchestra tuning up, and the musicians were coming in and hurrying past us, down a corridor.

Klaus turned to me. "There's a band call this morning. They're fitting a new Saffi in. This is the musicians' entrance. We'll go over to the artistes' entrance now. It's all fixed."

"Danke schön, Herr Fischer . . ."

The little man looked after us proprietorially as we walked down the corridor, miles long it seemed, which went right under the stage and came out on the other side of the building, leading to another stage door. Here we found a second man in a braided cap and repeated our performance with him.

I heard the word *Telephon* and the man offered Klaus the use of one in his office. But Klaus refused politely. The doorman pointed down the corridor. They spoke rapidly in German, the man pointing upstairs, before we left him.

"A problem," Klaus said. "There's one public phone here." He pointed to a bubble booth near the stage door. "But the artists have one on the floor upstairs. Come on."

Climbing a narrow stairway up two flights, we came out onto another long corridor, running at right angles to the stage. "Here," Klaus pointed to the row of dressing-room doors. "These are the male chorus rooms. And there"—he nodded to a recess halfway along one wall—"there is the phone." It was a few yards from the stairway down to the stage, in a fairly exposed position.

"How do we watch?" I asked. "We can't just hang around out in this corridor all the time."

But Klaus was already walking down to the end of the corridor now, opening the door of each empty dressing-room

309

as he passed along. Splendid gold-braided uniforms hung on hooks. There was a smell of stale makeup and old sweat.

"We can hardly pretend to be members of the chorus," I said. "Or was that what you had in mind—getting dressed up as a hussar?"

The orchestra started downstairs just then, the music coming up all round us faintly through the Tannoy system: the strains of *Der Zigeunerbaron.*

Klaus had disappeared through a door at the end of the corridor by now and when I got there I saw it was marked *"Herren."* I found him standing on the lavatory seat in one of the cubicles. There was a high partition all round these conveniences, but by standing on tiptoe one could identify anyone going down the corridor and into the recessed phone booth.

"Perfect," Klaus said, checking the angles and heights again. Then he started to hum with the music on the Tannoy *". . . 'doch treu und wahr' . . ."* I'd rarely seen a man in such a good mood.

"What? We lock ourselves in here?"

"Precisely. Go down there, and come out of the dressing rooms, then cross over to the phone. Just to make sure."

I did as he asked. And he shouted back down the length of the corridor, his handsome Gypsy head just visible above the partition. "Perfect! I can see everything."

"But what happens if someone wants to use the lavatory?" I asked.

"They'll have to wait, won't they?" He smiled. *"'Wer uns getraut' . . ."* He sang the words that we had heard on the tape, the beginning of the *Dompfaff* duet. "That's our cue. You wait and see."

I thought he must be wrong. What preposterous good humor, staking out a terrorist got up as a hussar from a lavatory seat! I was sure he must be wrong.

By three-fifteen, when the operetta was well into its second act, we'd come back up the stairs and locked ourselves into the little cubicle. The Tannoy sang faintly in the corridor for us, and only one person had rattled the door of our cubicle, though the *pissoir* outside was often filled with hussars and Gypsies—and the passageway beyond had frequently been a seething mass of elaborate lace and splendidly gilt uniforms charging up and down stairs.

And then, just after three-thirty—before the *Dompfaff*

duet started onstage—a rush of hussars emerged from all the dressing rooms, stamping their heavy boots as they made their way downstairs for their entrance.

Afterwards there was silence—just the weak sounds on the Tannoy, the beginning of the duet: "*Wer uns getraut...*" We literally held our breath. Then the Gypsy chorus joined the lovers, the velvet music rising on the air. But nothing moved in the corridor.

I suppose I expected some great galumphing hussar in tights to emerge from one of the dressing rooms, look both ways nervously, before making for the phone. But there was no one. The duet continued on the faraway stage, the woman's voice rising into ever-sweeter levels as the lovers exchanged vows. But nothing stirred and there was no sound from the empty corridor. Klaus looked at his watch. It was nearly a quarter to four. He was angry, fidgeting—a conductor on a podium that happened to be a lavatory seat, waiting for some tardy musician.

Then a door opened quietly halfway down the passage and a young man in a gray suit, carrying a brief case came out and walked confidently down toward the stairway. Would he turn into the phone recess? He did—and I could hear Klaus's sigh of relief.

"That's him," he whispered. "He must have been on half call—a chorus understudy, not needed. But that's him!"

"Are you sure?"

"It must be. That's why he's wearing street clothes: he makes the call, then leaves straight away."

The man was out of our sight for nearly two minutes. Then he emerged again and disappeared down the stairs.

"After him!" Klaus said. And I had to admit then to the excitement of the chase, even though it wasn't after a hussar in tight pants and braid.

So intent was I on keeping my eye on the gray suit that I lost Klaus almost at once among the crowds of tourists wandering about Philharmonikerstrasse in the hot afternoon light. This was, I supposed, a job I did better than Klaus. The young man crossed over the street behind the opera house and threaded his way along beside the terrace of Sacher's. Turning right at the end, he cut into a main artery of the city, walking past the Augustinerkirche toward the great pile of the Hofburg further down on the left, where the busy main road narrowed sharply, dividing into a clutter of little streets and alleyways, the heart of the old town. But once I'd caught up with him, after the first minute's panic, he was an easy trail. He walked steadily, without stopping or looking for reflections in shop windows. He was an amateur, I thought.

Opposite the huge Hofburg entrance he turned right into the narrow streets, crossed over a small triangular *Platz,* and went into an old shop with all sorts of expensive Austrian feathered hats and green capes and lederhosen in the neat windows. It was very crowded inside and the heat brought out the smell of fine wool and old leather. I thought I'd lost my man: he was nowhere to be seen among the wealthy tourists trying on long hunting-green capes and busy men crowding round small mirrors—admiring themselves, their heads surmounted by ridiculous little felt hats with chamois whiskers sticking out on top.

The air was filled with strident *"Bitte*'s" and *"Danke-schön*'s" and overattentive old saleswomen. One of them approached me, smiling heavily.

"I wanted—" I gestured unconsciously to my trousers for some inane reason.

"Ah! Lederhosen! Ja." She pointed up a narrow stairway at the side of the shop.

On the first floor was another small room, occupied entirely with silly men this time, fingering a variety of short leather pants, crushing them up brutally in their hands as if trying to mutilate them; others were throwing green felt capes over their shoulders dramatically and putting on hunting hats. They were Germans for the most part, exclaiming ecstatically as they gazed at their preposterous transformations in various mirrors.

These long mirrors were on the doors of little fitting cubicles, which opened now and then, the glass swinging round into the bright light, reflecting all the frenzied sartorial change, so that the room seemed like a stage for some mad sylvan ballet, where the mirror images of men in dashing hunting capes were superseded by others emerging from the fitting rooms with knobbly knees and lederhosen. But there was no sign of the perfectly ordinary man in the gray summer suit.

"Ja, mein Herr?" A salesman came up to me.

"I thought—a cape?" I said. "If I could look at some." I saw now that there were three cubicles, and the door of one of them hadn't opened since I'd arrived in the room. If my man wasn't inside it, he wasn't anywhere.

I went over with the salesman to the other side and tried on some capes. And then, to pass the time, I put on some of the fearful little feathered hats as well.

"Is a Styrian hat," the man told me, beaming.

"Yes. It's fine." I looked in the mirror. Moon-faced, capped and feathered, I was like some ogre in Grimm's *Fairy Tales*.

"Is right size?"

"Almost, but not quite, perhaps." I glanced in the mirror again, adjusting the horror. The cubicle door behind me opened and a young man in lederhosen, long white socks, and a frilly summer shirt emerged. He was carrying a brief case. He wasn't such an amateur after all, I thought.

He pushed his way downstairs and I apologized for the hats and capes and followed him: a fair-haired, broad-faced, well-built youth in his early twenties. He might—as I soon saw when we both got outside—have been one of any number of country boys up in the big city for the day, or there for some folk festival, for the streets seemed full of them that afternoon.

He walked back out onto the main street, down past the Hofburg, turning left along a parkway, where he eventually came to a tram stop. We waited ten or fifteen minutes in the rush hour, before he climbed aboard one marked "Grinzing." I pushed my way on after him.

Half an hour's ride took us out to the end of the line, to the northern suburb of Grinzing, an obvious tourist trap on the lower slopes of the Wiener Wald, with wine taverns and folksy restaurants every few yards. The man hurried away from the terminus and started to walk uphill, out of the city. But there were still many people about and it was easy to follow him.

Indeed there seemed a great number of us—tourists as well as commuters—all going in the same direction. At the top of the rise, after twenty minutes' hard walk, I saw what the attraction was: a folk-dance exhibition or festival of some sort, already under way in a kind of asphalt amphitheater that rose further up the hill toward a shabby old building immediately behind it. At first it seemed to be some small, run-down country palace, set on a peak with a stupendous view over the whole city, lying out beneath us now in a hazy dream of late afternoon light.

Several hundred spectators had already gathered above the dancers in a rising arc—a dozen men and women stomping about to the raucous strains of a silver band. And now that my man had begun to move among the other dancers, preparing to take over the platform next, it was almost impossible to keep him in sight as he bobbed away from me among waiting groups got up in an extraordinary variety of Austrian folk dress: men in tall golden stovepipe hats and peach-skinned women in richly embroidered lace set under fabulously decorated aprons and smocks. The silver band thumped vigorously and a small breeze on the hill made it less hot, but I was soaked in sweat after the long climb. Even though I had identified the man with the brief case I could hardly keep up with him as he threaded his way through the dancers.

Was he part of that group about to move on to the platform? Yes, he'd stopped and was talking to someone. But when I'd caught up and the man turned I saw it was someone else, equally fair-haired, identically dressed.

I was very near the silver band now, just behind the platform, and the blaring trumpets stunned me, the sun flashing on the instruments as they swayed with the jaunty folk tune. I'd lost him. The brief case had disappeared. And then I thought I saw him—or at least someone in lederhosen carrying something—high up above me on the skyline, beyond the circle of spectators, moving onto a terrace in front of the old palace.

Coming up toward it round the edge of the crowd I saw it wasn't really a palace at all, imposing though it looked from a distance. It must have been some kind of extensive nineteenth-century summerhouse in the old days—a long, single-storied, pavilionlike building, but the pink stucco was cracked now and the tall windows all boarded up. In front of it, looking down the hill, were rows of tables on a wide-stepped terrace, filled with people watching the dancers. Each table was surmounted with a rusty green metal lampshade like some rude mushroom. And then I realized that the place had been a summer night club in the more recent past; now the folk people occupied the outdoor dance floor below, and the tourists had taken over what had been expensive little tables for nothing.

But my man was nowhere up here. The music changed, moving into some easy Viennese lilt, a group of dexterous accordionists and a zither man taking up some sentimental melody.

I'd walked round the old building now, and was testing the louvered shutters. They'd been closed up for some time, nailed shut, the paint cracked and the hinges flaking with rust. And then, wandering round to the side of the pavilion, to the main entrance where it gave out onto a car park, I stopped in my tracks, almost falling over the hood of the car, parked as it was immediately round the corner. It was a large, maroon-colored Peugeot station wagon with Belgian number plates. I dodged back round the corner. But there was no one about. Looking again, I was almost certain. It was Pottinger's hired car, the one in which we'd left Brussels and gone down to Heidelberg in. Pottinger and the fair-haired youth must be somewhere in the building behind me.

But the main hall door, I found, was locked securely, so were all the other windows. I thought I must be wrong, until I moved away between the cars, down a small drive toward a twisting hill road. Then I saw it: a doorway, built into the side of the hill, giving immediate access to the roadway on one side and leading into the pavilion through a tunnel, I thought, under the forecourt on the other: an old servants' and tradesmen's entrance, so that the summer nobility would not be troubled with any chance plebeian encounters.

This old, nail-studded door opened fairly readily onto a storeroom filled with sand and bags of cement. A dark, flag-stoned passageway led out of it, sloping gently, as I'd expected, back uphill toward the pavilion.

Almost at once, after I'd closed the door and was standing in the half-light, I heard footsteps coming down the corridor. I took the little revolver out and crouched down behind a mound of sand. Seconds later a figure passed me, and when the door opened I saw the young, fair-haired man standing against the light for an instant, before the darkness came again. Was this where they were holding Lindsay? Surely I should leave and get the police now? But curiosity got the better of me and I found myself drawn almost involuntarily up the musty passageway.

At the top, above some steps, was another door partly open. Looking through the crack, I could just see a row of gas stoves and some old pots and pans on shelves above: the night-club kitchens. I nudged the door open very slowly and delicately; as I did, I could hear the strains of music drifting up from the accordion band, and just above that the slight murmur of voices—people talking somewhere beyond the kitchen.

Opening the door inch by inch, I moved into a large empty space, lit by clerestory windows above. A long table had been left by the far wall, just underneath two serving hatches, one of them ajar. Walking over to it, I found I could see out only as far as a green baize serving screen a few yards straight in front of me, so that a proper view into the big main room was blocked.

But I could hear the two voices much more clearly now— a rather bad-tempered English voice at first, familiar from somewhere, followed by incisive American tones.

"...*No* problem, now that we've got them to Vienna. We've only one more move to make..." I lost the next bit in a spurt of music. But there wasn't any doubt: it was Pottinger. Then the older voice came again: "...enough is enough. I can't go on roaming about Europe, writing them letters..." I thought for a second that it might be Lindsay. But then I had it. Of course it was that petulant, upper-class, slightly whiny voice that I had last heard in a Bloomsbury flat: the bearded expert in Slavonic studies—Professor Allcock. "...Simply can't. I've done enough, leading these wretched people on."

And then I saw what had been happening all these weeks. I'd been right in my very first estimation of these two rogues: Allcock and Pottinger were together in some Intelligence maneuver—had been scheming against us from the very beginning, leading us on through one European city after another, ever since we'd left Glenalyth. "Enough is enough—I can't go on roaming about . . . writing them letters . . ."

Why, it was the Professor we'd been following all this time, not Lindsay. It had been Allcock, the old family friend, who'd forged all the letters to Madeleine for some reason: Allcock doubling for Lindsay, using his long and intimate knowledge of the man and his family so that he could persuade us to follow him, persuade us that Lindsay was alive. And that was the worst kind of deceit.

So that it was sheer anger, not bravery, that led me silently through the kitchen door, where I stopped behind the serving screen, gun in hand.

They'd started walking toward me just then, coming straight for the screen. I stepped out from behind it like a waiter, leveling the revolver.

They stopped dead in the center of the old parquet dance

floor, next to a clutter of empty wine bottles and a stack of little gilt chairs, dust beams of light falling on them from the roof windows: lone dancers surprised amidst the tawdry rubbish of Gay Vienna.

They didn't recognize me until I'd stepped further into the room. "Back," I said. "Over to that table. Back!" I stumbled into a pile of champagne coolers and there was a fearful racket for a moment. But now they could see me and they retreated to one of the few tables left in the great, dusty room, sitting there like dissatisfied customers waiting for the show to start. Pottinger was a different man, wearing a smooth business suit, his hair smarmed down. Allcock I didn't recognize at all for a moment: his beard was gone, his deep-set eyes were bright with fatigue, the skin all sucked in under his old cheekbones. He was a gaunt, shorn man—a death's-head, somehow.

They looked at me calmly. Then Pottinger started to get up, smiling apologetically, like a man caught cheating at the gaming tables.

"No," I said, as if talking to a dog. "Down! This works. It's not a toy."

He sat down again meekly. I didn't know what else to do or say. And they said nothing. What was I to do? Kill them both? Leave them, and fetch the police? Or march them out at gunpoint into the crowds outside? I had no experience whatsoever in these lethal confrontations.

Finally I spoke to Allcock—and as I did so I found the anger rising in me again, saving me. "So you wrote those letters to Madeleine. Of course—who else could have known all the details? The silver bracelet, the nicknames? You got all that from the trip you made with them to Sweden before the war." Pottinger looked at me malevolently. Without the beard he was naked and frightened. And I was so angry at him that I raised the little revolver, holding it in both hands now, pointing it at his chest, about to fire. He put his hands up to his face, cowering.

"You bastard! You'd do this to Madeleine and Rachel. Your friends. They believed you, you know. They think Lindsay is alive somewhere down here. Well, let me show you..."

"I—" Allcock began. "I was forced—"

"Say nothing!" Pottinger interrupted him brutally. "He's not going to kill you."

I turned the gun on Pottinger. "No. Perhaps you first."

He looked up at me confidently. "You won't, Marlow. You're a good tracker. But not a killer—"

I fired the gun then. The music was loud enough outside to muffle the sound. The bullet hit the wall immediately above them. A lump of plaster fell on the table.

"Where is Lindsay?" I asked vehemently. "I'll kill you both. Don't think I won't." I was furious now, almost beside myself, and they could clearly sense it. All the pain of the previous weeks boiled up in me then and I'd have shot them both for two pins, and they knew it. Pottinger gripped the table, scratching the surface with his nails. The band played in the distance. Dusty motes rose in the disturbed air, climbing up the sunbeams from the high windows. But everything else was perfectly still in the decayed room.

"Where is he?"

"We—I don't know. We've been looking for him as much as you have."

"'We'?"

"Yes. The Americans. I'm CIA—"

"You're a liar, Pottinger."

"No—you can see, I have a card." He reached for a pocket.

"Don't!" I had the gun on him again. "If you're looking for Lindsay what are you doing putting us all on, tempting us through Europe like this, pretending to be the Free Croatia group?"

"Nonsense! We've nothing to do with them—"

"You're lying again, Pottinger—or whatever your real name is. I saw the little fair-haired bugger in leather pants coming out of here. And we already know it was he who made the calls from the opera house to Madeleine, saying he represented the Free Croatia group. You should have paid a pro to do your legwork for you."

Pottinger looked at Allcock with sharp annoyance.

"So what are you trying to set up?" I went on acidly. Pottinger didn't reply. The music changed again outside, another raucous silver band taking over and blaring up the hillside.

"Nothing," Pottinger said at last, as if resigning himself to the truth. "We've been looking for Lindsay Phillips, just as you have. Setting you up, if you like—yes, as decoys, that's all. Hoping he'd contact you, if he was in Europe."

"Or Moscow."

"Yes. Or Moscow. We thought maybe he'd come over—ask you to meet him in Berlin maybe, or here in Vienna."

There was a touch of truth in Pottinger's voice, but only a touch. "And the CIA want Lindsay as much as we do—is that it?"

"Yes."

"So you go to all the trouble of making out he's been taken by some Croatian terrorists? That doesn't add up."

"That was just to get you all over here. I told you."

"Yes, you told me. But not everything. First of all you're not CIA, Pottinger. Why should the Americans be so anxious to find him? That's rubbish. I think you're on the other side: Moscow is looking for Lindsay. He was one of theirs—and he's missing." I was getting tired of holding the revolver up in my right hand. I moved it to my left. Pottinger shifted a fraction. He was desperate to have a go at me, his bland face full of barely hidden anxiety and cunning. I took the gun again in my good hand and waved it at him ostentatiously.

"Think whatever you like," he said. "I'm CIA. I can prove it too, if you'd let me show you—"

He made a move toward an inside pocket again.

"No. Don't show me. Just sit!" I should have disarmed him. But again I'd no experience and didn't want to risk such a close encounter. We'd reached another awkward deadlock.

Then quite suddenly the Professor stood up, surprising both of us. He was a tall, emaciated figure in his old linen tropicals and sandals, with the air of some prewar Hampstead intellectual down from a tour of the Low Countries and a hike through the Black Forest. He seemed about to set off into the Wiener Wald—a socialist with Marx in his rucksack, quoting Strachey and *Das Kapital* in the intervals between *Biergärten*—a man once full of happy, radical certainties, now quite gone to seed. I moved the gun onto him.

"You can shoot me if you like," he said briskly. He had regained all his old pedantic authority now, as when he'd lectured me so confidently about Lindsay in Wigmore Hall a month before. It was as if he'd suddenly found his great Edward Lear beard again and put it on. "I can't go on with this anyway," he said to Pottinger, scrawny hands buttoning his creased jacket. "I told you: I've done enough."

Pain moved across his face. He winced suddenly, closing his eyes tight for a moment, as though against some imaginary blow. "I'm too old for all this in any case. Service ends—at some point." He looked at Pottinger calmly, smoothing out

319

the crumpled pockets of the old suit. "I'm leaving now. I'm going back to Bloomsbury."

He walked toward me. I simply couldn't shoot him. And as I turned to watch, just before he disappeared behind the serving screen, Pottinger shot him—a heavy-caliber bullet thumping into his back so that he collapsed over the screen like the victim of some fearful accident in a restaurant.

Pottinger had left the table as I threw myself to one side behind the pile of gilt chairs. And when I got to my feet he was running round to the other side of the dance floor, fast as a sprinter; I got a shot at him before he disappeared behind an old piano. But again he was better than I at these things: another shot from him kept me behind the chairs, and when I looked out again he'd moved right round by the far wall, behind some shabby curtains on a small stage. And from there he made a dash for it, through the kitchen doors and away.

I let him go. My first thought was that he hadn't shot at me when he'd had the chance, when my back was turned: he'd gone for the Professor in some vital preference. I was ignorant, of course. It was Allcock who had possessed some secret, some knowledge of Lindsay that had to be preserved at all costs—those other, deeper truths the Professor might have released but which Pottinger would never have told me.

The band thumped away outside. It must have drowned the gunshots. Allcock was pretty dead. The socialist millennium—and all the good, brave causes of the thirties—had come to an end in a pair of old sandals, sticking out from some dented champagne coolers in a ruined night club. I looked through his pockets. He was unarmed. There was an airplane ticket home, a lot of Deutsche marks and Austrian schillings and a well-rubbed, bulky leather wallet. Among other bits and pieces from a long life I found an old street photograph of Lindsay as a very young man, smiling awkwardly in a Fair Isle pullover, standing in the sun on the cobbled pavement of some foreign city, just beneath a circular kiosk with advertisements all over it in Cyrillic script. It must have been Moscow or Sofia or Belgrade in the early thirties. And the man next to him was Allcock himself: younger then by far, with only a mild beard, but nonetheless the happy father figure.

"I WONDER why I ever believed it—those Croats. It was too unlikely, all that way from Glenalyth. Too easy."

Madeleine was calm but dazed, like someone still in shock after an accident. She sat on a bench, a tortured baroque maiden rising up behind her, in the gardens of the Schwarzenberg-Palais. Klaus and Rachel were at a table opposite. "But I never thought...How could the Professor—?"

"The sneak!" Rachel interrupted bitterly. She was nervous, like a schoolgirl once more, using the playground slang, comforting herself with an old and secure language.

"He and Pottinger must have been together for a long time. With the Russians. They thought Lindsay would contact us over here."

"He's still in Europe somewhere then?"

"I think so. I think maybe in Zagreb." I'd told them now about my meeting with Mrs. Rabernak that morning.

"With Eleanor?" Madeleine shook her head. "I can't really believe that. That couldn't be."

I looked at Madeleine carefully. "It could, I'm afraid."

The garden was quiet and still very warm after the long heat. I'd come straight out to them on the lawn and now I wanted a shower and a beer inside in the cool bar. "Well, I've told you," I said, standing up. "I don't know about Eleanor. But I think he may have gone there. He's not in Moscow—else they wouldn't be looking for him. And we have to leave here anyhow. It's up to you. But that's where I'd look for him."

Klaus nodded. "You could be right—"

"Rubbish!" Rachel interrupted again. "How could he? How *could* he?" But she was speaking of Lindsay, not me. A vision had come to her of some real and awful betrayal by her father, and she wouldn't face it. But she knew it had existence at last; she had admitted the thought for an instant—and so now she herself would have to prove it wrong.

An hour later they agreed we should fly to Zagreb next day.

7

Klaus couldn't come with us, but he saw us off willingly enough, with many promises to Rachel about a position with the orchestra in Munich, which she took account of in a vague way; she was far more anxious that he should come with us at that moment.

"But I can't! We've another concert in Innsbruck tomorrow night." He said he'd try and join us in Zagreb at the end of the week. And we'd keep in touch—wouldn't we? I sensed his renewed suit with Rachel might have cooled—that he was anxious to be up and out of Vienna. And away from us too. At some time in the near future Allcock's body would come to light—a scene in his opera I think he had not yet imagined.

But no one stopped us at Zagreb Airport, where we picked up tourist visas without any trouble the following afternoon, before going on into the city. Ironically, the only hotel with three rooms available was the Palace, where Eleanor had fallen under the tram. It was still there—a staid old turn-of-the-century building, facing out over some fine public gardens right in the middle of the city. And the trams were still there, too, possibly the very same prewar coaches: little blue trams clanging up and down in the sunlight of the long green avenue outside.

The women had rooms in the back. Mine was in the front, like a tree house, perched high up on the top floor, looking directly out onto a tremendous cage of summer green—a double line of huge plane trees that almost touched my window. Beyond was a bandstand, fountains, and heroic statuary in the middle of the leafy gardens, with a long row of tall dark nineteenth-century apartment blocks looming up on the other side.

The hotel itself was from the same Belle Époque period, the time when Zagreb was "Little Vienna," the last civilized outpost of the Hapsburgs before the crude horrors of the Balkans proper took over. But the interior of the building had been partly and hideously redecorated in a selection of modern plastic veneers; the gilded cherubs and mirrors had gone, my room smelled of some choking floor polish and the hot water was no more than a rusty dribble in the bathroom.

But the view from the high window made up for everything. Over the trees, across to the sun-flecked square, the city was beginning to revive, it seemed, after the desperate heat of the afternoon. Up to my left on a hill I could just see a line of cream and terra-cotta roofs poking out steeply over the town, with two needlelike cathedral spires to one side; mica had been embedded in the slates, so that one roof shone like a mirror in the slanting light. Beyond the hill, a mountain was just visible, thunderclouds rolling in over it from the north: the first rain of the summer, I thought.

There was an oppressive stillness in the air below me, I noticed then, and soon the bruised skies began to tumble in over the city. And suddenly, after the endless heat of the past months, I wanted to be out in the open when the rain came—out and about like any tourist in a new place, letting the water fall over me and the thunder crack, cleansing the frustration and violence of the past days.

I left the hotel, skipped between the blue trams and into the park. I got to the line of trees on the other side just as the first peel of thunder echoed round the dry gardens and drops of rain fell delicately on the wilting herbaceous borders. In a few minutes the whole city went black as the rain came, the leafy streets emptied and the plane trees started to weep.

The dark storm swept along the roads in vicious little eddies of warm, damp wind and raindrops as large and bright

323

as pearls hammered on the cobble-stones. And I was happy, running before the weather, released at last from care.

But I was too carefree. I should have seen the two men following me earlier—with a head start I might have dropped them entirely. I'd been in the mouth of a shopping arcade at the top of the park, sheltering from the downpour, when I saw them moving toward me for the second time. And I had to run then, out into the storm and across a main street.

And I ran fast, appropriately, as others did, escaping the storm. But soon the only ones I saw, braving the weather in a similar gallop, were my pursuers. I set off madly, dodging great rivers of water flooding the gutters and puddles moving like tides, running further into a city where I knew no roads, where one turning might liberate me while another could end in a blank wall.

By the time I found some cover under the broad umbrellas of the little flower market I was soaked. Old women in head scarves and great billowing black skirts were tidying up for the day, waiting for the storm to die, as was a surrounding crowd, pressing together about the trestle tables, a damp crush of commuters, smelling heavily of salami and garlic.

It was difficult to hide among them, so tightly bunched were they in the middle of the tiny square that had a small baroque church at one end. I had circled right round to the far side of the market before I saw one of the men coming at me from the opposite side, holding his hat in the wind, blinded by the rain. I hid among the tables then, stooping down among the commuters. He hadn't seen me. I eventually managed to push my way right through the market. The church was immediately in front of me now, and I made for it, jumping the steps two at a time, pushing open the side door into a dark baroque interior, where several old women were kneeling. But there was nowhere to hide, apart from the few confessional boxes along one wall.

And it was in one of these that they got me in the end, one of the men pushing the grille aside violently and facing me with a gun, while his companion waited outside the curtain.

"Milicija," the taller one said, keeping his gun on me while his colleague frisked me, taking away my little revolver. Then they led me from the church and out into the storm again.

The police station was back in the middle of town, next the park, housed in a gracious nineteenth-century apartment block, now given over to harsher matters, the other entrances all down the street severely bricked up. I was pushed through a crowded hallway full of damp petitioners and grudging authority. There was that sour, acid smell of an animal cage, an air of bureaucratic delay and ready injustice that I remembered so well from my years in Durham Jail. I was angry. Though in a way I had expected it: luck couldn't hold forever and we'd all had a long run of it.

At least I wasn't delayed. I was taken upstairs at once and into an anteroom in front of the building, giving out onto the park: an office of some importance, with a male secretary tapping his way delicately on a new electric typewriter. The man picked up a phone and almost at once another small, agile fellow seemed to jump into the room through some large double doors. Although he looked very young, he was probably in his forties, not typically Balkan at all, but with rather fuzzy, fairish hair neatly parted at one side. He wore rimless glasses over narrowly placed eyes, and was dressed most smartly in a lightweight Windsor check. He gestured me inside casually, like a doctor vaguely welcoming a patient.

It wasn't an office but a long conference room, with a glass-topped table, old sofas down one wall and a large photoportrait of Tito in profile like a Roman emperor.

The secretary handed my little revolver to the man, closing the doors behind him.

"*Gospodin* Marlow?" he asked.

"Do you speak English?"

"Yes, I speak English. But I thought you would speak Serbo-Croatian—being sent all the way here specially. Sit down, please." He fingered Lindsay's revolver delicately, opening it, sniffing the empty chambers. The thunder cracked overhead, more faintly now.

"Fired quite soon. Quite *recently*." The man corrected himself. "Not normal issue, is it? Since when are British Intelligence using this?" He looked at me with quizzical interest, peering at me through his glasses like a careful scientist, as though here was an interesting case indeed.

"I'm not with British Intelligence." I wiped my face. The thunder broke again, much further away over the city. The storm was dying. The man went over to the better light by the window, looking down the barrel of the gun. "Strange weapon." He rubbed the ivory handle, then examined the silver chasing. "An antique." He turned to me quizzically again.

"I told you. It's not a police gun. It belongs to the friends of mine I came here with. At the Palace Hotel—"

"Yes, yes. We know about all of you. The Phillipses. The family of Lindsay Phillips, I assume." He put the gun down on the table and leaned toward me. "And you are Marlow. Peter Marlow—*also* with British Intelligence," he added punctiliously.

"No, I'm not. We've just been looking for this man Phillips. He was with Intelligence."

"Yes. We know about him. We've been waiting for him. He was to come here. But he never did. At least not yet, unless he did it—clandestine? How do you—?"

"Lindsay Phillips? Come here? How do you know? You're looking for him too?"

The man didn't reply. He just went on gazing at me carefully, his calm blue eyes magnified in the glasses. The thunder disappeared completely in the distance. The rain had stopped, and a shaft of sunlight suddenly brightened the gloomy room.

"Who are you?" I asked. But again there was no reply. Just that steady, inquisitive stare. He picked up the gun again. It glinted like a pretty thing in the sunlight.

At last he spoke. "No. Perhaps you are not with British Intelligence." His tone was deeply considered. "You would have a proper gun—not this toy. And you would be alone, not with this man's family." He walked back to the window. "I do not understand it yet. But we will. We will." He turned. "Tell me, who were you shooting at with this?"

"No one."

"But it has been fired recently."

"It came from Scotland. It belongs to Lindsay Phillips. Someone must have fired it up there."

The man sighed, sat down and opened a file on the table. "But you have needed a gun, yes? On your travels?" He looked at a typewritten sheet. "First we were to expect this *Gospodin* Phillips, chief of your Section Nine: the 'Slavs and Soviets,' is it not? He did not come. Then we learned that you would come instead. And it is so. That is good. You are here." He looked up, smiling.

"Warned? But I had no idea I was coming here until yesterday. Who could have warned you?"

326

"No, no! You go too fast." The man shook his head. "I am still thinking."

"Let me explain," I said, feeling he was a sympathetic listener and that I could help him out. "I *was* with British Intelligence. But only as a clerk, no more. I left it over ten years ago. The Phillipses are old friends of mine. I agreed to help them find Lindsay Phillips, entirely as a private matter..." And then I decided to explain the whole affair to him. Why not? There was nothing to lose. And explain I did, with very few omissions. I told him about Pottinger, too—how I was sure that we'd been led on by this man, by the KGB in fact, down through Europe, in a wild-goose chase after a man who had never been kidnapped by any Croatian terrorist group at all.

My man took an extreme interest in the story and I could sense he believed me. "So each time," I said, "we were led on by these letters. But not here. That was entirely my idea. You see, Lindsay Phillips once lived in Zagreb, with his first wife, in the thirties. And she was killed here, so they say— under a tram opposite the Palace Hotel. But I don't think she was killed..." And I ended my tale with an account of Eleanor and Zlatko Rabernak, and how I'd thought that Lindsay might have come back here to rejoin his first wife.

"So how," I said finally, "could you have known I was coming here?"

The man went over to the double doors. He spoke to the clerk outside. I heard the name "Rabernak." When he returned his bemused indecisiveness was gone. He was brisk and businesslike.

"I would not have believed you," he said. "But what you say fits very well with"—he glanced at the file again—"with our other investigation." He took up another, fatter file. "A few weeks ago we arrested one of our own men here—a very important man. The chief, in fact, of our Croatian *Milic̆ija*. We had thought for some time he was with the Soviets; then we were able to prove it. It was from him that we took our information about Lindsay Phillips—and yourself: that one or other would come here. You were then to be arrested, charged, exposed. It was part of a plan he and his friends in Moscow had to show that Western Intelligence was interfering in our internal affairs, so that they could promote a new, hard-line, pro-Soviet policy in the country, and eventually

327

replace President Tito with one of their own men. He was waiting to take you—our chief of police.

"But!" The man waved his hands ambitiously in the air. "But we took him first, this old man. We have trouble from every side, do you see?" he went on confidingly. "From the old men here who are still with Moscow—the Stalinists! And the other old men abroad here who are still with Hitler and Pavelić." He shook his head, almost mournfully. "Too many old men who will not let us alone. So you see—we are on our guard!"

The phone rang just then and he spoke rapidly for a minute in Serbo-Croatian. Then he turned to me. "We have no immediate record of any man called Rabernak in the city. Perhaps before the war only—"

"He had an antique shop here then, yes—"

"Ah, there are few such shops here now. The war." He gestured again, less confidently this time. "But we can check maybe with the old files. However, they are nearly all lost, too." The man was offhand now. "But for the moment—what are you to do here?"

"This Scotswoman—Eleanor Phillips: I wanted to see if she was still alive."

"I do not follow you there. She was killed by tram you said."

"Yes. And buried here, apparently, in some big cemetery on a hill."

"Mirogoj, yes."

"But I don't think she was killed. You see, her husband, this Lindsay Phillips—I'm almost certain he was a double all his life: he was with the KGB in fact, like Philby and the others we had in our Intelligence Service—"

"You say Phillips is with Moscow?" The man leaned intently forward now, suddenly interested again.

"I think so."

"Then perhaps his wife was, too—this woman you are looking for?"

"Perhaps," I said. "She was certainly very left wing before the war."

"But how could she be here? An *English*woman, even if she was alive?"

"I told you: she married this Zlatko Rabernak, I think—secretly, in Vienna. Then they came back to live here—or so

328

his relations in Vienna think. No one has heard from him since. So they may not have survived the war."

"They may have changed their names, of course." He was vaguely excited now, my man, dreaming of some Intelligence coup, his eyes alert, dancing behind the thick lenses. "You see," he went on, "we know for certain there are several others with Moscow living here in Zagreb right now. 'Deep-cover illegals' you call them?" I nodded. "Yugoslavs," he continued, "living and working here. And some, we know, who have been with the Soviets maybe since before the war. Other old people," he added distastefully. "I wonder maybe if this Rabernak and his wife are like this?"

"Perhaps." There was silence in the long room. The sunlight blazed in now, a golden evening light slanting over the huge trees in the park. "I should let my friends know," I said. "In the hotel. They'll be anxious." I looked out over the city.

"Yes." The man stood up and went to the window again. "Yes," he repeated slowly, gazing out at the moist trees and the glittering, rain-washed roofs and steeples rising on the hill away to the right above them.

"Lindsay Phillips once lived in a house here," I said. "Above the city, in some park. With trees. Cherry trees—"

"Tuškanac, for sure. The diplomatic area."

"I wondered if they might be living there, if they were here at all."

"Unlikely. It's nearly all diplomatic there. Consulates, Residencies, members of the government here. Too exposed for an agent." He turned to me now. He was authoritative, businesslike once more. "Good," he said. "We will help you look for this woman."

"She may be dead, of course. I could be quite wrong."

"Indeed. But that is easy to prove. She was buried in Mirogoj. You have her name? What it was at that time? And the date she died?"

"Yes."

"Then they will have the records up there. They will not have gone in the war. So it is simple. We can dig her up."

"I see," I said, alarmed at this precipitous, slightly macabre enthusiasm. "I don't know," I went on. "Maybe—"

"No, no! It is the answer. 'No stone unturned,' as you say. And I may assure you the need is urgent. It is our chief concern right now, to find these Soviet cominformists here.

These agents and sympathizers. If we do not—Moscow may easily take us when Tito is gone."

So I gave him the details on Eleanor and he came over to me afterwards, offering his hand. "Good. We will work together. Go back to your hotel. I will make arrangements with the cemetery. Perhaps this evening...And perhaps we can trace this Rabernak from before the war. My name is Stolačka. Brigade Commander Pedar Stolačka."

I shook his hand. "Pedar—Peter? My name too."

"Good. Good. We will work together. And I will keep this for the moment." He picked up the little silver revolver. Then he paused for a moment at the doorway. "Tell me—we are not so foolish: who were you shooting at?"

"At Pottinger," I said, admitting it, glad to be involved at last with someone whose interest in the truth appeared at least as great as mine. "A little trouble with the KGB in Vienna."

"Did you kill him?"

"No. He got away."

"Unfortunate. But then, of course, you are no Intelligence officer. And even if you were—with this!" He looked at the little revolver, shaking his head. "But remember, since his plan was to get you to Zagreb in any case, he may come on here himself anyway. Beware."

"He doesn't want to kill me. Just the opposite: he thinks I can lead him to Phillips. They want to get him home; back to Moscow, I suppose."

Stolačka laughed. "They want to *kill* him, Mr. Marlow— if what you say about him is true. Before his British friends get hold of him. A double agent for so long? He knows too much. Both sides must want him out of the way forever." He opened the door. "I'll keep your passports, too," he added.

"I didn't know you had them."

"We are not so inefficient. And, by the way, I should not speak of our business—to the British Consulate here, for example."

"I'll have to tell the two women."

"Yes. I suppose you will. Lies can come to nothing." He smiled, showing me out graciously, and I walked back to the hotel across the damp park, wondering what on earth the two women would make of it all.

They made very little of it, in fact, that evening over dinner in the hotel. They were numbed by the twisting course of events and tired by the strange travel. Without Klaus to support her, Rachel seemed almost acquiescent. Indeed she was flippant about Stolačka's plans.

"I don't know what the British authorities will say, digging up their graves like this," she had said quietly.

"They're not going to know."

"It's all the most awful, criminal nonsense," Madeleine had added. "Eleanor *can't* be alive." She looked at me incredulously, as she had so often done before after my comments about Lindsay. "She's dead, don't you see? She must be. Lindsay would have told me otherwise." She paused, seeing the implications. "Why, he'd never have married me if she had been alive. He *couldn't* have done."

Madeleine—faithful as always to her whole life with Lindsay—still believed in simple, straightforward answers. I wished I could have supported her in this. But it was too late.

"We've no alternative," I said—like a hanging judge, I suppose.

A police car called for me very early next morning, while it was still dark, and we drove through the silent streets up a long sloping avenue out of the city for several miles until we came to high walls and a great arched and columned gateway.

It was a vast place inside, too, like another city, with endless crisscrossed avenues stretching down the far side of the hill, back into the mists. Ornate tombstones and marble funerary groups lurked at every corner, granite violins, weeping angels and sad pet dogs cast in stone at Daddy's spatted feet; great family mausoleums sprang up at us quickly, one after the other, out of the morning dark like blind houses on a real street as we drove down the main avenue.

Then, in a dell of land on the far side, we saw the floodlights shining through the mist, illuminating a van. Piles of earth and shadowy figures were moving carefully round the site like patient archaeologists. We walked the rest of the way down a winding, cypress-bordered path and Stolačka emerged from a group—brisk and confident, like a sewage engineer in yellow oilskins and gumboots. His breath hung in wisps for an instant in the chilly air. "We've had no trouble. It was all clearly marked in the records."

I saw the headstone then, lying on its side at the top of the gaping hole, where they were still digging. It bore the same brief legend that I had seen on the window in Dunkeld church:

IN MEMORIAM
ELEANOR PHILLIPS
1912–1937

"When the day breaks,
and the shadows flee away..."

I felt a shiver of awful disgust at this desecration of simple love that I had helped to bring about. Even the dead were not to be free of my inquisitions.

A spade struck a stone—or a skull, I thought—and I turned away, suddenly pierced with the morning cold and hatred at myself. The sun rose just then, climbing over the cemetery walls, and the morning flooded over us quite suddenly in a lovely white-blue light, the mist dissolving all round me. But still I could hear the spades scraping on something hard behind me, scooping up the bones—and I could bear it no longer. I turned and pushed my way in among the circle of people. Stolačka was on the other side of the hole, bending down intently, hands on his knees, peering into the dark hollow.

"Bricks," he said. "Nothing but bricks." A man below handed one up to him and he threw it across to me—a badly eroded red brick. And I saw a line of them now, like stepping stones, running the length of the grave beneath me, covered in scraps of rotten wood. I stood up, dizzy, my trousers damp with mud. A first gold beam struck the hollow then, sloping over the walls like a spotlight illuminating the empty tomb.

My stories had come true. The vague ghosts I had conjured with throughout the last weeks had substance at last—and one, at least, had risen long before and might be out there, now, I thought, somewhere in the fresh blue morning, waking in the bright city beneath me.

"You may be right." Stolačka came up to me. "Anyone who made such bother to arrange all this—" He held a brick up. "Well, they must have had something big to hide. But where do we start to look?" We both gazed out over the town as the sun touched the cathedral roofs far below us and the slates brightened slowly into a fiery mirror.

* * *

AT first Madeleine and Rachel completely refused to believe what I told them, thinking I had become entirely malicious. It wasn't until Stolačka himself came to the hotel in the middle of the morning and confirmed the details that they began to accept the truth of the matter. And it was a bad few minutes when they did, for now at last they were faced with the incontrovertible evidence of some great lie directly involving Lindsay. They were refugees caught in what seemed most wicked machinations, a vast familial deceit they were part of through inheritance and love, but which they could only attempt to explain quite blindly now, still trapped in their original faith.

"Of course it's possible that my husband knew nothing about Eleanor's survival at all." Madeleine offered the rather limp excuse.

"Well, *he* certainly didn't push her under that tram," Rachel added, looking at me viciously—taking a small victory.

Stolačka was tactfully precise. "You mean, Mrs. Phillips, that your husband really thought she was dead?"

"Yes. He must have done."

"But he must have seen her, surely? Known that she was living? Either at the hospital or—"

"Someone may have 'arranged' her death," Madeleine interrupted. "Without Lindsay knowing."

"Yes—certainly someone arranged it. And it would not have been too difficult in those Royalist days here. All it would take would be a good bribe for the hospital workers, the funeral people. But are you really thinking your husband did not know of it?"

"I think it's possible, that's all. I didn't know my husband at the time, you see."

"Of course. I understand. It must be a very unhappy business for you, Mrs. Phillips. I am sorry. But you will see that we have to make our researches now."

He stood up. "Before you go," I asked him, "could you get hold of a list, a street directory perhaps, of the various shops here before the war? The antique shops?"

"We are doing that right now, Mr. Marlow. Many of the street records are gone in the war. But there are people here who will remember. I will let you know."

Stolačka left us then, courteous as ever, without any suggestion of keeping us under house arrest. We were free to go

333

and do as we wanted. But what was there for us to do? We knew now that some great confidence trick had been played out between Lindsay and his ex-wife, and with Zlatko too, almost certainly. But why? And were any of them still here—or alive at all? Despite the bitter revelations we were no further on into any real truths.

Rachel was blazingly angry. There was no help she would let me give her. Madeleine was stunned. I offered to get them a drink, but they refused. Rachel went to her room, retreating into one of those long moans of self-disgust and enmity, I supposed. Yet now she had real reason for her pain, I thought. And I wished she hadn't. I wished once more that I had never set eyes on the Phillipses at the Chelsea Flower Show—and all for the sake of a set of new radials and a sherry bill. For I had lied too, those lies of omission that in the end kill far more painfully.

"Look," I said to Madeleine, trying to absolve myself. "It doesn't really matter what went on here forty years ago. All we have to do is to see if Lindsay's here. That's all. If he is, then I'm sure he'll be able to explain everything."

"Yes," Madeleine replied vaguely. "I'm sure he will." But I wondered how any man could explain away a line of bricks, instead of his first wife, in an empty grave.

"I think I'll rest a bit," she said. "What will you do?"

It was midday. I was tired, too, but again I had a great urge to walk the streets, tempted by some truth I was convinced lay out there, in an antique shop, or an old house on a hill. "I'll take a look round outside," I said.

"For what?"

"I don't know."

Madeleine studied me for a moment, sadly. "Rachel is right in a way, you know," she said. "You have a kind of demon in you now, about Lindsay."

"Do I?" I was annoyed, for this was partly true. But there were other parts, not demonic at all, in my attitudes toward the man, which she seemed conveniently to deny now. "Remember," I went on, "you thought I could help find him. Are we to stop looking just because unpleasant factors arise?"

"Unpleasant?" Madeleine seemed surprised.

"Doubtful then. But it's ridiculous to expect perfection in any case. Surely you see—"

"Yes, of *course* I see that. But all this about Eleanor is much more than 'unpleasant' or 'doubtful.' If it's true it changes everything, don't you see?"

"Yes, I see that. But it's hardly my fault. Are you saying you'd prefer *not* to find Lindsay, rather than learn the truth about him?"

She didn't answer directly. Instead she prevaricated: "Is there such a thing as the truth?"

"I think so. But I'm not moralizing about it. As I said, what does it matter what he did in the past, if we can find out where he is now? If he's alive?"

"Of course," she agreed, and we left it at that. But I could see that what Madeleine feared was the final proof of Lindsay's death, where the fearful truth would have emerged all the same, without his then being able ever to explain it to her. Perhaps, at worst, my inquisitive demon could save her from that silent fate.

I HAD never seen a place so threatened by the sun as Zagreb that morning, unless it was Cairo years before. The weather had become a dangerous event; a state of war had come down over the city, and what few people were about moved quickly across the streets from one shadow to another, like a beleaguered rear guard under fire.

The plane trees opposite the hotel in Strossmayer Square gave some cover but by the time I'd reached Republic Square, the main crossroads of the city, I was nearly done for. Trams jostled to and fro across the huge expanse of concrete, pushing through dancing spirals of heat, and people avoided the soft puddles of tar like minefields, going to ground wherever they could—beneath awnings, in shopping arcades and in the interiors of dark cafés.

Beyond the square the red-roofed medieval town rose steeply, a glimpse of watchtowers and greenery poking out high above the melting pot beneath. Confusing steps and alleyways seemed to lead up to it, but further along I found a more inviting access—a little funicular. For a penny I went up with it to the heights. And here was a different world—a village of tree-lined walks and parapets, where heavy chestnut leaves leaned right out over the city, stirring in a faint breeze, with minute squares beyond and alleys that threaded their way back over the hill between shaky old houses and stately baroque buildings, small Venetian palazzos wreathed in tentacles of lime-green creeper, once the homes of a merchant aristocracy, now restored as government offices, museums and art galleries.

There were no cars, and it was almost silent up in this blazing summer perch, as families took their lunch in curtained rooms, bureaucrats scuttled along the shadowed side of lanes, back down the hill into the city, while a few sun-dyed tourists huddled in the cool of a church porchway. There were several shops—a state tourist office with curios and knickknacks in the window, and a number of inviting little restaurants. But there were no antique shops. It was an impossible search, I thought, as I crossed the square toward the tempting shadows by the tourist shop. I wiped my face and thought of a cold beer back in town, gazing vacantly at the thick, brightly painted Dalmatian pottery in the shop window. There was some cut glass as well, and a row of nicely carved wooden boxes—cigarette boxes, I thought.

I was just moving away when the door opened and someone came out; for an instant I heard the delicate tinkling of a music box. I stopped in my tracks and thought back to the weeks before, in Hyde Park Square, where I had last heard such music.

The shop was empty except for two middle-aged American women over by the counter with an assistant. They were examining what I had thought to be the cigarette boxes. I picked one up. They were little contemporary music boxes, I saw then, pretty modern things, hardly more than toys, latticed in matchwood on the sides, the lid roughly inlaid and with a fairly cheap mechanism inside.

"Don't they have any other tunes?" the big American woman asked. She was dressed in a kind of floppy toga which she hitched impatiently about her while her companion fiddled with the key.

"No." The Yugoslav girl smiled nicely. "Just those two: the 'Blue Danube' and 'Imperial Polka.'"

"Well, I don't know. Six thousand dinars—that's around ten dollars, isn't it?" Big patches of sweat stained the fabric under her arms. She seemed rooted to the spot, fatigue and indecision overcoming her impatience. "Play it again, Martha." Her companion set the music off once more, the sweet notes filling the room, a distant, gracious age renewed.

"Are they made locally?" I asked the Yugoslav girl, turning my box over, looking for a marking.

"Yes. Yes, here in Zagreb." The girl beamed.

"You don't know who makes them, do you? I specialize in this kind of thing in London, you see. I'd very much like to meet the man, to see how they do it over here."

"Oh, I don't know—"

"Well, look, I'll take this one in any case. And if you could give me their name. Or where you get them from..."

The girl melted a little. "I'll ask my friend."

The two Americans continued to ponder the quality of the merchandise against the financial outlay and the girl disappeared behind a curtain. A minute later she reappeared with a piece of paper.

"'Is a wood shop near here. A wood..." She searched for a better word.

"A carpenter's shop?"

"Yes," she said slowly. "Is not quite a carpenter's shop." She smiled awkwardly. "Is for *pompes funèbres*. You know? How you say. They make boxes for people as well."

"Coffins?" I asked.

"Yes." She beamed hugely. "Coffins. Is near here."

She gave me the name and address. "*Gospodin* Josip Radja. Is a little road going back to Republic Square: Radićeva." Then she found me a street map and pointed it out. Finally she wrapped up my box very neatly with a ribbon over coarse brown paper. She couldn't have been more helpful, and the place seemed only just round the corner. The only thing I missed when I came back out into the sun was my little silver revolver.

Of course, it was a remote chance—difficult too, for I had none of the language. But I had one of their music boxes to prove my bona fides, and I thought I could bumble my way through a few sensible inquiries with a bit of French or German.

There was no sign above the shop front in the narrow old street that twisted down back into the city, just grimy glass windows and a doorway wide enough for coffins, and I could identify the place only by carefully checking the street numbers of the other small secondhand shops on either side of it. The steep alleyway was a last bastion of private enterprise in the city, a shadowed place, covered by long eaves, where the sun hardly penetrated at all. And when I opened the door I came into an even darker world—it might have been a medieval workroom. A long narrow space like a cave led back into the hill, littered with drifts of sawdust and coffin sides and lids and brass fittings, the air cloudy with motes of wood and smelling of sharp new varnish. In the gloom they might have been making strange boats, little angular craft, golden-colored bathtubs, specially designed to sink without trace.

When my eyes became accustomed to the dimness, I noticed two men carefully tending a casket in the middle of the room. Two others, in the cloud of sawdust beyond, were stripping elm planks in a rotary sander, and there were other, unidentifiable thumps behind them in the invisible gloom at the end of the workshop. To my right was a glass-partitioned office with an old man inside, leaning over sheaves of paper—a man from the true Balkans, with a droopy white mustache, heavily lined peasant's face and sunken eyes like dark stones.

He came out at once, agreeing that he was Josip Radja. I showed him the music box and for a minute or two we stumbled through a variety of languages without getting anywhere. But he finally understood what I wanted.

"Yes," he said at last in halting English, "I have you one girl," and without knowing what he was up to, I followed him right down to the end of the workshop and out into a tiny sunny courtyard at the back. And there, sitting at a table beneath a stand of huge sunflowers, was a pretty schoolgirl, dark-haired, thin-faced, in a linen school smock, eating lunch from a tin canteen. She must have been fourteen or fifteen—an attractive girl, slim, in long pigtails, her hair parted severely in the middle. But when she stood up, at the old man's bidding, and looked at me, I saw that her beauty was marred by an awkward squint in one eye, a flaw in her vision, so that she gazed askance at the world.

"Is Enka. My big daughter. English! English!" The man waved his hands about, speaking to the girl in Serbo-Croatian.

"I speak English—leetle," she said in a shy way. "I learn now school. This is my grandfather," she added slowly. "We help you?"

"Well, I just wondered..." I showed her my music box. "I wanted to know how these were made here. I'm very interested. Who makes them here?" I turned to the old man.

"I make it." I turned back in surprise. The girl was examining the box carefully. "This one I make," she added confidently.

"Yes?" I queried.

"Yes! Yes!" The old man waved his hands vigorously in

the air again, encouraging the girl like a boat-race coach. "She make him!" He laughed out loud in pride now, pointing toward another wooden doorway on the far side of the postage-stamp garden. They brought me over. Inside, in a space as big as a lavatory, was a small workbench, a selection of wood veneers and match strips, fret saws, chisels and several medical scalpels: a complete miniature workshop. The old man picked up a little tissue packet and unwrapped it. Inside was the spring mechanism for the music boxes. *"Nematchka,"* he said.

"It is from Germany," the girl explained. "But everything other we make here."

"Marvelous," I said, looking at a half-completed box in a vise. "But how did you learn? Where did you get the idea of making these?"

"Pardon?" The girl looked at me queerly.

"How—did—you—start—making—these?" I almost spelled out the sentence, holding up one of the music boxes. "Who taught you?"

"Please?" Still she didn't understand and she looked over to her grandfather now for help. He spoke to her again, a slight note of urgency in his voice, I thought.

"Ah, yes," the girl went on much more confidently now. "I am learn it in my school. In woodtechnic studies." She smiled happily and the old man smiled too. Both of them seemed so friendly and willing to help that I decided to risk the next question.

"I wonder," I said, "if you remember a man here in Zagreb before the war, who collected these music boxes? A Mr. Zlatko Rabernak." I repeated the gist of the sentence again, even more slowly.

But the girl looked quite blank. "I don't know—" She turned to her grandfather again.

"Rabernak?" he said. "No—who is? No..." He spoke haltingly, shaking his head. I'd obviously come to an end; with the language problem there was no other real progress I could make. We'd come out again into the dazzling little concrete square and I'd started on my thanks and good byes when the old man patted me on the shoulder and said "slivovitz" several times, gesturing me to take a chair beneath the huge sunflowers. He spoke to the girl again in their own tongue and then said, *"Chekai, chekai,"* to me, in great good humor. I felt I could hardly refuse his hospitality, though the heat was uncomfortable in the enclosed space and I needed a cold beer far more than plum brandy.

I sat down as the old man went back into the main workshop. The girl watched me curiously, flirtatiously, it seemed now, flicking her pigtails over her shoulder, leaning against the wall a few yards from me, hands behind her rump.

"*'Chekai'*—it means 'wait,'" she said, smiling like a much older woman. And we waited. She crossed her legs as she stood there indolently, asking to be admired, hands still behind her back, her small breasts pushing through her smock, arched away from the wall, never taking her eyes off me. But was she really looking at me? It was hard to be sure because of her squint and the sun in my eyes whenever I looked up.

The whirr of electric machinery stopped suddenly in the workshop behind me. And something warned me then—the tempting schoolgirl with the cast in her eye, perhaps—that I shouldn't be here any more, that it was time to be up and away. I got to my feet quickly, making for the door.

But the girl was quicker still: in a flash she was round to the other side of the little yard, barring my way, and now I saw what she'd been hiding behind her back, as the scalpel in her hand glittered in the sun.

8

The girl didn't move; she stood very firmly against the door, holding the scalpel at arm's length, pointing it at me like a bayonet. Her knowing smile was gone but she wasn't frightened, and the smooth brick walls all round were impossible to climb. I was the one who was sweating. I hated knives anyway and here was a real tomato slicer. But there was the table, I saw, to keep me away from it. I picked it up, and using it as a shield with the legs outwards, moved behind it toward her. Then I lunged forward with it, pinning her to the door, trapping her between its legs on all sides as she jabbed about with the scalpel, narrowly missing my fingers. Then I gave the table a great thrust to one side, two legs catching her in the ribs and spinning her over onto the ground, where she lay stunned.

I was into the back of the workshop then, seeing nothing in the sudden gloom. There was no sound. The place was deserted, the men sent out for lunch, I assumed, by the old man, the machinery stilled and all the main lights turned off. I could hardly see my way at all. Suddenly I felt something soft coming up round my legs—a pile of sawdust, I realized, as I fell into it. I moved to one side then, feeling my way gingerly along what I thought must be the wall.

But my fingers came to a blank space almost immediately and I stopped. There was another room, it seemed, off to my right. Then I heard footsteps ahead. The old man, I presumed, was on the move—someone who knew the geography of the place intimately, a sure-footed walk toward me, between all the obstacles I remembered ahead.

But I couldn't see a thing, though my eyes had become used to the gloom by now. Then I realized why. The room I'd come into, off the main workshop, was a storeroom—and I was standing behind a tall pile of coffins, in all shapes and sizes, which had blocked my vision ahead.

The footsteps stopped then. He was waiting for me to move. Then the door from the backyard opened: the girl with the scalpel was up and about again. There were two of them now, one on either side of the long workshop, waiting for me in the dark. I was trapped in the little storeroom.

A diversion was required and the material for it was ready to hand. I got behind a coffin on the top of the stack and pushed it suddenly, with great force, out into the main room, then a second and a third, the light wood casings speeding away like torpedoes. There were smaller missiles available, too—little white children's caskets—and these I was able to pick up high in the air above my head and hurl like shot at my invisible, uncharitable hosts. Soon there was pandemonium in the stuffy cave as the wood splintered again and again on the hard floor beyond me. Now that the stack of boxes in front of me was depleted, I could see through the gloom into the workshop. But there was no one there. I got my hands behind another large coffin and shoved. It didn't move. I shoved again. Then I saw it was made of aluminum and had a lid on it. Someone or something was inside.

I was damp with sweat and fear and the energy suddenly ran out of me, bile rising in my throat, and I sagged to my knees. Someone called then, standing in the doorway, open now onto the street.

It was Stolačka, silhouetted against the light.

"*Gospodin* Marlow? Cease fire, cease fire!" He came toward me, walking jauntily through the splintered debris, in what seemed high good humor. I got to my feet, covered in sawdust, the wood sticking to my sweaty skin like breadcrumbs. He started to brush me down.

"It's good that we were following you," he said easily. "I told you: we are not inefficient."

"The two people—an old man, a girl?" I asked.

"Yes—they tried to run. We have them. Outside."

"And there's someone else," I said. "Here, in this coffin. Or maybe it's just some more bricks."

And I thought: It's Lindsay. It must be Lindsay.

But it wasn't. When Stolačka pulled the lid off I saw the dead features of Pottinger lying out flat in the bottom of the metal box, the keen, bright face that I remembered like a dark negative now, the skin faintly plum-colored.

"It adds up," Stolačka said to me later, when Josip Radja and his impudent granddaughter had been taken away. He had brought me to a workers' buffet a little further down the lane and bought my cold beer at last. "This man who you call Pottinger," he said. "They put him in that metal box because he was wounded. In the chest, some days ago. So you must have got him with your little gun in Vienna after all."

"How? If he'd been wounded in Vienna he'd have gone straight to the Russian Embassy there."

Stolačka shrugged. "Yes, maybe. So perhaps they killed him here then. Your friend Josip Radja. We will tell maybe for sure—if there is a bullet."

"Who is this Radja?"

"They are checking now, on the phone."

"You see, the moment I started talking about Rabernak—that's when he changed his mind about me. And of course—those coffins. That's his job. Isn't that how they managed the business with Eleanor Phillips? It could have been, if that workshop was there before the war."

"Maybe. We will find out. Come, we will see."

We went back out again. The police had blocked the alleyway off now and Stolačka's men were going through the workshop inch by inch. The place was brightly lit and there was a man on the phone in Radja's little glass office. Stolačka spoke to him for a minute before turning to me.

"They have checked this Josip Radja against our files. There is nothing wrong with him, at least on paper. This workshop has been here for many years. Yes—since before the war. We will question him. But he has a brother—which may be of more interest to us! Dr. Ivo Radja. He lives just up here above us, in the old town." Stolačka shook his head in surprise.

"What?"

"This man is distinguished; he is well known here for—what you say? A picture fixer?"

"An art restorer?"

"Yes. Restoration. Wall paintings in the church—"

"Frescoes?"

"Yes. And he is expert in the baroque time as well." Stolačka turned back to his colleague on the phone and took it from him, talking directly for a minute to some central registry, with long pauses as he jotted down various information.

When he'd finished he read from his notes: "Dr. Ivo Radja, professor at the Zagreb Academy of Fine Arts. Married to Liesl Radja, once Liesl Schlüsselberger, an Austrian woman, born in Vienna in 1913, now a naturalized Yugoslav citizen. They have two children: Stepan and Stanka Radja. He is a research chemist at the Scientific Institute here. And she, of course, is the pianist."

"Of course?"

"Yes, of course." He looked at me in surprise. "Stanka Radja—one of the best in Croatia."

The little office had become unbearably hot and we went outside into the road again. "Liesl Radja," I said. "Born in Vienna in 1913. That's very close to Eleanor Phillips's birthday. She lived in Vienna, too. And spoke German fluently." Stolačka had taken his glasses off, wiping them as I spoke. Now he looked at me carefully. "You are thinking what I think?"

"I wondered. Is this Liesl Radja perhaps—"

"Perhaps the woman who should have been in that grave?" Stolačka interrupted.

I shrugged. "Maybe. But it seems unlikely, if they're all so well known here."

"Come." Stolačka spoke quickly. "We may make our inquiries. They live only up the hill here." He called to a colleague and together the three of us moved up the little alleyway back toward the old town.

It was a small, two-storied baroque house, finely restored, the stucco delicately veined with Virginia creeper, set on the highest part of the hill. A graceful archway divided the building, which was now an art gallery and museum, representing the entire history of this medieval town. Stolačka spoke to a woman inside at a ticket desk. "Of course," he said when he returned. "The professor has an apartment at the back. But he is not here. They are away on holiday. Come."

We went through the archway, across a courtyard, and climbed some circular wooden stairs leading to an apartment above what must have been stables in the old days. At the top were two lovely arched barn doors, beautifully restored with their original latches and studs, but firmly closed now, with some tactfully modern locks. And there was no reply from a distant bell.

Stolačka sent his colleague back for the caretaker and a few minutes later we were inside a long and wonderfully decorated attic room, running almost the length of the building, a stone-vaulted hay or grain store, I supposed, originally, but now converted with taste and skill into a richly ornamented salon. A row of dormer windows gave out onto a jigsaw of umber tiles and beyond that a vision of the city beneath us; a sylvan tapestry ran along the other wall; a big refectory table piled with art books ran down the middle of the smooth pine floor. There were silver icons and other odd bits of baroque ecclesiastical decor set about on shelves, in niches between more books and small pictures. Two twisting barley-sugar sticks in yellowed wood, the remnants from some baroque pulpit, I thought, held up a mantelpiece over a grate at one end. There was a small grand piano in a corner, a Liszt concerto open on the music rack.

We wandered round the salon, the other two looking into the neat bedrooms that led off it. The place was empty and wonderfully cool, a glittering treasure house, edged in black and old gold and set off with fine Dalmatian pottery and bright red, peasant-weave chair coverings.

I shook my head when Stolačka came back. "It seems unlikely," I said. "It's all too grand, surely? People like this wouldn't be the sort..."

"The sort of what?"

"To play tricks with graves—all that. To work for the Russians. Besides, there's nothing English here. If she'd been Eleanor Phillips..."

"You'd expect—what?"

"I don't know. Tea, marmalade—something." We'd come into the kitchen and I was looking over the provision shelves. There was a great variety of bottled fruit, pickles and red cabbage, with hams and long bronzed sausages of old salami hanging from hooks. But there was no Twinings Best Darjeeling or Oxford coarse-cut.

A small study led off the salon. And there I saw the music box: just one, on a shelf above the desk—but a Fabergé of a music box, the sides ribbed in latticed gilt with an enameled lid depicting an airy bunch of cherubs flying through a blue empyrean, each one puffing a golden horn. I lifted the top and a tune emerged: the tone was extremely delicate, precise—a mazurka. There was a list of half a dozen other tunes, written in fine copperplate inside the lid. It was a perfect object.

But still I wasn't sure—even when Stolačka's colleague switched on a large transistor radio back in the salon. The crisp English accent immediately flooded through the room. It was the two o'clock news summary from London. The transistor had last been tuned to the BBC Overseas Service, and someone had been foolish enough to leave it on that wavelength; foolish, that is, if they were guilty of anything. But why should they be? And I disliked the spying then: it was like wartime in occupied Europe and we were SS men wickedly on the move, searching out the innocent, tuned to freedom.

I said, "Lots of people listen to the BBC abroad. It doesn't mean a thing."

"No. Perhaps not."

"Lots of Yugoslavs who want to improve their English—"

"Of course. I did that myself. I know. But here, look at this." Stolačka had picked up a little red-covered book. "This is perhaps not so typically Yugoslav." It was one of Ward Lock's Red Guides, I saw: *The Highlands of Scotland,* a fairly new edition, taken from the British Council's library in Zagreb. "You told me this Eleanor Phillips was originally from Scotland—no?"

"Perhaps the Radjas were just thinking of a holiday up there."

"Yes," Stolačka agreed. "Except that they have already gone on holiday. The caretaker told me. They have a *dacha,* you know—a place in the woods, north of here, near the Slovenian border. The castle of Trakošćan. It's a museum now. But there are some small houses in the forest. The Radjas have one. They are there now."

"Let me go there first, will you?" I said at once. "If we are right. Could we see them first?"

"Why not? They are not guilty of anything—yet. But we will be behind you. In case."

We left the fabulous apartment then. A music box, the BBC news, a guide to Scotland: it wasn't conclusive evidence, but it was just enough, I felt, to tip the balance.

Back at the hotel I went through the same routine with Madeleine and Rachel, taking the role of devil's advocate once more. Though now I was less insistent. I put it on a take-it-or-leave-it basis. "I'll go up there in any case," I said, after I'd explained all the day's events to them.

"It's not a lot of proof," Madeleine said.

"It's enough to take a look. And Lindsay may well be with them, hiding out there for some reason."

Madeleine's face twitched in pain. "Look," I said gently. "You have to face it one way or the other. And if you don't, what will you think for the rest of your life? It'll haunt you."

She didn't reply. Rachel had said hardly anything all along. She was calm, a steely calm like that of a gambler waiting over a roulette wheel. Now she shook her head in disbelief.

"It's all so unlikely, isn't it?" she asked me, smiling, looking at me in a friendly way for the first time in days. "It's just a story. It can't be true." And I saw then, in the depths of her face, way behind the solid calm, that she feared it all *was* true, because it was so unlikely. She had that confident look, with a great crack of unease running through it—like that of a faithful spouse, the last to realize her partner's infidelity.

She laughed, still shaking her head. "I'll go. Why not?" she said. "I'll do this one more thing before I leave—just to show how wrong you are."

"Fine. And you?" I turned to Madeleine.

"How can I refuse?" she replied. But she didn't smile.

Stolačka arranged rooms for us in the local tourist lodge at Trakošćan and a car for me to drive up there; it was several hours northeast of Zagreb, on the main road to Maribor, up in the hills. He showed me the route on a map back at the police station.

"Through Krapina," he said. "Then here at Donji Macelj, you turn right. It's a small road—not more than a forest track, I think, along the river valley here for about fifteen kilometers. At the end there is the hotel, the castle—and the woods. You can't go any further."

"And their house?" I asked.

"It is in the forest." He showed me another large-scale map of the Trakošćan area now that included, at the center, a rough triangle about twenty kilometers long, an outline of the old castle estates, an area colored almost entirely in green, with a few small lakes, the rest of it wooded and with what appeared to be a large marsh some distance beyond the castle.

"Is all forest now," Stolačka said. "Apart from this limestone quarry." He pointed to what I'd thought was a marsh. "Here—from this hill behind the castle, down to the river."

"Fine. But if it's all forest, how do I find their house?"

"Is not a house, it's a wooden *dacha*, an old converted hunting lodge. From what I learn from our forestry department there are three or four such places in the estate. Summer rest houses—they belong to the artists' unions, writers, painters. Are rented out—and are not on this map. But the Radjas' place is here, we think."

He pointed to a spot near a lake, several miles beyond the castle. "There are tracks," Stolačka went on, "with notices—all through the woods. And they will have a more detailed map at the hotel to help you. You will find them easily enough."

"And you?"

"We have already made arrangements. Happily, this terrain around Trakošćan is one where our military reservists take training every year. The local people are well accustomed to seeing soldiers in the forest all through summer. So we have just added to these reserve men—a group of our own, in uniform of course. They will never be far away from the *dacha*. They will have it in vision, in fact, be camping nearby. Here, I will give you this whistle. Blow hard if there is emergency. And this, too." He handed me back Lindsay's little revolver. "Perhaps you will feel better with it. There are field glasses in the car you will have."

"How many are at the lodge?"

"The caretaker said the whole family. That would mean five adults and the two grandchildren—the son, Stepan, is married."

"Quite a crowd," I said doubtfully. "I wonder if it's really possible, if we're right at all..."

"That is for you to find out. Remember, you asked to see them first. And I agreed, because of course you have a better chance than us to find the truth. With us they can easily lie, after all. But with you and Mrs. Phillips—you who know their history—they cannot so easily lie."

Stolačka nodded sagely, and I felt like a cheap police informer again, as I had with Basil Fielding when he'd first made his offers a month before. I thought of throwing the whole thing in there and then. But, as usual, it was just a little too late.

Madeleine, Rachel, and I drove out of Zagreb first thing next morning in a small Fiat, along a good main road for an hour or so, sloping gently up through broad valleys of vines and sweet corn, then rising higher through passes and over torrents of water, toward the hills, the last remnants of the Alps, near the Slovenian border.

After we turned right beyond Krapina—off the main road and along a narrow, twisting strip of tarmac—the landscape changed at once. The open, rolling valleys disappeared as we ran along the bottom of a long, heavily wooded defile in the land—beside a flashing stream that snaked down from the steep wooded crags and hills ahead of us. We were already in some lost country now, absolutely without habitation, a vast forestry preserve with no evidence of man but the road and a few loggers' tracks and firebreaks.

The women said little. The sun was fearsome again under the tin roof. But with all the windows open I could smell the watery marsh airs, touched with pine, and I looked forward suddenly to the future. What did it matter, I felt once more, what ugly deceits had transpired years before—in this fabulous green world of trees and strange wild flowers and rushing water under the pure white light?

"Cheer up," I said gently, to neither of the women in particular.

"Yes," Madeleine said, sitting beside me, sunglasses covering her eyes. But she said no more.

After twenty minutes the narrow pass opened out into a small valley, like a neat green saucer hidden between white crags and pine-crested hills crowding in all round. On one side, high up and dominating the whole valley, was the castle—a great fortified medieval keep in white stone circled with four wedding-cake turrets and a tall square tower rising up in the middle. On the other side, an open meadow where they were scything hay, was the tourist lodge, a low, flat building with a large terrace in front; a few people were sitting in wicker chairs over coffees and beers, looking over the miniature valley. And when we got out of the car it was like some childhood summer long before—a fragrance of freshly cut hay in the air and the remembered promise, in those better times, of some great summer adventure.

There was at least an hour to go before lunch, so I said, after we'd checked in and met again in the lobby, "We might as well go on now." I'd got the binoculars and a more detailed map of the estate from the receptionist.

"There," I said, "that must be the Radjas' lodge—up here beyond this lake."

"What do we do? Just walk in on them?" Rachel asked. "Saying 'You're Eleanor Phillips and Zlatko Rabernak, and I claim my five pounds'? Or 'Hello, Daddy, where have you been all this time?'?"

"What else?" I said.

"And if he's not there, and they've nothing to do with Eleanor or Lindsay?"

"We'll soon know."

"How will we soon know? They can lie to us as well as anyone. We don't even know what they look like now," Rachel added aggressively.

"I've a fair idea, from those old photographs. Besides, Eleanor must look a bit like Susan."

We were on the terrace, looking out over the valley, the sun burning us. "Come on," I said. "Let's not hang around here anyway. It'll be cooler in the woods." I looked at the two women. They were more shaken than I was. But then, of course, it was their family, in a way, whom they might possibly be meeting for the first time in their lives in half an hour.

We crossed the meadows through the haystacks and climbed some sharp steps, zigzagging through rhododendrons, up to the castle, where a few American tourists marveled at a portcullis. On the other side of the great squat building the land fell steeply away again, in a series of stone terraces and formal grassy slopes, toward a lake filled with weeds and lily pads. We took a flower-bordered path along the edge here, and soon the rather severe aspect of these water gardens gave way to a whole countryside of informal little lakes and twisting waterside paths that snaked beneath great stands of copper beeches.

Further on the lakes narrowed and stopped, and the land opened out into great stretches of virgin meadow set round with huge, haphazard clumps of oak and chestnut; a ruined English parkland, the trees gone way past full maturity.

A track led across this parkland to a much thicker ring of trees on the far side, and pushing through these we were soon by another lake again, a darker lake with deep, leaf-filled inlets and a little pagoda-roofed boathouse halfway along with a pier jutting out over the still water. Standing on this, just above a rubber dinghy, I could see faint, damp footmarks and a forgotten towel. There were wet bicycle tracks on the hot wood. And then, a few yards out in the bronze-colored water two great fish swam into view, moving very slowly just beneath the surface. We'd come into a place preserved, where there was no fear, it seemed: a world before the Fall.

We'd been walking for more than half an hour, twisting ever deeper into the forests. I got the map out. "This lodge, at least, is just off here, at the end of the lake: we turn right."

The two women were sitting by the boathouse, resting in the shade. Madeleine was tired.

"Do you want to stay here while I go and take a look?" I asked.

"No. We'll come too," she said at once. Before I had always gone on my own toward Lindsay, but now they were to be there as well—in at the kill, or as witnesses to my folly.

Two dark-haired boys on small bikes suddenly came dashing along the waterside path. They barely noticed us. We followed them down the path, further into the woods, a minute afterwards. I wondered where Stolačka's task force were hiding themselves.

A grassy track led away from the lake at right angles, through a long archway of trees, toward another open meadow in the distance. And here, stopping just before the end of the wood, we looked out across the wide field and saw a wooden lodge nestling in a clearing of trees on the far side, less than half a mile away. The two boys were riding across the center of this meadow now, their heads bobbing up and down in the grass. It was a space impossible to cross without being seen.

I took the binoculars out and focused them. The mop-headed boys came into vision and then, when I raised the glasses a bit, the lodge itself.

The first thing I saw was a big table on the covered terrace being prepared for lunch by two young women, one in a bikini, laying plates and cutlery, with what looked like a muslin-covered Moses basket to one side. I handed the glasses to Madeleine.

"I can't see," she said. "Just grass."

"Up a bit."

"Yes. There's someone in the background now." She handed me the glasses. "There—in the shadow of the doorway."

I looked again. It was a middle-aged woman, her back half-turned toward us. Then she came out into a better light and I could see she was carrying a big platter with something like a ham on it. She had a broad face with a peasant kerchief triangled over it. A nanny, perhaps, or a servant? A youngish man in bathing trunks, carrying a collection of bottles between the fingers of each hand, followed her.

The boys had arrived at the lodge by now. Throwing their bikes down, they started to mob the man—their father, I assumed—running round him in circles, the three of them doing a little dance before he managed to get all the bottles down on the table safely and cuffed them away. We could just hear the laughter then, drifting across the heat haze.

We stood there, in the cover of the trees, watching for a few minutes in silence. Then Rachel took the glasses.

"Well, there's no sign of Lindsay," she said with relief. "You must be out of your mind," she went on, gazing intently. "That fat old woman is nothing like Susan."

"No," I had to agree. "Perhaps she's just the babushka. Or a wet nurse. You see the Moses basket?"

"This isn't feudal Russia. She's the mamma. And she isn't like Aunt Susan." She handed the glasses back.

A much older man came out onto the terrace just then and seemed to confirm Rachel's point about the big woman, for he put his arm about her and squeezed her in a familiar way. I had a close look at him: it must have been Dr. Radja. He was small, sixtyish, with thin gray hair, wearing a pair of linen shorts and a string shirt. Was his hair parted in the middle? Zlatko's had been. I looked carefully; it wasn't, but simply because he had so little hair. It could have been, years before. And was the face impish? Yes, that was more possible, I thought. His eyes were close together, at least.

"Come on, let's go back," Rachel said. "Lindsay's not there. And it's not Eleanor. Or Zlatko. And we can't just push in on them in the middle of their lunch. It's rude. Come on, let's leave them in peace."

"Wait," I said. The older man had picked up a tin from the table, while the younger one started to carve the ham. It was a yellow tin of Colman's mustard: I saw the name quite clearly when I focused carefully on the bright yellow label.

"Rubbish!" Rachel said. "They sell Colman's all over the place now." But already I was out from the cover of the trees and into the light, starting to walk across the meadow. I'd had enough prevarications, a month of violent mystery and indecision. It was now or never.

They must have seen us as we walked across the open field, but they showed no sign of it until we were almost upon them, moving up a path into the center of the little clearing. They were all seated round a long table that was heavily laden with inviting salads and cold meats. I saw now that there were steaks barbecuing to one side of the wooden terrace. The table was littered with bottles: wine and Coke and mineral water. It was quite a feast—a family gathering of great intimacy and happiness.

I suddenly felt horrified at my interruption—a lout broaching this familial ease, a harbinger of pain. But I was in the lead. I felt like an actor, sagging at the knees with nerves, at curtain rise, about to embark on a part probably far too big for him.

"Excuse me," I said weakly. They stopped eating—just a blur of faces on the shaded terrace, gazing at me like an expectant audience. "Yes, I'm sorry—"

"Lost your way?" the older, white-haired man inquired politely in good, slightly accented English, a glass of deep-purple wine in his hand.

"Dr. Radja?"

"Yes. Can I help?"

Rachel and Madeleine were standing behind me and I couldn't see them. But I could see the large woman clearly now, sitting at the end of the table, presiding over the spread like an earth mother. She was looking intently over my shoulder—at Madeleine, I thought.

"Can we help? Are you lost?" the old man asked again.

A waft of blue smoke from the charcoal grill drifted over the table, a fine smell of singed garlic burning with the meat. The two pretty younger women tended to the boys' lunch in hushed voices—one fair-haired, wearing a print blouse, her hair up in a bun; and a much darker one in a bikini, with a thin, intelligent face. The baby in the Moses basket was still asleep. I turned back to Rachel and Madeleine.

"This is Madeleine and Rachel Phillips," I said in clear tones, like a toastmaster. "From Glenalyth, in Scotland." I looked carefully at the big woman as I spoke, and I was almost certain I'd hit home then, for the lady shuddered just for an instant, involuntarily, as if caught in a cold draft.

"Yes?" the old man asked. "So what should we...? I don't understand." But I think he did understand, for he suddenly stood up and he was leaning across the table toward us, tense, annoyed. He spoke in Serbo-Croatian to the old lady.

"Eleanor? Zlatko?" I asked before they'd finished talking together. But they heard me well enough. And there was silence then. Absolute silence. Only the meat crackled and spat in the background. The two boys looked round at everyone inquiringly and the younger man in bathing trunks sat quite still, his hands laid out in front like an animal about to spring.

But it was the old man who moved suddenly, the chair grating on the wood, turning back quickly into the lodge.

"No! Don't do that," the woman called after him in English. "It's too late." Then she turned to me. "You have come at an awkward time." She spoke very pleasantly, like a fine hostess from the Shires, the English pure as glass even after so many years of exile, with just a hint of Scots in it. "It's my daughter Stanka's birthday, you see." She leaned back in her chair and took the kerchief from her head, relaxing, twisting her neck about so that her still-dark hair dropped round her shoulders. Suddenly she looked quite a different woman—younger, the face much more finely cut, something chiseled about it as it became defined by the frame of hair.

"So," she went on. "You see: you must sit down and not disturb things for the moment. The others don't speak much English—we will say you are old friends. From London. Sit down and enjoy yourselves. You must be tired? You've walked all the way from the hotel. No?"

"Yes," I said. The old man had come back now and I had my eye on him. I don't know what he'd gone away for—a gun, I supposed. But the woman spoke to him in English then. "These are our old friends—you remember? The Phillipses. They will join us. We will talk later." The old man seemed to accept this meekly.

She addressed the rest of the family in their own tongue and happy introductions were made all round—to the two boys, the woman in the print blouse and her nervous husband, and to Stanka, bronzed and matchlike in her bikini, whose birthday it was.

Drinks were offered liberally then. I needed one, for it was an eerie situation, sharing this warm birthday feast with the family, pretending to be old friends for the sake of decorum, but with all the great questions hanging impatiently in the air about us. And though the family were friendly, asking polite questions in halting English, they were none of them fools and everyone sensed the strange pressures, keeping so many lids on that the calm couldn't last.

And it didn't. I suppose the fine local wine loosened tongues, so that at the end of the meal, when the boys had gone to play with their father, the mother had left to tend her baby, and Stanka had gone inside, the five of us remaining sat back and started to talk.

9

It was the big, generous-looking woman at the end of the table who took charge, offering us a slivovitz with our coffee, smiling at us all, particularly at Madeleine who sat immediately across the table from her.

"Mrs. Phillips." She raised her glass. "In a situation like this you either laugh or cry, don't you think? Forgive me—" She smiled broadly. "I think it better to laugh."

Madeleine didn't entirely respond to this toast, though she tried. "So you are Eleanor?" she asked, but not incredulously. It was more a polite inquiry, confirming an expected thing.

"I am Eleanor, and this is Zlatko. You are right." She waved a hand over toward the old man. "My husband." He was sitting rather hunched up, his eyes lowered over his coffee, saying nothing. He seemed, for the moment, to be entirely in the thrall of his wife. But I didn't trust him. I was sure he'd gone back into the lodge for a gun or a knife.

"You have been very clever finding us," Eleanor went on. "After all these years. Why did you bother?" Her voice fell. "We have been very happy." She looked around at the terrace, at the afternoon sun filtering through the trees beyond, where the boys were throwing a Frisbee with their father. There was a sense of peace, for the moment—far more powerful than the air of strife we had brought with us.

"I'm sorry. We were looking for Lindsay," Madeleine said. "He's disappeared. Three months ago." Madeleine's eyes were glassy with trapped emotion. She was not so calm at heart. "We thought he might be here." She looked round vacantly at the heavy canopy of trees.

"Disappeared? Like me." Eleanor shook her head good-naturedly, like a nanny sharing notes over a recalcitrant charge. "There's only us, I'm afraid. He's not come here. I'd be the last person he'd want to see in any case. But how did you find us?"

"A grave," I said. "We found an empty grave up at Mirogoj."

"I told you, Zlatko." She looked over at the little man reproachfully. "The police must know too." And she looked around again, peering through the beech trees toward the thick ring of fir beyond. "They're not here alone," she went on.

"No," I said. "We are not alone. The police know too. At least, about the empty grave."

"Why *on earth* did you do that?" Rachel spoke suddenly, with childish exaggeration, looking at Eleanor in amazement.

Eleanor turned to her slowly. "You are Lindsay's good daughter. I can see it, so well. Do you really want to know?"

Rachel didn't reply. It seemed, indeed, from her tense face that she'd been struck dumb.

"You were dead, run over by a tram opposite the Palace Hotel," I said, breaking the silence.

"Ah, yes. That too."

"And a memorial—a window in the church outside Dunkeld."

"Is there?" Eleanor asked lightly. "That would be Susan, wouldn't it? She was very formal, of course. Little memorials—very much her. She was like that."

"She still is. She's still alive, you know," I said.

"I didn't. You see I—Zlatko and I—have had no connection, obviously."

"But how could you have cut yourself off like this from all your own family, for forty years. With such—such..." Madeleine searched for a word. "Telling such fibs," she finally said, the nursery word starkly inappropriate.

The table indeed had become like some nightmare version of the Mad Hatter's tea party, in which there were so many crossed wires, and so much time now all to be re-accounted for, that it was difficult to know where to begin on this necessary rearrangement of old life and memory. It was as if the natural order of the world had been entirely contradicted, and we had come to a secret place in the woods where the dead lived again and all temporal order was completely confounded.

Eleanor sipped her coffee. She seemed completely at ease in her reincarnation for all of us. Indeed, she seemed to find it rather an original joke; there was a touch of mischief in her eyes, I thought, and I could see the prankster in her now, the funny, vital woman she must have been years before, embarrassing her hosts in Vienna—the darling girl of the diplomatic circle in that city before the war, pretending to be a Von Karlinberg. But why the ruse of the empty grave, which seemed just beyond a joke?

"Cut myself off?" she said brightly. "Yes, I did. I couldn't stand the family pretense anymore: the Phillips family and mine. Lindsay and Susan. The social pretense—and the worse lies behind that." She looked round at us efficiently. "The thirties at home weren't just a political cheat, you know—MacDonald and Chamberlain pulling the wool over everyone's eyes. It was a family betrayal as well, and by families like ours particularly: such a lot of rich, comfy, Christian do-gooders, pretending they didn't know what was happening with Hitler, keeping out of things. 'It's not *our* affair'—what frauds they were!"

Eleanor became vehement now, but in a perfectly controlled manner. She wasn't acting, merely intent on offering us, as clearly as she could, a whole part of her old life, a memorial revisited.

"You see, at heart they *knew,* these families—knew political right from wrong. Yet they didn't just *let* Chamberlain and all the other wishy-washy right-wing cowards take over, they actually encouraged them! Yes, I cut myself off—though in a way I had no choice. Lindsay wanted rid of me, for other reasons."

"We met an old friend of Lindsay's in Brussels," I said. "Ivo Kovačić. He thought Lindsay had pushed you under that tram."

"Oh, Ivo..." Eleanor beamed. "He was always so strong

and forthright. He's still alive? I'm glad. But he had no head for subtleties. He was gullible."

"Everyone seems to have been pretty gullible, except you and Zlatko. And Lindsay, I suppose. It seems a funny trick," I said. "Oh, and Willis Parker," I added, suddenly remembering the little diplomat. "He knew about it all, as well. He must have done—which is why they got rid of him."

"Willis?" Eleanor said, with alarm. "They killed him?"

"Yes. And they tried to do the same for me several times, too. Anyone who was likely to know was dangerous. But why? What was so vital that we might have found out about Lindsay?"

"What I found out here in Zagreb forty years ago, in the spring of 1937."

"That Lindsay was a double agent, really working for Moscow?"

"That he *wasn't*," Eleanor said triumphantly. Her husband interrupted her now, talking bitterly, excitedly in Serbo-Croatian, seeming to condemn her. But she took little notice of him, saying in English, "They know, Zlatko! They know about us already. The *Milicija* are somewhere out there in the trees, watching us now probably. They'd never have allowed the Phillipses to come here on their own. So what's the point?" She turned to Madeleine then. "And in any case I'm so tired of lies. It's been nearly fifty years now, my lies. And Lindsay's. While there's time"—she glanced out again into the trees—"you ought to know now. No one else will ever tell you—"

"It's not your business," Zlatko interrupted angrily.

"Whose then?" she said equally sharply. "My life is my business—and years of it was with Lindsay. And it was he, after all, who originally encouraged me, before you came. It was Lindsay who first persuaded me about Moscow, all that world—before I found out about him."

"Found out what?" I asked. There was silence again in the clearing. The boys had gone down to the lake and the two women were somewhere in the sun, sitting on the other side of the lodge. "Found out that he wasn't with Moscow?"

"No. He was something much more dangerous from their point of view. Like our old friend Philby—there were very few of them—he'd been specially created by the British a long time before, at Oxford, as a Trojan horse: to *pretend* he was a Communist, which he did very well, so well that while I was up at college with him, he persuaded me to take on the same cause. And of course, just as the British intended, he was duly recruited by the Soviets—by that professor friend of his in London. They told him to give himself suitable right-wing cover while he served his apprenticeship with them. And he did that very well, too: the Foreign Office took him on at once—though God knows I didn't understand why he changed his views at the time. It was the start of our rows. The fact is, I think, that Lindsay was totally loyal to his British masters from the very start—or at least to the few people in British Intelligence who knew he was this Trojan horse in Moscow."

The picture at last began to make sense. Of course, I thought, John Wellcome had been the initial recruiter on the British side, at Merton and in his father's little cottage with the model railways at Bletchley—and it had been David Marcus, latterly, who probably alone, with Wellcome and Willis Parker, knew of Lindsay's real stance and had thus been so determined to preserve the secret: Lindsay, whom the KGB had thought to be their most reliable man, at the heart of British Intelligence, had in fact been nothing of the sort. It was the KGB he must have so thoroughly betrayed over the years—a worm near the center of their apparatus. Or had he fooled them? There was a flaw in this, for of course one other person had apparently known of the ploy: Eleanor herself.

"But you—you knew this too?" I asked her.

"Yes. I came to suspect it. Then I knew it. You see, we were both with Moscow by then, after we were married. And there were things he wouldn't tell them—political matters in the embassy in Vienna, and here at the consulate in Zagreb. I knew it in the end—you do when you're that close, as I was, to someone. Which is why he tried to kill me. And of course he thought he *had* killed me: Ivo was right. He did push me under that tram. I survived, but it was a very dead-looking body in the nursing home apparently." She smiled, looking over at Zlatko. "My friends—we managed to fake it all very well, didn't we?"

"You must not say such things," he said curtly.

"Yes, yes, I must."

I looked at Zlatko. "Your brother Josip—of course, he must have helped arrange all that, with his shiny coffins. The police are holding him in Zagreb now."

"You see?" Eleanor turned to her husband. "I told you. It's all too late. They've even got Josip."

"And another man—who really *is* dead. Someone called Pottinger, who is certainly with the KGB. So you must all be associated with Moscow—you and Zlatko and Josip. You've been together for years."

Eleanor looked at me confidently. "Can they prove it?"

"I don't know. But you've told us."

"Since it's a family matter as well, I wanted you to know the truth, that's all. Wasn't that why you came here? To find out the real truth?"

"Yes, I—we wanted—" I looked at Rachel and Madeleine for help. But both of them seemed frozen in the heat—Rachel staring intently at Eleanor with her arms wrapped right round her ribs, like the sleeves of a straitjacket.

"Yes," I said. "We wanted to talk to you first."

"About Lindsay and me?" I nodded. "Well, he's not here. As I said, I'm the last person he'd want to see, I think. You see, on a purely personal level, we rather fell out."

She looked at us all inquisitively, staring, as it were, into a huge silence. "Forgive me," she went on in a lower but still decisive voice. "I can see you don't know. Susan never told you. But now that you've found me, there's really no point in lying any more. Patrick wasn't my child. He was Susan's, with Lindsay. How is he? Where is he?"

Madeleine's face had become quite expressionless. She sat there in the hot silence without stirring, eyes wide open, unblinking, like a woman about to sleepwalk. Rachel appeared to take no notice of this news whatsoever, looking with boredom out into the woods. But I felt it was the assumed uninterest of a clever child or someone deranged—plotting mischief or revenge.

"Patrick died," I said, breaking the silence. "Just after the war. An illness."

Eleanor was genuinely moved. "Oh! I *am* so sorry."

"I find that an unlikely story," Madeleine spoke calmly.

"Why should I lie?" Eleanor asked.

"I don't know," I butted in. "But on the other hand why have you told us all this about you and Lindsay in any case, throwing over a lifetime's commitment? That doesn't make much sense. After all, you could go back to Moscow. A *dacha* in the Moscow woods."

361

"It's too late and I'm too old. This is my world. Here. My home is here. And my family. I'm too old. I've done my stuff."

"But Lindsay? From what you say he never managed to do his stuff at all, did he? Though he must have thought he had, believing you were dead. But you weren't—and so you told Moscow about him, didn't you?"

"Yes," Eleanor admitted, looking unhappy for the first time. "I had to. They neutralized him, carried him. At least I assume they did."

"So Moscow fed him a lot of nonsense for more than forty years. What a waste of a life—trotting between the KGB and the British all those years with equally useless information."

It was sad to think of abilities so stupidly wasted: almost a lifetime down the drain. Yet I wasn't really surprised; the whole business, I'd known for years, was a mug's game. I suppose I was simply startled by someone of Lindsay's caliber being involved in such a charade. It wouldn't have mattered if he'd been a stranger, but he wasn't. He was someone I'd known very well—a sane, reasonable, loyal man as I'd kept telling myself. And yet now, I saw, it was exactly these qualities that were in question, for what sane, loyal person could have behaved in this way, putting away his wife, with a child by another woman, her sister? Here was madness, not sanity—the acts of someone else altogether.

"So now you know," Eleanor said, a note of tiredness in her voice, as she fanned herself with a napkin in the drowsy afternoon heat. But we were all still alert. "You know now, and they are out there, I suppose, waiting for us." She turned and looked at me.

"The trouble is," I said, "I feel I *don't* know. It all sounds so unlike the man I knew."

"Who *knows* the person we know? Not even that person himself. And he's someone different for each of us. That's not strange. Lindsay—he was a lot of other men, even for me, who lived with him. So how do you expect to 'know' him?" She leaned toward me intently, as if with some vital secret. "But you mustn't think it was all a betrayal. Only at the end. There were lots of other times."

"Yes, I know. I found your book—your *Comrade's Diary* by Maria von Karlinberg. 'The snow weddings'...Before Christmas that year, at Dunkeld, when the champagne was too cold. I spoke to your sister."

Eleanor nodded her head as I spoke, agreeing with me

happily, wordlessly. "But of course! You've seen already. So you mustn't take away the impression of lost lives entirely. We had two lives—and one of them was marvelous, as fine as you could wish for. But I couldn't compromise, settle for less, while Lindsay so doubted himself at heart. He always did—telling little lies about things. And about the big things, like Patrick. A wonderful man, but something of the coward there, too—like so many wonderful men."

Eleanor could see now the numbing effect her words were having on the two women—this old storyteller, a myth herself describing another myth, holding us all in thrall, giving us the true version, it seemed, of a man we had all entirely misunderstood.

"You're a lying, malicious old woman," Rachel said suddenly in a high voice, still with her arms tightly wrapped about her, like a precocious child, at the foot of a soothsayer, intent on exposing the fairy tale.

"We shouldn't deny the truth, you know—it's the one thing that can't finally hurt us."

As Eleanor spoke there was a strange, faint thundering sound in the distance, the noise approaching from somewhere deep in the woods beyond the lodge. I thought the weather was changing again. But the afternoon out on the meadow was still brilliantly fine.

"It's only the train," Eleanor explained. "The limestone wagons. There's a small railway down there that takes the stone out from the hill beyond the lake." The invisible wagons rumbled away from us then, a faint threat in the air. We were not so far away from real life after all.

"You talk of the truth," I said, trying to see the women's side of it. "That it won't hurt us. Yet you've gone to such lengths in your life to hide it: working for Moscow, and the elaborate ploy of that diary you wrote, in German, under an assumed name. It seems a lot of lies, doesn't it?"

"Yes—which is why I tell you all this: it can't 'finally' hurt us, I said. I think I've lied for too long."

"A convenient confession—before execution?"

"No. I don't expect necessarily to avoid the consequences of what I've told you. I meant that the truth is worth having anyway. Better late than never."

"You know," I said, "I can't really see you as a Communist, least of all as a Communist agent. You've got too much fun in you—and sense. I wonder if you're lying—even about that."

I had this image of double creativity about Eleanor: of a woman full of good sense among earthly things—fine hams, bronzed salamis and chunky glasses of purple wine—and yet someone of crystal-sharp vitality in the mind, as well of literary conceits, a sweet imagination. And none of these happy gifts sat easily with the criminal bureaucracies of Moscow.

"No, it's the truth," she said. "Or it was. But no longer, which is another reason for my telling you all this. It's an old story now."

"But how was it ever fresh for you? The horror was there almost from the start—Stalin, long before Hungary and Czechoslovakia?"

"Almost? You weren't there in the thirties. It was all very fresh for me. So fresh—even the memory makes it so, all over again."

"What? All that privileged socialism? Earnest, pimply youths in sandals, running through Daddy's money in East End soup kitchens for a month or two before they became Lloyds underwriters and said what a fine chap Chamberlain was. You said that's what happened yourself!"

She smiled. "There were others, lots of them, who weren't like that, who didn't change. If you'd been in Vienna in 1934 it would have marked you for-ever. Not in Hampstead, running through Daddy's money, but in Floridsdorf or Ottakring—you'd not have forgotten."

I could see the faith renewed in her eyes then—the dream of all the fair people in the thirties. She ceased to be myth, and I saw the white puffs of smoke from so many righteous guns of the times going off again in her mind: the workers behind the barricades at Floridsdorf, or in the Plaza Mayor in Madrid—or storming Franco's garrison on the heights of Teruel: the whole dirty decade made bright again for a moment in the old woman's vision.

"And now?" I said, cruelly perhaps. "You're just one more person who's seen the dreams go sour: a liberal without a belief in progress, common as clay. We have to do better than that, don't we? Even if it's nice to know the 'truth' in the end. Maybe it'd have been better if we stuck with Lindsay's world—cultivating his own garden, even if it was five thousand acres. The traditional virtues: a little grouse shooting, apples for the tenants at Halloween, and God always very much at home on Sundays."

Eleanor had leaned forward as I spoke and now she was

intent once more, on her way with another truth that we could never have guessed. "You know," she said, "the strange thing is I often wondered if Lindsay really believed in all those Tory virtues at all. There were so many times while I lived with him when I was sure, so sure, that at heart he actually believed in everything I did."

"Of course, being a Trojan horse, it wouldn't have been very difficult—would it?—to pretend he believed in the workers and so on."

"No, I don't mean that. He really *did* believe..." She shook her head in the certainty of memory. "I could feel it. He was like me—but really more so. In Vienna then, in '34—especially then. It marked him too. He believed entirely. And I suspect he never entirely lost that part of his faith either."

"He served his two masters, you mean—both genuinely?"

"Yes, I think he did. I think he must have done."

Here was a glimpse of the sensitive, civilized, fair-minded Lindsay that I remembered. What Eleanor had just said made me see him again in that way: as a man of real justice deep down, involved in some agonized search for the truth. And yet, if the other things she'd said about him were only half true, there must have been another quality in him, at a deeper level still—some horrific flaw that had betrayed his good sense and with which he had betrayed others. Eleanor had spoken of his true feelings just then, of his life at "heart." Yet for all her insight this heart of his remained as ambiguous as ever—at least for me, if not Rachel, who had come to bitter life.

"Now I've come all this way," she said, loosening her arms at last, relaxing like a defense counsel about to make a killing, "and I've listened to you, Eleanor—and it's all so stupid." She shook her head derisively, gazing down her long, straight nose with patrician disdain—as she'd looked at me in the old days, before our collapse in Notting Hill: a glance of ageless, inherited power, a look that attracted and repelled in equal measure, beauty in a heartless beast. "So stupid," she went on. "Talking about Lindsay's politics—and his family's, and all the dirty deeds of the thirties. *What does that matter?*" she nearly shouted. "Nothing. Nothing whatsoever. I know him *now,* as a person, not part of any manifesto or crusade or stupid theory about the rights of man. Someone who was such fun—"

"I knew him that way too, Rachel. We had an old blow

telephone in our house in Zagreb, from the bedroom to the kitchen. We sang arias up and down it all one evening."

Eleanor left this one incident from the past—which so well summed up their lives together in prewar Vienna and Zagreb, with all its youth and dazzle—hanging on the air, like a few chords in music so richly evocative that they bring the whole symphony to mind without another note being played.

This remark hit home, I think. But Rachel only swayed her head again—slowly, dismissively, a canny puritan critic who would not join the dance.

"I don't believe you," she said. "You had a few years with him. I've had nearly forty—"

"The length of time doesn't matter—if it did, everyone would love Christ by now. A week or a year can give you someone equally well. It's just that you and I have different Lindsays, that's all."

Rachel leaned forward intently, just as Eleanor had done. "*Exactly*. But your Lindsay is always in shadow. And Peter's too." She turned to me. "I see him quite clearly, in the light. And there's no need to doubt what I see. None at all. But you—you two—for the sake of your wretched political dreams and failures, you've tried to blame Lindsay, and fit him into *your* failure, into your whole shoddy scheme of things: about his being a double agent and all that nonsense—and having a child with Susan and trying to kill you. But all that is just your hurt, Eleanor. Don't you see? Because he didn't get on with you, or something." She glared at both of us, uncertain for a second. "You two can't see goodness when it stares you in the face—nor ordinary tact or decency. You see only corruption—because you are corrupt. You look for deceit in Lindsay, when it's your deceit. And you pass on the evil, people like you, like an illness. Soiling your own nest, you have to soil others', too. *You* carry the plague, not Lindsay."

"My dear, I haven't questioned your love for your father. Why do you try to rub out mine for him?"

Rachel was bright-eyed with woe and bruised faith—a grief-laden child without her father, dumbly snuffling late at night, long after he should have come upstairs and kissed her to sleep. She was living through the hour of the wolf now, where there is nothing and no one, rustling about desperately for something living to touch. And I thought she'd found it when she seemed to relax and said lightly, "We had music too, you know—he and I, ever since I can remember. Nursery rhymes and Scots ballads round the piano at Glenalyth—romantic nonsense about Bonnie Prince Charlie and the Road to the Isles. And polkas round the dining-room table on New Year's Eve, and flute cadenzas in London later on. Even—you won't believe it—a barrel organ that I turned in the square one frosty evening just after the war, going tinkety-tonk. That sudden frost in a city, after it's been warm, in autumn," she went on in a chatty way. "You know—when you hear the slap of people's boots a long way off, echoing so clearly in the dark."

She looked up at us serenely. But she was lost to us. "You see, there was nothing I didn't have with him—nothing."

And it seemed a truth. They may not have believed it, but I did. Rachel saw her father again with that perfect recall she possessed—as when she had remembered, a few weeks before, seeing him from the top of the copper beech at Glenalyth as a child, going down to the boat on the loch, to join Susan. But now they were purely happy incidents of her life with him that she rescued from time, once more stepping into and completely inhabiting an old holiday photograph—kissing to life all the marvelous things of the day.

Rachel was possessed by her magic again, by a knack of mind, or a need so inspired that with it, as in her music, she could reclaim vast landscapes of perfection, offering a world reachieved—the dross turned to gold, where all misdemeanor and even tragedy are shut out.

"You see, there was absolutely nothing—nothing I can't remember. I had everything..."

She had gone back onto one of her many pedestals now—one where she would not be reached any longer, living in some hermetic place, that playground where for years, with her father, she had happily committed herself to a lifetime growing up. Her brief hurdle at maturity, where there are lies to overcome and other people's inexplicable betrayals, had failed. And she was bright now—certainly she was bright now—but in a way I could never share.

It all happened very quickly then. Though I should have foreseen it, and would have done, I think, but for my concern with Rachel's terrifying isolation. She'd left the table and gone inside the lodge. Madeleine had followed her, as a comfort. The three of us were left at the table. The afternoon had begun to die a bit, the sun slanting on the waves of grass in the meadow in front of us. A minute breeze heralded the evening.

"I'm sorry—about everything," I said rather limply to Eleanor, limply because I couldn't see that anything that had happened was exactly my fault. But there was a need then, after the storms of revelation, for some polite inconsequential chatter. She didn't oblige me, however.

"Sorry? Perhaps it's us. We should never have started it all. But then you don't start a belief, do you? You catch it. That's the infection Rachel talked of—not corruption, just the opposite: the blinding-light department. We were all struck by it then, in the thirties. I was dazzled longer than most. I still am, in many ways. Though not Moscow's way."

She sat back in her high wooden chair then, kneading the two armrests gently with her fingers, looking at me candidly. "Of course, we never expected to be found. It's your fault there, from what I can gather, pursuing us so."

"We were looking for Lindsay, not you."

She smiled weakly. "Indeed—and after all this"—she gestured round at the lodge, the meadow and the woods as things already lost to her—"you seem as far away from him as ever. The body I mean."

It was a point I hadn't considered until she mentioned it— and it was thinking of it that took my mind off events about me. I never noticed Zlatko leave the table. And when I saw him again it was too late. He was in the doorway of the lodge, holding Rachel, dazed and uncomplaining, round the neck with one hand, the other with a gun or a knife at her back. He was barely taller than she was, in his short pants and string shirt, and the two of them looked ridiculous, standing there for a moment, frozen in this act of violence. They were like children, undecided about some mischief.

"Don't be silly, Zlatko. Let her go." Eleanor spoke so casually, yet authoritatively, that at first I really believed it was a game. But Zlatko didn't reply, and he didn't let her go. He shuffled away like a crab, holding Rachel in front of him, sideways down the back of the covered terrace, toward a small stone balustrade at the end where the barbecue was.

"It's so well—that you all talk the truth," he said as he went, glancing at us waspishly, an angry imp of a man again, peeping over Rachel's shoulder. "But you have forgotten me, Eleanor."

I saw he had a gun at Rachel's back. "I still have commitments, you know—matters to keep silent about."

He clambered over the barbecue pit, manhandling Rachel with him. Perhaps she thought he was going to roast her alive, but at any rate she started to resist and shout just then and a moment afterwards the fools started shooting from the woods to the front of the lodge—Stolačka's men, or some trigger-happy sniper, who seeing Zlatko over the balustrade and out in the open now, believed he could get him in one.

But he failed—and Zlatko managed to wrench Rachel away with him, using her as a shield, pulling her across the twenty yards of open space before the thick wood and undergrowth to the side of the lodge gobbled them both up.

The hidden store of soldiers burst from the trees in front of us and the long grass in the meadow beyond, bounding toward us, yelping with enthusiasm as they came, Stolačka in the vanguard, his Windsor check suit replaced now by a sort of floppy, ill-fitting commando's outfit.

"You have your little gun!" he shouted when he got to me. "Why did you not use it?" He was extremely excited, flourishing a heavy automatic like an officer leading his men over the top. It struck me that being in charge of these quite unaccustomed military maneuvers had gone to his head. In fact, it was soon obvious that he and his platoon of dressed-up urban secret police had little or no experience of these jungle search-and-destroy operations, for they thrashed madly about in the bushes all round the lodge for a minute or two, going in opposite directions, before I was able to persuade them of the right path. As a result Zlatko got a good head start on us, which he should never have had at all.

He'd gone into thick scrub to the side of the lodge and a tight fir plantation beyond that, an area of land that sloped down gently between long rows of trees, but with hillocks rising up here and there, so that it was impossible to get a clear line of vision for more than twenty or thirty yards ahead.

And Zlatko obviously knew his way round this land, which we didn't, a fact made very apparent by the nervousness of Stolačka's storm troops in this leafy wilderness, where the sun filtered through the layers of green and played strange tricks with the light, so that the men jumped at shadows, stumbled into drains, and generally behaved like city folk stampeding from a flash flood. Thus our general progress was slow. And soon Stolačka and I, unencumbered and perhaps more adroit on our feet, found ourselves dangerously ahead of the gun-toting heavy infantry behind us.

But then the land fell away sharply and we found ourselves on a steep slope. As the plantation thinned out I heard the distant rumbling of a train. A deep cutting opened up immediately below us, a few hundred yards away, and we saw the quarry railway line at the bottom of it, a broad-gauge single track running straight in this section, with a train halfway along—a great diesel shunter plowing heavily through it, with a snake of high-sided wagons behind. And there, running alongside it, was Zlatko, a tiny figure trying to grasp the sides of one of the wagons.

We were on our backsides suddenly, as the land slid away beneath us at a forty-five degree angle—slithering down the hill through brambles and gorse and little outcroppings of stone, Stolačka yelling at the engine driver as he went. But the man couldn't hear us.

Zlatko was still running along the rough track beside the rails when I last saw him, before a boulder caught me, twisting me over, so that I lost sight of him for several moments. And when I had my wits about me again, he was gone—and the train had passed, the last car disappearing into another turn in the cutting.

It wasn't until we were standing on the track itself, and looked down a small incline the other side, that we saw Zlatko—or several parts of him. He'd obviously stumbled between two trucks and the heavy car wheels had cut him up like a lot of bloodied twigs.

"Rachel?" I shouted, looking wildly around. But she was nowhere. The train rumbled away in the distance and the slanting sun glinted on the high white escarpment ahead of us, at the end of the cutting. Stolačka's men joined us, slinging their machine pistols, well pleased.

"Where is she?" I said violently.

Stolačka rubbed his chin doubtfully, speaking to his men. He shook his head. "Well, we came through the wood between the lodge and here very carefully," he said. "All the same, perhaps when he let her go she went back to the lodge. If not—well, she could not have gone up there." He looked across, up at the almost sheer rise on the other side of the cutting. "She must have gone that way—toward the quarries."

I ran along the track through the cutting, as fast as breath would take me, Stolačka behind—only to be faced with a tunnel round the next bend. "No!" he shouted. "No—up! Up there." And we climbed then, round the tunnel opening, up a path over the rock face, and a few minutes later were standing on top of the hill looking over an utterly changed landscape.

The woods had all gone, eaten away by the great white gash in the earth, a mile or more square, bounded all round on one side by the huge limestone cliff on which we stood, with old workings and flooded quarries some hundreds of feet immediately beneath us. A mile away, in the distance, were the newer cuttings, a jumble of cranes, great tongs and scoops and mechanical diggers all grinding away with a faint roar, the air about them dust-white.

But where we were, high up on the rim of land, the air was pure and cool and there was silence—a pleasant silence, where you could hear birds about again after the heat of the day.

"Beyond here she could not have gone," Stolačka said. "So she must have gone back to the lodge." But we both looked down at the watery pits beneath us, without saying anything. The sun slanted over the huge valley from the west, piercing a few thin clouds on the horizon like beams of the apocalypse, a fiery orange ball that turned the whole harsh place beneath us into sheets of blazing communion-white.

"Rachel?" I called, looking round me. But there was nowhere she could have hidden. I came to the rim of the crater again. "Goddamn you—what have you done now," I said under my breath, my stomach falling about inside me. "Maybe she went along the cutting the other way," I said. "Or into the tunnel."

"I hope not—for the train was coming in that direction. She is sure to be back at the lodge." Stolačka put his arm on my shoulder. "Come."

But Rachel was nowhere in or near the lodge when we returned, or further back along the track, or in the tunnel when they went through it later—or in the woods, which half a local army brigade dragged through high and low for a week afterwards. She'd disappeared just as Lindsay had. In the midst of life, another great hand had come out of the sky and scooped her up. And they couldn't find her in the watery quarry pits either, even though they used frogmen and all sorts of elaborate mechanical drags. Many others, we learned during the week we stayed on at the tourist lodge, had disappeared into this quarry without trace. It had been one of several convenient mass graveyards at the end of the war, where thousands in Pavelić's Croatian army had been consigned by the partisans—the men, like Ivo Kovačić and his family that the British had sent back from Bleiburg a hundred miles or so to the northwest. The British, of course, so ably staffed there by officers like Lindsay, packed them back into the cattle cars, and sent them across the border to their execution.

It was all the saddest, dirtiest business—that week and these memories. Eleanor was taken away, of course, though her children and grandchildren were spared. And my God, George's sudden arrival didn't help—George Willoughby-Hughes, who tracked Madeleine and me down to the Palace Hotel in Zagreb when we got back there. Marcus had had to release him in London and he'd managed to contact Klaus, who had told him where we all were. He stood in the lobby of the hotel, sweating horribly in his old linen tropicals, and made a scene. British officials from the consulate and the embassy in Belgrade stood all round us, as he shouted fearful old-fashioned abuse at me: "You louse!" "You cad!" He was mad with grief, his huge body twitching round on his little feet, like a monstrous clockwork toy once more—a masterwork of mourning now. As though he'd been the only one to love Rachel, I thought.

He left straight away, up to Trakošćan, to continue the search for Rachel himself. But even George's great skill—with which, like a water diviner, he had so often before successfully unearthed his love—would meet with no reward this time, I felt. Rachel was dead now—and Lindsay was still missing.

After a few days I took Madeleine home to Glenalyth.

EPILOGUE

Later that summer, in September, when the weather had cooled at last, I went up again to Glenalyth, to see how Madeleine was and offer what help I could. I can't say that even she had borne things well. She was a bright crusader, certainly; but a crusader fights for a special, saintly hope, and that cause was lost to her now. Her quality of fervent simplicity and the deep fund of expectation which was her real capital—these had died in her and now she was like so many other women who seek only to survive the day.

I had suggested that I help them with the honey crop just coming in then, for things were still active on the estate. Indeed it was this, from Madeleine's point of view, that was very much part of any cure she was likely to undergo.

And so she and I and Billy, the farm manager, and a few other local hands donned veils and gloves during those fine September days, out each morning about the gardens extracting frames, or going further afield on a truck to bring back the outlying colonies from the purple heather moors beyond the house.

The hives on the Oak Walk beside the house were the last we tended to. I was out there with Billy one afternoon, beneath the dry-leafed trees, taking the heavily laden frames out and putting them on a trolley. And it was then that we found one of the hives, halfway along the line, practically empty—the hive that Lindsay had been working on just before he disappeared. There seemed no explanation but that half the colony had left and swarmed somewhere else during the long summer, without anyone's noticing.

I was standing on the edge of the croquet court, immediately beneath the walls of the house, later that afternoon, when I saw where they might have gone. The day was so still you could hear sounds a long way off, right down to the plumblue mirror of the loch where someone was cutting trees over the far side—a day with a fine, almost crisp silence in it, autumn falling imperceptibly all round, leaves offering their bronzed and yellowed sides to the golden light. And it was in this silence that I heard the faint but persistent murmur of bees somewhere above me. Looking up, I saw the insects hovering in the bright air, against the blue, high above me, just beneath the eaves of the house, where the guttering divided, giving way to a leaded gully in the middle of the roof.

I told Billy about it and we went up together, with a flashlight and a bee skip and a smoker, to take a look—up through the little lime-washed servants' rooms and into the bone-dry attics beyond, where Lindsay's clutter of old papers still rested in so many boxes; a huge memorial library that I never wanted to read again. I put my foot on a twisted rail, a remnant from his old collection of model trains, and it snapped up at me like an animal. A butterfly, a fine Red Admiral, flapped uselessly against the small grimy window that gave out onto the lawn. But there were no bees. Billy managed to open the window and look out a fraction.

"They're further along," he said. "To the left. In the roof somewhere."

"The attics don't go that far, though."

"No. We'd have to take the slates off."

"Not worth it."

I had moved my hands carefully along the plasterwork to one side and up to the rough ceiling overhead. But everything was solid. There was no access. It was Billy who found the space—behind the great iron Victorian water tanks right at the end of the attics—an opening a few feet square where all the pipes ran from the tank to the bathrooms below.

He squeezed through it first and I followed, having pushed the bee equipment across to him. There was only a little light in the place, a gloomy nook set right up directly beneath the roof. Dusty beams fell from one or two cracks in the slates and there was another angle of light coming from a small circular opening, a stone gutter of some sort, down by the end of the joists. The air was breathlessly warm and dry and there was a deeply sweet smell. We could hear the bees now, buzzing about somewhere ahead of us, and see them coming in and out of the stone aperture. I trod on something—another model rail it felt like, crunching beneath my feet.

Billy turned on the flashlight, and I saw that it had been not just a rail I'd stepped on, but part of a whole layout, raised up carefully on the joists and circling the entire space. It was Lindsay's old model railway, I saw at once, complete with all the missing rolling stock—the prewar canary-colored coaches and boot-black engines; Lindsay's clockwork masterpieces that I had been unable to find earlier that summer. But here they all were, spread out lovingly, a branch-line train just arriving at a country station with a long banner Virol advertisement running down all one side of the platform: "Growing children need it."

The bees seemed to be concentrated among a pile of old sacks up by the stone guttering. Billy shone the flashlight on them now, moving toward them carefully, bee smoker at the ready. But he stopped halfway along, crouching down beneath the rafters, frozen.

The beam of light showed not sacking but what looked like an old suit laid out flat along the joists—a coat and trousers that some workman had thrown down there casually years before. It wasn't until he moved the light that we saw the sudden angular profile rising from one end of the cloth: a dark, leathery thing, the vague color and shape of an old Rugby ball. It was a skull, but with the flesh still there, a chocolate veneer, sunk tight as a bowstring against the forehead and down over the nose and chin so that the features were easily recognizable. It was Lindsay. In the six months' great heat up here he'd been mummified—dried out like a kipper under the burning slates and preserved, an almost identical shadow of his former self. And here was where the missing swarm of bees had made their home, we saw now, as they buzzed to and fro—from the stone opening deep into his dry entrails. Out of the strong comes forth sweetness, I thought—from a man now shrunken like a child, laid out among his dearest toys in the darkest, hidden shadows of his house.

The strong? Perhaps I'm wrong there. Though who can really say? I can't be sure even now, after all that I'd learned against him in the previous weeks, what horror had driven Lindsay to kill himself, for suicide it was: a vast overdose of Nembutal, as we learned from the autopsy. He left no note. Nor am I any more sure what had driven him back into his youth in this singular manner—why he should have chosen this remote, eccentric, self-inflicted crucifixion among the joys of his childhood.

It's not enough to say that we are all childish men. Though I think with Lindsay this aching dichotomy, which he must certainly have thought of as a disability, may have predominated: as a result of a childhood barely expressed at the proper time, caught, as he had been, in the severe expectations of his father, the wicked old general—a childhood ever since repressed, finding irresponsible outlet only in his lies and infidelities, and indeed in the nonsense of his secret work itself, which he had taken to so successfully in the first place, children being natural double agents.

Cast out from the playrooms beneath years before, he had—in however so strange a manner—sought re-entry to it by way of this hidden space beneath the roofs of the family home—a sharp revenge in the chosen site, so close to home, so appropriately childish, too. He had succeeded in these aims, perhaps. Or so I see it, when I remember that calm, bronzed face, with the spiky chin and nose bone, as of some musky, golden emperor, miraculously preserved, unearthed after thousands of years from a fabulous tomb filled with grave gifts of yellow coaches and little cars and coal-dark engines with which he would travel happily through eternity.

It's only theory, of course, such psychology. It's equally possible that his lies and infidelities—and the memory of men like Ivo Kovačić, whom he'd sent their deaths—may have caught up with him, and become, with age, an intolerable burden. Yet he might well have argued that these were either peccadilloes made necessary by his secret work or, in the case of the massacred Yugoslavs, a fault not his—a matter entirely within the evil fortunes of war.

Or the poison may have come as a result of the guilt he felt over what he thought was his first wife's death—a matter even a patriotism such as his could not easily have justified. Or perhaps, at the last, as Eleanor had suggested, he had become disgusted with all the compromises in his life, the hopeless indecisiveness of his political faith, a lifetime in which he had vacillated between East and West, a genuine double agent with a real dilemma, who could never really give his heart to either side; a man who saw too clearly the good and ill in either camp—and who gave his death as final evidence of the plague in both their houses.

These are all theories—there may be other reasons that even I know nothing of: only the horror remains fact.

Yet perhaps it wasn't all horror. Susan, after all, had gained a sister, risen from the dead, and Madeleine—though desolated beyond words by Rachel's death—had at last re-achieved her husband. His discovery must have been some sweet release: Lindsay, whom she had so loved, had been returned to her. The pain there, at least, was over, the mystery solved; the vessel of her joy had come home. I remembered Basil Fielding's remark: "People have an enormous need to tidy things up in that way." And now Madeleine could do this, and she did so with a relieved calm, offering Lindsay, in his emblematic return, all that she had given him in his life—the gifts of total faith, loyalty, and affection.

"You know," she said to me that same evening, with a return of her old, brave confidence, "I wonder if there's anything really strange in the way he went. What was strange was the complete content and trust we had in each other all along. It's a lifetime's warmth for me. The rest—the last few weeks, poor Eleanor—that's all nonsense by comparison. Oh, all she said may be true! But that's irrelevant."

I nodded. Her unquestioning love had, in the end, unbolted the dark: Lindsay's dark, where my persistent inquiries had led only to pain. And the truth, I saw now, could well be irrelevant also—the search we make for it so vehemently creating steps that finally take us away from it.

David Marcus, of course, managed to cast a real gloom over the proceedings. He arrived posthaste from London the next day, busy yet temporizing as ever, a man with obvious lies in his heart, but who, unfortunately, would never kill himself.

I said, "Well, you have your man at last." We were in the morning room. He was fingering the books on the shelves again—ever the sly investigator—just as he fingered people's lives, wondering how much they were worth or what you could borrow on them.

"Yes, indeed," he said. "A tragedy."

But I could see he was really immensely relieved. Lindsay would never embarrass him now, turning up at some staged press conference in Moscow a few months hence.

"A brave man—which makes it all the more inexplicable," he went on—as though suicide was an act of cowardice.

"You know damn well, Marcus, it can't be all that inexplicable."

"You'd so like to know," he murmured secretly under his breath.

I was about to tell him that I knew already. But I changed my mind. "You tried to get me," I went on. "You succeeded with Willis Parker. You didn't want Lindsay found for some reason, unless he was dead, as he is now."

"What nonsense you speak," he said gravely, turning to me, very formal in his dark pin-stripe—a man usurping genuine old decencies, in language and dress, thus to give weight to his deceit.

But I didn't press my luck with him, and thought no more of telling him that I already knew the truth about Lindsay's Intelligence operations. He would learn the uselessness of that whole long, elaborate business in due course, perhaps, when the matter came to light at Eleanor's trial. Until then he could pretend that Lindsay's work for British Intelligence had been the one shining success in that deeply flawed organization. Though even there, I don't know how they can ever establish a true profit-and-loss account in such cloudy matters as this Trojan-horse ploy—but let them try—it's suitable work for their narrow souls.

They buried Lindsay later that week in the family plot to the side of the little granite church, high on the moors—the laird come home at last. The whole neighborhood attended, the real people of the estate and locality, less real friends, pillars of the county society—and a few far worse men from Whitehall, pretending loss, though more intent, I think, on making sure Lindsay didn't jump from the box and escape them a second time.

It was a perfect afternoon, the sun with a touch of wind flowing over the blue landscape, the clouds funneled into strange white spirals, miles tall, very far away in the distance. It wasn't a formal or military funeral—there would be a memorial service in London for all that nonsense later on, in some Wren church off the Strand. But a local bagpiper played him out, after all the numbing obsequies: the last expected musical homage for a Scots officer and gentleman, "The Flowers of the Forest," a funeral dirge I have always found awkward and atonal, though thus certainly all the more effective in creating a chilly mood. Enough to say that it's a kind of music I've never been able to understand or connect with, and thus it may be an appropriate reflection of my failure to really understand the man they were burying. Or is it the other way round perhaps? Did this lonely, harsh, and unmelodic line reflect the true lack of any melody at the heart of the world, a dark Lindsay always felt and which in the end he could not bear?

ABOUT THE AUTHOR

JOSEPH HONE was born in 1937 and educated in
Dublin. A former BBC producer and member of
the UN Secretariat in New York, Mr. Hone still
writes and broadcasts on East European and
other international affairs. Two of his novels, *The
Private Sector* and *The Sixth Directorate,* have
been published in this country. Married, with
two children, Mr. Hone now lives in
Oxfordshire, England.

CURRENT CREST BESTSELLERS

CURRENT BESTSELLERS
from POPULAR LIBRARY

THRILLS * CHILLS * MYSTERY
from FAWCETT BOOKS

GREAT ADVENTURES IN READING